FROM THE ASHES

A NOVEL

LENA NOTTINGHAM

FROM THE ASHES

ISBN 978-1533683458

Cover Art by Bev Johnson

"Life and death, energy and peace. If I stop today it was still worth it. Even the terrible mistakes that I made and would have unmade if I could. The pains that have burned me and scarred my soul, it was worth it, for having been allowed to walk where I've walked, which was to hell on earth, heaven on earth, back again, into, under, far in between, through it, in it, and above."

Gia Marie Carangi

CONTENTS

Chapter 1

FAR FROM HOME

Dakota hates hospitals. She hates the bright lights, the overbearing nurses, the "rate your pain" scale, and most importantly, she hates the stupid questions that they ask over and over. She'd intended on never setting foot in one again, but this time she didn't really have a choice.

Come to think of it, Dakota doesn't really have a choice in much of anything. At least, that's how she feels as of late.

She shifts uncomfortably on the plastic bed, paper crinkling underneath her. Her hand is wrapped in a neon pink cast, a color that she didn't even get to pick. She scowls, extends her arm out in front of her, and tries to wiggle her fingers. Wincing, she huffs and let her hands fall back to her sides. Her hand hurts like hell. She had literally felt the bones shatter upon impact.

Alright, she admits this is probably her fault, considering she was the one who decided to block someone's face using her fist. But technically it's the fault of the kid who just *had* to make a jab at her mother. He knew exactly how to get a reaction out of her. She probably shouldn't have let him provoke her to that point, but she's pretty sure her bones weren't the only ones she felt crack. Maybe his broken nose will give him something to think about.

There's a knock in the doorway and someone pokes their head into the small room. It's not a nurse. It's a tall woman dressed in a black pant suit. Her heels click against the linoleum floor as she walks across the room to shake Dakota's hand. (The non-broken one).

"Remember me?" she smiles at Dakota as if they're long lost friends. Dakota just stares back at her. The woman laughs as if she's just made the joke of the century, and takes it upon herself to sit at the end of Dakota's bed. The mattress shifts and Dakota bites her tongue.

"I'm your social worker," she explains. "I've worked with you before. After the—,"

"I remember you," Dakota mutters after the realization hits her. This isn't really a topic she enjoys making light conversation about.

"I remember *you* from that night," the woman continues, oblivious to Dakota's discomfort. "Spiderman pajamas." She laughs and shakes her head. "You wouldn't let go of your brother."

Dakota keeps her eyes low.

"Anyway," the woman's voice is chipper, as if they're not sitting in a hospital room because Dakota just punched someone in the face. "The family isn't pressing charges. You got lucky this time."

"I want to see my brother."

"You will," she reassures her, flipping through a stack of papers she's brought along with her. Dakota wants to take her sacred clipboard and throw it across the room. "There's just one problem…" she continues paging through, tapping her nail against a pale yellow sheet. "It says here you live with your uncle in… Cape Cod?"

Dakota stiffens.

"I thought maybe it was a mistake on someone else's part so I did some research, but..." the woman's voice has lost its chipperness. "He's been dead for ten years, hasn't he, Dakota?"

Dakota's jaw clenches. This woman is asking her questions that she already knows the answer to. She curls her good hand into a fist and doesn't move. She doesn't speak. Silence seems to be her best option. The woman sighs, shakes her head, and turns back to her clipboard.

"So it's just been you and your brother in that house all along, huh?" There she goes again with the questions she already knows the answers to. "Taking down the 'For Sale' signs, boarding up the windows... You guys just moved right back in after all the renovations."

"No one wants to buy it anyway," Dakota mutters. "Everyone thinks it's haunted."

"That's a criminal offense, Dakota," the woman flips the papers back over, sending a rush of air in Dakota's direction. She shivers. "Squatting in an unoccupied residence, tampering with state property... I could go on."

"Don't," Dakota huffs.

"You're a minor, Dakota."

"Hudson isn't."

"I'm aware," the woman turns to face the girl. "But he's not your legal guardian. He could apply, but the court would turn him down the moment they find out he's not in school or working a stable job. I—,"

"He's working on getting a job," Dakota interrupts her, desperately trying to plea her case. "He's got a buddy down in Arizona that's—,"

"I'm talking about right *now*, Dakota," the woman stresses her words. "With your uncle being dead, you're technically under the state's care."

"What's that mean?" Dakota lifts her head. Reality starts to set in. At first she hadn't been sure where this conversation was going, but now she feels fear rising in her stomach.

The social worker sighs. "I don't know how you got this one past the system. And for *eight years*, Dakota."

"Obviously you didn't care enough about us to check in for eight years," Dakota quips back, shaking her head. "So now what? Fine us and send us off to live with some distant relative we've never met?"

"We've located a home in California, a girl's home, they've got—,"

"What?" Dakota stands up in a panic.

"*As I was saying*," the woman sets her clipboard down, her eyes sending icy daggers in Dakota's direction. "There's a group home in California that's so graciously offered to take you in for the time being. I know it's far away, but finding a place for a seventeen-year-old girl on such short notice is near impossible."

Dakota just stares at her, mouth agape in disbelief. Who knew punching someone would get her shipped off to some hellhole in California. She racks her brain for some sort of excuse or escape plan but comes up empty. All she can muster is a bitter "*fuck you*," thrown in the woman's direction.

"We've packed your things for you," the social worker stands up, still full of fake professionalism as she so effortlessly ignores the girl's words. *So easy to pretend I'm just another case number*, Dakota thinks, clenching her jaw. "We leave for the train station in an hour."

"My brother..." Dakota takes a step forward before the woman reaches the door. Now, all her fight has drained, and she's just drowning in disbelief. "What about my brother?"

"He's over eighteen, he's out of our hands. He has the number of the home you'll be staying at. But... we think it's best you two don't see each other for the time being."

"Who's we?" Dakota moves forward, anxiety rising in her chest. "Who's making all the decisions for me? I've survived this far, shouldn't I get a say?"

"Arguing about this will get us nowhere, Dakota," the woman sighs. "We leave at six."

Dakota opens her mouth to argue, but by then the heavy door has already slammed shut. She holds up her fist, reeling back, but thinks better of punching the wall with an already-broken hand. Instead, her resolve crumbles, and she stumbles a few steps to fall onto the bed, burying her head in her hands. Forcing herself to take deep breaths, she slowly lays back and squeezes her eyes shut. If this was all just a dream, she swears she would reverse time and right all of her wrongs.

The only thing she can think of is how this was all her fault. She just *had* to get in that fight. If she hadn't had punched the kid, she wouldn't have been in the hospital, and they wouldn't have gone over her records.

She's suddenly reminded of the same feeling of fear she was plagued with as a young girl, following her brother down the side of a highway with only a small backpack and a pair of Spiderman pajamas to her name. The same terror that made her cling to her brother is still there, but now she's alone. And there's no one she can turn to for answers.

She just wants to see her brother. She wants to go home. She wants to be six years old again, waking up from a nightmare and crawling into bed with her mother. But those are all luxuries that life has not afforded her. No, instead what little she *does* have is being torn out from underneath her. And she can't do a thing about it.

"The girls are in school. They'll be back in an hour or so. I told them to be expecting a new guest when they got home."

The wooden door creaks open and Dakota takes a few hesitant steps forward. From the outside, her new home sticks out like a sore thumb. It's an old Victorian, painted in muted greens and yellows, circled by a huge wrap-around porch. It's been a long car ride from the train station to the middle-of-nowhere, California, and her legs are still wobbly.

"Your room is this way," Loretta, the house advisor, walks in beside her. Dakota's already sized her up. Her coarse hair is pulled back into two braids that wrap around the top of her head. She has some kind of shawl pulled over her shoulders—bright purple—in contrast to her dark skin. There's a motherly feel to her, Dakota thinks, but she has no intentions of bonding with these people.

The home smells of stained wood and pumpkin candles. Dakota's eyes scan her surroundings—the stain glass windows, the large brick fireplace, and the knitted blankets thrown over the back of an olive green couch. It's got personality, she'll give it that much. Loretta reaches out to help her carry her suitcase, but Dakota shakes her head and tightens her grip on her things. They're all she has left.

Her room is the first one at the top of the stairs. Dakota wanders inside and lets her bags slump to the ground at her feet. It's pretty plain. The walls have the slightest tint of blue to them, but it might as well be white. There's one window across the room, covered in wooden shutters. Dakota notes the two twin sized beds and glances back to Loretta.

"Usually we have roommates," she explains. "The house can fit six girls, but we've only got four right now. You included."

"Got it," Dakota nods, shrugging a bag off of her shoulder. It thumps to the ground beside her and she nudges it toward the wall with her foot. She sighs. This is home now.

"Would you like to see the rest of the house?" Loretta stands in the doorway. Dakota just shakes her head and sits down on the bed, feeling all too defeated.

"I just want to be alone," she runs a hand through her hair, dark brown and still slightly damp from the shower she'd taken at the hospital that morning.

"Long day?"

Dakota nods. Loretta gives her a sad smile. "Bathrooms are down the hallway. Doors aren't allowed to be closed all the way during the day, standard practice." She glances down to Dakota's things. "The girls will be home in around an hour. You can call me Red, by the way. Everyone else does."

"Thanks," Dakota sighs. She sits on the edge of the bed, counting the footsteps that echo as Loretta—*Red*—makes her way back downstairs. Exhaling slowly, Dakota walks over to her window and struggles to pry it open with her good hand. Eventually, though, the sound of the outdoors echoes through her room and she feels a little bit more at ease.

For the next hour, she sits on her bed across from the open dresser and tosses her clothes in one by one. Red passes by her door once, holding a laundry basket, and raises an amused eyebrow at her little game. But besides that, she's left to herself for a while. After shoving her suitcase under her bed, she digs through her backpack and pulls out a worn leather journal. She tries to write something, tries to get her feelings down, but she just ends up drawing trees sprouting from the corners of the page.

An hour passes quicker than she thought, and Dakota's startled by the sound of the front door opening. The creak seems to rush through the entire house, aching the walls, and she bites her lip when she hears a stampede of footsteps barrel into the foyer.

"Oh, Finley, another package came this afternoon. It's in the kitchen." *Red.*

Dakota hears a pair of footsteps scurry excitedly across the floor beneath her. At the same time, she hears the sound of someone trudging up the stairs. She untucks her hair from behind her ear, letting it fall in front of her face like a curtain in hopes she'll be invisible.

The first person that trudges past her door is a blonde. Her hair is thrown up in a half-assed bun, wavy strands poking out, and there's faint, faded streaks of pink at the ends. Her sweatpants seem two sizes too big for her. She doesn't even look in Dakota's direction, and Dakota can hear her heavy footsteps enter one of the bedrooms, and something—a backpack, she supposes—is thrown onto a bed carelessly.

Another pair of footsteps hurries up the stairs, much lighter than the latter. Dakota watches quietly as a tinier girl appears, barely visible behind the large cardboard box she's carrying. She turns into the room directly across the hall, and Dakota catches a glimpse of her wavy sandy-brown hair, almost perfect ringlets. Again, Dakota remains unnoticed, to her relief.

She's just turned her attention back to her journal when she hears someone else coming up the stairs, slower… and… heavier? She pauses, tapping her pen against her lip.

"Ryland?"

The footsteps stop. "Hm?"

"Play nice." It's Red.

"Yeah, yeah," the voice replies sarcastically, and then the crooked-sounding footsteps continue. Dakota quickly looks away when a girl half-walks, half-limps past her door, swinging a lanyard around her wrist. However, the footsteps pause, and when Dakota looks up, the girl has turned around and peered back into her bedroom. Awkward eye contact ensues, and Dakota looks away quickly.

"I see they gave you your own room," the girl notes. Her dark hair is tugged up into a ponytail. Dakota's confused by how pretty she is, considering she's expected everyone here to be absolutely psychotic. Her eyes travel down to the metal-looking brace on the girl's leg, black straps holding tightly around the material of her jeans.

"Quit it, Ryland," Red appears at the top of the stairs, her voice firm. She glances over her shoulder. "Finley, door."

Ryland's eyes scan Dakota's bedroom while the door across the hallway is quickly pulled open. "Sorry." The curly haired girl pokes her head out into the hallway. It's only then that she notices their visitor.

"Looks like you're not the newbie anymore, Finley," Ryland leans against the doorframe and glances across the hallway. Finley's head quickly shies back into her bedroom, leaving her door open a few inches.

Red sighs and shakes her head. "I see you've met Dakota," she turns to the girl. "Dakota, this is—,"

"*Ryland, nice to meet you,*" the girl interrupts Red, faking a smile and giving Dakota one last glance before she pushes off of the doorway, disappearing from sight. Red rolls her eyes half-heartedly.

"That's Ryland," Red explains. "She'll warm up to you. She just—,"

"*Dakota*," another voice appears. The door across the hallway is nudged open with a foot and Finley moves to stand beside Red in the doorway. Her eyes scan a large, mustard-yellow book that she holds with both hands, propped up against her chest. "Dakota. Your name isn't in here," she furrows her eyebrows, eyes fixed on the book. "Oh, wait. Here's something." She clears her throat, licking her thumb before flipping the page.

"*North Dakota, a state with an area of 70,665 square miles, is bounded by the Canadian provinces of Manitoba and Saskatchewan to the north, Montana to the west, and South Dakota to the south.*" When she finishes reading, she looks to Red and sends a shy glance in Dakota's direction.

"Finley," Red laughs and places a hand on the girl's shoulder. "You're on dinner duty tonight. Why don't you run downstairs and start getting it ready?" This earns a quick nod from the girl, who slams the book shut and tucks it under her arm before hurrying down the stairs. Dakota raises a questioning eyebrow at her odd behavior, but Red ignores this. It must be normal for her, Dakota thinks.

"I'm assuming you'll be starting school with the girls tomorrow," she nods softly. "Unless you have any reservations…?"

"M'fine," Dakota shakes her head, closing her journal and shoving it under the bed. She makes a mental note to find a better hiding place.

"Alright," Red nods once. "Just let me know if there's anything I can do to help."

Once Dakota's left alone again, she wanders over to the window and peers out. There's a garden in the back of the house, just barely visible from her room. California is much greener than she's imagined it to be. She stands on her tiptoes, noticing the lattice that runs up the side of the house and keeping it in mind. It'd make a good escape route, if things took a turn.

Eventually, her solace is interrupted when the same curly haired girl—Finley—peers into Dakota's room. "Dinner," she says quietly, offering a shy smile before disappearing down the hallway to collect the other girls. Dakota quietly follows her downstairs, through the living room and under a large archway that leads to the kitchen. There's 5 plates on the counter, and Dakota copies Finley, grabbing one and following her over to the table.

"That's Gia's chair," Finley pipes up just as Dakota is about to sit down. She pauses, moving a side-step towards another empty seat. Red gives her a soft nod, letting her know it's okay. Sighing, Dakota sits down. Ryland—the hostile girl from before—appears moments later, sliding into the seat directly across from her. Dakota keeps her head low, nervously moving her food around on her plate.

Someone else trudges down the stairs. Dakota still doesn't know her name. The blonde doesn't throw a glance in their direction, instead she just grabs a plate from the counter and turns back around to go upstairs.

"You know the rules, Gia," Red speaks up, her voice echoing around the lower level. "No food upstairs."

"I have homework," the girl mumbles back without hesitation, not even looking behind her. Red just rolls her eyes as the girl—Gia—makes her way back upstairs.

"Was worth a try," Finley shrugs and offers Red a small smile.

Dinner carries on awkwardly. Dakota's not hungry, but she makes an effort to move her food around on her plate and occasionally take a bite. At this point, her plan of action is to lay low. The last thing she needs to do is draw more attention to herself. For a while, the only thing that can be heard is the clinking of forks against plates, and Finley's foot tapping incessantly against the leg of the table.

"So, *Dakota*," the girl across from her speaks up, slowly sounding out her name. Dakota stills. "Where'd you come from?" Red sends a warning glare in Ryland's direction, who looks back innocently, knowing she hasn't done anything condemnable.

"Michigan," Dakota mumbles, twirling a long noodle around her fork before letting it uncoil back onto the plate. Ryland raises an eyebrow.

"Isn't that on the other side of the country?"

"Yeah, well…" Dakota shrugs one shoulder, keeping her broken hand in her lap. She trails off, not wanting to offer an explanation. Finley's eyes travel back and forth between them.

"You a senior?"

Dakota nods. Finley mumbles a half-hearted "me too," from across the table.

"We all are," Ryland reminds her. Finley just nods and taps her fork against her plate. Ryland turns her attention back to Dakota, her ponytail spilling over her shoulder.

"How long are you here for?"

Dakota finally looks up, tilting her head to the side. "What do you mean?"

"*Ah*, we must've got ourselves a first-timer," Ryland hums in acknowledgement. "Kids come and go all the time in places like these," she explains, gesturing back and forth with her fork. "You either pass through for a few days while mommy and daddy pay lots of money to get you back, or you're stuck here for life like the rest of us."

"*I'm* not stuck here for life," Finley pipes up, her posture straightening. "I'm going home soon."

Ryland rolls her eyes so only Dakota can see, ignoring Finley's comment and turning back to the girl. "So what is it? They gonna ship you back to Missouri in a few days?"

"Michigan."

"*Michigan, Missouri,* same difference," Ryland dismisses it with a wave of the hand. "Or did you just get out of jail like Finley here?" she nods to the girl at the head of the table. Finley's mouth falls open.

"*Did not,*" she gasps. Red sends Ryland a warning glare.

"You're no fun," Ryland shakes her head and turns back to Dakota, propping her elbows up on the table and giving the girl her full attention. "So what is it, tiny? You part of the dead parents club?"

Dakota tenses, the water glass in her hand shakes and she quickly sets it back down. It's been years, yet those words still manage to spark something inside of her.

"Ryland," Red hisses, her fork clattering against the plate. "*Enough.*"

"*My* parents aren't dead," Finley mumbles. Dakota hangs her head down, her grip on her fork tightening. Luckily, Finley gets up to excuse herself from the table, and Dakota's quick to follow her lead.

The nighttime sounds in the house consist of the hiss of showers being turned on, the thump of clothes being thrown down the laundry chute, and the crackling of the old fireplace in the living room. Dakota's writing in her journal again after having changed into an old hoodie and brushing her teeth. Her peace and quiet is interrupted when someone taps on her door, swinging it open and peering in.

"Group's in five," Ryland nods. A toothbrush hangs out of her mouth and she glances around Dakota's room for a moment before she disappears. Dakota doesn't even have time to ask what she's talking about.

"Get your ass outta' bed, Dawson!" Ryland calls from the other end of the hallway. Dakota peers out of her room, finding Ryland banging on the doorway to get Gia moving. Ryland disappears into the bathroom, rinses the toothpaste out of her mouth, and makes her way back down to the hallway. She pauses in front of Dakota. "You coming?"

"What?"

"We have a meeting every night before bed," Ryland shrugs, grabbing a towel from one of the banisters and tossing it into her bedroom. "It's supposed to promote 'bonding' or some shit. Been doing it for as long as I can remember." And with that, she's off. Dakota notes how she maneuvers down the stairs, an iron grip on the railing and her free hand clutching the knee of her brace.

Shaking it off, Dakota tugs her hair up into a half-assed ponytail before making her way down the stairs after the girl. In the living room, the couches and chairs have been arranged into a circle. Finley sits cross-legged on the couch, an aztec patterned blanket tugged around her shoulders. She has both hands wrapped around a coffee mug, and she's blowing on the steam, following it with her eyes. Dakota quietly takes her seat on the kitchen chair that's been pulled into the mix.

Eventually Gia and Ryland make their way downstairs. Gia—the blonde—falls into a knitted beanbag on the floor and Ryland lowers herself down on the couch, tapping Finley's leg to make her scoot over. Dakota pulls her legs up underneath her in an attempt to make herself as small as possible. Red clears her throat while Ryland waves her hand through the steam coming from Finley's mug.

"Alright," Red clasps her hands together and places them in her lap. "So, since we have someone new with us today, I want you to go around the circle and introduce yourselves." She turns to Dakota, motioning for her to continue.

"Me?"

Red nods. Dakota looks down at her hands awkwardly, picking at a string unraveling from her cast. All she can offer is a small shrug. "Dakota."

"That's it?" Red raises an eyebrow. Dakota nods. Sighing, Red turns to Ryland and waits expectantly.

"You already know my name," Ryland crosses her arms and leans back in the couch.

"Her name's Ryland," Finley speaks up, holding the string from her teabag and moving it in circles around the rim of her mug. "I'm Finley." She points to the blonde. "That's Gia."

"Thank you, Finley," Red sighs. "Would you like to start us off for highs and lows?"

"Sure," Finley nods. She takes a sip from her mug before leaning forward to place it on the coffee table. She then turns to Dakota. "Highs and lows is where we say one good thing about our day, and one bad thing," she explains, smoothing out her wavy hair and tugging her blanket around her shoulders. She thinks for a few moments, pursing her lips and tilting her head to the side.

"I got a new package," she offers, looking to Red with bright eyes. "That's a high."

"And a low?" Red nods. Finley crinkles her nose.

"School."

"Just school?"

Finley nods, then adjusts her position on the couch so she's looking to Dakota. "Your turn."

"I don't get it," Dakota looks down and picks at her nails.

"We'll start with your low," Red nods in her direction. "What's been the low point of your day?"

"Being here," she mumbles, digging at her hangnail so hard that it draws blood. She doesn't see it, but she hears Red sigh from across the room.

"And your high point?"

Dakota raises an eyebrow. "Nothing."

"You have to have a high point," Finley pipes up, tilting her head to the side. "It's the rules." For some reason Dakota looks to Ryland for confirmation, who just shrugs, a smug smile on her face. She's enjoying this, Dakota thinks.

"I really don't have one," Dakota shakes her head. Her entire day has just been a low point, if she were to be honest.

"Just pick something and get on with it," Gia groans from her spot on the beanbag. Finley glares at her, but Dakota shrinks back in her chair.

"It doesn't have to be something monumental," Red meets Dakota's eyes. "But every day has a high point."

"Does breaking my fucking hand count?" Dakota clenches her jaw, tilts her head to the side, and holds up the heavy cast on her arm. Her voice is cold. Finley flinches and the room falls silent. With a sigh, Red turns to Ryland.

"Your turn."

Ryland tugs on her ponytail, running a hand through her loose hair, a dark brown with shades of caramel. "My leg kinda hurts," she shrugs. Finley furrows her eyebrows, leaning forward to offer Ryland one of the butterscotch candies on the table. But Ryland shakes her head softly, so Finley pops it into her mouth instead.

"My high…" Ryland pauses to think, her eyes scanning the room. Her gaze lands on Dakota, and her lips curve into a smirk. "My high is her broken hand, too."

Finley giggles quietly but quickly shuts herself up when Red glares at Ryland. Dakota just rolls her eyes, praying that this will be over soon.

"My high is sleep and my low is everything else," Gia speaks up loudly, rushing her words and clapping her hands together. She hops up to her feet. "Is that it? Can we go to bed now?"

Red shakes her head, pinches the bridge of her nose, and sighs. "*Goodnight*, ladies."

Gia's the first one upstairs. Dakota slowly rises to her feet.

"Finley," Red adds, standing up to rearrange the chairs. "Remember you meet with your social worker tomorrow afternoon. And Dakota…" she nods towards the girl. "You're allowed to close your door overnight. Just don't try anything and you won't lose that privilege."

"Got it," Dakota sighs. She tugs her hair out of its ponytail and hurries up the stairs. All she wants to do is fall asleep and sleep for another million years. Or at least until she turns eighteen, so she can finally have control over her own life.

However, when Dakota leans against her door to push it shut, she's met with resistance. Then, she's stumbling a few steps backward when the door is pushed open. She glares at Ryland, who forces her way into the room and closes the door shut behind her.

"What do you want?" Dakota sighs.

Ryland just ignores her and walks around the room, studying the walls. "You don't plan to stay long," she notes. Dakota raises an eyebrow.

"You haven't hung anything up," Ryland explains, motioning to the nearly empty room. "You haven't made yourself at home."

"I couldn't hang anything up even if I wanted to," Dakota shrugs, sitting cross legged on her bed and digging her hair brush out of her suitcase. Ryland watches her for a few moments.

"They pack your stuff for you?"

Dakota nods. "You're observant."

"Been here a while," Ryland brushes it off. She lowers herself onto the bed across from Dakota, and Dakota can hear the creak of the metal brace on her leg as it moves with her knee. She looks away.

"Alright," Ryland claps her hands, the bed bouncing slightly. "What do you need to know?"

Dakota raises a questioning eyebrow.

"C'mon, it's your first day here. I know you have questions."

Dakota just stays silent, shrugging and running the brush through her hair. Ryland sighs.

"Fine," the girl across from her leans back on her hands and studies Dakota. "I'll go first. What'd you do?" she motions to Dakota's cast.

Dakota stills, slowly setting the brush down beside her. She's not sure if she should trust Ryland, or anyone here, for that matter. But someone is actually making an effort to make conversation with her, so she shrugs. Maybe it'll scare her off.

"Punched someone."

"Why'd you—?"

"*Finley*," Dakota blurts out, interrupting her by posing another question. She sees a smile play on Ryland's lips. "Is she…?"

"She's a… special case," Ryland lowers her voice. "Mom's in the crazy house cause she's schizophrenic. Tried to kill her own daughter cause she thought someone was hunting them down. The poor kid is still convinced she's gonna come back for her."

Ryland pauses, watching as Dakota's mouth curves into a frown. All she can manage is a "*that's unfortunate*," before leaning backwards to toss her brush onto her dresser.

"What? Not gonna ask about me?" Ryland jokes, but Dakota just shakes her head and crawls to the other end of her bed, retrieving her journal from underneath.

"This place is fucked up," Dakota mutters, untying the leather straps around her journal and pushing it open. She leans against the headboard of her bed, well aware that Ryland's still sitting there watching her. She hopes that if she's abrasive enough that the girl will get the message.

"It's a hell of a lot better than any of the other places they could have sent you," Ryland speaks up, her voice sharper. Dakota just rolls her eyes.

"I don't belong in any of these *places*," she makes air quotes with one of her hands, not even bothering to look in Ryland's direction. She stiffens when she hears the other girl push herself up to her feet.

"Yeah, well you're no better than any of us, either," Ryland's voice is cold as she throws the door open, yanking it shut behind her. Dakota winces when it slams closed. She hears Finley try and interrogate Ryland in the hallway, but the slamming of another door signifies that Ryland hadn't said a word. She hears a sigh, soft footsteps, and then Finley's door shut gently. The hallway lights flicker out.

Dakota rolls onto her back, clutching her journal against her chest. The dim light coming through her window melts across her ceiling and she traces it with her eyes. *This isn't home*, she keeps telling herself. She squeezes her eyes shut.

This isn't home.

Chapter 2

BRAVADO

Dakota manages to get an hour or so of sleep, *maybe*, before she's waking up again.

Her nightmares aren't anything like the ones seen on TV. She doesn't wake up screaming. She doesn't sit straight up in bed and gasp for breath with wide eyes like she's just seen a ghost. She doesn't bolt awake in a cold sweat.

No, instead, she just fades back into consciousness, swearing that she smells smoke. It takes her a few seconds to come to, realizing where she is. Sitting up, Dakota rubs her eyes and presses her hand to her chest. Her heart is beating a mile a minute.

Taking a deep breath, she walks over to the window and leans forward, hanging her head out. She breathes in the fresh air, closing her eyes. Everything feels unreal at this point. So much has changed in such little time that she hopes it's some sort of cruel joke.

She knows she won't be able to fall back asleep, so she quietly opens her door and peers out into the hallway. Tiptoeing downstairs, she rummages through the cabinets until she finds a box of cereal. She's just pouring the milk into her bowl when another set of footsteps pads down the stairs. Dakota freezes, turning around slowly.

Finley doesn't even look at her. She's got an old quilt tugged around her shoulders and she wanders over to the TV. Dakota watches as the girl sticks a VHS tape into the slot underneath the television. Finley hits the power button once, twice, three times before she's content. She curls up onto the couch, wrapped in her blanket, and watches intently as the Jeopardy theme song begins to play.

Dakota half-smiles with a mouthful of cereal. She leans against the counter, spooning food into her mouth and watching as Finley calls out the answers to the game show.

"*What is valence*?" Finley repeats to herself quietly. Dakota sets her empty bowl down in the sink and wanders over to the front window, trying to stay out of Finley's eyesight. The street is pitch black except for the light coming off of their front porch. It's quite eerie, actually. Her eyes move over to the front door.

She could leave right now, she thinks. Disappear off into the night and never look back. It's all too appealing. Dakota takes a step toward the door.

"I wouldn't do that if I was you."

Dakota jumps, whipping her head around to look at Finley. The girl's eyes are still fixed on the screen.

"You'll set off the alarms," Finley glances over at her before turning back to the television. "*What is The Sound of Music*?" she mumbles under her breath, humming contently when the blue square on the screen reveals the right answer.

Sighing in defeat, Dakota reluctantly plops down on the couch beside Finley, who's too entranced by the show to pay much attention to her. She hugs her legs to her chest, scooting back to the furthest corner of the couch.

She doesn't mean to fall asleep there, but she does. The next thing she knows, someone's nudging her shoulder and gently coaxing her awake. When her eyes flutter open, she's face to face with Finley, holding a piece of toast in her mouth.

"Time for school," the girl mumbles, taking another bite and standing up. Dakota rubs her eyes, looking around the room and realizing where she is. Finley scurries back into the kitchen, already dressed and ready. Sighing, Dakota peels herself off of the couch and makes her way upstairs.

She takes her time getting dressed, digging through her things and eventually deciding on a pair of leggings, a maroon tank top, and a flannel thrown over it all. She's running a brush through her hair when she walks into the bathroom to find Ryland bent over the sink, brushing her teeth and simultaneously running a brush through her hair.

Rinsing out her mouth, Ryland spits in the sink before turning around and looking Dakota up and down as she wipes her chin. She raises an eyebrow. "Trying to make a good first impression?"

Dakota shrugs, studying her reflection and running a hand through her hair, trying to shake some sort of volume into it.

"Don't," Ryland shakes her head, tossing her toothbrush back into a cup on the counter. "S'not worth the effort. Once they find out where you're from they'll chew you up and spit you out."

Dakota pauses, watching as Ryland disappears down the hallway, effortlessly yanking her hair into a ponytail. She grabs her toothbrush from the counter and shoves it into her mouth. "That's comforting," she mumbles, to no one but herself.

It's fixing to be a long day.

They walk to school like a funeral procession.

Finley's in the front, holding tightly to both straps of her backpack and walking with a skip in her step. Dakota's a few feet behind her, and Ryland follows them both half-heartedly. Gia trails behind all of them, taking as much time as she pleases. Dakota takes the chance to study the old neighborhood, the narrow sidewalks, the ancient trees that seem to be holding hands over the street, the brick walkways to the houses. There's an odd sort of charm to it.

"You're not going to punch me if I walk too close to you, right?"

Dakota slows her pace when she realizes Ryland's caught up to her. She can hear the brace on the girl's leg make a clanking noise every time she takes a step. Dakota tries to tune it out.

"Not a morning person, I suppose," Ryland mumbles under her breath. Dakota just shrugs as they come to a crosswalk. Finley presses the button on the stoplight once, twice—four times. Dakota looks to Ryland for an explanation but she just shrugs.

The school looks like something straight out of The Legend of Sleepy Hollow. The dark bricks are overgrown with vines and moss, and one of the letters is missing from the sign, spelling out *HIGH SCHOO* and leaving a faint spot where the 'L' is supposed to be. Finley glances over her shoulder to make sure they've kept up.

After she gets her schedule, Dakota finds her first class. The whole school just looks depressing. The lockers are a dark orange color and the walls are made of the same dark brick that covers the outside of the school. The lights only serve to cast an ugly yellow glow across the entire campus. She hates it already.

Finley's in her first class, World History. Dakota notices her in the back of the classroom, pushing a pair of glasses higher up on her nose and twirling a strand of hair around her finger, buried in a book. When Dakota drops her backpack down on the seat in front of her, Finley flinches, but she recovers quickly when she looks up and sees who it is. She just offers the girl a small smile before turning her attention back to her book.

Dakota takes her time to study the other kids in the room. She feels like an outsider. It's a different sort of feeling. None of them have a clue what has happened to her in the past few days. She thinks back to what Ryland had said that morning.

Finley's quick to slam her book shut when the bell rings, and someone clears their throat from the front of the room. The teacher walks over to the board, scrawling the date in the corner with a squeaky blue expo marker. Then, he turns around, clears his throat again, and lets the eyes scan the room.

"I notice we have a new student," he nods when his eyes land on Dakota, who suddenly wants to shrink down into her chair and disappear. "Care to introduce yourself?"

"Dakota," she just shrugs, running a hand through her hair subconsciously.

"Are you new to the neighborhood, Dakota?" he asks, turning around to write his name on the board. Mr. Jonson.

It just kind of spills out of her after that. "I-I, yeah," she nods quickly, keeping her broken hand hidden in her lap. "We moved down here a few days ago from New York—me and my uncle. He got a promotion and his company sent him out here."

"Where's he work?" someone asks from across the room. It's all too easy to lie.

"He's a director," she's quick to respond. "We move a lot, whenever he's working on a new movie."

"But you said—,"

Dakota whips her head around and glares at Finley, whose eyes widen. The wavy haired girl quickly clamps her mouth shut and looks down, as if she hasn't said a thing.

"Well, we're glad to have you, Dakota," the teacher walks over, placing a textbook down on her desk. "If you see me after class, I can catch you up on what we're working on."

Dakota just nods, tracing her fingers over the picture of a globe on the front of the book. She surprised even herself by how quickly that story spilled out of her mouth, almost involuntarily. She glances back at Finley apologetically, but the girl doesn't move to look at her, she just keeps her eyes glued on the open book laid out on her desk.

The first half of the day drags on. But eventually, it's lunchtime. Realizing she didn't pack anything, Dakota just stands awkwardly in the entrance to the courtyard. Since it's a nice day, everyone is eating outside.

"Hey, new girl!"

She jumps, looking around quickly. Someone waves her over at one of the picnic tables and she walks over hesitantly. All of the boys are wearing the same white and blue football uniform. The few girls who sit at the table have white and blue bows in their hair, and Dakota slowly gets the gist.

"You're new, right?" one of the guys asks. Dakota nods quietly.

"You should come to our game tonight," he motions to the girls seated across from him, and they scoot over to make room for her. Someone hands her a flier about the football team, and Dakota finds herself sitting down at the end of the bench.

When she looks up, she notices Finley across the courtyard, sitting cross-legged on the brick wall that surrounds them. She seems perfectly content by herself, spreading peanut butter onto crackers and taking small bites, humming softly.

"Dakota?"

"Hm?" She snaps out of it quickly.

"I asked what you did to your hand," the boy across from her laughs, nodding in her direction. Dakota purses her lips, holding up her cast and turning it back and forth, studying it.

"Back home we go out on the water a lot," she lies again, finding it all too easy to fall into this routine. "One of my friends has a boat and I fell when we were waterskiing. Nothing too serious." She shrugs.

When she looks up again, Ryland's leant up against the wall next to Finley, who hands her an apple slice. Dakota offers her a small smile, but Ryland just rolls her eyes and looks away. Biting her lip, Dakota folds the football flier into a little square and shoves it into her pocket. Maybe she will go. Maybe Ryland doesn't know what she's talking about.

The walk back home is silent aside from Finley's humming.

Ryland doesn't try to catch up and walk beside her. Instead, she trails behind with Gia. Dakota's still confused, but she does her best to shrug it off. Who needs them? She's made a few friends at school and they're not as bad as she thought they were.

Red greets them at the door. Finley wiggles in past her, immediately digging into the refrigerator. Dakota follows, tossing her backpack onto the couch as she passes.

"Oh, Gia, there's a message for you," Red speaks up as she closes the door behind them. "Your probation officer called."

"*Great*," the blonde mumbles under her breath. She claps her hands, gaining Finley's attention, and then claps her hands again. Finley holds up an apple and Gia nods for her to throw it, catching it with one hand before plopping down onto the couch. Holding the apple in her mouth, she dials voicemail on the old cord phone and takes a bite.

Finley pulls her head out of the fridge and turns to Dakota, offering her a bag of carrots. Laughing quietly, Dakota takes it from her and rips it open. Finley leans over to steal one from the bag, chomping down on it and leaning against the counter beside her. Dakota doesn't mind Finley's company, if she's being honest. She seems the least hostile out of the girls. The phone rings on speaker a few times.

"*You have 2 messages*," the phone's monotone voice fills the room, and Gia just rolls her eyes and motions for it to hurry up. Dakota takes a bite of her carrot. There's a long beep, and then the first message begins to play.

"*Hey, Koda… it's, uh, it's Hudson.*"

Dakota's entire body stills.

"*They, uh, they told me I could call you here. Listen, they're going to start asking you a lot of questions—they already did it to me—about mom, and the fire, and—,*"

The voice is cut off when the phone is slammed back down onto the receiver, ending the message and letting an eerie sort of silence fall over the room. Gia glares at Dakota, who'd yanked the cord from her grip to end the message, but the dark haired girl doesn't dare look at anyone in the room. She just snatches her bag from the couch and storms upstairs, the entire house shaking when her door slams shut behind her. Finley jumps, nearly dropping the food in her hand.

Ryland, standing in the kitchen, looks to Red, who just shrugs at her. Gia rolls her eyes and dials voicemail again, now skipping to the second message. The room is still uncomfortably silent.

"Did you know William Howard Taft was the fattest president?" Finley offers hopefully with a mouthful of food, trying her best to cut through the tension in the room.

Dakota never cries.

That's one thing she prides herself on. When she fell off her bike and had to get three stitches above her eyebrow, she didn't cry. When Hudson accidentally broke her favorite action figure, shattering The Incredible Hulk's arm to pieces, she didn't flinch. When her mother died, she didn't even shed a tear. The guidance counselor at her old school thought this was a bad thing, but Dakota prides herself on it. She's not weak.

After the whole episode downstairs, she's holed herself up in her bedroom, closing her door as much as she can without warranting a warning from Red. She's sprawled out on her bed, laying on her stomach and reading through a chapter in her history book, trying anything to occupy her mind. But her thoughts keep trailing back to her brother. Where is he? Did they take the house away? Is he in trouble?

She slams her book shut and shoves it off the bed. At the same time, there's a quiet knock at the door. Dakota pulls herself together and sits up.

It's Gia. "We've got dinner," she says softly, nodding towards the stairs.

"Huh?"

"We're on dinner duty, me and you," Gia raises an eyebrow. "Did you not see the chart in the kitchen?"

Sighing, Dakota shoves her things aside and follows Gia downstairs. As always, Finley's on the couch, hugging a pillow to her chest and studying another mustard yellow book that she's balanced on the arm of the chair. Gia digs through the fridge, shoving a handful of ingredients onto the counter. Dakota hangs back by the doorway, still becoming accustomed to her surroundings.

"Here," she tosses an onion to Dakota, who scrambles to catch it. "Chop this. Dice it, whatever. It's for soup." Dakota nods quickly.

"Alright, Finley," Gia calls out as she searches through the cupboards. "What's today?"

"*M*," Finley doesn't even bother looking up. Dakota moves to the sink to start peeling an onion, and Gia ducks underneath her to retrieve a pot from one of the drawers.

"Meteor," Gia calls out. Immediately, Finley flips through the pages of her book, brow furrowed in concentration. Dakota looks at Gia questioningly, who shrugs.

"It's her thing," she glances to Finley. "Encyclopedias. She sends away from them every month. Reads em' front to back."

"It's a long one," Finley notes, clearing her throat before she begins reading. "*A meteor, otherwise known as a "falling star", is the passage of a meteoroid, micrometeoroid, comet or* asteroid *into the Earth's atmosphere, heated from collisions with air particles in the upper atmosphere and shedding glowing material in its wake to create a visible streak of light.*"

She keeps reading while they cook. Dakota slides the diced onions into the pot with her knife and Gia tosses her a green pepper.

"Next!" Finley calls out, tapping her fingers against the spine of the book. Gia thinks for a moment.

"Mustang."

"Got it."

For a while, all that can be heard is the turning of pages and Finley reciting articles from the encyclopedia. For Dakota, it's better than the alternative. She doesn't feel like talking. Not now, not ever.

Dinner is quiet. Painfully so.

Red asks Dakota how her first day of school was, and when she talks, Finley quickly looks away, keeping unusually silent. Almost everyone notices this. It was only a matter of time, Dakota supposes.

And, of course, Ryland swings her door open later that night and leans up against the frame. "So how's that rich uncle working out for you?" Her voice is teasing. Dakota freezes.

"I got it out of Finley. It wasn't too—*hey*... What are you doing?" Ryland takes a step forward, suddenly concerned.

Dakota pauses, looking down at the heavy duty kitchen scissors she swiped. She doesn't say anything, just holds her breath, adjusts them one more time, and then her pink cast is cracking in half and small chunks of plaster rain down on the bed. Ryland just watches as Dakota carefully removes her hand from the cast she'd practically sawed through, holding it up in front of her. She tries to move her fingers, immediately wincing.

"Well that was stupid," Ryland quips from the doorway. Dakota glares at her.

"It was too tight," she mutters, turning her attention back to her hand. It's bruised, dark blue and purple melting all across her knuckles and down to her wrist. It looks even worse than she thought.

Dakota doesn't even notice Ryland leave, but moments later Ryland's reappearing from the hallway with a first aid kit in her hand and plopping down onto the bed beside the girl. Dakota watches hesitantly as the girl digs out an ACE bandage. Ryland holds out her hand and looks to Dakota expectantly.

Reluctantly, the girl extends her broken hand towards Ryland, who holds her wrist and turns her head to study it. "God, you really fucked this thing up," she shakes her head, carefully uncoiling the bandage around Dakota's hand, pulling it tight a few times and earning a wince from the girl beside her.

"Shoulda' seen the other guy," Dakota breathes out. Ryland pauses, looking up and raising an eyebrow.

"Did you really punch someone, or is this another one of your lies?" She smirks. Dakota glares at her, whatever trust she has built up for the girl still depleting. Ryland just laughs and ties off the end of the bandage.

"Group!" Finley's voice rings out from downstairs. Dakota rolls her eyes, studying the new bandage on her hand. Ryland stands up.

"Should probably put ice on that, y'know, now that you went all Frankenstein on your cast," Ryland advises before heading downstairs for group. With a sigh, Dakota pushes herself up to her feet and follows her down.

Finley and Gia are already on the couch, and Dakota crinkles her nose when she smells smoke. She feels nauseous when she sees the cigarette in Gia's hand. But unfortunately, the only seat left is the one next to Gia, so she sits down reluctantly after grabbing a drink, trying to only breathe through her mouth.

Finley studies Gia's box of cigarettes, running her finger over the words. She pauses, grabs her book from the coffee table, and pages through it.

"Menthol," she reads aloud. "*Terpene alcohol with a strong minty, cooling odor and taste. It is obtained from peppermint oil or is produced synthetically by hydrogenation of thymol. Menthol is used medicinally in ointments, cough drops, and nasal inhalers. It is also used as flavoring in foods, cigarettes, liqueurs, cosmetics, and perfumes.*"

"That sounds gross," Finley crinkles her nose and glances to Gia, who just shrugs and flicks the end of her cigarette over the ashtray on the end table.

Red emerges from the kitchen with two cups of coffee, handing one to Finley and keeping one for herself. She sits down in her usual chair—a dark red loveseat with golden embellishments, and takes a sip of her drink before addressing them.

"I got some good news this afternoon," she announces, warming her hands around the outside of her mug. "Finley..." she turns to the girl, who immediately perks up. "Your social worker called today. You have a visit with your mother next week."

Upon hearing this, Finley nearly spills the coffee in her lap. Her eyes widen and she leans forward. "For real?"

"For real," Red nods. "I didn't want to get your hopes up until it was final, but they said she's been having a good spell lately and she's been asking about you."

"She has?"

Meanwhile, Dakota notes the silent conversation going on between Gia and Finley, who both roll their eyes and shake their heads. She tries to get Ryland's attention, wanting an explanation, but she fails.

"I'll tell you more later," Red gives Finley a soft smile. Then, her attention turns to Gia, who blows a cloud of smoke out in front of her. Finley grimaces and waves it away, but Gia just laughs and blows another towards the girl.

"*Gia*," Red warns her, and the girl holds both hands up as if she's surrendering. "Care to share what your probation officer had to say?"

"Nothing special," Gia shrugs. She digs the end of her cigarette into the ashtray beside her and circles it around a few times. Dakota watches, clenching her jaw. "He just said that the court date got moved back again."

"Again?" Finley furrows her eyebrows. Gia just shrugs, unfazed.

Meanwhile, Ryland watches from the other side of the circle as Dakota looks around to make sure no one is watching before leaning over and pouring a few drops of her water into the ashtray. She quickly sets her glass down. Ryland raises an eyebrow.

"Alright," Red claps her hands, snapping both Ryland and Dakota back to attention. "Time for high and lows. Finley?"

Finley takes another sip of her coffee and thinks for a few moments. Gia cups a hand around her lighter, new cigarette in mouth, and lights it. Dakota's grip on her glass tightens.

"My high is getting to see my mom soon," Finley nods quickly, an excited smile on her face. "And I guess... I guess my low would be not getting to see her even sooner." She shrugs. She turns to Gia. "Your turn."

"Tomorrow's Friday," Gia shrugs, blowing out another puff of smoke. Dakota feels sick to her stomach.

"And your low?"

"That *today* isn't Friday?" Gia offers. Red just rolls her eyes and looks to Ryland.

"Mine's the same as Gia," Ryland laughs softly. "And, uh, my low is my leg, again."

"You've got an appointment next week," Red reminds her. Now it's Ryland's turn to roll her eyes.

"Yeah, like that'll fix shit."

"*Language*," Finley mumbles. Ryland just sighs and slumps back in her chair. All eyes turn to Dakota, who quickly looks away.

"Highs and lows, Dakota?" Red prompts her.

"Don't got any," she mutters. Red sighs.

"I imagine hearing from your brother must fall into one of those categories," she offers, trying to be helpful, but this triggers Dakota's anger. She glares across the room.

"That's nobody's business but mine," she hisses. Finley sinks further back into the couch, nervously.

"Well on that note, I'm going to bed," Ryland claps her hands together, interrupting the tense silence. She pushes herself up to her feet. Gia quickly follows. Dakota stands to disappear upstairs as well, but Red meets her eyes and motions for her.

"The message is still on the machine," she says softly, pulling Dakota aside. "You can delete it, if you'd like."

Dakota just nods. As everyone clears out of the room, even Finley, who quickly catches on, Dakota's eyes turn to the old phone sitting beside the couch. Glancing around one last time, she sits down slowly, and holds the phone to her ear. It rings the voicemail, once, twice, before there's a beep and her brother's voice appears.

"Hey, Koda… it's, uh, it's Hudson. They, uh, they told me I could call you here. Listen, they're going to start asking you a lot of questions—they already did it to me—about mom, and the fire, and how we kept quiet all that time."

Dakota bites her nails, holding the phone tightly against her ear. She squeezes her eyes shut.

"Just tell them the truth, okay? No more made up stories like before. I'm going to figure something out, Koda, I promise. I'm eighteen, I can get you out of there somehow. I'll figure it out."

There's voices in the background that Dakota can't make out, and there's a long pause over the line.

"Alright, Dakota, I've got to go. Don't freak out. I love you."

The line goes dead and Dakota hangs up as quickly as she can in order to avoid the awful hiss of dead air. She sits on the edge of the couch for a moment, rocking back and forth to calm herself down. Impulsively, she grabs the phone and clears the voicemail.

By the time she gets undressed and falls into bed, it's started storming. Dakota quickly comes to learn that the old house doesn't take well to storms. With even the smallest gust of wind, the walls creak and the windows sound as if they're caving in. She rolls onto her stomach and smothers her head with her pillow to try and block it out.

"Psst."

Dakota thinks she's hearing things, but when she lifts her head, the door creaks open slightly and Finley pokes her head inside.

"Wanna hear about materialism?" She holds up her encyclopedia hopefully. Dakota doesn't miss the quiver in her voice. She sits up slowly, rubbing her eyes.

"Don't like storms?"

Finley must take that as enough of an answer, because soon she's closing the door behind her and hurrying over to the unoccupied bed. Sitting cross legged, she turns to a dog-eared page in the book and starts reading.

"Materialism," she nods softly. Dakota lays on her back, gazing at the ceiling. "*Materialism, also called physicalism, in philosophy, the view that all facts are causally dependent upon physical processes, or even reducible to them.*"

Finley clears her throat and flips to the next page. And somehow, Dakota finds it easier to fall asleep with Finley's voice draining out the storm. By the time they get to "*martian,*" Dakota's long gone.

Chapter 3

DAMAGED GOODS

The next morning, Dakota's stirred awake by the hiss of a shower being turned on. She's quick to grab her things and make her claim to the second bathroom, relaxing as soon as she steps into the shower and the hot water soothes her muscles. It's a bit of a struggle to wash her hair with one hand, but she manages.

Holding her towel around herself with her free hand, Dakota stumbles out of the shower and digs through the drawers in search of a comb. Coming up empty, she huffs and turns to the medicine cabinet adjacent to the mirror. Something else catches her attention, though, and before she can stop herself she's studying the translucent orange bottle of pills, turning it around in her hand.

Ryland Moreno. Take by mouth as needed for pain.

Dakota winces and quickly puts the bottle back, shutting the medicine cabinet a little more forceful than necessary. Suddenly she feels guilty for having found them.

By the time she gets dressed and goes downstairs, everyone's just getting ready to leave. Finley offers her a shy smile, handing her a piece of toast. Dakota thanks her, holding it in her mouth as she tugs her backpack over her shoulders. And with that, they're off.

"You're telling me it's nearly 80 degrees out and you're wearing a jacket?" Ryland raises an eyebrow at Finley, who shrugs one shoulder.

"I like it," she hums, smoothing out the hem of the floral peach sundress she's wearing. Over it, she's clad in an olive green jacket that serves as more of a parka. Ryland just laughs, and Finley hops down the front steps and down the sidewalk. Ryland and Dakota exchange glances, but Ryland just shrugs and follows her, kicking the gate open with her good foot.

Finley peels an orange as they walk, tossing the peel into the grass beside them. She offers Dakota a slice, who takes one and keeps her eyes focused on her feet, stepping on every crack in the sidewalk. Gia diverges from them, taking a left turn when they hang a right. Dakota opens her mouth to call after her but changes her mind at the last minute—this must be normal. Finley just shakes her head and keeps walking.

"Was your dad a smoker?"

Dakota jumps when Ryland appears beside her, and she moves to walk in the grass so the girl can have more space. Mouthful of orange, she raises an eyebrow at the girl.

"Saw you putting out Gia's cigarettes yesterday," Ryland shrugs, glancing over at the girl. "Figured you had something against smokers."

"Oh," Dakota whispers, her eyes quickly diverting away. She hates the tense silence between them, though, so she just shrugs one shoulder and keeps her gaze focused on the ground. "If he was, I wouldn't know. Never met him."

"Join the club," Ryland laughs under her breath. Taken aback, Dakota glances over at her, and Ryland just offers her a sad smile and a shrug. Dakota's mind starts to race, filled with questions, but she keeps her silence, afraid to break Ryland's trust. She's just beginning to earn it.

Finley pushes the crosswalk button four times.

"Finley, hey."

Dakota weaves through the crowd of students, grabbing onto the arm that she'd spotted poking out of an army green jacket. Finley flinches, turning around quickly and looking at her in confusion.

"I'm not walking back with you guys," Dakota explains, pausing to catch her breath. "There's this party, I got invited, I'm getting a ride there," she motions with her hands. Finley furrows her eyebrows.

"You'll miss dinner," the girl whispers, lowering her voice and looking around to make sure no one's overheard them.

"Doesn't matter," she shakes her head. "Just let Red know where I am."

Finley nods reluctantly, tugging at the straps of her backpack. Dakota flashes her a thankful smile before disappearing back into the sea of people surrounding them.

When Dakota returns to the house, it's just a few minutes shy of midnight. And it's pouring rain. She ducks under the front porch, coughing and shaking the water out of her hair. The blue light coming through the windows signals that Finley's awake. She tries the door, but it's locked. Sighing, she taps on the window, drawing Finley's attention. Dakota points to the door, and Finley pads over, opening it just a crack and peering out at the girl.

"Can I come in?" Dakota raises an eyebrow, annoyance in her tone. Finley shies backwards, leaving the door open and taking a few slow steps back towards the couch. She glances over her shoulder at Dakota, concern flickering in her eyes.

"Are you—?"

"*Don't*," Dakota sighs and shakes her head. Biting her lip, Finley offers the girl a nervous smile before sinking back down onto the couch in front of her television. Dakota's up the stairs and collapsing in her bed within seconds.

She's been home for less than a minute before there's a knock at her door. Dakota lifts her head half-heartedly, her messy wet hair thrown across her pillow. A beam of light from the hallway seeps into the room as the door is pushed open a crack. *Ryland.*

"Hangover cure," the girl says softly, holding up a small glass. "Doesn't taste too great going down, but it saves you a whole lot of trouble in the morning. I'll just leave it here." She takes a few steps forward to set the glass down beside Dakota's bed.

"I didn't drink," Dakota mumbles. She rolls onto her back and focuses her eyes on the ceiling. She feels Ryland still beside her and holds her breath. Ryland's eyebrows stitch together when she notices the gash on Dakota's forehead, blood smeared down her cheek.

"Did they find out?" Ryland's voice softens. All Dakota can offer her is a slight nod. With a sigh, Ryland sinks down to sit on the edge of the bed.

"Two days, damn," she shakes her head. "Think we've got a new record."

"You make no sense," Dakota mumbles. She brings a hand up to her head and presses two fingers to the cut, holding them in front of her and grimacing at the red stain they leave behind.

"Everybody here lies about where they're from," Ryland shrugs. "Even Finley."

Dakota shifts her position slightly so she can sit up, blinking a few times to let her eyes adjust to the darkness. "Did you?"

"Yep," Ryland laughs softly. "Used the same rich uncle schtick that you did. Cept' mine was the owner of a restaurant." She motions for Dakota to scoot closer and reaches over to grab a handful of tissues from beside the bed. Holding Dakota's chin in one hand, she carefully dabs at the cut on her forehead with the other. "So who was it?"

"Huh?"

"Who did this?" Ryland nods once, showing Dakota the bloody tissue. Dakota grimaces.

"That would be me," she mutters, rolling her eyes. "I walked home. I took a shortcut but then I got lost. It was dark and I ran straight into one of those diagonal electrical wires."

"Smart move," Ryland laughs and shakes her head. "So they didn't retaliate?"

"Huh?"

"You know..." Ryland thinks for a moment, setting her hands down in her lap. "When they found out.... they didn't like... go after you?"

Dakota shakes her head.

"That's a first."

Tilting her head to the side, Dakota takes a moment to study the girl. "I take it you've been here a while?"

Ryland stands up, throwing the dirty tissues away and keeping her back turned for a few moments. She shrugs. "Depends on what you consider *a while*," she slowly sits back down on the edge of the bed. "Been here since I was fifteen. Jaden used to have me beat by a year but then she aged out of the system. This was her old room." She pats the bed. "How's the hand?"

Dakota doesn't ignore the fact that Ryland tried to change the subject. She looks down at her hand, shrugging with one shoulder. "Hurts more without the cast." Looking back up, she nods to the girl's leg. "When does yours come off?"

She regrets it as soon as she says it—something in Ryland shifts. The girl lifts her leg, looking at it, and then laughs under her breath. "Doesn't," she shakes her head. "Wish it did."

Immediately, Dakota's rushing to apologize. "No, oh my god, I'm an idiot," she shakes her head and holds up a hand as if she's surrendering. "That was so inconsiderate of me—,"

"I've heard worse," Ryland interrupts her, trying to keep the mood light. "Trust me. When they first brought Gia here, her first words to me—if i remember correctly—were '*who kicked your ass*?'"

Dakota frowns, but Ryland just laughs softly, unaffected. "She's improved since then, as you can see."

Nodding softly, Dakota picks at the bandage on her hand. "So how'd *she* get here?"

"Shoplifting," Ryland scoots back on the bed. "And then resisting arrest when she was *caught* shoplifting." This makes Dakota laugh quietly.

"That's when they found out she'd run away from home," Ryland glances out to the hallway. "She threatened to throw herself off a bridge if they even *thought* about sending her back to her parents."

"Shit," Dakota mumbles. Ryland just nods.

"Yeah. Her dad was a pastor of some sort," she rolls her eyes. "I think he got a little too aggressive with his kids sometimes, but I'm not sure. Gia refuses to talk about it."

"*Oh*," is all Dakota can say, her eyes moving down to her hands. The bed shifts and Ryland stands up, grabbing the glass from the nightstand.

"I take it you won't be needing this anymore," she laughs. "There's aspirin and shit downstairs if your head bothers you," she adds with a small nod. Dakota lays back in the bed when Ryland turns for the door. But then, her footsteps stop and there's a few moments of silence.

"T'was a car accident," Ryland's voice is quiet, and she leans against the doorway, keeping her back turned to the girl after answering her silent question. "My leg got caught in the door. Crushed all my nerves."

Dakota's breath catches and her eyes go wide. She sits up slightly, taken aback by Ryland's sudden confession. "I…" she struggles to find the right words. "I'm sorry…"

"Everyone is," Ryland shakes her head, still not making eye contact with the girl. She pushes off of the doorframe. "Night."

And with that, she's gone, leaving a confused Dakota in her wake. As soon as she's left alone, Dakota slumps back in the bed and curses herself. *Sorry*? Really? That's the best she could do? She groans, rolls over, and tugs the blankets over her head.

All night long she can hear the faint sound of Finley calling out Jeopardy answers.

The next morning, Dakota slowly makes her way down the stairs. It's earlier than she usually wakes up, but she'd barely gotten a wink of sleep anyway. Rubbing her eyes, she pauses at the bottom of the landing. Finley sits on the couch with her wet hair tied up in a bun. A Wheel of Fortune rerun plays on the TV, and Dakota wanders over to sit on the couch next to her.

"Morning," Finley mumbles, a mouthful of cereal. Dakota watches curiously as the girl digs her hand into the box of Fruity Pebbles between them. Carefully, Finley picks through the cereal, dropping three red flakes into her bowl of milk, dunking them under with her spoon, and then scooping them up into her mouth. She repeats this with every color. Orange, then yellow, then green. Somewhere in between, Dakota digs her hand into the box and grabs a handful of dry cereal for herself, leaning back on the couch as Finley mumbles the answers to the contestants on the screen.

Some time later, Ryland wanders downstairs, hugging a knitted blanket around her shoulders. She stands behind the couch for a few moments, yawning and studying the television before slipping past them and into the kitchen. She returns shortly after, cupping her hands around a coffee mug and lowering herself down into one of the old armchairs.

"Gia snuck out again," she finally speaks up, tapping her pointer finger against her mug. "Didn't even bother to close the window."

Finley furrows her eyebrows. "Will she get in trouble?"

"Not if she's back before Red realizes she's not asleep," Ryland shrugs, turning to glance down the hallway where Red's bedroom is. They're the only three awake, it seems.

Dropping another three flakes into her bowl, Finley taps her spoon against her bottom lip and shakes her head. "Where does she even go that's worth breaking probation for?"

"Who knows," Ryland shrugs. She takes a sip of her coffee, clears her throat, sets her mug down on the table. "Is this the one where they lose the million dollar prize?"

"Shh," Finley shakes her head and nods to the screen. "Don't spoil it."

Dakota looks to Ryland with a raised eyebrow, but the girl just laughs quietly and leans back in her chair. Finley drops three green flakes into her bowl.

“That’s Jaden.”

Dakota jumps when a voice appears from behind her, feeling as if she’s been caught doing something she’s not supposed to. But, in all actuality, she’s only been studying the pictures scattered above the fireplace, standing on her tiptoes to get a better look at them.

“She’d been here since she was eleven,” Ryland continues, moving to stand next to Dakota. “She was one of Red’s first girls. Taught me how to survive in this place.”

“What happened to her?” Dakota can’t help but ask. Ryland taps another picture—a now older Jaden adorned in a red cap and gown.

“Graduated and aged out of the system,” Ryland nods. “The last I heard of her she was visiting her brothers in Florida. God knows where she is now.”

“You don’t keep in touch?”

Ryland just shrugs. “No one really keeps in touch. Once you’re outta’ here, you don’t want to look back. Most of the kids that leave this place just pretend it never happened.”

Pursing her lips, Dakota stays quiet as her eyes trace over the rest of the pictures. She points to another one, a collection of girls sitting in front of the house. “Who are they?”

“I took this one,” Ryland notes, plucking the picture from the wall and holding it in front of her. She traces it with her finger until it lands on a girl with jet black hair. “Recognize her?” she smirks, tapping her nail against the figure.

"Gia?" Dakota's eyes widen.

"Yep," Ryland laughs and tapes the picture back up. "She came to us with black hair and a nose piercing. Red told her she could only keep one," she shakes her head. "So she kept her hair, took out the nose piercing, and snuck out to pierce her eyebrow."

"You're kidding."

"Do I ever kid?" Ryland laughs to herself. "That's when Red made her dye her hair back to blonde and scrap the piercings altogether."

Before Dakota can say anything else, Ryland snatches another photo from the wall and studies it closely before passing it over to her. "This was Finley's first week," she nods. "Took this one, too."

"Where is she?" Dakota tilts her head to the side. The picture is of three girls decorating a Christmas tree, but there's no Finley in sight.

"Look closer," Ryland slowly drags her finger to the top corner of the picture, tapping once. "See those shoes?"

Dakota nods.

"That's her," the girl explains. "She never came downstairs. But sometimes she'd get too curious and just watch us from the top of the banister. That's about as close as we got to her for a month or so."

"It was that bad?"

"That wasn't even the worst of it," Ryland shakes her head, but she doesn't elaborate. She sets the picture back down and takes a step back to admire the wall. "I don't even remember half of these faces," she admits. "And I probably shared a room with most of them."

Confused, Dakota tilts her head to the side.

"People come and go all the time," Ryland dismisses it with a wave of the hand. "You don't have time to learn names. Trust me.

I used to be like Finley—making friends with every new person that came here. But then I learned."

"Learned what?"

"That it's better not to get attached," Ryland states matter-of-factly, making Dakota frown. "Most kids don't stick around for long. They get their court date and then go back with their parents, or off with some relative—if they have them. It's not worth wasting your energy."

Dakota's shoulders drop slightly and she keeps her gaze fixed on the photos on the wall. "I wish that was the case for me."

"Parents in jail?"

Dakota shakes her head, scrambling to change the subject. "There's just… nowhere else for me to go. Legally, at least," she shrugs, looking down at her feet. "Unless my fairy godmother appears to save the day, I'm pretty much stuck here."

It's silent between them for a moment. But before it can get too uncomfortable, Ryland speaks up. "Well, then it's a good thing I remember your name," she nods once, pushing off of the fireplace and leaving Dakota in her wake. Alone again, Dakota's eyes land on a picture tucked behind one of the frames, and she carefully slides it out.

In the picture, Red sits on the couch next to a younger girl—one who Dakota quickly realizes is Ryland. Her entire leg is in a hard cast, and she's covering her face with a pillow, flicking off the camera with her free hand. For some reason, Dakota feels guilty for finding it, and she quickly slips it back into its hiding place on the mantle. There's a web of unanswered questions running through her head, and she's not so sure who she can turn to for answers. She feels as if everyone here is shrouded in mystery. Dakota figures they've all seen their share of evils if they've ended up here. This home, to her, seems like a last resort for people like her—a holding tank for the kids society has given up on. The thought scares her more than she's willing to admit.

Red digs out enough lunchmeat and bread so they can have sandwiches for lunch. Finley and Dakota sit on the edge of the island, their feet hanging down, and Ryland leans against the counter across from them. Red pauses as she's cleaning up, looking back and forth between all three girls.

"Getting along?" she raises an eyebrow. Finley nods quickly. Ryland just shrugs.

"Where's Gia?"

"Asleep," Ryland's quick to reply. Finley tenses from beside them. They all exchange glances when Red heads over to the bottom of the stairs.

"Alright, Gia!" she calls up, tapping her hand against the banister. "It's almost noon, come down and eat something." Finley looks to Ryland worriedly when silence follows.

Just as Red's about to make her way up the stairs, they hear heavy footsteps above them. Finley sighs, letting her shoulders drop in relief. Gia trudges into the kitchen moments later—her hair a mess, dark circles around her eyes from her makeup. Ryland stifles a laugh.

"Thanks," Gia mumbles, snatching the half eaten sandwich out of Finley's hands. The girl looks shocked at first, but she quickly recovers.

"It's spicy mustard," Finley warns her. Gia just shrugs, shoves half the sandwich in her mouth, and steals what's left of Ryland's orange juice. Dakota looks at Ryland questioningly, but all she gets is a roll of the eyes and a shrug in return.

"I've got to run out to the grocery store," Red announces, grabbing her keys from a hook on the wall. Finley quickly hops off the counter.

"Me too?"

Nodding softly, Red turns to the rest of them. "Be good," she warns them, her gaze resting on Gia. Ryland just dismisses her with the wave of a hand, and Finley's already got the front door wide open. As soon as they hear the car start in the driveway, Gia's headed back upstairs.

"Goodnight!" Ryland calls after her, a smug smile on her face. Gia flicks her off from over the banister.

Now just the two of them, Ryland makes herself busy by collecting their dirty dishes and rinsing them off in the sink. Dakota sits quietly on the counter, thinking pensively for a few moments.

"I can't believe you've been here the longest," she speaks up, spurring Ryland to pause and lean against the counter, drying off a plate in her hand. The girl tilts her head to the side.

"Why? Figured I'd have offed myself by now?"

Dakota nearly gasps, and then she quickly shakes her head to clear herself up. She stops though, when she sees Ryland laughing. So, rolling her eyes half heartedly, she just shrugs and hops off of the counter. "S'not that. I just… you're so…" she stumbles over her words, motioning to Ryland with one hand. "*Normal.*"

Ryland finds this hilarious, and she tosses the rag over her shoulder. "If only you knew…" she shakes her head.

"Then tell me," Dakota's suddenly pushes forward, and she takes a step closer to the girl. "Make me know."

Ryland glances back to her, raising an eyebrow. "No can do, kiddo, I like to keep my friendships for more than a week."

Dakota's left standing in the kitchen as Ryland wanders over and falls back onto the couch, surfing through the channels.

"So we're friends now?" Dakota notes, raising an eyebrow. Ryland doesn't respond, and Dakota huffs in frustration.

It's silent for a while as Dakota digs an ice pack out of the freezer and unwraps the bandage around her hand. She hisses when she presses it to her bruised knuckles, and bites down on her lip as she flattens her hand out on the counter.

"So how'd your grand old lie get exposed?" Ryland clicks off the TV, finding nothing of interest, and turns around on the couch to watch Dakota. The dark haired girl sits down at the island, icing her hand, and shrugs.

"I told them."

This effectively confuses Ryland. "You told them?"

"You heard me," Dakota mumbles. Knowing Ryland will keep pushing the topic, she just shakes her head and turns to disappear upstairs. She hears the girl sigh in frustration, but blocks it out as best as she can. No one scolds her for having her door all the way closed.

The rest of the day passes by quickly, mostly because Dakota barricades herself in her room to try and catch up on the stack of make-up work her teachers have assigned her. After dinner, she ends up falling asleep halfway through a math worksheet, her broken hand hanging off the bed and her hair sprawled over her textbook.

It's around midnight when the alarm sounds. Ryland's jolted awake when she hears the four telltale warning beeps, and then the alarm blares throughout the whole house. Gia stirs in the bed across the room, and they both sit up in confusion. It takes them a moment to understand what's going on, but when they hear rushed footsteps downstairs, they exchange wide eyed glances.

Just as Ryland stands up to go see what's going on, Finley bursts into the room.

"She wouldn't listen to me," Finley shakes her head quickly, visibly distressed.

"What are you talking about?" Ryland rubs her eyes. Gia groans and falls back onto the bed, covering her face with a pillow.

"Dakota," Finley throws her hands down to her sides, not knowing what to do with them. "She... she... I told her but she didn't listen, I..."

"Alright, calm down," Ryland grabs Finley's shoulders. "Show me."

Finley drags Ryland down the hallway, peering around the corner of the wall before nodding for Ryland to follow her. They lean over the banister adjacent to the stairs that gives them a view of the living room. Quietly, the two girls watch as Red leads a solemn Dakota back into the house, a blanket around her shoulders. She helps the girl sit down on the couch and then quickly closes the door behind them. Even in the dark, Ryland can see the girl is shaking.

"She just went outside," Finley whispers. "I tried to tell her not to."

Ryland nods slowly, holding a finger up to her lips to silence the girl. Finley clamps her mouth shut, leaning further over the railing. Ryland practically has to pull her back to keep her from falling face first. She tugs the girl back down the hallway.

"Just go back to bed, Finley," she says quietly, glancing behind them. "Red will get mad if she knows we're eavesdropping."

"But—," Finley starts, but quickly takes her words back when she sees how serious Ryland is. With a quick nod, she tiptoes back down the hallway and shuts her door as quietly as she can. Ryland takes a deep breath and sits down on the edge of her bed, rolling her eyes when she realizes Gia's already fallen back asleep.

Dakota doesn't even know what happened. All she knows is one second she was mid-nightmare, and then suddenly she was rushed forwards into reality with Red grabbing her by her shoulders and repeating her name over and over. When she had looked down, her feet were planted in the middle of the street.

So she let Red lead her back inside, and now she's sitting anxiously on the couch, hugging a pillow to her chest and trying to slow her breathing. She still feels like she's in the dream, she still feels like she's just ran a marathon, she still smells smoke. It always takes her a while to recover after a nightmare, but now she's just in a haze of confusion.

"Here," Red walks back over, handing her a mug of something warm. "Drink."

It's tea. Dakota takes a few sips and nods softly. Red sits down on the arm of the couch and studies the girl for a few moments.

"Another girl who passed through here was a sleepwalker, but the most she did was wander downstairs and fall asleep in a different room," Red laughs softly. "I guess we've got our hands full with you."

"This has never happened before," Dakota clears her throat and brings a hand up to her pounding forehead. "I don't even remember… I…"

"You're probably not even fully awake," Red notes. "It's best you just try and go back to sleep."

Dakota simply nods, standing up and wiping her eyes. "Thanks."

"You're alright?"

"M'fine," she mumbles. "G'night."

When she goes back upstairs, though, she doesn't go into her bedroom. Instead, she grabs one of the towels from the hall closet and slips into the bathroom. Something pushes her to take a cold shower. Her whole body feels numb, but her forehead is burning up. She's desperate to just wash it all away.

The shower squeaks as it comes to life, spitting cold water out and slowly turning into a stream. Dakota takes a deep breath, closing the door behind her and stepping under the water. It's cold at first, but she ends up cranking the knob to the side, making the water even colder. She wants to scrub her skin until it falls off.

She's slowly starting to remember what the nightmare had been about. Normally, her nightmares end with her being cornered by the fire, but this time she'd managed to run through it and get to the front door. When she escaped the house in her dream, she realizes, she must have also been doing the same in real life.

"*Shut up*," she mutters to herself, pressing her hands against her forehead and squeezing her eyes shut. The water drips down her face, and she forces herself to take a deep breath. It feels like she's gasping for air at this point. Everything's catching up with her. She just wants to go home.

Eventually, she hugs a towel tight around her small form and tiptoes out of the shower. When she slips across the hallway to grab a comb, she nearly gasps when Ryland's in the other bathroom, digging through the medicine cabinet. They look at each other for a few moments in awkward silence.

"I won't ask," Ryland mumbles before tossing a pill in her mouth and throwing her head back to take a swig of water. She swallows and then looks back to Dakota, who just nods softly.

Once Ryland disappears back into her bedroom, Dakota gets dressed and wanders down to the other end of the hallway, having noticed the light coming from underneath Finley's door. She knocks quietly.

"It's me," she whispers, pushing the door open slightly and peering in. Sitting cross legged on her bed, Finley looks up from her book and gives Dakota a nervous smile.

"Wanna watch Jeopardy?" Dakota bites her lip. Within seconds, Finley's on her feet and hurrying downstairs.

Dakota falls asleep in the middle of their second episode, curled up in the beanbag chair.

Chapter 4

THE GHOSTS WE KEEP ALIVE

On Sunday afternoon, all the girls are sent to their rooms so Gia can meet with her social worker in the living room. Dakota's working on homework when there's a knock at her door.

"Hm?" she lifts her head, expecting Finley or Ryland. However, she quickly sits up when an older woman pokes her head in the door.

"You must be Dakota," she smiles. "May I come in?"

"Who are you?"

"Your new social worker," the woman walks over to shake her hand. Dakota clenches her jaw when she takes a seat on the bed beside her. "I read over your file this morning."

"And?" Dakota slams her textbook shut and shoves it aside.

"It's… a lot."

Dakota just scoffs.

"I thought you'd be happy to know that your brother isn't in any serious trouble," she continues, and Dakota stiffens. "As far as I know he's currently staying with a friend of his in the neighborhood."

"And the house?" Dakota's voice softens.

"What about it?"

"What's happening to it?" the dark haired girl looks down at her hands.

"My guess is they're going to continue trying to sell it," the social worker shrugs. "The electricity hasn't even been on for… for *years*, Dakota. How did you two manage?"

"We made do," Dakota shrugs, clenching her fist. "No one's gonna buy it," she adds. "It's haunted."

"I was under the impression that you and your brother started that rumor to keep people away from it."

Dakota looks away. "It's *our* house."

"I know you may have an emotional attachment to your childhood home, Dakota. We all do," the social worker sighs. Dakota scoots away from her. "But legally, the house isn't yours. Or your brother's. The state repossessed it. The state's the one who funded all the repairs after the fire. The state—,"

"*I get it*," Dakota mutters. If it wasn't for her broken hand, she'd probably have already punched something by now. She pauses to take a deep breath before looking back to the woman. "When can I see my brother?"

"I looked into that," she nods. "But the state wants to get court approval before I can schedule a visit for you two. They're concerned you may negatively influence each other."

"He's my *brother*," Dakota gapes, her shoulders rising. "And '*schedule a visit*?' What the hell does that mean? You can't just keep us apart!"

"It's out of my hands, Dakota."

Dakota shuts off at this point. The rest of the meeting consists of her just nodding and agreeing with whatever the social worker says, paying more attention to the fraying string on her jeans than anything. Eventually, the visit ends awkwardly, and she follows the woman back downstairs.

Dakota stands in the doorway, absentmindedly turning the knob back and forth as she watches the social worker start her car and drive off. Clenching her jaw, she whips her head around and slams the door shut. The walls shake and something falls over on one of the shelves. When Dakota turns to go back upstairs, she pauses when she realizes Finley's been here the whole time, laying upside down on the couch with a book in her hands.

"Listen to this," Finley offers Dakota a sad smile, sitting up and tracing her finger over the book. "*Blades of grass are called 'blades' because they actually do cut your skin, just so small that the naked eye cannot see. That's why sitting on grass can cause skin irritation.*"

"Awesome," Dakota mutters under her breath, disappearing without another word.

Ryland gets home from lunch with her social worker later that afternoon, feeling no more motivated or inspired than she had before. She tosses her bag aside, but pauses when she sheds her jacket. There's commotion upstairs. She looks to Finley for an explanation, who's still hanging upside down from the couch and reading. The curly haired girl just shakes her head, a stoic look on her face.

Ryland raises an eyebrow, but hangs her jacket up and quickly makes her way to the stairs. Finley sits up quickly.

"Bad idea!" she calls after Ryland, but her words are ignored. Ryland's already halfway up the steps.

She pauses outside Dakota's door, flinching when something hits the other side and causes it to slam shut. Unsure of what to do, Ryland listens as something else is thrown across the room, and footsteps hurry to follow it. She pushes open the door and just narrowly dodges the dresser drawer that skids past her. Standing in the middle of the room, Dakota freezes. There's a split second where they both stand there, staring at one another, but it's over when Dakota shakes her head and continues digging through her drawers.

"You don't understand," Dakota mutters, throwing a handful of clothes to the ground. "You don't—,"

"Dakota..." Ryland takes a step forward, but the girl flinches away from her.

"Don't!" she glares at Ryland. "Don't touch me."

So instead, Ryland takes a slow step backwards, watching as Dakota clears out the last drawer from her dresser and kicks it across the floor in frustration. Ryland wants to ask her what she's doing, but she knows better.

"You don't understand," Dakota repeats herself, moving over to her nightstand. Her path is interrupted, though, when she nearly trips on something sticking out from underneath her bed. She pauses, immediately sliding to her knees and tearing through the suitcase. Her eyes widen when she pulls out a manilla folder, and she empties it onto the floor. The whole entire mood in the room shifts.

Ryland catches a glimpse of something pink before Dakota snatches it up, hugging it against her chest. Suddenly, she isn't throwing things across the room anymore. Her disposition has completely changed. The dark haired girl quietly sits on her bed, pulling her legs up underneath her and taking a deep breath. Ryland watches awkwardly from the doorway.

Dakota places the paper in her lap, holding her breath as she runs her fingers across it. Ryland takes a cautious step forward, and then another, and then, slowly, she sits down a foot or so away from Dakota on the edge of the bed.

Dakota doesn't move away, so Ryland quietly looks at the picture in her hands. It's a crudely cut heart, made out of pink construction paper. "Mother's Day," is written in purple crayon, and wiggly circle of glitter glue outlines a picture in the middle. Leaning closer, Ryland recognizes one of the two faces.

"That's her?" she whispers, biting her lip.

Dakota doesn't even look at her, she just keeps her eyes on the picture, pressing her fingers against it and giving Ryland the slightest of nods. With a sigh, Ryland scoots closer and puts an arm around the girl. And, surprisingly, Dakota doesn't shove her away. Instead, she leans over and rests her head on Ryland's shoulder, still looking at the picture.

"You look like her," Ryland says softly, gently squeezing the girl's shoulder. She feels Dakota exhale slowly. "Even there. Same dark hair and blue eyes."

"It was a fire," Dakota blurts out before she can stop herself. She can feel Ryland tense beside her, but she forces herself to keep her eyes down, to keep talking. "It was a fire," she repeats herself.

"You don't have to—,"

"My brother was the one who woke me up," Dakota continues, allowing herself to confide in the girl. "After everyone went to bed I used to sneak downstairs and watch TV, and I always fell asleep on the couch. If I hadn't had been downstairs I don't think I would've… you know…"

Ryland nods softly. Dakota runs her thumb over the picture, her hands shaking slightly from how tight she's holding it.

"The fire was on the upper level, but it spread fast. The entire front door was like… red hot," she shakes her head, gesturing as if she's pressing her hands against a door. "My brother burnt his hand trying to open it."

"I was screaming for my mom the whole time but… I never knew how *loud* fire was. It was roaring. I couldn't hear anything." Ryland looks down. "We were young… we didn't really know what to do so we started going back upstairs to find her. But it was so smokey and I couldn't see, I just kept coughing."

"I don't really remember the rest, but apparently one of our neighbors broke a window on the first level and yelled for us to follow his voice, then helped Hudson climb through and carried me out."

"The next thing I remember clearly is sitting on the back bumper of the police car and refusing to let go of my brother," Dakota runs a hand through her hair, drawing in a shaky breath. "He said I kept trying to hit any of the officers that came near us because I thought we were being attacked or something."

Ryland doesn't say anything, but she nods, listening intently. There's something different flickering in her dark brown eyes. Dakota can't quite put a finger on what it is.

"We weren't supposed to find out she was dead right then. But I guess one of the neighbors was yelling at an officer and Hudson overheard him say something like '*What are these kids gonna do without a mother*!?' And I remember my brother… he stood up so quickly and everyone turned to look at us. I can still hear his voice when he asked them if she was dead. And then I just started screaming for her and… and running towards the house. One of the firefighters had to make a grab for me and his arm ended up knocking the wind out of me, and I was just coughing and screaming her name over and over and punching him to try and get out of his arms…"

Dakota trails off when her words start to jumble together, catching her breath and looking away. "We didn't even go to the funeral. We were supposed to stay at the neighbor's house overnight but Hudson waited until they went back to bed and then made me climb out the window with him. We'd watched a lot of movies about siblings who got separated, you know? He didn't want that to happen."

"Did they ever catch you?" Ryland speaks up for the first time. Dakota shakes her head.

"Not until last week," she presses a hand to her forehead. "It was all him, he somehow kept us under the radar. He was thirteen at the time, but he always kept me sheltered from it. I don't know how he did it. Somehow they believed we were staying with our uncle in Massachusetts. I've never even been to Massachusetts." She laughs bitterly.

"How old were you?"

"Just turned seven."

Ryland takes a deep breath.

"We slept in the dugout of a baseball field at an elementary school for the first month. The school didn't even have a baseball team so… we were pretty hidden. Then they fixed the house and put it up for sale and we just… kinda… moved back in." Dakota shrugs lightly.

"How'd you pull that off?"

"Kept all the curtains closed. Never used the front door. Electricity was out so no one ever saw lights on or anything," she bites her lip, and Ryland notes how she recites these like a list of rules. "We walked two miles to a new school every morning to avoid our old one."

"I guess we kinda took on alter egos to stay hidden, you know?" Dakota thinks for a moment. "Hudson cut his hair really short and you couldn't even recognize him, because he used to have this wild mop of curly hair that he got teased for. He got everyone to start calling him by our last name, Quinn. Made me tell people my name was Danielle and just go by 'D.'"

"We got more careless as we got older, though. Hudson used to dig up the 'For Sale' signs and just shove them in the garage. Once some guy caught us in the backyard and started yelling at us for trespassing. We had to spend a night away from the house just to be safe," she shrugs. "But in high school most of my friends knew who I really was and kept it a secret. By then I was old enough to take care of myself."

"Not according to the state," Ryland notes. Dakota rolls her eyes.

"Unfortunately not," Dakota shakes her head. "You know, you manage on your own for nine years, and for some reason they think it's in your best interest to separate you from your only family and strip away any sense of familiarity," her voice grows cold and she turns to look at Ryland. "Makes perfect sense, right?"

"None of this makes sense," Ryland sighs. Defeated, Dakota leans into her side and clutches the picture between both of her hands.

"M'sorry for dumping that on you," Dakota mumbles after a short period of silence. Ryland just laughs softly.

"Don't be," she shakes her head. "I hear everyone's stories at one point or another. They make mine seem a little less fucked up."

Dakota's about to ask Ryland what her story is, but she's interrupted by the sound of the front door being opened and closed, and someone calling up "*Dinner*!" Dakota sits up quickly with wide eyes.

"You clean this up," Ryland's on her feet within seconds, motioning around the room. "I'll cover for you downstairs." All

Dakota can muster is a soft nod, and then Ryland slips out of the room.

(Later that night, there's a knock at her door, and when Dakota opens it, she almost steps on the plate of food left in the hallway for her. Raising an eyebrow, she looks across the hallway into Finley's room, but the girl sitting on her bed just points to herself and shakes her head.)

"Alright Finley, you start us off for highs and lows."

Dakota's seated cross-legged in one of the kitchen chairs, next to the couch where Ryland and Finley sit. Finley's drinking her tea as always, and Ryland's combing through her wet hair, flicking water across the circle to Gia every few seconds until Red sends a warning glare in her direction.

"My low is that we have to go back to school tomorrow," Finley thinks for a moment. "And my high…"

"I talked to my social worker today," she nods. "I get to see my mom on Wednesday. *Wednesday at twelve o'clock*, she said." The girl looks around the circle and then smiles widely. "That's in three days."

They all offer her smiles of excitement, but Ryland glances over to Dakota and shakes her head. Dakota raises an eyebrow, but by then Finley's already nudged Ryland to let her know it's her turn.

"My low is the same as Finley," Ryland nods once, high-fiving the other girl. "And I turn eighteen in five months, does that count as a high?"

"Hell yeah it does," Gia speaks up from across the room. Ryland laughs but Finley scolds her for 'language.'

"And Gia?" Red turns to the girl.

"My low is this stupid headache," Gia furrows her eyebrows together and shakes her head. "A high…" she looks around the room, thinking. "The weather's nice?" She shrugs. All eyes then turn to Dakota, who shyly looks away.

"Dakota?" Red prompts her. Ryland watches hesitantly.

"They're keeping me away from my brother," Dakota admits, surprising even herself. Finley tilts her head to the side curiously. "That's a low."

"And a high?"

Dakota bites her lip and looks down at her hands, picking at her bandage. "Is it okay if I don't have one?" she asks quietly, looking back up. Surprisingly, Red just gives her a soft nod from across the circle and changes the subject.

Ryland reaches over to squeeze her shoulder, and Finley offers her a butterscotch candy from the middle of the table. Dakota smiles shyly back to them.

That night, just as Dakota's about to go to bed, someone slips into her room from the dark hallway. She looks up and tilts her head to the side. It's the same pair of brown eyes from earlier that day. Avoiding her gaze, Ryland holds something in both of her hands and sits down on the end of her bed. She pages through the book—a photo album—and then places it in Dakota's lap.

"That's mine," she says softly, pointing to a picture of a woman in a floral sundress, holding a smaller girl on her hip. Dakota studies it for a moment.

"That's you?" she points to the child in the picture. Ryland nods. "And that's your…?"

"Mom," Ryland finishes her sentence for her, taking the album back into her lap and flipping to the next page of pictures.

"These are some of the only photos I've got of us. Probably one of the only good memories, too."

"How old were you here?" Dakota points to another picture.

"Six," Ryland nods. "I only got these a year or so ago." She points to a blurry picture of the beach. "We went on this vacation… at least, that's what she called it. We were on the run from another one of her psycho ex-boyfriends and made a stop in Ocean City for a few days."

Dakota nods softly, glancing at the pictures and then back to Ryland.

"It's funny, actually," Ryland half-smiles. "At the time I didn't really understand the concept of paying for things in a store, so when we went to the boardwalk, I just slipped this camera into my mom's purse thinking it was free. She thought it was the funniest thing when we got back to the hotel and found it. Even after it ran out of film I would pretend it was a real camera and point it at everything." She holds up her fingers as if she's holding a camera and turns to Dakota, making a clicking noise with her mouth. The dark haired girl laughs softly.

"Last year they sent it back to me along with a bunch of other shit of my mother's, I guess the people investigating her suicide never considered there'd be someone she left behind," Ryland's voice grows softer. "If I hadn't have investigated her case when I got older I would've never gotten any of this back."

There's a few seconds of silence and Ryland slowly realizes what she's said. Dakota slowly traces her fingers over the pictures. "Did… did she…?"

"*Yeah*," Ryland's voice is barely a whisper. She closes the photo album and shoves it aside, and Dakota braces for her to storm out of the room. But instead, Ryland just sighs and lays back on the bed. "It's a long story."

Taking a chance, Dakota mimics her and lays back, both of them staring at the ceiling with their arms crossed over their chests. "I've got all the time in the world."

"You sure?" Ryland turns her head so she's looking at Dakota, who does the same. "This is your last chance to back out."

"I'm sure," Dakota laughs softly and nudges her shoulder. "I told you mine, remember? You owe me one."

Ryland nods, gazing back up at the ceiling. "Alright…" she thinks for a few moments, suddenly forced to revisit an onslaught of memories she'd tried to forget. "Well. It was a week or two after that vacation I told you about."

"The psycho ex-boyfriend finally got arrested for a DUI," Ryland nods. "She had a lot of those, by the way," she pauses. My mom… she was… *alright.* I don't think she ever really loved me in the way that you'd expect a mother to love their daughter, you know? She loved men a hell of a lot more than she did me."

Quietly, as she listens, Dakota slides the small photo album between them and starts paging through the pictures. She tries to put herself in Ryland's shoes, studying the small girl who seems so happy and carefree in the photographs.

"She had her good days. Occasionally. The bad days were a lot more common, though. Like, one time… I remember one of her boyfriends brought me this brand new bike for my birthday. It was bright red. Had streamers coming from the handles and everything," she laughs softly. "But when I woke up the next morning it was gone. She sold it for drug money."

"You're kidding me."

"Wish I was," Ryland just laughs and shakes her head. "She'd drink or snort or smoke anything she could get her hands on. She used to inject stuff, too. But she stopped doing it in the house after she found me playing with one of the used needles," her voice grows softer. "It was… confusing, you know? I remember wanting her approval so badly and doing whatever I could to get it. It was never enough."

Dakota hums softly, looking up from the photo album and realizing she's never seen Ryland look this vulnerable. She shivers.

"Anyway," Ryland clears her throat, trying to shake off her nerves. "I woke up from a nap one day after we got back from the beach. Found her in the bathtub. Her fingertips were turning blue." Ryland pauses to hold up her own hands in front of her, studying them.

"Was she…?"

"Dead. She was dead," Ryland nods once. "There were pills all over the floor." She pauses. "I don't think I had a moment like you did… I didn't scream or try and shake her awake or anything. I honestly don't remember too much of it. They tell me they found me the next morning curled up next to her. Apparently I'd cleaned up all the pills, too. Put them back in the right bottles and everything."

Ryland sniffs, and Dakota sees her squeeze her eyes shut and press her palms against them. She looks back and forth from Ryland to the picture in front of her—of tiny Ryland hanging upside down from the bed in the hotel room, her mouth open in a wide smile.

"I'm sorry," Dakota whispers, shaking her head. "I know that sounds stupid, but… I don't know. I'm sorry."

"S'fine," Ryland shakes her head and gives her a sad smile. "They just shuffled me through the system after that. I lost count after six foster homes, I think," she furrows her eyebrows. "A lot of families take in kids thinking that they'll fit in right away, you know? Like they could just go to the store and pick out the perfect child and they'll be the perfect family. They don't want to make the effort to fix the broken kid." Her voice cracks and she pauses.

"And then I got older and gave up on ever bonding with any of these families, that was about it for me," she shrugs. "And now I'm here. This home's the closest thing to family I've got."

"M'sorry," Dakota mumbles again.

"Stop apologizing," Ryland laughs and pushes the girl's shoulder. She sits up, trying to lighten the dark mood that's fallen over the both of them. "So there. Now we're even. Not so normal now, am I?"

Dakota pushes herself up to sit beside Ryland and shrugs. "Are any of us?"

Ryland thinks about this for a moment before sighing. "Good question, tiny."

Chapter 5

Black and Blue

Dakota really hates school.

It's not that she doesn't like learning, because she does. But she hates feeling like an outsider around her peers. Something's put a wedge between her and most of them unconsciously, as if she just can't find any way to connect with these people. Her situation seems so different from theirs.

With a deep breath, she keeps her head down and ducks around the back of the courtyard. After Friday night, she doesn't dare go near anyone else. So instead, she's the first to the brick wall where Finley usually sits.

When Ryland slips outside, she immediately notices Dakota, sitting awkwardly by Finley's usual spot, alone. She feels equal parts happy and guilty. Making her way over to the girl, she offers Dakota a sad smile and hops up to sit on the wall beside her.

"How's Monday treating you?" Ryland laughs softly, digging a brown paper bag out of her backpack.

"Average," Dakota shrugs. Ryland holds a half of her sandwich up, raising an eyebrow at Dakota, who takes it gently. "Thanks."

"Hi," another voice appears. Finley pops up from behind them and climbs over the wall, sitting cross legged. She offers them both a small smile before stealing a drink from Ryland's water bottle.

"You're unusually cheerful for a Monday," Ryland comments. Finley just shrugs.

"Today's not so bad," she mumbles, a mouthful of food. "No one's said anything to me."

"That's a good thing?" Dakota speaks up. Finley nods contently.

"She gets a lot of shit from some people," Ryland tosses a grape in Finley's direction. "Some more than others," she adds quietly, nudging Dakota and then pointing across the courtyard to a table full of guys.

Dakota just nods softly, but Ryland pauses when she notices something different. A dark back eye on one of the students she's motioned to. She couldn't miss it if she tried. Ryland turns to look back at Dakota, but the other girl quickly looks away.

Once they throw away their trash and Finley disappears in search of her next class, Ryland grabs ahold of Dakota before she has a chance to slip away. Pulling her aside, she raises an eyebrow at the younger girl. "*What did you do*?"

"I don't know what you're talking about," Dakota quips back, a little too quickly.

Ryland just grabs Dakota's non-bandaged hand and turns it over. Of course, there's tell-tale bruises on her knuckles. Dakota yanks her hand away.

"And what would have happened if you broke that hand too?" Ryland tilts her head to the side.

"I didn't," Dakota mutters, shaking her head. "I didn't aim for the nose."

"I can tell," Ryland laughs, glancing over her shoulder. "Seems like his eye took most of the beating."

"I have to go to class," Dakota tries to hurry away, but Ryland's too quick for her. The girl grabs her backpack and pulls her back, coming face to face once more with a now-annoyed Dakota.

"Why'd you do it?"

"He deserved it," Dakota huffs and shrugs her backpack out of Ryland's grip. "He doesn't know anything…" she mutters under her breath. "Not a damn thing."

"Did he say something?" Ryland crosses her arms. Dakota just sighs.

"It was at the stupid party I went to. He started saying shit about this girl in his math class. And then I realized it was Finley," Dakota rolls her eyes. "He got what was coming to him, okay?"

"So you defended Finley."

"I defended *myself*," Dakota shakes her head. "We all come from the same place."

"So *that's* why no one's messed with her today," Ryland notes.

Dakota groans and leans against the wall, her shoulders dropping in defeat. "It's also why no one sat beside me in history." She rolls her eyes. And then, on a last minute's impulse, looks to Ryland hopefully. "Can we leave? I hate it here."

"You want to skip?" Ryland raises an eyebrow, an amused smile forming on her face when Dakota nods.

"Follow me," Ryland laughs softly, nodding towards the door and then hurrying to blend into the sea of students. Dakota sticks close behind her, eventually reaching out to grab a hold of her backpack so she doesn't get lost. They catch Finley at her locker, and Ryland leans beside her.

"We're leaving early today," Ryland gains Finley's attention, who hugs a textbook to her chest and tilts her head to the side. "Wanna come?"

"You're just… not going to class?"

"Yep," Ryland nods. "You coming or what?"

"I…" Finley hesitates, pausing to glance up and down the hallway. "I mean… I'd rather not have to walk home alone…" Dakota can see the slightest of smiles tugging at her lips. And Ryland reaches out to squeeze the girl's shoulder.

"C'mon, kid, you deserve a day off," Ryland laughs, nodding to the end of the hallway.

And so, with that, Ryland's digging through her backpack and holding up a keycard in victory. Dakota raises an eyebrow when she scans it next to the back exit, and it works. The locks click off and Ryland smirks, holding the door open as they make their way outside.

"How?" Dakota laughs, glancing back at the building.

"It's all magnets," Ryland shrugs, tucking the card back into her pocket. "Pretty easy to manipulate if you have the know-how," she points to her head jokingly. Dakota rolls her eyes.

"If we go home Red will be mad," Finley notes, kicking a pebble as they walk. She glances at her watch. "She doesn't leave until exactly… 12:43."

"We aren't going home yet," Ryland shakes her head. "I figured we'd walk down to the tracks."

Finley nods quickly. "I'm fine with that," she smiles softly, kicking an empty can across the parking lot.

After ducking behind a dumpster, hopping a fence, and taking a shortcut through someone's backyard, the three girls end up wandering down a seemingly-endless set of train tracks. Finley's a ways ahead of them, balancing on the metal rods, while Dakota and Ryland trail behind.

Eventually they sit down on the tracks by a small pond, where Finley skips rocks absentmindedly. Dakota leans back on her hands, closing her eyes and feeling the sun warm her face. This beats being in school any day.

"Dakota?" Finley tosses another rock in the pond before turning to look at the girl.

"Hm?"

"What was your mom like?"

Dakota's taken aback by the question, but she just shrugs. "She was cool."

"Yeah, but what was she *like*?" Finley prods. "Was she pretty? Was she a good mom?"

Dakota nods. "Yeah. I, uh… I don't know how to describe her. She was always patient with us. She never really yelled or raised her voice. Always made sure to tell us how much she loved us…" she trails off. "She was basically the opposite of everything I am."

"I doubt that," Ryland speaks up. Dakota just glances over at her and shrugs. Finley tosses another rock, creating a series of ripples in the pond.

"What about you, Finley?" Ryland changes the subject. "You nervous to see your mom?"

Furrowing her eyebrows, Finley shakes her head. "Nope," she smiles. "I haven't seen her in a while. My social worker says she's been asking about me." The curly haired girl pauses, turning a stone around in her hands. "Maybe we'll get to go home soon."

Ryland looks at Dakota nervously before turning back to Finley and nodding softly. "I'm sure you'll get to go home before you know it, Finn."

"It's *Finley*," the other girl corrects her.

"Is Finley short for Finnegan?" Dakota raises an eyebrow. Almost immediately, Finley's head drops and she doesn't reply.

"It's short for Muffin," Ryland answers for Finley, exchanging glances with Dakota. "Her mom told the doctors that was her name."

"Like the food?"

Ryland nods.

"It's not her fault," Finley mumbles. "They wouldn't put her on the good medicine because she was pregnant with me." She tosses another rock and then leans her head back. "Schizophrenia…" she speaks softly from memory. "*A psychotic disorder marked by severely impaired thinking, emotions, and behaviors. The term schizophrenia comes from two Greek words that mean 'split mind.' Schizophrenia is the most chronic and disabling of the severe mental disorders, associated with abnormalities of brain structure and function, as well as disorganized speech and behavior, delusions, and hallucinations.*"

"So Muffin turned into Fin, and then Fin turned into Finley. Get it?" Ryland explains to Dakota, who nods quickly in understanding.

"What about your middle name?"

"Don't have one," Finley whispers, absentmindedly nudging the tip of her shoe into the dirt. "M'just Finley Brown."

Ryland and Dakota look at one another. Dakota raises a questioning eyebrow but Ryland just shakes her head, as if to dismiss her further questions.

"Alright," Finley hops to her feet, brushing off her hands on her jacket. "We should get going. House is…" she glances to her watch. "*Empty*. Coast is clear."

Dakota stands up and offers Ryland her hand, earning a confused glare from the girl. However, she allows Dakota to help her to her feet, giving her a shy half-smile.

Gia's sitting on the front step when they arrive back to the house. A cigarette hangs out of her mouth as she aimlessly flicks through the mail. She looks up, mumbling a "*finally*" when Finley hops up the stoop to unlock the door.

"Red only trusts Finley with the key," Ryland glances to Dakota. "For obvious reasons."

Dakota just laughs, shaking her head and following the other girls into the house. She goes out of her way to step on Gia's cigarette, digging her heel into the ground. This doesn't go unnoticed by Ryland, either, who slips inside behind her.

"Tonight's pizza night," Finley announces as she digs through the wicker chest behind the couch. Smiling triumphantly, she holds up a game of Monopoly and looks to the other girls hopefully. "Wanna play?"

Gia looks to Ryland, who looks to Dakota, who shrugs and plops down on the couch.

"I call the thimble."

Tuesday comes and goes uneventfully. Wednesday is when things start to get interesting.

"Hit me," Dakota mumbles, holding out her bowl to Finley, who fishes in the box of cereal and drops a handful into her milk. Dakota mumbles a thank you and hops onto one of the stools at the island, rubbing her eyes.

"I see my mom today," Finley nods excitedly, tapping her spoon against her bowl.

"We know," Ryland's raspy voice appears, making her way down the stairs. She yawns, stretching out her arms. "You woke me up last night to remind me." Dakota laughs from across the room.

Grabbing a spoon, Ryland leans over the counter and steals a bite from Dakota's bowl, who doesn't flinch. She's used to it by now.

"I don't have to go to school either," Finley hums, dropping three more pieces of cereal into her milk. Ryland rolls her eyes in Dakota's direction, earning a soft laugh from the girl.

"Neither do I," Ryland reminds her.

"That reminds me," Red speaks up from her seat at the kitchen table, a laptop and papers spread out around her. "Dakota, do you have your license?"

"It's upstairs. Why?"

Red thinks for a moment, looking to Ryland and then to Finley. "I forgot Ryland had her appointment today and I've got to take Finley to see her mom. If I take the bus and leave you the car, can I trust you to drive Ryland to the doctor?"

Ryland's eyes widen. "But—,"

"I'm not rescheduling it again, Ryland," Red warns her. Ryland's eyes flicker downwards.

"I can drive her," Dakota shrugs. "It's no big deal."

"That means you get to skip school, too," Finley informs her from across the room, giving her a thumbs up. Dakota laughs, but Ryland just tosses her spoon into the sink and disappears back upstairs without another word.

"What was that all about?" Red looks to Dakota for an answer, getting nothing but a shrug in response.

"Ryland hates physical therapy," Finley mumbles with a mouthful of food. "She says it's '*stupid, useless, and painstakingly demeaning*,'" she nods. "She said a couple bad words about it, too."

Sighing, Red closes her laptop and turns to Dakota. "Can I count on you to get her there?"

"I'll try my best," Dakota hums.

With a soft nod, Red glances to the stairs. "Should I even bother waking up Gia?"

"If you have a death wish," Dakota mumbles. Finley shakes her head.

"There's no use. If she has to walk to school on her own, she'll never even make it to the crosswalk."

"*Alright*," Red holds up her hands as if she's surrendering. "I guess you all have the day off." She moves to the fridge, plucking a purple sticky note from it and holding it out to Dakota. "That's the address. Car keys are on the front hook."

"Gotcha'."

"If we're taking the bus we better head out now," Red turns to Finley and snaps her fingers. "Go grab your things, c'mon." Within seconds, the curly haired girl is scrambling upstairs. Dakota sees them off, earning an excited hug from Finley. When the door closes, she turns around and glances to the stairs. She has a feeling this is going to be a long day.

Dakota manages to get Ryland into the car, but it takes a bit of convincing on her part. Ryland tries to coax her into lying and just skipping the appointment altogether, but Dakota doesn't let up. So, eventually, they're pulling out of the driveway, a grumpy Ryland in the passenger side of the car.

"This is it," Ryland mumbles her first words as they pull up in front of a large brick building. "You can just let me out here."

"You don't want me to come in?" Dakota raises an eyebrow. "I can just sit in the waiting room…"

"No," Ryland shakes her head, a little too quick for Dakota's comfort. "Just… just be back in like an hour."

"Are you s—?" Dakota starts, but is cut off by Ryland's door slamming shut. With a heavy sigh, she watches the girl disappear into the building before pulling into an empty parking spot and turning off the car. She finds a book in the glove compartment leans her seat back, figuring she has an hour to kill.

When Ryland returns, it's abrupt. Dakota's startled when the door is thrown open and Ryland slides in, slamming it behind her. The whole car shakes. Tossing the book aside, Dakota turns to look at the girl, concerned.

"What's wrong?"

"Appointment's over," Ryland mutters, not even looking in Dakota's direction. There's defeat in her voice, and Dakota hesitates with her hand on the keys for a moment, debating whether or not she should say something. When Ryland leans against the window and sighs heavily, Dakota quietly starts the car.

It's silent between them for a while, but Dakota can't hold it in forever.

"Does it hurt?" Her voice is hesitant, and she sees Ryland tense out of the corner of her eye. The girl sits up slightly and looks to Dakota questioningly.

"Your leg," Dakota nods once. "Can you feel it?"

"S'complicated," Ryland shrugs, leaning forward and squeezing the knee of her brace. "It's just… complicated." Dakota hears her take a deep breath.

"Is the guy in jail?"

Ryland raises an eyebrow.

"The guy who did this… the other driver," Dakota stumbles over her words. "Is he in jail?"

She hears Ryland sigh and lean back against the window, and she kicks herself for being too nosy. Ryland picks at a hole in her jacket for a few moments, before shaking her head.

"There was no other driver."

"What do you m—?"

"T'was an old pickup," Ryland sighs. Dakota pulls into the driveway of the house and parks the car, but neither of them make a move for the door. There's a long pause of silence before Ryland squeezes her eyes shut.

"I was with my old foster father at the time. I was fifteen," she opens her eyes and exhales slowly. "We were supposed to be going to pick up one of his kids from a soccer game but he went down this unfamiliar road. Started getting all… you know…" she motions with her hand.

"I don't…"

"*Touchy*," Ryland grimaces at the word. Dakota shivers. "He started talking about how… how he didn't understand why someone let a *pretty girl like me* end up in the system. Saying I needed someone to take care of me." She pauses again, swallowing hard. "He started reaching over, trying to… you know…"

This time Dakota catches on.

"And then… he just… he kept on getting frustrated when I moved away," Ryland continues. "Like it was my fault, you know…?" Dakota nods softly, but the other girl doesn't dare meet her eyes. "Started going on about how he made *all these sacrifices* to bring me into his home… saying I should be *thankful…*"

Her words are sharp, lingering in the air between them and making Dakota hold her breath.

"I don't know what I thought it would do..." Ryland sighs, closing her eyes once more. "I was just... so... *jumpy*. My heart was racing." She holds a fist to her chest and raps it a few times, Dakota mimics her. "He started to pull me closer with one hand and reach over with the other.... He was driving with his knee. So I just panicked... you know? I just panicked and I... I grabbed the wheel."

Dakota's eyes widen.

"I just wanted to scare him, you know? Show him I'd retaliate if he messed with me," Ryland anxiously tugs at her ponytail. "But then... I guess we swerved into the opposite lane, cause the next thing I know someone's laying it down on their horn and he's yanking the wheel in the opposite direction."

Dakota can almost see it, small slivers flashing through her mind. It makes her feel sick to her stomach, and she slowly pulls her knees up to her chest, hugging her arms around them. Ryland takes a shaky breath, looking down.

"The in-betweens are blurry," she admits, bringing a hand to her forehead. "All I know is the truck flipped over the guard rail and my door was the point of impact." Dakota's jaw tightens. "Basically, somehow, my leg had gotten wedged between the door and the seat. So when we hit..." she snaps her fingers. "Crushed it."

Dakota can't help but wince, imagining the god-awful sound of metal against metal. She shakes her head and looks away. "But he's in jail, right?" is all she can ask, seeking some sort of justice.

Ryland laughs, it's a bitter sort of laugh and it makes Dakota feel stupid for even asking. "I was the one who grabbed the wheel, remember?" Ryland shakes her head. "It was all too easy to blame it on the unstable foster kid."

"They blamed it on you?"

Ryland nods. "Sent me away and reimbursed him for a new truck."

Dakota's hand curls into a fist. "But he was about to..." she trails off, motioning vaguely. "Did you tell anyone? Did you fight it?"

At this point, she notices the tears in Ryland's eyes and bites her lip. The girl beside her just shakes her head, inhaling shakily.

"Been fighting it all my life, kid. Never works," Ryland just blinks through her tears and eventually gives in, reaching up to wipe her eyes with the cuff of her jacket. "If I'd have told them, they never would have believed me." She sighs. "I guess sometimes you just get fed up with swimming upstream."

Unsure of how to respond, Dakota looks down and breathes in deeply.

"Fucked up, right?" Ryland's voice is cold. "Should've just let him do it. No one would've believed me either way." She's muttering, now, her voice barely audible, but she's heard loud and clear.

Her words hit Dakota straight in the chest, and she feels as if she's struggling to catch her breath. "Don't say that," she mumbles, shaking her head.

"Say what?"

"That no one would've believed you," Dakota squeezes her eyes shut.

"Well..."

"I would've," Dakota nods. "I do."

Ryland tenses, glancing to Dakota before looking away and nodding slowly to herself. Reaching for the door, she pauses. "We should get back inside," she looks up. "Looks like it's gonna storm."

The air between them deflates like a balloon, and Dakota just nods quickly. "Yeah, yeah, sure," she mumbles, shaking her head and pulling the keys from the ignition. She's out of the car before Ryland is.

Just as she's unlocking the house, Ryland grabs her arm. "Hey, wait." Dakota turns around slowly.

Taking a deep breath, Ryland just gives the girl a soft nod. "*Thank you.*" And right away, Dakota can tell that those words are almost foreign to the girl. A sad smile tugs at her lips. She just nods, unlocking the door.

"If I ever see the guy, let me know, okay? I'll punch him with my good hand," she gives Ryland a soft smile and pushes the door open.

"Shut up," Ryland can't help but laugh, shoving Dakota's shoulder as she slips inside past her. Pulling the door shut, Dakota just smirks and kicks off her shoes.

"I'll hook him with both hands if this thing ever heals," she adds, holding her her bandage and grimacing. Ryland rolls her eyes.

"Just don't aim for the nose this time."

"Oh, shut up."

Chapter 6

SMOKE SIGNALS

Gia orders pizza, and for once the three girls are left home to their own devices. With Finley and Red gone, they crowd into the living room, kicking their feet up on the table and arguing over what to watch.

"If you change the channel one more time I swear to g—,"

"Hey, look, *Hell's Kitchen,*" Gia interrupts Ryland, a teasing smile on her face. She turns up the volume, causing Ryland to shrug, figuring it could be worse. Dakota sits cross legged in the beanbag chair, amused by the playful banter between the two. It's the first time she's ever seen Gia in a good mood, she realizes.

They watch an episode of *Hell's Kitchen* and then Ryland steals the remote, turning on some sappy Hallmark movie just for the sake of annoying Gia. They're mid-argument, with Ryland about to throw a pillow, when they hear keys in the door. The look Ryland and Gia exchange doesn't go unnoticed by Dakota.

The door swings open and soon Finley's swiftly crossing the room, headed for the stairs. Dakota perks up.

"How was t—?"

Ryland clamps a hand over the girl's mouth, making Dakota's eyes go wide. She waits for the heavy footsteps to disappear up the stairs before she moves her hand away. Dakota opens her mouth to question her, but then a door slams so hard that the entire house shakes. Dakota flinches.

"Again?" Gia speaks up. Dakota follows her gaze to Red, who stands in the doorway, looking defeated.

Red just sighs and shakes her head. "Every time."

Dakota, confused, looks to Ryland for an explanation. But she doesn't get one. The other girl just gives Dakota a look that tells her not to ask any questions. Gia mumbles something under her breath and shuts off the TV. The silence that follows is deafening.

Finley's door remains closed for the rest of the night. Even Red doesn't make a comment about their usual rule. When Dakota passes by her room before going to bed, she presses her ear against the wall quietly, searching for any signs of life. All she can hear is the steady hum of the air conditioning.

She should've known she wouldn't be able to fall asleep. Her body has started training itself to stay awake after she's constantly shaken from sleep by nightmares. It's as if she's scared to fall asleep because she knows the way in which she'll wake up. So she tosses and turns until she's had enough. Frustrated, she resists slamming her door shut as she slips out into the hallway and navigates the stairway in the dark.

Something's off. She pauses. Finley isn't on the couch like usual. There's no Jeopardy rerun on the TV. It's nearly pitch black. Dakota crinkles her nose. She doesn't like this.

The dark haired girl digs through the fridge and holds a leftover piece of pizza in her mouth, tiptoeing across the kitchen and searching for the remote. However, she nearly gasps when she turns around and there's a figure on the couch. Narrowing her eyes, she takes a cautious step forwards. *Ryland*?

The girl's asleep, one leg curled underneath her, her head tucked in her arms which rest on the arm of the couch. Furrowing her eyebrows, Dakota hesitates for a moment before carefully moving to sit on the far end of the couch, giving Ryland as much space as possible.

She curses under her breath when the figure beside her stirs. Dakota, remaining completely still, watches awkwardly as Ryland comes to, rubbing her eyes and blinking a few times.

"I didn't mean to wake you up."

Ryland jumps when Dakota speaks, and she quickly turns to look at the girl. Confused, she squeezes her eyes shut and turns to scan the room again. "Why aren't you in bed?" she asks, her voice scratchy.

"I could ask you the same thing," Dakota nods to the girl, motioning to her with her piece of pizza. Ryland looks down and then back to Dakota, eyebrows furrowed.

She shrugs. "T'was tired."

Dakota just nods and takes a bite of her pizza, kicking her feet up on the coffee table. "Me too."

"That's odd," Ryland raises an eyebrow. "You're tired and yet you're down here eating a slice of pizza."

Dakota pauses, her eyes darting downwards. "My body's tired. It's my mind that isn't," she taps the side of her head. Ryland hums in understanding.

"You're preaching to the choir," the other girl sits up carefully, biting her lip as she adjusts her braced leg. Dakota notices this and raises an eyebrow.

"You good?"

"*Fine*," Ryland grits her teeth, but replies a bit too quickly. It's defensive, almost. Dakota purses her lips. She wants to say something, but she knows better. Sighing, she shoves the last of her crust in her mouth and stands up, dusting her hands off.

"M'headed upstairs," she nods softly. She makes her way around the couch, but pauses. "You coming up too?"

She sees Ryland hesitate. The girl doesn't turn to look at her, but instead she just shakes her head. "I can't."

"What?" Dakota takes a step back towards the girl.

"The stairs," Ryland's voice is quiet, laced with embarrassment. She gestures vaguely and then lets her shoulders drop. "I can't."

Now Dakota moves to stand in front of her, her eyes darting back and forth from Ryland to the staircase. "Oh," is all she can muster, the word coming out as a small whisper between them.

"It just… does this sometimes," Ryland shakes her head and lifts her leg with both of her hands. Her wincing doesn't go unnoticed by Dakota, who holds her breath. "They call it '*phantom limb*' or something," she explains, continuing to ramble nervously, still unable to meet Dakota's eyes. "Happens to a lot of people like me." She reaches down, massaging around her ankle. "It's like… I can't move the leg, but I can feel the pain. Does that make sense?"

"I…" Dakota bites her lip. "Do you need an ice pack?"

Ryland can't help but laugh at this, and she shakes her head. "I wish that could fix it, kid." Dakota looks away.

"If you balance on one foot I could help you," she offers, trying to come up with a solution. The younger girl holds out her hand to Ryland, hoping to help her to her feet, but Ryland just looks at her, a sad smile on her face, and shakes her head.

"It's not worth it," her voice is small. "I'm fine, Dakota," she waves the topic away with her hand, trying to dismiss the girl to leave. But instead, to Ryland's surprise, Dakota glances to the stairs one last time before resuming her spot on the couch beside Ryland.

"Well, then I figure you could use some company," she resolves, offering her a shy smile. Ryland isn't sure how to respond.

And so, Dakota snatches the TV remote from the coffee table and starts flipping through the channels.

"This place only gets like five stations," Ryland mumbles. Dakota turns to a 1980's horror movie, rolls her eyes, and continues searching.

Eventually, Dakota gives up and they end up watching infomercials. The younger girl slumps back on the couch, scoffing and shaking her head.

"That could *never* work," she motions to the television. "Look at it! That's so fake."

"Shh," Ryland giggles, nudging the girl's shoulder. "People are sleeping."

"This is bullshit," Dakota lowers her voice to a whisper, managing to make Ryland laugh even harder.

"There's a simple solution to that, you know," Ryland shakes her head. "You just don't buy it."

"But it looks cool," Dakota mumbles. "Imagine if it really *did* work."

"And what would you ever need night vision goggles for?" Ryland raises an eyebrow.

"*Two pairs* of night vision goggles" Dakota corrects her, pointing to the TV. "It's a special deal if you call within the next five minutes. We could both have one."

Ryland reaches over and unplugs the phone, making Dakota laugh and bury her head in a pillow.

Some time passes, with both girls half-heartedly throwing out insults to the television to make each other laugh. Dakota pulls her legs up to her chest, resting her chin atop them and yawning. "Ryland?"

"Huh?" the other girl looks over, turning down the TV a few notches.

"Does it still hurt?" Dakota asks quietly. "Your leg?"

Ryland just nods slowly. "Unfortunately."

"What's it feel like?"

"I…" Ryland thinks for a moment. "It just… well, right now it feels really hot. But like… not." She shakes her head, unable to articulate. "The best way I can think to describe it is… like a cavity, but in my leg. You know?"

Dakota grimaces and brings her hand up to her mouth, remembering the countless times she'd had cavities as a child. Ryland looks away, suddenly feeling embarrassed.

"Where's it hurt?" Dakota inquires again.

"You ask too many questions."

"I'm serious."

Sighing, Ryland leans down and feels around her ankle. "Mostly where I start gaining the feeling back," she explains, moving up and digging her thumbs into the skin above her knee. "But… it just depends. Some days it's worse than others."

And then, gently, Dakota's scooting over and laying back, resting her head in Ryland's lap. "Does this hurt?"

Taken aback, Ryland shakes her head quickly.

And so Dakota yawns, content. "M'kay," she mumbles, wiping her eyes. Ryland can tell she's tired. Ryland, on the other hand, is now wide awake and caught off guard. She doesn't know what to do with her hands and she's practically afraid to move.

Dakota looks up at Ryland, the blue light of the television reflecting in her pupils. "What're you gonna do when you leave this place?" she asks quietly. Yet another question. Ryland isn't used to this.

"I…" Ryland hesitates. "I haven't thought about it much." As she ponders this, she absentmindedly reaches down to brush Dakota's hair out of her face. Dakota shivers.

"Me and Gia have talked about renting a place together," Ryland thinks out loud. "A small apartment or something." She shrugs. "I'll probably get a job. College is pretty much out of the picture for me. I don't have that kind of money."

"When you were little what'd you say you wanted to be when you grew up?"

Ryland laughs at the memory. "An astronaut." Dakota can't help but smile.

"I could see it," she nods softly, feeling Ryland's fingers still in her hair. "I wanted to be a police officer until I found out that they all don't drive motorcycles."

"So technically you just wanted to be a motorcycle driver," Ryland notes. Dakota laughs.

"Yeah, but you can't make a living on being a badass."

"Why not? Tons of people are badass for a living."

"Like who?" Dakota raises an eyebrow.

"Chuck Norris."

"I'm nothing close to Chuck Norris," Dakota giggles. Ryland furrows her eyebrows.

"You wouldn't stand a chance against him."

"I can't argue with you on that one," Dakota shrugs. She turns slightly to look at the TV. "Look at this bullshit," she motions. "They're still trying to make Shamwow a thing."

"I think Finley has one somewhere," Ryland laughs softly.

"Of course she does." Dakota yawns, pausing in thought for a few moments. "How many of those things do you think it would take to clean up an entire pool?"

"Is this all you think about at 2 am?"

"Occasionally."

Somehow, amidst their playful banter, Dakota ends up falling asleep. The next thing she knows, she's waking up on the couch, with one of Ryland's hands still tangled in her hair. With a quiet yawn, she studies Ryland's sleeping figure—noting how she appears at peace in her sleep, her face free from worry. Dakota could have laid like that forever, had she not been startled by the sudden sound of something scraping across the kitchen floor.

She lifts her head to find Finley, eyes dark and sullen, standing atop a chair to retrieve something from the pantry. Dakota keeps quiet, not alerting Finley of her presence just yet. Across the room, the curly haired girl grabs a box of cereal and hops back down to the ground. It's only then, when she turns around, that Finley meets Dakota's eyes and realizes she's awake.

"Good morning," Dakota's voice is soft. She rises from her spot on the couch, about to join Finley in the kitchen, but freezes when Finley's grip on the cereal box tightens. Panic flickers in the girl's eyes. And then, she's hurrying back upstairs, abandoning the bowl and carton of milk she'd laid out on the counter. The slamming of her door reverberates throughout the house, loud enough to wake Ryland from her slumber. And when she stirs, the first thing she sees is Dakota, who stands staring at the stairs, a puzzled expression on her face.

"We have school," is the first thing Ryland says, rolling back her head and working out the kink in her neck. Dakota glances over to the girl. Images of the night before slowly come back to her. She gives one last fleeting look to the stairs before groaning.

"Don't remind me."

And just like that, last night seems to fade away. Since neither of them addresses it—the fact that Dakota slept half the night with her head in Ryland's lap—it suddenly becomes unspoken, something they're both well aware of, yet neglect to mention. Which is why a tense silence follows, leaving Dakota tugging anxiously on the sleeves of her shirt.

Luckily, Gia trudges downstairs moments later, simultaneously yanking her hair up into a bun. She pauses at the landing, looking back and forth between the two girls. "Sleep well?" The knowing smirk on her face doesn't go unnoticed by Dakota, who hurries to look away.

"Here," Gia tosses a handful of clothing in Ryland's lap, dropping a purple toothbrush atop it. "I didn't know if you wanted jeans or leggings, so I just grabbed both," she shrugs. Watching this, Dakota begins to realize that Ryland's night on the couch might not be a rare occurrence.

"Thanks," Ryland's voice is barely audible. Gia holds out a hand, and soon Dakota's hurrying over to help pull Ryland to her feet. However, once she's standing steady, Ryland shoves them both away when they try to lead her forward.

"*I've got it,*" she hisses, her voice sharper than usual. Both girls are quick to move aside, well aware that Ryland doesn't mean it personally. It kills Dakota to watch Ryland—holding tightly to the clothes Gia had brought down—wince and limp her way over to the bathroom. Everything in Dakota screams for her to do something, but Gia tugs on her sleeve, shaking her head. She knows well enough that trying to help Ryland would only result in another outburst.

Only once she hears the bathroom door shut does Dakota jog upstairs to get herself ready, and even then she rushes to get dressed and hurry back downstairs. Ryland's leaning against the entrance to the kitchen, her hands fiddling with the adjustments on her brace. Quietly, Dakota slips past, keeping her distance while still maintaining a watchful eye on the girl. Knowing Ryland's frustration, she's settled on staying quiet until the girl makes a move. She fears she'll end up angering her even more if she insists on helping her.

"We've got ten minutes," Gia reappears, nodding to Dakota. "Toaster's under the island. You know where the bread is?"

Dakota nods, quick to follow her instructions. She lugs the shiny metal toaster onto the counter.

"Throw one in for me," Ryland finally speaks up, motioning to the toaster. Dakota obliges, and soon she's piling a stack of toast on a plate and grabbing one for herself. Gia takes two, one for herself and one for Ryland, who hums softly in thanks.

"You good to walk?" Gia asks carefully. Ryland just nods and insists that the worst of it is over, that she's done this a million times before.

As Ryland's talking, footsteps storm down the stairs. All of their heads turn, but before anyone can get a word in, Finley's already out the door. Dakota flinches when it slams shut.

Gia's the first to break the silence that follows, sighing heavily and grabbing her backpack. "I guess that's our cue to head out."

The walk to school is silent aside from Ryland's occasional request to take a break. So when they arrive, they're already late—the first bell has rung and the hallways are desolate. Dakota, however, still stays behind to make sure Ryland gets to her first class, taking the long way around the building to escort her.

As they walk, Dakota pauses, noticing a familiar face in one of the classrooms. She offers Finley a soft smile, but the girl looks away quickly, pretending she hadn't seen. When Ryland glances back and witnesses this, she sighs heavily. Dakota frowns, then hurries to catch up.

"How long will this last?" Dakota looks to Ryland as they walk. All she gets in return in a one-shouldered shrug.

"You haven't even seen the worst of it."

Chapter 7

DOWNPOUR

And unfortunately, Ryland's right. It only gets worse.

The next three days pass quietly, granted. All the other members of the house tread cautiously. Dakota feels as if she's walking on eggshells. Finley hasn't spoken to—let alone *looked at* anyone in days. She moves like a ghost, only appearing to dig through the fridge in the middle of the night. The rest of the time she's disappeared in her room, making no sound. Yet Dakota notices that her light remains on at all hours of the night.

Night. That's when things go downhill.

It's another rainy Friday, forcing everyone inside. Even Gia, who rarely sets foot in the house on Friday nights, is holed up in her room thanks to the violent rainstorm. They eat dinner in silence, each one waiting on the edge of their seat, quietly listening for any signs of life in the bedroom above. Dakota feels like they're waiting for a bomb to be diffused. If only she understood the irony.

And then—inevitably—night falls. Dakota finds a bottle of sleeping pills in the bathroom and downs two, praying she'll actually be able to sleep soundly. Which she does, for an hour or two. But then it happens.

Dakota hears it first, brought out of her sleep by the sound of something shattering. Quickly sitting up, she strains to hear over the sound of wind whipping around the house.

It happens again, this time it's a bang strong enough to shake the walls. The glass of water beside her bed vibrates, water rippling within. Now wide awake, Dakota's on her feet and out in the hallway within seconds.

That's when she realizes—*Finley*. Now, Dakota's hurrying forwards, knocking on the door. "Finley? Are you—?"

Just as she starts to push the door open, something slams it shut from the other side, making her jump. She has to yank her bandaged hand away to keep it from getting crushed. There's another thud—louder this time, and Dakota starts to panic.

"*Guys*?!" she calls out, looking to both ends of the hallway for help. She jiggles the doorknob, ramming her shoulder against the door, but coming up empty. It's locked. She looks around anxiously. "*Red*!"

To her relief, the door at the end of the hallway swings open and Gia hurries out with Ryland not far behind. Dakota's pushed aside as Gia slides to her knees in front of the door, fishing a bobby pin out of her messy hair and snapping it in half. Ryland places a hand on Dakota's shoulder as some sort of consolation, drawing the girl's nervous gaze.

"What's going on?" Dakota looks to her for an explanation. But by then, Gia's wedged the bobby pin into the knob and managed to unlock the door, which she nudges open a crack. Looking back to Ryland one last time, she takes a deep breath before pushing the door wide open. And there stands Finley, shattered remnants of her window scattered across the room.

For less than a split second, the girl pauses to acknowledge their presence. But within an instant, she's back to tearing the sheets from her bed, wide eyed and manic.

"Finley…" Gia begins, holding out a hand and stepping forward. Dakota immediately moves to follow her, but Ryland catches hold of her arm and pulls her backwards. Just in time, too. Moments later, Finley's grabbing her bedside lamp and winding it around. It crashes into the wall, right where Dakota would have been standing, shards of blue clay scattering across the room and into the hallway.

"She's insane!" Finley speaks—no, *screams*—for the first time in days. Her voice is gravel, rough in the back of her throat. Dakota catches her eyes for just a second—red and bloodshot—dark enough to make her stumble back into Ryland's arms, shocked.

Just as a shelf of encyclopedias topples down to the floor, leaving a nasty hole in the wall, Red practically sprints up the stairs. Ryland and Dakota immediately move aside.

What happens next only confirms to Dakota that tonight is far from this first time they've dealt with this. Because as soon as Red meets eyes with Gia, they silently nod to one another before pushing their way into the room.

Gia grabs a hold of her first, catching Finley's arm before she can yank the drawer from her nightstand. Panic flashes in Finley's eyes when she turns to look at Gia, and just as Red reaches for her other arm, Finley starts thrashing, desperately trying to pull herself out of Gia's grip. Red has to duck in order to avoid being stuck by Finley's arm. Her entire body reels away from Gia, her shoulder slamming into the wall. Dakota winces, unable to even focus on the fact that Ryland's holding her back, both hands wrapped around her arm protectively.

"Let me go!" Finley cries out, yanking her arm downwards. Gia nearly stumbles, but manages to hold on. "You're hurting me!"

Dakota can barely recognize Finley. The girl's head slams back against the wall, but Red's finally able to grab her other arm. Together they're able to hold Finley still against the wall, pressing her shoulders back to keep her from thrashing. The girl still fights, though, throwing her weight forwards. Gia and Red practically have to slam her back against the wall to prevent her from breaking free. The impact sends something crashing to the ground in the adjacent room. Ryland's grip on Dakota's arm tightens.

"I hate her!" Finley screams, her voice cracking. "She's insane! She's insane!"

And then, as if she's run out of gas, Finley starts to crumple. Her fight dissolves, and suddenly her knees shake. Her weight seems to drop, sliding her down against the wall and onto the floor. Both Red and Gia, like routine, kneel down beside her. They still hold her back, but she's no longer struggling to break free.

"She's insane."

Finley's voice is barely a whisper now. Her shoulders drop, as if her body is suddenly caving in on itself. With her head hung forward, tousled hair covering her face, Finley just continues to repeat herself. "She's insane. She's insane."

Red finally lets go of the smaller girl, no longer a flight risk. She sits back on her heels, inhaling slowly and pinching the bridge of her nose. Gia, however, still holds loosely to Finley's wrist, shaking it gently to try and gain her attention.

"Finley," Gia's voice is gentle, seemingly out of place after all that's happened. "Finley, listen to me."

"She's insane," Finley shakes her head. "I'm not insane. I'm not. She is. It's her."

"*Finley*," Gia pushes. "It's Gia." She moves to kneel in front of the girl. "We're in the house, see? In your bedroom. Red's here too." She squeezes Finley's wrist.

Dakota almost misses it, but she catches when Finley looks up slightly, her breathing starting to even out. The mood seems to have deflated like a balloon, leaving them in the aftershocks of what's just happened.

"You're sitting on the floor by your bed," Gia continues. "It's Friday. We don't have school tomorrow."

"She's grounding her," Ryland says softly so only Dakota can hear. The two girls watch from the hallway, backed up against one another, lingering in the doorway. "When she comes down from these things, it helps to remind her of where she is. Brings her back to reality."

And Ryland's right. As Gia talks to her, Finley slowly holds her hands up in front of her, as if they're foreign objects. She turns them back and forth, studying her palms, acting as if she's just now realizing that they're an extension of herself. And then her hands drop to the floor beside her, knuckles against wood echoing around the room. Her eyes stare straight forward.

"I'm not crazy," she shakes her head, her voice rising an octave as the tears finally spill forward. Within seconds, she's a different person—curling into a ball, her knees to her chest, and burying her head in her hands. And finally, as she rubs Finley's back through her sobs, Gia exhales heavily. The worst of it is over.

However, now someone else is filled with unexplainable fear. It hits Dakota like a wave, crashing into her chest and knocking the wind from her lungs, spilling over her. She stumbles backwards, pressing one hand against the wall. It's as if facing Finley has also forced her to face a projection of herself, recognizing her own anger and desperation mirrored in the girl.

When Ryland, confused, reaches out for her, Dakota pulls away. She meets Ryland's eyes, shakes her head, and then she's gone. Ryland tenses when Dakota's door swings shut.

"You're okay," Gia sighs, still comforting Finley. She steals a glance behind her to Ryland, just now noticing Dakota's absence. She raises an eyebrow in question, but all Ryland can do is shake her head. They both scan the room, taking in the mess left in the wake of Finley's breakdown. Cold air rushes through the window, making Ryland shiver. Now standing in the aftermath, she has to keep reminding herself that the worst is over.

Dakota completely tunes out the quiet voices in the hallway. The sound of Red taping bags over the broken window to keep the rain out, the scrape of glass against the floor as Gia tries to clean up the shattered remains of Finley's lamp, the squeaking sound of Ryland's brace as she moves to and fro—Dakota shuts it all out. She just sits on the edge of her bed, feet tucked underneath her, watching the flicker of the lightning outside her window.

Glancing back to her door, she inches over to the window, clenching her jaw as she heaves it open. A gust of wind hits her face, whistling through the room. She shivers.

The thing about storms is that Dakota's never been scared of them. As a kid, she only used it as an excuse to crawl into bed with her mother, hugging her hands around her neck, burying her head into her shoulder, inhaling the smell of her coconut shampoo and the faintest hint of oil paint from her hours in the studio. She'd make her tell her the story about the sky—how thunder was just the stars bumping into each other, how lightning was nothing but stardust being sent down to the Earth. She would press her palms against the window, watching the storm as it rolled in. And in the morning, she'd drag her brother outside, searching for any stardust the lightning may have left behind.

But now that she's older, the magic is lost. It died with her mother, she supposes. Storms aren't stardust to her anymore. They're wind and rain, anger and desperation, lashing out against the dry Earth. Storms are exhaustion, rooted deep in the sky, making her bones ache. Yet they still don't scare her. They're magnetizing, pulling her in closer. What's she got to be afraid of? Dakota figures she's already become the eye of the hurricane.

And so, somehow, she finds herself crawling onto the roof, wind whipping her hair around her face as she scoots to lean against the side of the house. All around her, trees sway back and forth, their leaves hanging on for dear life. Rain, riding the strong wind, pelts against her bare legs, soaking through her clothes and weighing down her hair. But here, in the chaos of it all, she finds that she feels much less anxious than she had trapped in her bedroom.

She could climb down right now. The lattice that runs from the garden up the side of the house could easily hold her weight. But she doesn't run. Partly because she doesn't know where she would go, and partly because she's beginning to feel tied to this place. This isn't a conscious action on her part. Ryland, the only person she's ever opened up to, seems to hold a part of her now. By confiding in this girl, Dakota feels as if she's handed a part of herself over. Leaving Ryland would be like leaving herself behind. As if suddenly—she isn't the storm anymore, she can't come and go as she pleases. Now, she's the ocean, still raging and flowing, but always pulled back in with the tide when the waves crash to shore. Ryland's begun to have a hold on her, in the same way the moon turns the tides.

But also, *literally*, Ryland's got a hold on her.

"What the hell are you doing?" Ryland hisses. She's leaning out of the window, looking to where Dakota sits, a foot or so away from her. Something flashes in her eyes—something that involuntarily sends chills down Dakota's spine. And suddenly, Ryland's hand is tight around her forearm, her nails practically digging into her skin. Her voice is cold. "Don't you dare."

Dakota opens her mouth to question the girl, but by then Ryland is already yanking her closer, grabbing her by the shoulders once she's within reach and practically pulling her through the window. Dakota struggles to find her footing and ends up stumbling forward once she's inside, groaning and rubbing her shoulder after she hits the ground.

"What the hell was that for?" she looks at Ryland in confusion. The other girl slams the window shut so forcefully that Dakota's surprised they didn't break *two* windows that night. Silence follows. Ryland's eyes find hers once more, and again, Dakota's met with something she can't decipher. It's practically radiating off of the girl.

"Are you fucking stupid?" Ryland raises her voice. "Are you really *that fucking st*—?"

Dakota, back on her feet, grabs both of Ryland's shoulders. "Stop *screaming*," she hisses. "You're going to wake everyone up." Her worried eyes dart to the door.

"Well maybe I should," Ryland lowers her voice, now whisper-yelling, but her words remain just as sharp. "Maybe I should go get Red right now and have her ship you off to the crazy house with Finley's mom," her face is red as she flings her arm in the direction of Finley's room. "Is that what you want?"

"What are you—?"

"That wouldn't even kill you! God, Dakota!" Ryland shakes her head, bringing her hands up to her face. "You'd just break every fucking bone in your body and end up in a wheelchair for the rest of your—,"

"*Ryland*!" Dakota shakes her, wide-eyed. "What the hell are you talking about?"

"You!" Ryland raises her voice again, gesturing to the window, her eyes wide. And suddenly, it clicks. Dakota gets it. Her whole body stills, understanding beginning to wash over her, concern rushing through her veins. She looks from Ryland to the window, and then back to Ryland, her eyes widening as she searches the girl's face.

"You thought I was..." Dakota swallows. Her tongue suddenly feels too heavy for her mouth. The words fade out with her voice. "But I wasn't... I wasn't..."

"You weren't jumping?" Ryland's voice is suddenly soft again, words laced with confusion, her head tilting to the side like a lost puppy. Dakota's quick to shake her head, squeezing Ryland's shoulders.

"Of course not," Dakota's voice is wrought with disbelief. "I was just thinking," she tries to explain. "I do stupid shit like that all the time. I wasn't trying to—,"

She clamps her mouth shut when she realizes Ryland's not listening. Instead, the girl has turned away, with a deep breath so heavy that she practically deflates like a balloon. She lowers herself down on the bed, slamming her fist atop the nightstand, her whole body rigid as she brings a hand up to her forehead.

"Ryland," Dakota manages a whisper, the girl's name sounding like silk in her mouth. Delicately, she lowers herself to sit beside the girl, who's practically shaking. Dakota can tell it's taking everything in her to hold back tears, because she's breathing so heavily through gritted teeth that it sounds painful. Dakota can feel the lump in her own throat.

"Ryland," she whispers again. "Did you think I was...?"

Ryland doesn't respond, but Dakota doesn't need an answer. Seeing the girl like this—so small and afraid—triggers something protective deep within her. Reaching out, Dakota grabs Ryland's hand with her good one, turning so their knees are touching.

"It reminded you of her," Dakota states. She knows her words are risky, but Ryland nods shakily a few moments later, her bottom lip drawn tightly between her teeth. It's enough to make Dakota shudder.

"I'm not going anywhere," Dakota shakes her head. She can feel how tightly Ryland's grip on her hand has gotten and slowly runs her thumb over the ridges of the girl's knuckles, feeling how the girl's shaking down to the bone.

"I'm sorry," Ryland's voice is fleeting, sandpaper in the back of her throat. With her free hand, she reaches up to wipe her eyes using the back of her wrist. After she exhales shakily, Dakota moves to sit cross legged, facing her and resting her forehead on Ryland's shoulder. As she watches her own thumb move back and forth across the girl's hand, she starts to realize just how exhausted they both are.

"I hate this," Ryland speaks once more. Rolling her head to the side, her cheek resting on the girl's shoulder, Dakota looks up to her.

"Hate what?"

"*Caring*," Ryland's free hand lifts only to fall back into her lap, a gesture of defeat. "And then acting like I don't."

"You don't have to act around me," Dakota lifts her head, her words lingering between them. With delicate fingers, she reaches up to brush Ryland's hair out of her face. Maybe it's because it's nearly 3am and nothing feels real anymore, but Dakota's inhibitions have begun withering away. Her hands touch Ryland like she's handling broken glass, all soft and light, fingertips barely brushing her skin as she tucks her hair behind her ear. Silence follows, a few painful seconds, before Ryland groans in frustration.

"I hate this stupid thing," she hisses, punching the top of her leg. Their hands detach as Ryland moves forward, yanking the straps on her brace, becoming more and more flustered when she can't undo them.

"Let me," Dakota shakes her head after taking a deep breath. With shaky hands, she pulls Ryland's own away, scooting closer. One by one, she frees the clamps on the brace. The metal slowly begins to loosen, and Dakota eases it off from her leg. As she moves to set the brace aside, Ryland breathes deeply and digs her thumbs into the skin around her knee, pushing circles into the flesh.

"Hurts?"

"A little."

Dakota nods, looking around the room absentmindedly. However, she pauses when her eyes catch the pillow and blanket tossed at the head of the bed. "Ryland?" She looks to the other girl, who glances behind them.

"Finley's in my bed," she breathes in slowly. "Red told me to come in here." She looks away.

"And that's when you thought I was…"

"*Yeah.*"

Dakota clears her throat, knowing it's a touchy subject. She stands up. "We should probably sleep," she says quietly. Ryland just nods.

And so, the lights are turned off and Dakota's soon back in her bed, arms crossed over her chest as she stares at the ceiling. She hears Ryland shift in the bed next to her, mumbling something under her breath about her *stupid fucking leg* and rolling over once more.

But, eventually, the room falls silent. Dakota can hear Ryland's soft breathing and she tries to match her breaths to hers. She wonders what the girl is thinking in that moment, if she had really been that panicked at the idea of Dakota jumping. With one hand, she reaches up, feeling the crescent shaped marks from Ryland's nails in her arm when she'd grabbed her on the roof. She traces her fingers over them, shivering at the thought of Ryland being that desperate to keep her from the edge.

She gives in.

"What are you doing?"

"Scoot over," Dakota whispers, tugging at the edge of Ryland's blanket. "I'm cold." Ryland mutters something to the likes of *shouldn't have climbed on the fucking roof, then*. But she still moves to make room.

And that's how Dakota ends up squeezing herself onto the bed beside Ryland, the blanket barely covering them both. She shivers, not at the cold, but at the feel of Ryland's arm pressed up against hers, both of them squished into the tiny twin bed.

Ryland, on the other hand, is frozen, too taken aback by Dakota's sudden intrusion of space to say anything. Not that she minds it, though. They both lay with their backs facing one another, eyes locked on opposite walls.

"Hey Ryland?" Dakota's voice breaks the silence not moments later, soft and hesitant. The bed shifts beside her.

"Hm?"'

"Can I ask you something?"

"You just did."

A smile tugs at Dakota's lips but she shakes her head. "Do you think we stand a chance?"

She feels Ryland tense beside her at the seriousness of the question, well aware of the multiple meanings her words hold. There's a long pause between them, where Dakota wants to hit herself in the face for saying anything. But Ryland eventually breaks the silence.

"I like to think we do," her voice is gentler now, still rough and wrought with exhaustion, but more vulnerable. Dakota carefully rolls onto her back.

"I wouldn't have jumped," she blurts out, trying to ease her anxiety. "I was just thinking. Trying to disappear," she pauses. "In the metaphorical sense."

"Thinking about what?"

"Everything," Dakota sighs. She feels Ryland shift beside her, rolling on her side and propping herself up on her elbow to face the girl. A leg brushes her own, and she tenses, but quickly realizes the other girl can't feel it.

"Everything?" Ryland's voice is closer now. Dakota nods.

"Everything I've lost," she says quietly, holding her hands up and studying the shadows that run across them. "My childhood, my house, my mom, my brother…"

As she goes on, Ryland absentmindedly reaches over, pulling one of Dakota's hands down and closer to her. With her pointer finger, she traces the lines in the girl's palm, a smile tugging at her lips when she feels Dakota shiver.

"You have me."

The words spill out of Ryland's mouth effortlessly, like water. And when Dakota turns to look at her, caught off guard, both girls can feel the mood in the room shift.

"What's that supposed to mean?" Dakota whispers.

"Just that…" Ryland shrugs. "You're not completely alone." She curls Dakota's fingers into a fist and traces her fingers across her knuckles like tiny mountain ranges. "I don't know if that counts for anything, but…"

"It does."

Ryland's hand stills. "Huh?"

"It counts for something."

When Dakota finally rolls out of bed the next morning, she turns around just in time to see Ryland's sleeping figure shiver at the loss of body heat and reach across to hug her pillow. It takes Dakota a minute to recall the chain of events that had happened the night prior, in the moments before she drifted off to sleep. And when she does, she's well aware that her face turns bright red. Something's happening, she realizes. She's not quite sure what it is just yet, but all she knows is that she doesn't mind it at all.

When she forces herself to peel her eyes away from the girl, all calm and glowing in her sleep, Dakota slips out of the room as quietly as she can. Judging by the absolute silence, everyone else is still fast asleep, recovering from the night before. Dakota, however, takes comfort in the quiet of the early morning—the stillness of life downstairs, the orange trails that the sun leaves across the dark hardwood floor. The only sound is the hiss of the coffee maker as she pours herself a cup, plain black the way she likes it.

Quietly, she pads across the living room, leaning up against the windowsill of the big bay window that hugs the front of the house. After the violent rainstorm last night, branches scatter the yard, and the grass still shines from the buckets of rain they'd received.

Before she can even take a sip of her coffee, though, something else steals her attention. It's enough to make her abandon her drink, hurrying barefoot into the front yard. Carefully, to avoid the glass scattered about, Dakota grabs the book, which was strewn wide open in the middle of the lawn. Brushing dirt from the cover, she hurries back inside.

The encyclopedia, mustard yellow, is practically dripping wet. Part of a page peels off in Dakota's hand when she tries to assess the damage. However, she's able to flip the book to a single dog-eared page. Her eyes are immediately drawn to a highlighted portion of the writing, pink highlighter faded and bleeding down the page. She traces her finger over the words.

"*Schizophrenia, a psychotic disorder marked by severely impaired thinking, emotions, and behaviors. The term comes from two Greek words that mean 'split mind.' Schizophrenia is associated with abnormalities of brain structure and function, disorganized speech, behavior, delusions, and hallucinations.*"

Without hesitation, Dakota tears the page from the book, folding it up into a tiny square and stuffing it into the pocket of her sweatpants. And then, she sneaks back upstairs into Finley's bedroom. Pretty soon, the collection of thick bound encyclopedias is stacked against the wall, arranged in alphabetical order. It makes Dakota feel a bit better.

By the time she heads back downstairs, her coffee is cold.

Still the only one awake, Dakota's sprawled out on the couch doing homework, with the TV turned low to fill the silence. The last person she expects to see is Finley, who startles her when she hops over the back of the couch, plopping down cross-legged in the space beside her. There's a wide smile on her face for the first time in days.

"Mornin'" she hums, reaching over Dakota to grab the remote and turn up the volume. Dakota, however, just continues to gape, staring at her in confusion.

"Is this history?" Finley leans over to look at her book, oblivious to Dakota's disarray. She answers the question for herself when she skims the page, nodding softly. "I finished that last week. Everything you need is in the back of Chapter 15."

"I-I, uh… thanks," Dakota clears her throat, shaking her head and flipping to the next chapter. She pulls her highlighter out from behind her ear, tapping it against her bottom lip. Out of the corner of her eye, she studies Finley, who's now contently watching the television as if last night had never happened.

"What is *Yellowstone National Park*?" she calls out the answer, nodding once when the contestant on the screen answers correctly. Dakota shakes her head in disbelief.

As soon as Ryland comes downstairs, Dakota's scrambling to her feet and following the girl into the kitchen.

"What happened?" she asks hurriedly, grabbing Ryland's arm. Groggily, the girl turns to look at her.

"Well good morning to you, too," she slurs, pouring herself a cup of coffee. Without even thinking, Dakota passes her the creamer, knowing exactly how Ryland likes her coffee—a dash of sugar and enough of her french vanilla creamer to make it turn light brown, just a shade lighter than her eyes. Dakota watches as a tired Ryland lazily stirs her drink, taking a sip before leaning against the counter to eye up Dakota.

"Alright," Ryland nods. "What're you freaking out about?"

"Finley," Dakota's eyes widen, drawn out of her trance. "She's acting perfectly normal." She motions toward the living room, where Finley still sits, intently watching the same Jeopardy rerun she's seen countless times before.

Ryland raises an eyebrow. "And that's a bad thing?"

Dakota shakes her head quickly. "No, no, she just…" she huffs in frustration. "Did you not see her last night? She was so…" she gestures vaguely. "And now she's so…"

"Normal?" Ryland looks to her. Dakota nods. "I know," Ryland drums her fingers against the counter. "That's how it works."

"This happens every time she visits her mom?" Dakota's shoulders drop in disbelief.

"Like clockwork," Ryland nods, confirming Dakota's suspicions. "I could practically plot it on a graph for you." Setting down her coffee, she traces a curve in the air with her pointer finger. "There's the visit, then the return, followed by the three or four days of silence, and finally… the breakdown." She drops her hand back down to her side. "And then, of course, the return to normal."

"But what happens when she sees her mom again?"

"The relapse," Ryland retraces her curve in the air a few times over, an endless cycle. "And then we're back to step one. Right where we started."

With a heavy sigh, Dakota leans back against the counter. Tilting her head to the side, Ryland holds out her mug to offer some to the girl. Dakota just shakes her head softly, to which Ryland simply shrugs and takes another sip.

"What's with the whole house waking up at the asscrack of dawn on a Saturday?" Gia trudges in, stretching her arms above her head and yawning loudly. She looks absolutely exhausted. All the stress from the night before seems to weigh heavy on her shoulders, showing in her puffy eyes and tousled hair. Ryland offers her some of her coffee, and, unlike Dakota, Gia snatches the mug from her hand and practically downs the rest of it within seconds. Dakota and Ryland exchange glances.

"You're welcome," Ryland mumbles, shaking her head and grabbing a new mug for herself. Dakota passes her the creamer once more, and this time Ryland notices. She looks down to Dakota's hand and then back to Dakota, taking the creamer with a raised eyebrow and an amused smile on her face. Dakota has to look away to hide the flush in her cheeks.

Chapter 8

THE OUTSIDE WORLD

Once Red's awake, she warns the girls not to cause trouble and then heads out to run errands, leaving them with the house to themselves. Finley locks the door five times behind her, leaning against the window and waving goodbye.

Dakota hangs upside down in the armchair, her head dangling just inches above the floor. Absentmindedly, she tosses an apple up and down with her good hand, feeling the full extent of her boredom.

"So what's on the agenda for today, tiny?" Ryland strolls by, catching the apple in mid-air and tossing it to her other hand before she takes a bite. Dakota glares at her, but Ryland just smiles innocently and tosses it back to her. As Ryland plops down on the couch across from her, Dakota pulls herself to sit upright, her messy hair spilling back down her shoulders. She looks at the bite in the apple, rolling her eyes half heartedly before chucking it back at Ryland, who catches it with one hand and grins.

"I have an English project to work on," Finley plops down on the couch beside Ryland, hugging a pillow to her chest.

"You have all weekend for that," Ryland shakes her head. "C'mon, guys, let's do something fun," she nudges Finley's leg with her own. Gia perks up from across the room.

"What do you have in mind?" the blonde raises an eyebrow, waltzing over to lean against the back of the couch. Playfully, she ruffles Finley's hair, making the other girl duck out of her reach.

"Depends," Ryland shrugs. "What do *you* have in mind?"

Gia tilts her head to the side, a mischievous smile tugging on her lips. "I guess it depends on if we're following Red's rules or not."

Dakota lifts her head, raising an eyebrow. "What's that mean?"

"It means she wants to sneak out," Finley looks to Gia knowingly. Gia just smirks.

"If Red left us money for dinner that means she'll be out long. Besides, what's the worst that could happen if she finds out? We get sent to a group home?" Gia raises an eyebrow and then looks around them. "Oh, *wait*."

"Where would we sneak out *to*?" Ryland takes another bite of the apple.

"It's the week before spring break," Gia nods. "Which means the boardwalk will be packed. We can go to the beach… make a few friends…" she nudges Finley's side, earning a glare from the girl. "And if we try hard enough—free alcohol."

"*I don't like the sound of this*," Finley mumbles under her breath. Gia ruffles her hair again.

"C'mon, Fin," she whines. "Live a little."

"It's *Finley*," the other girl sighs, furrowing her eyebrows at looking at the other girls. "Are you guys going?"

Dakota shrugs. "I'm in."

"Why not?" Ryland smirks. Finley looks away.

"I'm not drinking…"

Gia hops up. "But you'll go?"

"Well there's no way I'm letting you leave me here to face Red's wrath on my own."

Punching the air in victory, Gia's halfway up the stairs before the other three girls even know what's hit them. She calls back down, urging them to hurry up and get ready. Finley and Ryland look to one another apprehensively, but Dakota hurries to follow Gia. She's been aching to get out of the house.

"Red's gonna have our heads," Finley sighs, rising to her feet in defeat. Ryland just shrugs, arguing that if they die, they might as well die tan and happy.

Within an hour, all four girls sit at the bus stop, with Gia leading the way for once. Finley's leaning against the stop sign, hugging a beach ball to her chest and frowning. While she's dressed for the beach, Gia and Dakota obviously got ready with other things in mind. Ryland, on the other hand, is clad in her usual t-shirt and jeans, insisting on keeping her legs covered, even in the blistering heat.

"When we go to jail I'm using my one phone call to tell Red this was all your idea," Finley mumbles, pulling her sunglasses down. They're silver, the reflective kind, and Gia leans over to fix her hair in the reflection.

"We'll be fine," Gia laughs. "Don't make yourself miserable."

Meanwhile, Ryland glances to Dakota out of the corner of her eye. The dark haired girl has adorned a black romper and cork wedges. Ryland knows the last thing on her mind is a friendly game of beach volleyball. She looks the girl up and down. "Dressed to impress?"

Dakota turns to her and cocks her head to the side, then looks down at what she's wearing and shrugs. "It's Gia's," she nods back to the girl. “I didn’t have anything so she let me borrow it,” she pauses to tug at the bottom. “It is kinda short, isn’t it?” she realizes, pursing her lips.

Ryland just shrugs. “Unless you’re wearing the world’s smallest bikini under that, I’m assuming you’re not swimming.”

“I could say the same for you,” Dakota quips back.

“Does it look like I’m a competent swimmer?” Ryland taps her brace with a raised eyebrow. Dakota’s mouth forms an ‘O’ in realization, but she quickly recovers.

“Gia said she was gonna show me around.”

“I bet she did,” Ryland mutters, leaning back against the bus stop bench. Dakota furrows her eyebrows, but before she can question the girl, Gia’s waving down the bus. Dakota moves to help Ryland up the stairs, but she’s met with a cold glare and quickly moves out of the way.

It’s an hour bus ride into the city, and Ryland spends it squished against the window next to Finley, the beach ball shoved between them making it impossible for her to move her arms. Across from them, she can hear Dakota and Gia talking, and for some reason it’s driving her crazy. Finley, completely oblivious to Ryland’s discomfort, continues going on about how Red will never let them live this down.

“Listen to this one,” Finley clears her throat, her lips and tongue dark red from the popsicle she’s just finished. “Why did the policeman arrest the baseball player?”

“Because he stole 2nd base,” Ryland digs her toes into the sand. “Heard it before.”

Finley frowns, tossing the popsicle stick aside. “You’re no fun.”

They've been at the beach for a little over an hour, and Gia has already dragged Dakota off to god-knows-where, doing god-knows-what. Ryland and Finley, on the other hand, have laid out towels in the sand at the top of the beach. After paying the bus fare, Gia split the rest of their dinner money among them. Finley's already spent hers on a second popsicle. Ryland keeps hers rolled up in her pocket.

"You know, it's not too bad here," Finley leans back on her hands. "That is, if you try not to think about the fact that we'll be put on permanent house arrest the moment Red finds out."

"Way to kill the mood."

"Sorry," Finley mumbles, lifting her sunglasses and looking around them. "Where do you think they ran off to?"

"Your guess is as good as mine, kid," Ryland glances behind them. "There's no telling with Gia."

Scrunching her nose, Finley hops to her feet, pulling the last of her money from her bra. "Might as well go get another popsicle, then." Ryland watches as she wanders off down the beach, sighing heavily and letting the sun warm her skin. Usually, she's able to enjoy days like this—the smell of the beach, the sound of the waves—but right now, her mind seems to be elsewhere.

Eventually, Ryland and Finley wander down the boardwalk and find a pizza place whose line isn't miles long. They end up using Ryland's money to buy something to eat, trying to find a way to pass the time. By now, Red has probably returned home to find them gone, so they're in no hurry to go back.

After a while, they end up back on the beach, befriending a group of college students trying to fly a kite. Well, more like *Finley* flies the kite while Ryland sits on a driftwood stump and watches.

By then, it's gotten darker, and someone's already started setting off fireworks.

"Did you see that?" Finley jogs back over to her, out of breath. Another firework hisses and squeals in the distance, and she points to it excitedly. With a soft laugh, Ryland nods.

"I think I like the beach," Finley sits down in the sand, leaning back on her arms. "I never got to go as a kid. It's cooler at night."

"Y'think Gia's passed out yet?" Ryland asks, raising an eyebrow. Finley just shrugs.

"Who knows."

Another firecracker goes off and Finley perks up. "Hey!" She turns to Ryland. "That one was closer! Let's go find them!"

And so, that's how Ryland allows herself to be dragged down the beach by Finley, on a wild goose chase to find the fireworks. Ryland slows them down a bit, though. Walking in sand isn't exactly her strong suit. It's uneven and heavy and she keeps dragging her leg.

They walk for a while, with Finley trailing ahead to collect seashells. Eventually, she jogs back over to Ryland, a frown on her face. "They haven't set off any more fireworks."

As if on cue, something near them hisses. "You may wanna get out of the way!"

Ryland and Finley look to one another in confusion.

"Hey! You!" the group of guys from further up the beach call out to them. "Move the fuck out of the way!"

Finley grabs Ryland's wrist, hurrying to tug her forward, away from the fireworks being lit. Ryland almost falls, her foot catching in the sand, but Finley quickly grabs onto her.

"Oh, shit, dude," one of the guys slaps his friend's chest and motions over to the girls. "You just yelled at a cripple."

The firework goes off moments later, whistling on its way up and bursting into golden crackles in the sky. Finley gasps and gazes up at it, not noticing how Ryland stands frozen behind her, jaw clenched. She'd heard them loud and clear—heard them try to muffle their laughter as all eyes turned to her, her brace sticking out like a sore thumb.

"What the hell did you just say?"

Someone else storms between the groups, straight for the cluster of guys up the beach. Finley's head whips around.

"Dakota?" Finley looks to Ryland in confusion, but the girl looks just as confused as she is.

"What the *hell* did you just *say*?" Dakota repeats herself through gritted teeth, balling her hand into a fist and getting right up in the face of the boy who'd commented on Ryland. He mumbles something under his breath, and then Dakota's shoving him, both hands against his chest. "Huh?" She cocks her head to the side menacingly and takes another step forward.

"I didn't say anything," he speaks up, standing his ground. "Who the hell are you—?"

He's cut off when Dakota lunges for him, and he has to duck out of her way. She moves to hit him again, but one of the other guys catches her by the waist, pulling her backwards before she has a chance to grab him.

Now, Ryland, who's just been gaping at the scene, suddenly feels something protective wash over her. "*Hey,*" she takes a step forward, her voice raised and firm, a growl in the back of her throat. "Don't *touch* her."

Before Finley can grab her, Ryland's on the way over to the group of guys, grabbing Dakota's arm and shoving the guy who has a grip on her.

"Yeah, fuck you!" Dakota calls out over her shoulder as Ryland tugs her back over to Finley, who just looks utterly confused.

Dakota rolls her head to the side to look at who's holding her, recognition flashing in her eyes. "Ryland!" her lips curve into a smile. "I was just looking for you!"

"She's drunk," Ryland deadpans, pulling them to a stop in front of Finley, who just sighs and shakes her head.

"Am not," Dakota mutters. Rolling her eyes, Ryland makes eye contact with Finley and then lets go of Dakota, who immediately stumbles to the ground, proving her point.

"Okay, ouch," Dakota mumbles, bringing a hand up to her forehead. "What was that for?"

"You're drunk," Ryland affirms, watching Finley help Dakota stand back up. "You just tried to fight someone a good two feet taller than you."

Finley nods. "You had to stand on your tiptoes just to be eye level with his adam's apple."

"We need to start placing bets on when she breaks the other hand," Ryland raises an eyebrow. Dakota frowns.

"He deserved it," she mumbles, letting Ryland guide her back to the boardwalk, Finley following them. "I forget why."

"She's an angry drunk," Finley notes, making Ryland laugh under her breath. When they get to the boardwalk, Dakota furrows her eyebrows and looks down.

"Where'd my shoe go?" Dakota's lips stitch together. She lifts her bare foot, wiggling her toes and letting her shoulders drop in confusion.

Ryland sighs and looks to Finley, who just shrugs, as if to say she's just as lost as Ryland is. Ryland breathes in deeply.

"Alright, Cinderella," she turns to Dakota. "Where's Gia?"

Dakota pauses, tilting her head to the side and thinking. Her eyes light up as if she's remembered something, but then she quickly shakes her head. "I dunno."

"Well that's helpful," Ryland mutters.

"I'll find her," Finley sighs. "I know where she'll be"

"You sure?"

Finley nods. "I'll meet you at the bus stop."

Ryland watches as Finley hurries off down the boardwalk, realizing the girl has probably done this time and time again. Her eyes then travel down to Dakota, who just looks up at her in confusion. Sighing heavily, Ryland nudges her forwards to get her to start walking.

"What are we gonna do with you, Dakota Quinn?"

Ryland learns a lot of things about Dakota that night.

To start things off, when Dakota's drunk, she doesn't shut up. Unless she falls asleep. And that's exactly what happens. She babbles on and on about her night on the walk back to the bus stop, somehow losing her other shoe in the process.

Soon, Finley returns with Gia in tow, who informs them that Dakota is the *lightest* lightweight she knows. Finley argues that make she's just a heavyweight, and Gia simply giggles.

Somehow, they manage to load themselves onto the bus. Dakota's the only one talking, and Ryland has to keep shushing her. At one point, Dakota's nearly yelling, and Ryland clamps a hand over her mouth. But for some reason Dakota finds this outrageously funny and ends up laughing even louder than she'd been talking. The bus driver glares at them through the mirror.

Eventually, Dakota falls asleep, using Finley's half-deflated beach ball as a pillow. Gia's able to draw a unibrow on her face before Finley confiscates her eyeliner and chucks it under the seats, which results in Gia crossing her arms and pouting for the rest of the ride.

It's at least 1am by the time they arrive home. Finley and Ryland exchange knowing glances, well aware that Red will be waiting for them.

And, of course, she's standing in the foyer with her arms crossed, flicking the lights on and clearing her throat after the girls funnel into the house. Startled, Dakota stumbles backward into Ryland's arms. Gia just groans and covers her eyes.

"Do you girls have *any* idea what time it is?" Red narrows her eyes at them. Dakota hides her face in Ryland's shoulder, mumbling something about how it's too bright.

They probably would've gotten more of a lecture if Gia hadn't interrupted them by suddenly clutching her hands to her stomach and running to the bathroom. Red sighs, warning them that they'll be revisiting this in the morning.

"Who's the lightweight now?" Dakota calls out down the hallway as they make their way up the stairs. Ryland clamps her hand over the girl's mouth, but stifles a laugh of her own.

"Scoot over."

Ryland groggily mumbles something, stirred from her slumber. Dakota whines from where she stands next to the bed.

"*Rylaaaand,*" she nudges the girl's shoulder. "*Scooooot.*"

"What are you doing?" Ryland's voice is dry and wrought with exhaustion. She lifts her head to look at the girl. Dakota's woken her up, wearing nothing but an oversized t-shirt that nearly comes down to her knees. Ryland groans and lets her head fall back on the pillow. "You're still drunk."

"And *you're* still not *moving*," Dakota grumbles, trying to tug the blanket from Ryland's grip and stomping her foot impatiently. With a heavy sigh, Ryland reluctantly rolls onto her back, giving Dakota just enough room to crawl under the blankets. And she does, humming contently. Ryland holds her breath as the other girl makes herself comfortable.

"Can you feel this?" Dakota whispers, poking Ryland's leg with her foot and tilting her head to the side.

"That's my good leg."

"Oh," Dakota pauses. "Can you feel this?"

"Still my good leg."

"Oh," Dakota furrows her eyebrows, confused. "Where'd your other leg go?" She lifts the covers to search for it.

"*Dakota*!" Ryland gasps, yanking the covers from Dakota's grip.

"What?"

"Don't do that," Ryland mutters. Dakota grows confused.

"Why?"

"I'm not wearing pants," Ryland glares at the girl, speaking through gritted teeth. Dakota tilts her head to the side.

"Why not?"

"I was planning on sleeping undisturbed," Ryland lets her head fall back onto the pillow. "But then you showed up."

"I don't think I'm wearing pants either," Dakota whispers, giggling and then pausing for a moment. Ryland can still smell the alcohol on her breath. Vodka, she thinks. Lifting her head, Dakota abruptly looks to Ryland, as if she's suddenly had a revelation. "Wanna see something?"

Ryland sighs heavily. "Not if it has to do with you not wearing any pants."

"You're funny," Dakota shakes her head, already sitting up to show her. "Look," she hums, lifting her shirt and peeling something away from the curve of her hip. Ryland squints to see in the dark.

"What is that?"

"Saturn," Dakota nods once, tracing her fingers over her skin. Ryland's eyes shoot wide open.

"You got a tattoo?" she gasps, sitting up quickly. Giggling, Dakota leans forward and cups her hand over Ryland's mouth.

"*Shhh*," she whispers, leaning closer and shaking her head. "*It's a secret*."

"*Dakota*," Ryland hisses, pushing the girl's hands away and lowering her voice. "How did you…?" She sighs and shakes her head. Leaning forwards, she studies the tattoo, running her thumb over the red skin. Dakota shivers.

"It's Saturn," the other girl whispers, breathing in deeply and holding it in her chest. "That tickles."

Ryland quickly pulls her hand away, looking to Dakota in disbelief. Unable to come up with anything, she just sighs heavily and falls back onto the mattress. "That's it, Dakota. That's it. You're insane. Absolutely insane."

"You smell like the rain," Dakota whispers, lying back down beside the girl.

Ryland rolls her eyes. "You're drunk."

"I know."

Sighing for the millionth time that night, Ryland rolls onto her side, her back facing the girl, who just looks at her curiously. "Go to sleep, Dakota."

"But why?"

"*Dakota*," she warns.

"Fine," Dakota mumbles. Ryland feels her shift in the bed beside her, and then tenses when she feels the girl playing with her hair, brushing her fingertips over the strands that lay across her pillow. Ryland opens her mouth to say something, but just ends up sighing and closing her eyes.

Once the room falls quiet, she's asleep within five minutes.

Ryland had planned on sleeping until oblivion, but she's woken up at the break of dawn when the bed shifts heavily beside her. Through half lidded eyes, she rolls over to find Dakota sitting up with her back against the headboard, both hands pressed to her forehead. Noticing Ryland's awake, she groans and slumps down to bury her face in her pillow.

"I'm never drinking again." Her voice is muffled.

Ryland stifles a laugh. "You sound like my mother."

Her words just slip out, and she doesn't even realize what she's said until Dakota lifts her head slowly, looking at her through the mess of hair that hangs down in her face.

"*That's* why you don't drink," she notes in realization, brushing her hair out of her face. Ryland just nods. Sighing, Dakota lies her head back down and mumbles something about how she feels like shit.

"How's your hip?"

Dakota lifts her head and raises an eyebrow, but groans and brings a hand to her forehead when it serves to make her headache worse. Ryland, with a sigh, moves the blankets aside and points to the small tattoo that Dakota had shown her the night before. The girl's eyes widen.

"Woah," she whispers, sitting up to study it. "It's Saturn."

"You don't remember getting it?"

Dakota shakes her head, tracing her fingers over the design. An amused smile tugs at her lips. “But I like it.”

“Well *great,*” Ryland rolls her eyes. “God knows where you got that done. For all we know you could end up with some infection and die within minutes.”

Dakota just laughs, her throat raspy. “You would love that.”

“Shut up,” Ryland hits her with a pillow and rolls back over, tugging the blankets over her head. Dakota’s just about to grab a pillow, but before she has a chance to retaliate, the door bursts open.

“We’re dead,” Finley shakes her head, wide eyed and out of breath. “We are so dead.” She then pauses, eyes darting back and forth between the two girls in the bed, who look like a pair of deer caught in headlights. Dakota tugs the blanket back up to cover her tattoo, her chest rising and falling quickly.

“It’s not what it looks l—,” Ryland starts, but Finley shakes her head, cutting her off with a panicked look in her eyes.

“Gia’s probation officer is here.”

Chapter 9

SOMEWHERE FAR AWAY

"You're in my way."

"Then scoot over."

"I can't *see*."

"*Shh*," Ryland hisses, glaring at the two other girls. They're squeezed in front of the railing at the top of the stairs, trying to listen in on the conversation happening in the living room.

"You sure that's her probation officer?" Dakota looks to Finley, who nods quickly.

"I think Red called him," she says softly, leaning forward and craning her neck to see.

"Did she break probation by being out last night?" Ryland raises an eyebrow.

"Technically, yeah," Finley furrows her eyebrows. "This can't end well."

"Shh," Dakota nudges both of them. "Listen." All three girls lean forward.

"I can't hear anything," Ryland mutters. Finley, cupping a hand to her ear, holds up a finger to signal for them to be quiet.

"He's saying something about..." she listens for another moment. "Detention?" She turns back to them in confusion.

Ryland's eyes widen. "Juvenile Detention?"

"Juvie?" Dakota gasps. Finley shushes them, still listening.

"Red sounds surprised," she turns to them. "I don't think this is going to end well."

Before they can eavesdrop any longer, Dakota's huffing in frustration and ducking under Finley's arm, descending the staircase. Ryland's eyes widen.

"*Dakota*," she hisses. "Where are you going?"

But Dakota's already at the bottom of the staircase, disappearing into the living room. Finley and Ryland exchange anxious glances before hurrying to follow her.

"What do you mean it was your idea?" The two girls slide into the doorway just in time to hear Red turn and address Dakota, who stands only a few feet in front of them.

"I was the one who made them go," Dakota shakes her head, glancing over to Gia, who sits on the couch, feigning indifference.

Red raises a stern eyebrow at the girl. "I find that hard to believe."

"I'm serious," Dakota jumps to defend herself. There's a moment of hesitation, which Ryland notices, but then Dakota's sighing, lifting the hem of her shirt with one hand, and rolling down the waistband of her sweatpants with another, revealing her tattoo in all its glory. "I was getting this."

"She got a t—?"

Ryland squeezes Finley's arm to silence her. Red, now confused, looks to the probation officer and then to Dakota.

"It's Saturn," Dakota says quietly. She hears Ryland sigh from behind her.

"But all four of you snuck out, Gia included," the probation officer speaks up.

“And so sending her to juvie is the solution?” Dakota takes a step forward. Ryland has to fight the urge to reach out and grab her.

“That’s the next step for someone who repeatedly breaks the rules,” he explains, his arms crossed as he nods in Gia’s direction. “Like Miss Dawson here.”

“Juvie isn’t going to solve those problems,” Dakota resists the urge to roll her eyes. “Those are the people she *wants* to be around.”

“And you consider yourself a good influence?” he looks to Dakota, earning a cold glare from the girl in return. Luckily, Red speaks up before she can.

“Her record is clean,” she motions to Dakota and then turns to nod towards the two girls in the doorway. “Finley’s a member of the National Honor’s Society and Ryland’s got a 4.0.”

Upon hearing this, all other three girls turn to look at Ryland in shock, but the girl just shrugs sheepishly.

“So you’re saying these girls are good influences on Gia?”

“I’m *saying* she’s improved drastically since she first came here,” Red replies with a firm nod.

Sighing, the officer pinches the bridge of his nose and thinks for a moment. “My biggest concern is the repeated sneaking out,” he explains, motioning to the girl on the couch, who flicks him off when he isn’t looking.

“Oh, she sneaks out *all* the time,” Finley speaks up, making both Ryland and Dakota wince. Ryland grabs her arm to shush her but she pulls away.

“Like, once she snuck out to get more fish food for my goldfish, or else he woulda’ died,” Finley nods. “And another time, she had to sneak out to the library to print out Ryland’s science report that she forgot was due." Dakota glances back to Ryland, who simply shrugs.

There's a long, awkward pause before the probation officer sighs heavily. "One more chance, Miss Dawson, you got that?" he points to her threateningly. "One more slip up, and I won't be easy on you."

The moment the front door shuts behind him, Finley whips around and tackles Gia in a hug, relieved. Ryland glances to Dakota and raises an eyebrow, but the girl just shrugs and looks away shyly. Red shakes her head at them.

"I trust you won't be sneaking out anymore," she points to Gia. "And you—," she turns to Dakota, who tenses up. "There's a tube of A&D lotion in the bathroom. Keep the tattoo clean. I'm not paying for a doctor's visit if it gets infected."

Dakota raises an eyebrow. "You know this from experience," she notes.

Red just gives her a look before clapping her hands, addressing them all. "Even though Gia got off easy doesn't mean there won't be punishment," she nods. "All four of you are on house arrest until further notice." There's a collective groan throughout the room.

"But," Red holds up a finger. "You will be allowed outside." Finley perks up.

"As long as it's to complete the chores on this list," she concludes, handing Ryland a sheet of notebook paper. The other three girls crowd around her, groaning when they see the checklist, stock full of housework for them to complete.

"I expect them done by dinnertime," Red nods, leaving them alone in the living room. With a frustrated sigh, Dakota snatches the list from Ryland's hands, rips it into four sections, and then hands each girl a strip.

"You owe me," she mutters to Gia, shoving the paper into her hands. She then looks to her own list and disappears off to her first chore, trudging up the stairs. Ryland's eyes scan the paper in her hand, sighing and groaning when she realizes she'll be mopping until oblivion. Gia must be feeling the same, too, because she mumbles something under her breath and shoves the list into her pocket.

Finley looks to the two other girls, then to her list. Her shoulders fall. "Looks like we better get started."

"Hey, stranger."

Dakota looks up from where she's kneeling, tugging weeds from the garden. She holds up a hand to block out the sun and raises an eyebrow at Ryland. "How's it going?" she nods to the list in her hand.

Ryland rolls her eyes. "It's… going," she motions to the girl. "Weeding?"

Dakota nods, standing up and brushing her hands off. "M'almost done though. What about you?"

"I'm supposed to repaint the fence," Ryland points behind them to the old picket fence that surrounds the backyard. It used to be white, Dakota thinks. It's so cracked and peeled that it's hard to tell anymore.

"Isn't that a two person job?" Dakota tilts her head to the side. Ryland smirks.

"Do you want it to be?" she raises an eyebrow. Dakota shrugs, a playful smile on her lips.

"C'mon, tiny," Ryland laughs and shoves a can of paint into the girl's arms. "I could use someone small enough to reach the tight spaces."

"*Very funny,*" Dakota rolls her eyes. Ryland just grins and taps her nose with a paintbrush.

"So," Dakota pauses, wiping her forehead with the back of her hand. "A 4.0?" she turns and raises an eyebrow at Ryland, who's sitting beside her, running her paintbrush over the fence. The girl just shrugs.

"I don't really pay attention to my grades."

Dakota furrows her eyebrows. "So you just casually maintain a 4.0 GPA?"

"I just do my homework," Ryland dips her brush into the paint and pauses to look at Dakota. "Why is that so surprising to you?"

"Cause' it's impressive," Dakota laughs, sitting back on her heels and adding another coat of paint to her section. "I knew you were smart, but I didn't know you were 4.0 smart."

"Oh, shut up," Ryland waves her hand to dismiss the girl. "Finley's smarter than all of us combined."

"*Finley* doesn't have a 4.0," Dakota quips back. Ryland smears paint on the edges of the fence.

"That's because *Finley* failed art class," she chuckles.

"How do you fail art class?"

Ryland shrugs. "She just couldn't get the abstract part of it. For someone who's obsessed with numbers and patterns and repetition, she just didn't like the concept of making art that didn't follow any sort of rules."

Dakota purses her lips. "Fair enough," she scoots over to start on the next pillar of the fence. "You're still smart, though."

"There's a bee on your shoulder."

Dakota immediately freezes, her eyes shooting wide open. "*Get it*," she hisses, not even moving her head. "*Ryland*!"

"Shoo," Ryland waves her hand to scare off the bee, who buzzes off and circles into a neighboring yard. She turns to return to her work, but pauses when she realizes Dakota hasn't moved an inch.

"Thanks a lot," the girl mutters. Upon seeing Dakota, Ryland bursts into laughter. Apparently, the hand she swatted the bee with was also the same hand as her paintbrush, and she'd splattered paint not only all over Dakota's face, but also down the entire side of her shirt. Ryland manages to apologize through her laughter, and Dakota just rolls her eyes, trying to wipe off her face. Unfortunately, this only makes it worse, and she ends up with white paint smeared all over her cheeks and her hands.

"Nice move," Ryland fights back laughter. Dakota glares at her, but suddenly her frown morphs into a mischievous smile. Ryland's eyes widen.

"Don't you dare, Dakota, I just—," she starts, but is cut off when a paint covered hand slaps her cheek, splattering it all down her neck and across the front of her shirt. Ryland's mouth drops open, and she brings a hand up to her face, now sticky and covered in paint. Dakota sits in front of her, a glob of paint dripping from one hand, and the other hand covering her mouth to stifle her laughter. Ryland moves to grab her paintbrush, but Dakota jumps backwards and holds up her hands in surrender.

"We're even!" she shakes her head through her laughter. Ryland glares at her. The other girl lowers her hands carefully, catching her breath. "We're even," she repeats, fighting back laughter when she sees just how much paint is on Ryland's face.

"I hate you," Ryland mumbles. But Dakota doesn't miss the smile she tries to hide.

"Touché," Dakota grabs her paintbrush and resumes painting. Ryland steals a glance at the girl when she's not looking, and she can't help but laugh at her paint-splattered shirt. Dakota just crinkles her nose at her.

When the two girls finally venture back inside, dinner's in the oven and Gia and Finley have both already finished their chores. As soon as Red turns to see them, sweaty and covered in white paint, she sends them straight upstairs to clean up. Both girls find this hilarious and can't stop cracking up until they disappear across the hall into separate showers. Dakota accidentally leaves a white handprint on the inside of her door.

Dakota's done first, and after she gets dressed and throws her wet hair up into a bun, she wanders downstairs to find that everyone's already finished eating. With the kitchen to herself, she grabs a plate of food and hops up to sit on the counter.

Ryland eventually saunters down, joining her in the kitchen. She raises an eyebrow at Dakota, who looks ridiculously adorable perched up on the counter, wet hair and an oversized t-shirt, with a mouthful of fried rice. She shoots Ryland a soft smile.

"I practically had to sandpaper my face to get that paint off," Ryland rolls her eyes half-heartedly, making herself a plate and sitting on one of the stools at the island so she can face Dakota. "How's Saturn?"

"Itchy," Dakota nods, lifting her shirt a few inches to look at the tattoo again. "I put some of Red's cream on it. That helped a lil'."

"You got lucky," Ryland notes, pushing her food around on her plate. "I've heard stories of people who wake up after a night of drinking and find their ex's face tattooed on their left asscheek or something."

Dakota laughs softly and shrugs, but Ryland quickly grows aware that something's different. Dakota runs her fingers over her hip. "Mine has more meaning than that," she nods gently. Ryland sets down her fork.

"You didn't just drunkenly get a random planet tattooed on your body?" She raises an eyebrow. Dakota shakes her head.

"The timing was random. Planet wasn't," she laughs softly. "I've wanted a tattoo like this for a while. I mean, I figured I'd have to wait until I was eighteen, but apparently my drunk self found a way around that one."

"Why Saturn?"

Dakota looks away. "My mom."

"Oh," Ryland whispers, unsure of what to say. "I'm sorry."

Dakota just shrugs. And before their conversation can continue, Finley wanders into the room, holding up two VHS tapes and making them vote on which movie to watch that night.

There's the rustle of blankets. The creak of a doorknob. The patter of soft footsteps down the hallway. Another door creaks open.

"Ryland?" Dakota's voice is a soft whisper, unsure. There's no reply. Biting her lip, she takes a few hesitant steps forward and nudges the girl's shoulder.

"Psst. Ryland. It's me."

The girl finally stirs, mumbling an incoherent string of words and gazing up at Dakota groggily.

"I can't sleep."

Slowly coming to, Ryland rubs her eyes and sits up slightly. "What's wrong?"

"I can't sleep," Dakota repeats herself. "I, uh," she motions behind Ryland to the other occupied bed. "Gia's in here."

"And?"

"Could you…" Dakota stumbles over her words. "Can you…?" she shakes her head. Ryland sits up.

"Is something wrong?"

"Don't," Dakota's voice wavers. "Can you just…" her voice trails off and she huffs in frustration. Ryland just sighs and shakes her head.

"Help me up," Ryland says softly, extending a hand to the girl. She could act clueless as to what Dakota was hinting at, but they both know well enough that when Dakota wakes her up in the middle of the night, there's a common theme. It's becoming a pattern.

And so, surprised, Dakota quickly pulls Ryland to her feet.

"Is it hard to walk without your brace?" Dakota asks as she slowly helps the girl maneuver down the hallway. Ryland shrugs.

"It's different," she nods softly, letting out a deep breath when they make it to Dakota's bedroom, and the girl helps her lower herself to sit on the bed.

Squeezing her knee, Ryland nods. "Yeah, next time just get me *before* I take my brace off," she laughs softly. Embarrassed, this spurs Dakota, who begins apologizing over and over.

"Dakota," Ryland reaches out, placing a hand on the girl's wrist. "I was joking." She notices how Dakota tenses at her touch and stitches her eyebrows together. "Something's wrong."

Shaking her head, Dakota hurries over to the other side of the bed. Using her hands, Ryland scoots herself backward to lean against the headboard. Dakota's afraid to look at her.

"Hey," Ryland grabs her hand without thinking. "Breathe." All she gets in return is a nod.

"*Alright*," Ryland takes a deep breath, giving in and pulling Dakota closer. She snakes an arm around the girl, who instantly starts to melt into her. Quietly, she places her hand on top of Dakota's, and then guides them both to the hem of the girl's shirt, tracing their fingers over the skin just above the tattoo. Dakota shivers.

"So when are you gonna tell me about it?" Ryland's voice is gentle, just barely breaking the silence. Dakota finally looks over to her.

"What?" her voice is raspy, just a whisper.

"Your tattoo," Ryland nods softly. "Are you ever gonna tell me what it means to you?" She holds her breath when silence follows.

Dakota looks back down at their hands and shrugs. "You never asked."

"So if I ask, will you tell me?"

"You want to know?" Dakota looks back to her, tilting her head to the side. She isn't used to this—to someone wanting to know about her. It's new.

Ryland laughs softly. "Course' I do," she squeezes the girl's hand. "It means something to you," she pauses. "Especially if it has to do with your mom." Dakota shifts beside her.

"It was our favorite song," the girl starts out softly, keeping her eyes trained on their hands. Ryland's hand is laid on top of hers and she traces the lines of her fingers with the tips of her own. Dakota memorizes the pattern.

"It's an old Stevie Wonder song," Dakota nods. "She had the old record of it and everything. We used to play it over and over while I would help her cook dinner," she laughs quietly at the memory.

"The whole song is about how he wants to leave Earth and move to Saturn, because everyone on Saturn is happy," Dakota half smiles. "And I guess it just became our thing. We..." she pauses, swallowing hard. "We didn't have much... so, whenever she'd come home from a late shift and we only had bread and butter for dinner, we'd have a picnic on the living room floor and plan how our life would be on Saturn." There's a light in her eyes when she talks, Ryland notices, and it isn't just from the tears threatening to spill over.

She squeezes the girl's hand. "And what would life on Saturn be like?"

Dakota smiles. "Peaceful," she nods. "We'd live in a house with a spiral staircase—that was Hudson's idea. We'd have a huge backyard with a pool. And a trampoline right next to it. So we could do flips into the water."

"Your idea?"

Dakota giggles. "Yeah," she looks to their hands. "Mom never cared about what the house would be like. All she cared about was that all three of us were there, she said," Dakota glances down. "But me and Hudson always told her that we'd build her a huge art studio. With all sorts of colors of paint that didn't even exist on Earth. I think she secretly liked when we said that."

Ryland smiles. For some reason she feels lucky to have Dakota open up to her like this. She knows the girl would never do the same with Gia or Finley. She can't mess this up—whatever "this" is. It's too different from anything she's had before. Too rare, she thinks.

"There's a double meaning, though," Dakota speaks up again, drawing Ryland out of her thoughts.

"After she... *you know*," Dakota swallows, motioning vaguely with her hand. "We used to have to find warm places to sleep during the winter, cause' our house didn't have any electricity. I mean, we could bundle up on some nights and be alright, but it used to snow so much that the cold was just... unbearable." She shivers at the thought.

It's hard for Ryland to imagine this past version of Dakota, so young, yet faced with such an adult world. She wants to wrap up that girl, to shelter her, to keep her from going through the things that have stripped her of her innocence. But Dakota isn't fragile anymore, Ryland realizes. The girl next to her is shaped from the things she's seen, molded from the fire and brimstone meant to destroy her. She's tough, and Ryland knows that, yet she's not unbreakable.

"One winter we spent a lot of nights at the library," the other girl continues. "We would hide in the bathroom while they locked up, and then we'd have the whole place to ourselves."

"That sounds kind of awesome," Ryland comments, making Dakota laugh.

"It was cool," she agrees. "Hudson used to read books all night. But I remember this one night I was using the computer to download songs onto this old mp3 player I had." She pauses to take a deep breath. "I remembered that song, and so I searched it and downloaded it. But I guess I chose a *different* song called Saturn."

"When I listened to it I just... It made me think of her right away. There's this lyric..." she pauses to collect herself. Ryland squeezes her hand.

"Take your time," she whispers. Dakota gives her a sad smile, but Ryland can tell she's still fighting back tears.

"There's this lyric," Dakota continues, taking a deep breath. "It goes '*You taught me the courage of stars before you left. How light carries on endlessly, even after death.*'" Her voice wavers and she holds up a hand to make Ryland wait. Leaning over, she reaches under the bed to retrieve her journal.

It's worn and the leather is cracked. Random pages fall out as she flips through it, and she shoves them back in. Ryland watches, catching glimpses of sketched trees and flowers. Eventually, Dakota smooths down a page and passes the journal over to Ryland, running her fingers across her own writing.

"That night I wrote down the lyrics," she says quietly. Ryland's eyes scan the words, understanding right away why they resonated so deeply with the girl. "And then…" Dakota flips the page.

Ryland's eyes widen, finding the two-page spread covered in tiny handwriting, the entire song scrawled over and over. There's a model of the solar system sketched in the upper corner, with Saturn shaded in using orange highlighter. Dakota nods, allowing her to turn the page.

"It became a nervous habit," Dakota nods, watching as the girl turns through page after page of the lyrics. She looks away shyly when Ryland glances over to her.

"You just wrote it over and over?"

"Still do, sometimes," Dakota nods, taking the journal back and pausing to scan her writing again. "I just… it was comforting."

"No, I get it," Ryland nods as Dakota puts the journal back. "I used to draw circles over and over when I was in elementary school. The repetition is comforting, I know. I always got in trouble for filling my worksheets with drawings, but it was the only way I could keep myself awake."

Dakota raises an eyebrow.

"She threw parties at night," Ryland answers the silent question. "Sleep was impossible."

"Oh," Dakota whispers, trying to fight back a yawn by failing. Ryland laughs softly.

"Tired?"

"A little," the girl mumbles, sinking down in the bed and melting even further into Ryland's arms. "It's late."

"It's barely midnight," Ryland chuckles, her gaze following the girl.

"*Shhh*," Dakota reaches up blindly to cover Ryland's mouth, but ends up nearly poking her in the eye. "Sleep."

"Yes ma'am," Ryland raises an eyebrow playfully. Shifting slightly, she tugs the blankets over both of them. Dakota's practically pressed up against her, and Ryland knows the arm she has wrapped around the girl will be killing her all day tomorrow, but it's the last thing on her mind.

"Hey Ryland?"

Ryland's pulled out of her thoughts when the younger girl speaks up once more. "Hm?" she hums.

Dakota lifts her head to look at the girl, a sleepy smile on her face. "You're not half bad."

"Go to sleep," Ryland laughs and pushes Dakota's head away to keep the girl from seeing the smile she's failed to fight back, but she ends up just threading her fingers in the girl's hair and playing with it. Dakota hums contently and settles back down into the mattress.

Long after Dakota's dozed off, Ryland remains awake, still running her fingers through the girl's damp hair. She smells like shampoo and peppermint, and Ryland feels intoxicated. She's starting to realize something; that she's never felt like this over a guy—let alone a girl. And although it scares her more than she knows, it's still not enough to even make her consider going back to her own room.

Chapter 10

DON'T LOOK BACK

When Ryland wakes up, she's alone. However, her brace seems to have magically appeared, propped up against Dakota's nightstand. For Dakota to go out of her way to remember something as little as that astonishes Ryland, probably because no one's ever made the effort before.

Once she's dressed, Ryland makes her way into the commotion downstairs. Finley's taken on the challenge of making pancakes, and Dakota's currently joking around with her, trying to flip one by throwing it in the air from the pan. Both girls crack up when the half-cooked pancake ends up splattered on the floor.

Meanwhile, Gia spots Ryland in the doorway, watching the girls. She raises an eyebrow at her and then looks back and forth from Ryland to Dakota. Ryland's bed had been empty when she woke up, she's noticing a pattern.

But like always, they don't talk about it. In the morning, it's back to the usual friendly banter, as if Dakota hadn't been the one who fell asleep in her arms the night before. It's a habit they've slowly fallen into.

Ryland chugs half a glass of orange juice and leans against the counter. Finley turns around, holding up a plate in question, but Ryland just shakes her head. She's never hungry in the mornings.

"The countdown to spring break begins right now," Dakota announces, uncapping a marker and scrawling a series of exclamation marks across the following week on the calendar. Ryland rolls her eyes.

"Does it even count as spring break if we're all going to spend it on house arrest?"

"You don't know that," Dakota furrows her eyebrows. "She might lets us off easy." Upon hearing this, Finley laughs from across the room.

"Knowing Red, we'll be on house arrest until we die," she takes a bite of her pancake and rolls her eyes. "Or until this place burns down."

Ryland sees Dakota tense from across the room.

"Even then we'd still be in trouble," Ryland speaks up, changing the subject and setting her glass in the sink. "It's time to head out." Dakota glances over to her, a shy smile on her face.

"I'm going to fail this stupid science exam," Finley huffs, slinging her bag over her shoulder. Gia rolls her eyes.

"You studied *all* last night."

"Still gonna fail," Finley mumbles. Ryland glances behind her, noticing the look on Dakota's face and raising an eyebrow.

"I'm guessing *someone* forgot to study," she waits for Dakota on the front porch, picking up the pace beside her. Dakota rolls her eyes.

"Wouldn't have made a difference either way," she shrugs, kicking a pebble as they walk.

"What's it on?"

"Plate tectonics."

"No it's not," Finley speaks up from in front of them. "This week is isobaric maps."

Dakota looks to Ryland as if to say '*told you so.*' She lets her hands fall to her sides in defeat.

"Did you pay attention in class?" Ryland asks. Finley answers for her.

"When she's *in* class, maybe," she earns a glare from Dakota. Ryland turns to her and raises an eyebrow. "She always gets a pass to go to the nurse's office."

Ryland looks to Dakota, who shrinks in her jacket. "Why?"

"There's this kid—,"

"*Finley*!" Dakota snaps, startling the girl. "*Leave it alone.*" Finley's eyes widen and she clamps her mouth shut, looking to the girl apologetically before hurrying to catch up with Gia.

"What was she talking about?" Ryland asks cautiously once they're alone.

"Nothing I can't handle," Dakota mutters, picking up her pace as they near the school building. Before Ryland can push anything else, she's gone, disappearing into the sea of students.

"*The Tell-Tale Heart sums up the kind of horror that Poe implemented in his stories.*"

Ryland's only half listening. She taps her pen against her bottom lip and doodles aimlessly in her notebook. She's already read the story, twice over, and completed the comprehension questions in the back of the textbook.

"Ryland."

She glances up, looking to the boy sitting across from her. He meets her eyes and then nods to the back of the room. Glancing over her shoulder, Ryland grows confused when she sees Dakota, who perks up when Ryland turns around. She motions for her in the hallway.

Ryland glances back to the teacher and then to Dakota once more. "Me?" she mouths, pointing to herself. Dakota rolls her eyes, and Ryland knows if she could talk she'd be saying *Of course, you idiot. Who else*? Confused, Ryland looks back to the teacher before raising her hand and asking to be excused.

The teacher pauses, looking to the clock. "We've got ten minutes left, Moreno, can it wait?"

"It's, uh… it's my…" Ryland searches for an excuse. "It's my leg."

Upon hearing this, the teacher is practically shoving her out of the room, asking if she needs someone to walk her to the nurse. She shakes it off, ducking into the hallway and quickly pulling the door shut behind her.

"Took you long enough," Dakota appears by her side, grabbing Ryland's arm and leading her behind a row of lockers, out of view. Before Ryland can get a word in edgewise, the girl sidesteps behind her and starts fishing through her backpack.

"What are you doing?" Ryland hisses, pulling her bag out of the girl's reach. Dakota freezes.

"I need your keycard," she looks to Ryland hopefully. "You know, the magnet card you used for the back door?"

Ryland crosses her arms. "And what exactly do you need that for?" Dakota seems to shrink under her incriminating glare, and right away, Ryland knows something's up.

"I just need it, okay?" Dakota huffs in frustration. She moves back to dig through Ryland's bag, but Ryland's already slipped something out of the side pocket, holding it in her hand.

"Looking for this?"

Dakota's eyes light up and she makes a grab for the card, but Ryland moves at the last second. Dakota, confused, hurries after Ryland when she starts walking.

"So where're we headed, tiny?" she asks once Dakota catches up to her. The other girl quickly shakes her head, realizing what she's doing.

"Ryland, you can't—,"

"I have the key, don't I?" Ryland holds up the card once more. "You really think I'm letting you sneak off on your own?"

Dakota huffs. "I was hoping you wouldn't ask any questions." This makes Ryland laugh.

"Do you *know* me?"

They reach the door and Ryland pauses, raising an eyebrow at her. "You're sure about this?" Dakota glares at her.

"Fine, fine," Ryland shakes her head and scans the door. As soon as the locks click, Dakota is gone. Ryland's quick to follow.

Even though Dakota's practically sprinting, and Ryland's limping at a significantly slower pace, she turns the corner to the front of the school just in time to see Dakota practically tackle someone into a hug. She pauses, standing still in confusion. All she can make out is a mop of dark curly hair. Until Dakota pulls away, and then Ryland finds herself clenching her jaw. It's a guy.

Then, both of them are looking back at Ryland, and Dakota suddenly hurries over to her, grabbing her wrist and nearly dragging her back to the old pickup truck where the stranger stands. Ryland tenses, knowing well enough that his eyes have moved down to her leg.

"This is my brother," Dakota squeezes her arm and then lets go. "Hudson."

"*This* is your brother?" Ryland raises an eyebrow. They look nothing alike, she notes. The man standing in front of her is significantly tanner than Dakota, his hair is curly and in need of a haircut, and he has freckles blending in around his nose. Her eyes move back and forth between the two.

"Different fathers," Dakota quickly explains. She then turns to Hudson, nodding to the other girl. "This is Ryland. She's a friend."

Hudson nods to her, but it's clear his mind is on something else. There's a look of urgency in his eyes and it's unsettling Ryland. He glances to the front of the building and then back to his sister. "We need to hurry, Koda."

Ryland's not the only one who's confused, either. Dakota herself pauses and furrows her eyebrows. "What are you talking about?"

Hudson looks to Ryland in passing and then lowers his voice, as if it's a secret. "You think I drove all the way out here just to talk to you?"

"That's what you said on the phone…" Dakota hesitates. Ryland looks back and forth between the both of them, feeling like she's intruding on something private. She moves to take a step away, but Dakota grabs her wrist.

"Don't," she glances to Ryland. "Stay."

"Dakota," Hudson shakes his head. "We need to go."

"Go?" she tenses. "Go where?"

Again, Ryland feels like she's intruding, but Dakota still hasn't let go of her wrist. Hudson digs something out of his pocket.

"Fake passports," he explains. Dakota stiffens. "We can start over again, once we get to the border, the hard part is over." Ryland feels Dakota's fingers loosen around her wrist. She takes a step forward and looks at the passports.

"You're serious?" she looks up to him. Hudson nods. Letting go of Ryland's wrist completely, she pages through the passport in her hand and then swallows hard. "I…"

"We've done it before, Dakota. We can do it again."

Hesitating, Dakota looks back to Ryland, who remains cold as stone. Dakota's eyes search hers for some kind of answer, but the girl just shrugs and looks away.

"You didn't say anything about this on the phone," Dakota repeats herself again. Ryland doesn't know what to do. Dakota turns to her. "What will Red say?"

Ryland shrugs once more. "How should I know?" Dakota bites her lip and looks back to the passport. Her brother jingles the keys in his pocket impatiently.

"What do you think?" she turns back to Ryland.

"I think it's your decision," Ryland cross her arms and shrugs, feigning indifference. Dakota's eyes search hers pleadingly, but Ryland looks away. The younger girl takes a deep breath.

"Alright," Dakota takes a step forward, swallowing her fear and nodding to her brother. "Let's go." Hudson nods, opening the truck door and sliding in to start the engine.

"You'll be okay?" Dakota turns to face Ryland. She knows the moment she gets in that car, anything she's been building here will be gone, no more than a speck in the rearview mirror. Ryland included.

Ryland holds up the keycard, forcing a smile. "I can get back in the way I came."

Dakota shakes her head. "Not that. I mean… cause I'm…. *going…*" she takes a hesitant step towards her.

Ryland just shrugs. "He's your brother," she says softly, shoving her hands into her pockets. "I get it."

And she gets it, she really does. She doesn't want it to happen, obviously. But in the little amount of time she's gotten to know Dakota, she knows the girl needs freedom to make her own decisions. Although, it doesn't make her leaving any easier. Ryland figures that's what she gets for getting attached so easily.

"I'm sorry," Dakota whispers, and her words are more than just an apology to both of them. Ryland simply shrugs again, but then she's taken by surprise when Dakota's arms are suddenly around her and she's being pulled into a hug.

But within minutes, they're gone. Ryland watches the truck disappear down the street until it's out of view. In the passenger side of the truck, Dakota does the same, kneeling backwards in her seat and squinting her eyes for as long as she can, before the school is only just a memory, a speck in the distance.

When Ryland finally turns to make her way back into the school, she ends up chucking a glass bottle she finds by the dumpster. It shatters against the brick wall, shards scattering across the asphalt. But Ryland just sighs heavily. It'd only made her feel worse.

What bothers her the most is the fact that she understands why Dakota left. Ryland's one who holds grudges—and getting over this would be a hell of a lot easier had she and Dakota parted ways due to some kind of fight. But she's not bitter. She's not angry at the girl. She's just disappointed, because just when she thought she had something going for her, it drove away in the passenger seat of a navy blue pickup truck.

"Where's Dakota?"

It's the first thing Finley asks when they meet up to walk home. Ryland mumbles some excuse about her staying after class to get help with homework—the same one she'll give Red when they get home. Ryland refuses to be the one who "discovers" that Dakota's gone. At this point, she just wants to forget about her altogether, to erase her from their timeline and move on as quickly as possible.

Even though the only thing she wants to do when they get home is lock herself in her bedroom and sulk, she's on dinner duty with Finley, which means she spends the next hour grating cheese and browning ground beef. As the time passes by, even Finley starts glancing to the door, anxiously awaiting Dakota's return.

Red starts questioning them around dinnertime. Ryland stays quiet, shrugging and giving the occasional nod of the head if provoked. Looking to the clock, Red declares that if they don't hear from Dakota by tomorrow morning, she'll go to the police.

"Why so long?" Finley furrows her eyebrows, obviously concerned. Ryland sinks down in her chair and wills herself to disappear.

"We try and wait 24 hours before reporting a missing person from the house," Red explains. "We've had a fair share of false alarms."

Ryland mumbles something about how she wishes this were a false alarm. Red raises an eyebrow at her, but she quickly excuses herself from the table.

It's pouring rain.

Dakota shivers, pulling her brother's jacket up over her head. It doesn't do much to help her, though. She steps off the curb and huffs in annoyance when she lands ankle-deep in a puddle, soaking her shoes and the ends of her pants.

The further away from the city she walks, the narrower the sidewalks become, and the darker it gets. There's been a lump in the back of her throat since she left Hudson. But she knew she couldn't do it. The minute she'd seen the first checkpoint sign, she started to panic, and had Hudson cursing as he turned around and pulled over. She couldn't do it—she told him over and over, shaking her head desperately—she's already had to start over too many times, and as soon as she was gaining her footing, everything was changing again. Things are good in California, she'd promised him, and she'll be 18 soon and then she's free to roam wherever she pleases. But for now, she'd told him—fighting back tears—for now, she just can't go with him.

And that's how she ended up in the back of an almost-empty bus, headed on the long journey back to the home. She wouldn't call it *her* home just yet, but it's become a safe place to her, a chance at something normal.

Dakota would be lying if she said she hasn't been thinking of Ryland this whole time. After the screaming match she had with her brother in the car, he eventually realized there was no changing her mind. Things were tense between them on the drive to the bus stop, but they promised to meet again when she was eighteen and the law couldn't keep them apart anymore. So after losing her brother in that sense, she's been silently clinging to the only other person she seems to have left—Ryland.

Would she have returned to the home if it hadn't been for Ryland? Maybe. But did the thought of Ryland being there make her hurry back a little faster? Definitely.

Just as she reaches their street, a car comes whizzing by, screeching as it turns the corner—skidding right through a puddle and sending water flying everywhere—effectively soaking Dakota from head to toe. Wiping her face, she wants to cry right then and there, to throw her bag to the ground and quit. But she doesn't. She trudges uncomfortably down the sidewalk, feeling water pooling in the bottom of her shoes. And when she's eventually standing in the front of the house, she wants to cry again, just from pure exhaustion.

The lattice in the garden finally comes in handy. Making sure her backpack is secure, she carefully starts to climb. It's more difficult in wet shoes, but she navigates her way up and scrambles onto the roof, catching her breath.

After some initial struggle, she manages to scale over to her bedroom window. It's still pouring, harder than before, and the wind is pelting her with raindrops, so hard that it's painful against her bare skin. Breathing deeply, she presses her palms against the glass and maneuvers the window open, relieved that it wasn't locked. She swings in, feet first, and exhales heavily when she's standing on solid ground.

"Dakota?"

She flinches, accidentally slamming the window shut. Whipping her head around, her heart jumps in her chest when she sees Ryland move to sit up in one of the beds, rubbing her eyes.

"*Dakota*?" the girl repeats herself again, disbelief in her voice. She's still not convinced this isn't some sort of dream.

"I didn't mean to wake you..." is all Dakota can manage. Ryland just stares at her.

"You came back?"

But Dakota's too distracted. "Why are you in my—?"

She's cut off when Ryland tries to stand up, and Dakota practically has to dive forward to catch her when she stumbles. She has to hold both of Ryland's shoulders to keep her balanced. Just as she's about to repeat her question, Ryland grabs her face with both hands, her eyes searching, as if she's making sure she's real.

"You came back?" she asks again. And although Dakota's fought back tears countless times before, she's too exhausted to do it this time. She just nods.

"You should sit d—," Dakota starts, but then Ryland's arms are flung around her and she's hugging her so tightly that Dakota stumbles a few steps backward.

"Please don't do that again," Ryland's voice is barely a whisper, and Dakota almost doesn't catch it. But she does, and she's left confused by Ryland's words.

"Do what?" she whispers.

"Leave," Ryland mumbles into her shoulder.

Dakota freezes, unsure of how to process Ryland's words. She hesitates for a moment, but then all resolve falls and she squeezes the girl tighter, cupping the back of her head with one hand. "I won't."

Ryland pulls away, studying the girl's face again. "Are you hurt?"

Dakota shakes her head.

"Are you *okay*?"

Dakota shrugs. "I made him go without me."

It's then that Ryland notices. She pauses, slowly using her thumbs to wipe Dakota's cheeks. "Are you crying?

"*No*," Dakota quickly shakes her head, turning away to wipe her eyes. "It's raining."

"I know," Ryland nods, not pushing the subject. "I'm in here cause' Finley stole my bed. The water's leaking in through her window."

"Oh," Dakota nods softly. Ryland lowers herself down to sit on the edge of the bed. They both seem to notice that Dakota's dripping wet at the same time, because soon Dakota is shaking her head and hurrying over to the dresser.

"I'll be back," she says softly, grabbing a handful of clothes and disappearing out into the hallway. Ryland's left sitting on the bed, her mind suddenly reeling from everything that's just happened.

She brings a hand up to her forehead and makes herself take a deep breath. She'd just come so close to kissing Dakota. So close. It was just a spur of the moment thing, she tells herself. When she stood up, Dakota had been *right there*. She'd almost leaned in and kissed her just out of pure relief. Now, she has to calm down, because her heart is beating like crazy. And now, she's left to sit and wonder what would have happened it she had just went for it.

Ryland's so on edge that when the door squeaks back open, she jumps and whips her head around. And of course, like always, the sight of Dakota makes her heart flutter. The dark haired girl has changed into an old hoodie and lazily thrown her hair up.

"Cold?" Ryland quickly composes herself and turns to face the girl. Dakota just yawns, scrunches her nose, and plops down on the end of the bed. Sniffing, she glances over to Ryland.

"M'tired," she mumbles, crawling over to the top of the bed and laying on her stomach, burying her face in her pillow. Ryland, unsure of what to do, waits for a few seconds before slowly scooting back to lay on her stomach beside the girl. Dakota mumbles something into her pillow.

"Hm?" Ryland hums. Dakota rolls her head to the side to face the girl.

"Are you staying all night?" she asks hesitantly.

"Do you not want me to?"

Dakota quickly shakes her head. "No, no, I just—," she pauses. "If you wanted to… I wouldn't mind."

Sighing, Ryland scoots over and starts absentmindedly tracing her fingers over the girl's back. Dakota lays her head back down on her pillow and gives the girl a sad smile. Ryland, resting her chin on her free arm, studies Dakota's face.

"So you're staying?" she can't help but ask again. Somehow her hand ends up under Dakota's hoodie, and she traces small circles across her back, making the girl shiver.

"I'm tired of running," Dakota admits. "And… I guess this place isn't as bad as I thought it was," she yawns. "You guys keep things interesting."

"That means you're staying?"

Dakota can't help but laugh, and she props herself up on her elbows to look at the girl. "Yes, Ryland. I'm staying. Happy?"

Ryland nods. "Very. Because you're in charge of dinner tomorrow night." Dakota rolls her eyes, her head falling back onto her pillow. There's a few seconds of silence before Ryland works up her courage.

"Hey Dakota?"

"Hm?"

"Since you're staying…" Ryland pauses. "If, uh… If Red 'un-grounds' us by next week, do you maybe wanna… do something? Just me and you?"

A smile tugs at Dakota's lips that she's too tired to hide, so she just nods softly. "I'd like that."

"Yeah?" Ryland's surprised. Dakota laughs softly.

"Yeah." Dakota yawns and reaches over, absentmindedly twirling a strand of Ryland's hair around her finger. "M'glad you're here, you know."

Ryland has to look away to hide the smile on her face.

"Dakota?"

There's a dip in the bed and Dakota brings a hand up to wipe her eyes. Ryland sits in front of her, her hands hugging a cup of coffee.

"What time is it?" Dakota's voice is raspy and she clears her throat. Ryland shrugs.

"Everyone already left," Ryland says softly. Upon hearing this, Dakota sits up quickly and looks to the girl in confusion. Ryland just hands her the cup of coffee.

"Don't worry," she laughs. "I already took care of Red." She notices the girl studying the coffee and squeezes her knee. "It's black."

"Thanks," Dakota whispers, taking a sip and giving her a shy smile. "So Red… she knows?"

"She knows that you got sick and spent the night at a friend's house, yeah," Ryland smirks. "Remember? You tried calling home a bunch of times but our phone was unplugged."

"The phone was unplugged?"

"You're welcome," Ryland nods. "So now, you're taking a sick day."

Dakota furrows her eyebrows. "And you?"

"Stole a spare key and hid in the backyard until Red left."

"Smart," Dakota laughs softly and takes another sip of her coffee. Ryland nods, absentmindedly tugging at a loose string on her sleeve.

"So… what's happening with your brother?" she can't help but ask. Dakota looks down and sighs.

"We fought over me coming back," she confesses, tapping her fingers against the side of her cup. "But he's still going down without me. When I turn eighteen any of the charges against him will be dropped, though, so he's free after that."

"And then what do you do?" Ryland asks. "When you turn eighteen?"

"Good question," Dakota mumbles with a shrug. "I've never really given it much thought. I mean, before we got found out I just figured I'd end up working at the garage with Hudson. But then…"

"Things changed," Ryland softly finishes her sentence. Dakota looks back to her and nods.

"Exactly."

Ryland thinks for a moment. "Well what do you want to do?"

"I'm seventeen," the girl sighs. "How am I supposed to know? At this point all I want to do is survive."

"Don't we all."

Chapter 11

PEOPLE LIKE YOU

They make it through the next week of school, just barely. Spring Break comes around just in time. For Dakota, a week off of school means a week without any worries. The only problem is that they've been confined in the house for the first two days, and there's practically nothing left for them to do. Even Finley—who's managed to coerce them into playing six full games of Monopoly—starts to grow restless.

However, Gia soon has other plans. And with Dakota on board, they go over without a hitch.

So that's why Ryland's peace and quiet is interrupted at noon on a Wednesday, when Dakota comes barreling up the stairs and bursts into her room. The smaller girl flings herself onto the bed next to Ryland, a wide smile on her face.

"Pack a bag."

Ryland, who'd been in the middle of finishing her homework, just stares at Dakota in utter confusion.

"Come on," Dakota shakes her shoulder. "We're off house arrest. We're going out."

Ryland arches an eyebrow. "Who's we?"

"All four of us," Dakota hops off the bed and catches her breath. "Me and Gia convinced Red to let us spend a night at the beach. There's a huge carnival going on. Ferris wheel and everything. Hey—did you know Red's got a tattoo on her shoulder?"

"*Dakota*," Ryland laughs and shakes her head. "Slow down." She stands up, placing her hands on the girl's shoulders. Dakota takes a deep breath.

"Red's letting us go into the city for a night," she nods. "We're allowed to go as long as Finley goes too, she says. And Finley will go as long as Gia doesn't drink."

Ryland quirks an eyebrow.

"I know, crazy, right? But Gia promised she wouldn't," Dakota shakes her head. "She called and got us hotel rooms and everything."

A smile finally graces Ryland's face. "You're serious?"

"Dead serious," Dakota nods quickly. "We can split up when we get there. Then we can hang out. Just us, remember?"

"How'd you manage to pull this off?" Ryland laughs. Dakota just shrugs, fishing around under Ryland's bed until she finds her duffel bag.

"Hurry up and get packed," she pushes the bag into the girl's arms. "We're leaving in 10." And with that, she's gone, running over to her bedroom to get herself ready.

Dakota's excitement rubs off on Ryland, because she actually finds herself looking forward to this—more than she had with their trip to the boardwalk. It's probably due to the "*just us*" Dakota had thrown in. It had made her heart jump.

And before they know it, all four girls are seated on a two hour bus ride into the city. Even Finley, who normally despises these kinds of outings, is practically bouncing on the edge of the seat. They've squeezed into the back row, tossing their duffel bags underneath of them and getting comfortable. Dakota makes herself at home immediately, spreading out with her head on Ryland's lap and her legs across Gia and Finley's. She has a bag full of almonds balanced on her chest and tosses one at Finley every few minutes out of boredom.

"How much longer?"

"We're halfway there," Ryland laughs, looking down at the girl. Dakota frowns.

"I'm out of almonds."

"I know," Ryland hums. "You threw them all at Finley."

"It's no fun when she's asleep," Dakota lifts her head. Finley had passed out not even fifteen minutes into the trip, and Gia fought off sleep for as long as she could, but the lull of the bus eventually caught up with her.

"Do you think they know?" Dakota blurts out, arching her head back to look up at Ryland.

"Know what?"

Dakota looks away, pursing her lips. "Nothing."

"What are you—?"

"Hey!" Dakota giggles. "An almond!" She sits up, plucking something out of Finley's hair and bursting into laughter when she holds it up to show Ryland.

Ryland's immediately overwhelmed when they step off the bus and she can practically hear the roar of the crowd at the carnival. It takes place on the boardwalk, and she knows it's the perfect setting to be pushed and shoved around like a school of fish. Dakota's hand on her wrist distracts her, though, and she tugs the girl down the sidewalk, following Gia and Finley.

"So what are we doing first?" Finley asks, craning her next to try and catch a glimpse of the lights as they walk.

"Checking in," Gia holds up the bag in her hand, then nods to the other girls. "I don't know about you guys, but once we get rid of these, I'm set on eating three full pizzas. Or more."

"I like that idea," Finley nods quickly. Ryland looks to Dakota.

"You hungry?"

Dakota shakes her head. "I ate too many almonds." She shrugs. "You?"

Even though she hasn't eaten since breakfast, Ryland lies and says she's not hungry to avoid being split up from Dakota.

Once they get to the hotel, they find their rooms. Ryland's not disappointed at all when she finds that Gia's booked them two separate rooms, each with a queen sized mattress. Dakota quickly claims the bigger one and does some sort of somersault dive onto the bed. She's quickly distracted, though, taking her time to look around the new room.

Ryland finds it funny how the girl is fascinated with the air conditioner under the window, because she turns it up as high as it can go and her eyes widen when she's blasted with cold air. But then, Ryland remembers that Dakota's spent more than half of her life in a home with no electricity, and then it makes a little more sense—and becomes a little less amusing.

"We're ordering room service," Gia kicks open their door with one foot and leans in the doorway, a phone pressed to her ear and the cord stretched all the way from her room. Dakota ducks under her arm, running across the hallway and tackling Finley onto the other bed, both girls giddy at the prospect of adventure. Ryland and Gia look at each other, rolling their eyes.

"I'm good," Ryland shakes her head. "Just save me whatever."

"Red wine or white wine?" Gia looks up from the menu in her hands. Ryland raises an eyebrow.

"What happened to no alcohol?"

"It's just wine," Gia shakes her head. "It'll be before I go to bed."

Ryland crosses her arms.

"Shut up," Gia throws the menu at her. "It's spring break."

"Are you guys staying in?" Dakota jogs back in, noting the fact that Gia isn't wearing any makeup. The other girl just shrugs.

"We've got all day tomorrow and it's already getting dark," Gia nods. "Plus I think Finley's set on pigging out and watching movies all night."

"Who are you and what have you done with Gia Dawson?" Ryland looks at her in astonishment. Meanwhile, Finley throws something at Dakota from across the hallway and the dark haired girl ducks behind the door.

"Oh come on," Gia rolls her eyes at Ryland. "It's a *carnival.* What am I supposed to do? Rave on a ferris wheel?"

"Hell yeah," Dakota speaks up, sliding in place beside Ryland and placing a hand on her shoulder. "We're off to have fun without you. Don't wait up for us."

"Didn't plan on it!" Gia calls after them as Dakota pulls Ryland off down the hallway. Finley comes barreling after them, throwing an ice cube at Dakota just as the elevator doors slide shut. Ryland raises an eyebrow at the other girl, who just laughs and shakes her head.

"She started it."

"Sure she did," Ryland rolls her eyes playfully. "Where are we going?"

"I dunno," Dakota shrugs as they walk out into the cold night air. She looks around. "What do you feel like doing?"

They start to walk in the direction of the boardwalk, which is lit up with lights and drowning in music. Ryland just shrugs.

"Hey," Dakota grabs her arm, making her wait. She glances over to the boardwalk and then back to the girl. "I want you to tell me if your leg is bothering you."

Confused, Ryland looks at Dakota quietly.

"I don't want to like… drag you around thinking you're fine while you're actually in pain," Dakota explains, shaking her head. "You would let me know if we need to stop, right?"

All Ryland can do is look away and Dakota hesitates, taking a half step backward. "I didn't mean to—,"

"You're fine," Ryland shakes her head. "M'just… not used to it."

"Not used to what?"

"People…" Ryland thinks for a moment. "People like you."

"Like me?" Dakota cocks her head to the side.

Ryland nods softly. "You just… *get it*," she struggles to explain herself. "Like when you knew how I drink my coffee," she shrugs. "Most people don't pay attention to stuff like that. You make an effort."

"Don't most people?" Dakota furrows her eyebrows.

"Not for someone like me."

Confused, Dakota reaches out to grab Ryland's wrist. "Like you?"

"You know…" Ryland looks down, digging the heel of her shoe into the ground. "Just like… *me*." She motions to herself with one hand.

"I don't get it," Dakota's voice is soft. "What's so different about you and me?"

Ryland laughs to herself, shaking her head. "If only you knew."

"Then *tell* me," Dakota takes a step forward, pleading with the girl. "Stop saying that and help me get to know you."

"You'd leave," Ryland mumbles. She feels Dakota's hand let go of her wrist and keeps her eyes trained on the ground. There's empty air between them and Ryland's counting down the seconds, waiting for the girl to walk away. But she doesn't.

"Listen, Ryland," Dakota's voice is near-desperate, pleading with the girl to believe her. "I'm not your mom. I'm not any of the shitty people who you've lived with. I'm not some half-assed social worker who doesn't even remember your name," she takes another step forward. "I'm not *any* of those people," her voice is firm, pushing her point. "And I'm sorry that they left... I really am..." she shakes her head, taking a deep breath. "You know what I think?"

Ryland doesn't look up. She just hums a low note, allowing Dakota to go on.

"I think you're scared," Dakota nods. "I think you're scared because people use you like a revolving door, they just... come and go and come and go," she gestures with her hand. "And I think it's happened so much that you just shut yourself off from *everyone* because it's easier than getting attached and then losing them."

Her words hang between them, truthful and heavy. Ryland breathes in deeply and holds it in her chest. Her voice comes out so quiet that Dakota barely hears her. "You left."

There's a long pause of silence as Dakota processes her what she's said. Her words just spill out after that.

"I came back because of *you*!" Dakota finally throws her hands down to her sides, startling Ryland. "You think I came back for Gia and Finley? You think I would have missed the shitty kids at school? Do you really think I gave up my brother for that?"

Ryland's shoulders rise and fall in a soft shrug. Dakota sighs and takes another step forward.

"I spent that whole entire car ride trying to list out the pros and cons of leaving," Dakota speaks up after a moment of silence, her voice quieter. "And the whole time I was trying to forget that you existed because I *knew* how much harder that would make it." She pauses. "*You*, Ryland, you were the one who tipped the scales. I thought about you being all alone in the house and I just… I couldn't leave without… at least… giving this a shot." She motions between them. "Whatever *this* is."

"So I'm here, alright?" Dakota lets go of the girl's wrist. "I know that you feel like you're unloveable, or just not good enough, but I…" she sighs and shakes her head. "You're gonna have to let me in sometime, Ryland."

She's not sure why she starts to walk away. Maybe it's because Ryland stays quiet and doesn't acknowledge anything she's said, and then Dakota feels like she's just said too much, or overstepped a boundary of some sort. Maybe she hinted at too much. Either way, before she can get two steps away from the girl, it happens.

"Dakota, wait," Ryland exhales the breath she's been holding in and takes a step forward, grabbing Dakota's wrist before she can move any further. The girl tenses and freezes in place, but she doesn't turn around until Ryland tugs on her wrist gently.

"You're serious?" Ryland's voice is rough, yet gentle. They're suddenly inches apart. If Dakota takes a step forward, she'd be pressed up against her. She suddenly forgets how to breathe, and her eyes tentatively flutter up to meet Ryland's.

"What you said…" Ryland whispers. "You're not just making that up… right?" It's only then that Dakota realizes the other girl has tears in her eyes. But, unable to find her words, all Dakota can do is shake her head softly.

Yet the look in Dakota's eyes must be enough for Ryland, because soon their faces are terrifyingly close, and her hand slides down from Dakota's wrist to lace the girl's fingers with her own. Ryland's eyes flicker down to Dakota's lips, lingering for a moment before meeting Dakota's eyes once more, a silent question.

And as if making a statement of her own, Dakota doesn't give Ryland the chance to kiss her. No, *she's* the one who closes the gap between them. *She's* the one whose hand slides around to rest on the small of Ryland's back, pulling her closer. It's *her* eyes that fall shut first, it's *her* lips that find Ryland's, it's *her* that breathes in every inch of their closeness.

Ryland's suddenly the one who almost stumbles backwards when Dakota kisses her. She kisses her back, struggling to breathe as her entire body seems to turn to static. It all happens without hesitation, though. She finds it effortless. Dakota's kissing her and she's kissing Dakota, and everything else around her fades away.

And *Dakota is kissing her*. She's actually kissing her. Dakota had leaned in. Dakota had pulled her closer. So maybe, Ryland thinks, maybe Dakota's been wanting this, too.

When the kiss separates, Dakota's forehead is pressed against Ryland's and she breathes in deeply, her heart beating so fast that she's embarrassed Ryland might feel it. And she does. She doesn't say anything, but Ryland brings one of her hands up and presses her palm right under Dakota's collarbone, near her heart. Then, she just laughs breathily, finding Dakota's hand and bringing it to her chest, flattening it against her own heart and letting the girl feel that they're both equally as enthralled.

"Was that okay?" Dakota suddenly grows worried, starting to move backward. "That I…?"

"I was going to do it if you hadn't," Ryland tugs on her wrist, not allowing her to move away. Dakota's eyes meet hers once more, as if she's searching for any sign of hesitation in the girl. It's not just Ryland who feels inadequate at times. Dakota, too, is fearful of being the only one who falls.

"Is something wrong?" Ryland notices the girl's eyes scanning her own and loosens her grip on her hand.

"Are we…?" Dakota breathes out, gesturing back and forth between them. Ryland furrows her eyebrows.

"What?"

"You and me…" Dakota starts, growing flustered. "That wasn't… that wasn't just a one time thing, right? Like… you think we can do that again?"

Ryland can't help but laugh at the girl's nervousness. "I think you ask too many questions," she half-smirks, a playful look on her face.

Seeing Ryland at ease seems to calm Dakota down significantly, and she quirks an eyebrow at the girl. "I think *you* ask too many questions," she laughs softly. Ryland grabs both of her hands and pulls her forward.

"I think we both have some work to do," she whispers, so close to Dakota's face that her breath practically paints goosebumps across her skin.

And then they're kissing again, and this time it's Ryland who leans in. In this way, both girls suddenly have the confirmation that they've been searching for. And, in this way, Dakota forgets all about the Ferris Wheel. It's nothing compared to the high she feels in this moment.

They spend *maybe* an hour at the carnival, and mostly only because Dakota had promised to bring back cotton candy for Finley. To kill some time, they end up wandering around the games, and Dakota winds up spending way too much money to help a little girl win a large stuffed dog. When it's over, she ends up winning the stuffed dog *and* a stuffed owl, which she presents to Ryland, because "*it's got brown eyes, just like you.*"

In the end, Ryland has to practically drag her away from the ping pong goldfish game, because she's come to learn that Dakota has *very* good luck, and they don't need her bringing a bag full of goldfish back to the hotel room.

They kiss in the elevator. It's quiet at first, but then they accidentally lock eyes in the mirror across from them and Dakota just starts giggling, and then she's pulling Ryland closer to kiss her. When the doors ding open, they both burst into laughter, and Dakota starts twirling in circles around the hallway.

As Dakota tries to fish her room key from her pocket, Ryland surprises her by pushing her against the door and kissing her again. Giggling against her lips, Dakota manages to get the key while kissing the girl back, and when she kicks the door open, she playfully ducks out of the girl's reach and goes to dive on the bed.

"Wacko," Ryland mumbles, her cheeks bright red. She nudges the door shut behind them, wandering over to set the stuffed owl on the nightstand. Dakota, laying on the bed, rolls over to try and grab Ryland's arm, tugging her closer.

"You're in a mood," Ryland notes, but Dakota just laughs, shakes her head, and leans up to kiss her again.

"It's spring break," she giggles when they pull away. "Let me live."

"I'm not arguing with you," Ryland quirks an eyebrow at the girl. Just as Dakota moves in for another kiss, the door bursts open and they both jolt backwards.

"Finley—," Gia's right behind the girl, trying to grab her, but it's too late. Finley, squirt gun in hand, has already sprayed Dakota, startling the girl and making her fall backward off of the bed. Finley bursts into laughter, and Gia takes the opportunity to snatch the toy from her hands.

"Where the hell did you get that?" Dakota looks at Finley in confusion, wiping her face with the front of the t-shirt.

"She brought it," Gia answers for her. Ryland raises an eyebrow at the girl.

"You're not drinking," she notes, nodding to Gia. This earns an eye roll from the blonde.

"*She's a child,*" Gia throws her hands up, letting go of Finley when Dakota dives for the girl with a pillow. She walks to sit next to Ryland, on the other side of the room, away from the pillow fight that's breaking out.

"What?" Ryland furrows her eyebrows.

"I turn my back for ten minutes to take a shower and she finds the '*grape juice,*'" Gia sighs heavily and plops down onto the bed. Ryland stifles a laugh.

"How much?"

"Half the bottle," Gia shakes her head. "Now look at her."

Both girls turn to look at Finley, who ducks to avoid Dakota, chucking a pillow at her from behind the bathroom door. Just as Dakota peeks out, Finley flings a pillow in her direction, hitting her smack in the face.

"Gentle!" Gia warns them. Ryland bursts into laughter.

Raising an eyebrow, Gia turns to study the girl next to her, all red-faced and giggly. "What'd you do?" she asks, suspecting something.

Ryland's almost too fast to reply. "Nothing," she shakes her head, acting confused. "What are you talking about?"

"That's cheating!" Dakota cries from across the room, where Finley's hoarding all the pillows behind her. Dakota, defenseless, hides behind the bathroom door.

"Did you get her drunk?" Gia glances to Dakota and then to Ryland, but the girl quickly shakes her head.

"She's just hyper," Ryland shrugs. "Did you save me any food?"

"Food?" Dakota perks up. She's distracted for just long enough that Finley's able to chuck another pillow at her, whipping through the air and hitting her right in the middle of the stomach. Dakota grunts and falls to her knees in mock pain, which makes Finley laugh so hard that she topples off the bed and onto the floor, in turn making her laugh harder.

"It's in the fridge," Gia stands up and motions for Ryland to follow her. "C'mon."

"What'd you get?" Dakota hurries after them, abandoning her pillow. Finley, a pillow in each hand, barrels after her, but Dakota turns around just in time to grab the girl's wrist, startling Finley.

"Truce," Dakota nods once. "For food."

"For food," Finley's quick to agree, abandoning the pillows and racing the girl across the hallway. Gia and Ryland exchange amused glances before following them, making sure to hide the squirt gun under the bed.

Chapter 12

PLAYING WITH FIRE

The girls wind up ordering even more room service, because Ryland's starving and Dakota's craving macaroni and cheese. So, half an hour later, they're all camped out in Gia and Finley's room, eating from the roll-out cart in front of them as Finley searches through the channels.

"Go back," Gia mumbles with a mouthful of food, nudging Finley's arm. "I saw Jeopardy."

"We have over 270 channels and we're going to watch *Jeopardy*?" Dakota deadpans from her seat in the middle of the bed. But Finley's already clicked on the show, and her eyes light up as the intro begins to play.

"*Hey*," she tilts her head to the side, standing up and walking over to the TV. "It's different."

"It's a new episode," Gia tries to explain, but Finley shakes her head. Dakota and Ryland look to one another, but Ryland just shrugs and steals a bite from the girl's mac and cheese.

"It's different," Finley repeats herself a minute or so later, furrowing her eyebrows. "Why is it different?"

"It's a different episode than the one we have on tape at home," Gia raises an eyebrow at the girl. "There's hundreds of episodes. You know that, right?"

"*Valence*," Finley ignores her, watching as the card on the screen flips over. Her shoulders drop when it isn't the answer she's been expecting, and she lowers herself down to sit on the edge of the bed, confused.

"Finley," Gia laughs and shakes her head. "It's a TV show. There's tons of episodes." She pauses, her eyebrows stitching together. "Have you only ever watched that tape? Back at the home?"

The girl nods slowly. "It's mine."

"It's yours?"

"Well, it was my mom's," she shrugs. "But I brought it with me when she... went on vacation."

Gia sighs. "You know you can stop calling it that. We all know—,"

"She's coming back!" Finley jumps to her feet, snapping at the girl. Dakota and Ryland both freeze. A noodle falls off of Dakota's fork.

"She's coming back," Finley repeats herself, composing herself and then grabbing the remote. She shuts off the TV, letting silence wash over the room before she grabs her bag and makes her way into the bathroom, mumbling something about how she's going to take a shower. The door slams shut behind her.

"That was weird," Ryland mumbles. Gia sighs.

"It happens a lot."

"What does?" Dakota speaks up, tilting her head to the side.

"*That*," Gia motions to the bathroom. "She gets mad when she doesn't understand something."

"It was just an episode of Jeopardy," Dakota shrugs, confused.

"Not for her," Gia shakes her head. "You have to remember she hung onto her mom's every word for most of her life. And her mom was..."

"*Abusive, negligent, delusional, completely withdrawn from society…*" Ryland finishes for her, gesturing with her hand. "Need I go on?"

With a sigh, Gia nods. "The world Finley grew up in was a completely different reality than ours. Or anyone else's, for that matter," she motions to the room, turning to Ryland. "Remember her first week here?"

Ryland nods. "Food started disappearing from the kitchen," she explains. "She'd been sneaking down at night and hiding it under her bed."

"She's also the reason we didn't have locks on our doors," Gia adds.

"And she refuses to wear a seatbelt," Ryland continues. Dakota raises an eyebrow. "She's convinced they're made by the government to slowly bend your spine and kill you."

"You're serious?" Dakota looks back and forth between them. Gia nods.

"Finley's not schizophrenic. But because her mom was the only person she interacted with growing up… she still doesn't really understand what's real and what isn't," Gia explains. "She just picked up on everything her mom did and assumed it was normal."

"Her first month was hell," Ryland nods. "We had to take the locks off of all the doors cause she kept locking herself in our bedrooms. And then Red had to put this huge chain lock on the refrigerator to keep her from stealing food. It took weeks just to get her adjusted to going to school every day."

"But she's fine now, right?" Dakota raises an eyebrow.

"She's a hell of a lot better," Ryland shrugs, looking to Gia. "Give us a run down?"

"Last time I checked there was a box of granola bars and a bag of animal crackers under her bed," Gia glances over to the bathroom door when they hear the hiss of the shower. "And her breakdown the other week only fared a broken window… so… we're improving."

"What could be worse than a broken window?" Dakota feels like she's been clueless this entire time.

"A broken human," Ryland laughs softly.

Gia sighs and shakes her head. "The first time she got to see her mom after she was locked away… she *really* lost it. That was the only time they let her have a private visit with her mom because after that they figured out she was coaching Finley to run away to come break her out."

"Shit," Dakota mumbles.

"Anyway," Gia glances back to the bathroom door. "So in the middle of the night she tried to climb out the window. She used to be in your bedroom—by the way," she nods to Dakota. "But she moved across the hallway because it's impossible to climb out of that window."

"But basically, she fell part of the way down and ended up breaking her elbow," Gia continues. "No one heard her, though, and she just kept going. She made it halfway to her mom before Red realized she was gone and called the police."

"Was she okay?"

"She had a cast for six weeks," Gia shrugs. "And she refused to talk to anyone for like… a week afterwards."

"Her mom sounds fucked up," Dakota pushes her food around on her plate. "That's so unfair."

"What's unfair?" Ryland scoots closer to Dakota so she can steal a bite of her food. Dakota shrugs with one shoulder and passes her plate to Ryland.

"Her mom gets to treat her like complete shit and live," she mutters. "And ours are dead."

"Mine isn't," Gia speaks up while she absentmindedly searches through the channels. "Mine's alive and well."

"Is she in the crazy house too?"

Ryland pinches Dakota's arm, glaring at her to stop asking questions. But Gia just shrugs.

"Depends on your definition of a crazy house."

Before their conversation can continue, the bathroom door is nudged open and Finley wanders out in a t-shirt and pajama pants, tugging a brush through her hair. All three girls watch her, holding their breath and waiting for someone to snap. But she just pulls something out her bag and smiles hopefully.

"Wanna play Apples to Apples?"

"It's your go."

Ryland studies the cards in her hand, but then pauses when no one answers her.

"She's out," Gia laughs, motioning to Dakota, whose head has slumped over to rest on her deck of cards, fast asleep.

Sighing heavily, Ryland tosses her cards into the middle of their circle and scans the room. Finley's asleep at the head of the bed, and now Dakota's sprawled out in the middle of their Apples to Apples game, her feet resting on Finley's back.

"They're children," Gia rolls her eyes half-heartedly, shoving the game back into the box and putting it away. Ryland stands up, slowly easing her weight onto her leg and giving herself a minute to adjust.

Gia glances to the bed and then back to Ryland. "Well," she laughs. "Looks like we're rooming together again."

And so, the two girls wind up sharing the bed originally intended for Dakota and Ryland. And, unlike Dakota and Ryland would have, Gia and Ryland split the bed down the middle with pillows and stay on their respective sides.

However, Ryland's roused from her slumber a few hours later by a knock at the door. Lifting her head, she looks around the room in confusion. Another knock, louder this time. Groggily, Ryland reaches over and nudges Gia's shoulder.

"Hey," she yawns as the girl stirs awake. "Someone's at the door."

"Then get it," Gia mumbles, rolling onto her back and pulling a pillow over her face.

Ryland rolls her eyes. But Gia doesn't budge, so she leans over and fishes around beside the bed for her brace. As she hurries to get it on, there's another knock.

"Coming," Ryland mutters, yanking the final strap on her brace and slowly easing herself off of the bed.

"It's me," there's a voice. "Hurry."

"Finley?" Ryland furrows her eyebrows. When she pulls the door open, the light from the hallway blinds her, and Gia groans from where she lays in the bed. Finley stands in front of them, accompanied by Dakota, who has her arms hugged around her torso and is looking straight down at the ground.

"What's going on?" Ryland suddenly wakes up, studying Dakota in confusion. She looks like she's shivering.

"She did it again," Finley motions to the girl beside her. "She was sleepwalking."

Gia sits up behind them, rubbing her eyes. "What's going on?"

"She's awake now, but..." Finley shrugs with one shoulder. "She's like this."

“Are we switching rooms?” Gia speaks up again. Ryland looks back and forth between all three girls before pushing the door open wider with her foot.

“You don’t mind switching back across with Finley?” she asks Gia, who just shrugs and trudges out of bed, dragging a pillow with her. Finley turns to follow her but pauses to glance back at Ryland.

“Do you know what to do?” the girl asks quietly.

“No, but I’ll figure it out,” Ryland dismisses her with a wave of the hand,” Finley hesitates, but Ryland promises her she can handle it. When the door across the hallway shuts, Dakota still hasn’t moved from where she stands.

“You can come in…” Ryland says softly, holding the door open. But Dakota doesn’t move. Ryland hesitates for a moment, pushing the door open wider and motioning to the room, but the girl still doesn’t budge.

“Dakota,” Ryland reaches and and places a hand on the girl’s arm. “C’mon,” she pulls the girl forwards, and thankfully Dakota allows her to lead her back into the room.

But once they’re in the room, nothing changes. Dakota stands by the door and an awkward silence falls over them. Ryland feels completely powerless.

“Are you cold?” she asks quietly, noticing the girl is shivering. She quickly moves to grab a blanket from the bed and wrap it around Dakota’s shoulders. With a deep breath, Dakota hugs the blanket around herself and finally moves over to sit down on the edge of the bed. Ryland stands awkwardly for a few moments before quietly taking a seat next to her.

“Do you wanna talk about it?” Ryland asks softly. She wants to reach out and hug the girl, or simply take her hand, but she’s never seen Dakota like this before and she doesn't want to overstep her boundaries.

"There's nothing to talk about," Dakota mumbles, her eyes locked on her hands as she picks nervously at her nails.

"That's a lie," Ryland speaks before she can think. "You look like you've just seen a ghost."

The small girl beside her sighs and pulls her legs underneath her, sitting cross legged. "Technically, it doesn't count as a lie if we just don't talk about it."

"But then you'd be contradicting yourself," Ryland notes. Confused, Dakota finally looks up at her. Her face is flushed, eyes dark and bloodshot.

"You're the one who told me that I should work on opening up to you," Ryland nods softly. "Shouldn't you do the same?"

"It's different," Dakota mumbles. Ryland tilts her head to the side.

"How could it possibly be any different?"

Dakota shakes her head. "You don't get it."

Furrowing her eyebrows, Ryland finally gives in and reaches over to place a hand over the girl's own. "Dakota—,"

"You don't get it!" she snaps, yanking her hand away from Ryland's reach. The girl immediately recoils. "You just…" she sighs heavily, waving Ryland away with her hand and averting her gaze. "You just *don't get it.*"

"Alright, fine," Ryland shakes her head and rises to her feet. "You're right. I don't get it," she moves to the window, pinching the bridge of her nose to try and calm herself down. "You happy?"

"Ecstatic," Dakota mumbles into her hands, her elbows resting on her knees.

"Sorry for making an effort," Ryland draws the curtains open, but it's too dark outside to see a thing. She sighs heavily.

"Tonight wasn't supposed to be like this," the dark haired girl looks down. Ryland raises an eyebrow.

"You're telling me."

Dakota finally whips her head to look at Ryland, frustrated. "Stop it!"

Ryland turns and looks at her in confusion. "Stop what?"

"I-I—," Dakota huffs and shakes her head. "Making me feel bad."

"I just want to know what's wrong," Ryland sighs, her shoulders dropping. "I just want to try and help you."

"That's the thing," Dakota's eyes land on her. "You won't."

"I won't want to help you?"

Dakota just nods into her hands. Ryland takes a step forwards.

"Don't do that," she shakes her head. "Don't put words in my mouth."

Dakota doesn't respond. With a heavy sigh, Ryland sits on the bed, a foot or so away from the girl.

"I'm not good at this either, Dakota," her voice is softer. "I'm just—,"

"It's my fault, okay?" the girl throws her hands up in the air, startling Ryland. Her whole disposition changes. The fight in her eyes fades and suddenly she feels infinitely smaller.

"What are you talking about?"

Dakota's eyes move away from Ryland's, too nervous to look at her. Her voice is barely a whisper. "The fire."

Ryland's eyes widen. "You think it was your fault?"

"I *know* it was my fault."

"You were seven."

Dakota shakes her head. "The fire started in the upper level."

"So how could it have been your fault?" Ryland's voice is gentler now, and she slowly scoots closer to the girl. Dakota hugs the blanket tighter around her shoulders.

"We weren't supposed to play hide and seek in her bedroom," the girl keeps her eyes locked on the floor. "But I thought it'd be a good idea to hide behind the curtains. And so I did. And it was an old house… so we had this bulky heater backed up against the same wall. I guess when I was moving around in the curtains they probably got stuck… and then…"

"You *guess*?" Ryland raises an eyebrow.

"I mean…"

"Dakota…" Ryland whispers, shaking her head. "I…"

"*Don't*," Dakota's voice is raspy. "Don't. I already hate myself enough for it."

"*Dakota*," Ryland repeats herself. She finally gives in, scooting closer and taking Dakota's hand in her own, ignoring when she feels the girl tense up. "It was not your fault."

"You weren't there."

"Do you hear yourself, Dakota?" Ryland shakes her head. "You were seven. Seven. You're just trying to come up with some explanation for the fire. A seven year old hiding behind curtains isn't enough to somehow tangle them in a heater."

"But then what—?"

"How long have you blamed yourself for it?" Ryland cuts her off. Dakota looks away.

"Since the night it happened."

"Dakota…" Ryland squeezes her hand. "You've carried it with you for *that long*?"

"It's the only explanation that makes sense."

"You said the fire felt like it was traveling through the walls, right?" Ryland pauses. "You told me that the door was hot even before you saw the actual fire."

Dakota just nods softly, not sure why it matters.

"You think that would have happened that quickly if it had been the curtains that started the fire?"

Confused, Dakota looks back to her with furrowed eyebrows. "What are you saying?"

"I'm saying that you lived in an old house. If the fire travelled through the walls that fast, it had to be caused by something electrical inside them," Ryland shakes her head. "Not some kid that ruffled the curtains around a bit."

"But..."

"You blame yourself because it's less scary," Ryland now grabs both of her hands, meeting Dakota's eyes. "It's easier to say 'it's my fault' than to admit that you had no control over it. Because then at least you have an explanation. Isn't that the first thing you asked when it happened? *Why*?"

Dakota nods.

"Then of course you're going to think of every single little thing you could have done to cause it," Ryland squeezes her hands. "At seven years old the idea that a fire could start randomly, out of the blue? That's terrifying. Your house is supposed to be a safe place."

"You really don't think it was me?"

"Listen, Dakota," Ryland sighs. "When my mom died, I did the same thing. The police came and found her body and said that she'd been dead for almost 24 hours. And right away, I thought I was a murderer. Because *I'd* fallen asleep by her body when I found her. And maybe if *I'd* called the police right away, they could have saved her."

"But you're not a murderer," Dakota furrows her eyebrows.

"Try telling that to six year old Ryland," the girl laughs softly. "Because I was so sure that her death was all my fault, and that if the police knew what I had done they'd think I was the worst damn kid they'd ever met and then they'd lock me away for the rest of my life."

"And then one day I was playing in the street with a bunch of my foster siblings and neighbors, and they kept throwing rocks at me, and I got so frustrated that I told them they wouldn't want to mess with me because I was a criminal," she laughs under her breath, shaking her head at the memory.

"My foster mom came out from the front porch and pulled me aside and asked what was wrong, and I guess I must have just started crying and begging her not to send me away to jail," she looks away. Dakota frowns.

"And she just laughed at me and said something like '*Honey, your momma was dead long before you found her. It was just a matter of time before her body caught up with her mind. Even if you'd'a saved her that time, there's no telling when she would've run off and done it again*," Ryland puts on a fake southern accent, trying to lighten the mood. Dakota half smiles.

"She sounds nice," Dakota notes. "Why'd you leave her?"

"Her husband got arrested for selling illegal narcotics," Ryland nods. "I remember they used to give us 'medicine' to help us sleep when we went on long road trips and we'd all be out within minutes."

"That's insane," Dakota's eyes widen.

"I've seen all types of insane," Ryland shrugs. "That was nothing."

Dakota just purses her lips and looks away. "M'sorry for waking you up."

"Was it a nightmare?" Ryland asks, tilting her head to the side. Dakota nods.

"Some nights they're worse than others."

"Are you feeling a little better at least?"

Dakota nods. "Thank you."

"Do you want to try and sleep?"

Dakota yawns, mid-nod, making Ryland laugh.

"I'll take that as a yes," the older girl smiles, squeezing Dakota's hand. "And next time this happens, we'll talk about it, okay? No matter how hard you try you won't be able to scare me away, I promise," she smooths out the girl's hair. "I've seen all kinds of crazy and you're not it."

Cheeks turning red, Dakota just nudges Ryland's shoulder. "Stop talking and come lay with me."

Chapter 13

WHEELS AND WINGS

"Alright guys, highs and lows and then you're free to go to bed."

They've been home from their little vacation for about two hours, arriving back just in time to eat dinner with Red and then sit down for group. They'd walked around at the boardwalk for most of the day, stopping to get lunch and rest for a bit. Now, they're gathered back in their circle in the living room for the usual group meeting.

"High was the beach," Finley nods quickly, a soft smile on her face. "And I guess my low is the kink in my neck because I slept on the bus." She squeezes her shoulder. Red nods to Gia.

"High is the beach, too," Gia nods. "Low is the fact that spring break is halfway over." Dakota groans in agreement from her spot in the beanbag.

"My high..." Now Ryland's turn, the girl just shrugs, although her eyes can't help but drift over to Dakota. Right away, they both know they're thinking the same thing, and Dakota quickly looks away to fight off a smile. "My high was our trip," Ryland nods. She pauses to think. "I can't really think of a low."

"I'll let it pass for now," Red nods and then turns to Dakota, motioning for her to go on. The dark haired girl purses her lips in thought.

"My high is the same as everyone else's," she motions around the room. "Thank you, by the way, for letting us go," she gives Red a soft smile. "And I guess… my low…" she hums in thought. "I've gotta pass on this one too."

"And with that, it's time for bed!" Gia claps her hands and jumps to her feet before Red can even get a word in edgewise. Dakota and Finley are quick to follow her upstairs, exhausted from the past two days. Ryland, however, stays put. Red raises an eyebrow at her.

"I slept on the bus," Ryland shrugs, grabbing the remote and clicking on the TV. "I'm not tired yet."

"You just let me know if you need anything," Red nods and squeezes the girl's shoulder. "I'm glad you had a good time this weekend." Ryland gives her a thankful smile.

And so she remains on the couch, listening to the sound of footsteps and three bedroom doors being shut above her. However, as soon as Red's door shuts gently, someone clears their throat at the top of the stairs.

"You think I'd forget about you?" Dakota smiles playfully when Ryland turns around. She then slides down the banister, making a show of landing at the bottom of the stairs.

"Dakota," Ryland bites her lip. "I can't—,"

"I know," the girl shakes her head, wandering over to the couch and flinging herself down beside the girl. "I saw you messing with the brace at dinner. How bad is it?"

Ryland, surprised that Dakota noticed her discomfort, just shrugs. "We walked a lot today."

"You could have told me," Dakota furrows her eyebrows.

"You were having fun," Ryland shakes her head. "So was I. It was worth it."

"I would've had just as much fun if we were sitting on the beach and building sand castles," Dakota laughs softly. "Do you want something? I think there's Tylenol in the kitchen somewhere."

"I, uh, I have something upstairs," Ryland admits. "In the bathroom cabinet."

"Oh, right," Dakota nods and hops to her feet.

"Right?"

Dakota pauses. "I was looking for a comb and accidentally saw it one day," she shrugs softly. "No big deal." And with that, she's hurrying back upstairs.

When she returns, she's got a blanket thrown over one shoulder and Ryland's pills in her hand. After handing them to the girl, she retrieves a glass of water from the kitchen.

"Do they really help?" Dakota asks, sitting back down as Ryland throws her head back and swallows the pill. The girl beside her just shrugs.

"A little," Ryland sets the glass on the coffee table in front of them. Dakota hugs a pillow to her stomach.

"There's nothing else they can do for the pain?"

"There's surgeries," Ryland admits, shaking the bottle of pills and watching the last few roll around. "But they all run the risk of making things even worse. Plus the effects may not last forever." She sets the bottle down on the coffee table.

"You don't even think it's worth a try?"

"Not a chance," Ryland shakes her head. "At least right now I can walk with this thing," she taps her fingers against the brace. "What happens if I wake up from the surgery and they just decided to cut off my entire leg?"

"Wouldn't they have to ask you first?" Dakota furrows her eyebrows.

"It's happened before," Ryland shrugs. "I saw it on Oprah once." Dakota can't help but laugh at this. Ryland leans back in the couch and Dakota quietly scoots closer, slipping her arm underneath Ryland's and finding the girl's hand.

"Well what about acupuncture?" she asks, tilting her head to the side. "Maybe that could do something to ease the pain."

"You don't have to fix me, y'know," Ryland looks to the girl, laughing quietly. Dakota just shrugs softly.

"I just read some stuff the other day about how it might help, that's all."

Ryland raises an eyebrow. "You did what?"

"They have a whole medical section at the school library," Dakota shrugs, feeling embarrassed. "I had a free period one day so… I was just curious."

"And what'd you learn?"

Dakota purses her lips in thought. "That it hurts like shit," she nods once, making Ryland laugh. The older girl flips Dakota's hand over in her lap, using her other hand to trace circles in her palm, flattening out her fingers.

"You know, my doctor in the intensive care unit told me that if the car had hit the railing just a foot or so higher, it would've been my chest that got crushed," Ryland says softly, her eyes fixed on the girl's hand. Dakota winces.

"Would that mean…?"

"I wouldn't have had a chance," Ryland nods once. "But for some reason I'm here."

"That's… wow," Dakota breathes out.

"I guess," Ryland shrugs. "Sometimes I can't help but think, though, that if we'd hit the railing just a little lower, the truck would have flipped completely and I would have only walked away with a few bruises." She breathes in slowly. Dakota frowns.

"But you're here," the smaller girl offers, studying Ryland's face. "And you're alive. That counts for something, right?"

"I guess."

"I mean, I prefer Ryland with a brace over no Ryland any day," Dakota offers her a soft smile, leaning against the girl's shoulder. She pauses, deep in thought for a few moments before nodding softly. "I think you're the strongest person I know."

Ryland's taken aback by this, and she turns to look at the girl. "I am?"

Dakota nods. "I've thought about it before," she admits. "Just think, you were only six when you lost your mom. And I mean... she didn't really set a good example for you. And along with that, you dealt with the shitty foster system and your leg, to top it off. But you're still here," she smiles sadly. "All signs pointed for you to fail. But you didn't." She pauses. "I think *you* deserve an episode of Oprah."

Ryland laughs softly, thankful it's dark enough to hide how red her face has gotten. "Eh, Oprah's overrated," she shrugs. "But you know what I do deserve?"

"Ellen?" Dakota smirks, tilting her head to the side. But by the way the girl tugs her closer by her shirt, she knows well enough what she means.

"No, you idiot," Ryland laughs, their faces suddenly inches apart, thanks to Dakota's impatience. "This," she whispers, leaning in and capturing the girl's lips with her own.

It's risky, they know, kissing like this when Finley's prone to wandering around the house at night. But it's the last thing on their minds. Dakota's hands cup Ryland's face, as if she's trying to pull her even closer than they already are. She breathes in deeply, pulling away and lingering inches away from Ryland's face.

"Would you look at that," Ryland laughs softly, her words ghosting across Dakota's skin. "My leg is healed." There's a smirk playing her lips, and Dakota rolls her eyes playfully before leaning in to kiss it off.

(Ryland realizes that kissing Dakota has quickly become one of her favorite pastimes.)

The next morning, Finley's the one who finds the two girls asleep on the couch. And luckily, she shakes Dakota awake to warn her that Red's just woken up, judging by the sound of her shower being turned on. Dakota's flustered when she realizes she's been curled up next to Ryland this entire time, but Finley doesn't act any different. She just smiles and offers to make Dakota a bowl of cereal.

As soon as Red emerges from her bedroom, Dakota's on her heels like a puppy.

"So we're off house arrest for good?" she asks, sliding over to lean against the counter as Red pours herself a cup of coffee.

"That's what I told you," Red nods, having just woken up.

"And that means we're allowed to go out, right?" Dakota tilts her head to the side.

"As long as you're home before dinner," Red nods. "And don't do anything illegal."

"Perfect," Dakota slaps her palm against the counter. "That's all I need."

Before anyone else can get a word in edgewise, the girl is disappearing upstairs. Finley looks to Red, who looks to Ryland, who just shrugs. She's on the same page as they are. She glances out the window once more, but any traces of the girl are gone.

A few minutes later, while Ryland's washing out a mug for her coffee, a blur drops down past the kitchen window. Ryland catches it out of the corner of her eye. From behind her, Finley furrows her eyebrows.

"Did she just…?"

"I think so," Ryland nods. Finley tilts her head to the side.

"She knows we have a front door, right?" the girl taps her spoon against her knuckles.

"I'm not so sure anymore," Ryland laughs. She takes a sip of her coffee—black—and grimaces. She doesn't understand the appeal Dakota sees in drinking her coffee plain.

"Where do you think she's going?" Finley asks, scooting over when Ryland pulls a chair up to the island.

"Beats me."

"Yo," Gia wanders into the kitchen. "Dakota just went full on Spiderman down the side of the house." Finley can't help but laugh, and Ryland just rolls her eyes half heartedly.

Although Ryland's curious about where Dakota's disappeared to, she's distracted by Finley, who recruits both her and Gia to drag out an old picnic table from the shed and into the backyard. However, when two hours pass and there's still no sign of the girl, Ryland lingers around the kitchen just to keep an eye on the window.

But, what interrupts the silence later that day doesn't come from the backyard. This time, Dakota makes her presence known. A car horn blares from the driveway.

"Hm?" Finley and Ryland both look at each other at the same time, and Finley's scrambling to the front door.

"*Woah*," Finley breathes out, her eyes widening when she peers out the window.

"What?" Ryland pushes her aside and opens the door. She's immediately as stunned as Finley is, because in the driveway stands Dakota, leaning up against the door of a bright red car. The girl smirks now that she has their attention and reaches inside to honk the horn again.

"It's red," Finley nods, hopping down the front stairs and hurrying over to Dakota's side to check out the car. Ryland, however, remains in the doorway, her arms crossed as she raises an eyebrow at Dakota.

"What's this all about?"

Dakota turns around and looks to the girl, a soft smile on her face. "It's mine."

"You're serious?" Ryland takes a step down. Finley's already slid into the driver's seat, admiring the interior. Dakota nods.

"You're looking at a 1967 Chrysler Newport," Dakota motions to the car. "I got it for a steal. All I've gotta do is toy with the transmission and then this hunk of metal will run like a dream," she drums her fingers against the roof.

"And *you're* gonna fix it on your own?"

Dakota leans against the door, a cocky smile on her lips with an eyebrow raised playfully. "There's a lot you don't know about me, Moreno."

"Oh really?" Ryland matches her disposition, taking another step closer and tilting her head to the side. "I'd love to find out sometime. That is, if you can find the time in your busy schedule," she teases. Dakota just laughs and rolls her eyes.

"What the hell?" Gia appears in the doorway. "Who dragged this outta' the seventies?"

"*Sixties*," Dakota corrects her, ignoring Gia's tone. The girl wanders over, peering in the windows and shaking her head.

"There's a hole in the floor," she notes.

"Which I will fix," Dakota's quick to reply, pointing to the girl. "Along with the rust."

Gia opens her mouth to speak but Dakota's quick to cut her off.

"*And* the shit paint job," she nods in finality, making Gia clamp her mouth shut. Ryland stifles a laugh. Gia just furrows her eyebrows and takes one last look at the car.

"Did you at least get a good price?"

Dakota nods. "It was practically free."

"Don't blow it up," Gia hums, giving Dakota a nod of approval before wandering back into the house. Finley honks the horn at her.

"Is she always like this?" Dakota turns to Ryland, who just laughs and shakes her head.

"Spring Break's coming to an end, she's just grumpy," she rolls her eyes, wandering around to study the back of the car. "How'd you pull this off?"

"Huh?"

"Buying a car," Ryland nods. Dakota just shrugs.

"I *was* saving up to get a Harley," she shakes her head. "But that was before all this happened," she gestures vaguely to the house. "So my Harley fund turned into this," she slaps the roof of the car and nods to Ryland.

Ryland laughs, raising an eyebrow in disbelief. "A Harley?"

"Yeah," Dakota nods. "You know, like the motorcycle?"

"I know," Ryland shakes her head. "I just never took you for the motorcycle type," she pauses, laughing softly. "I guess I really do have a lot to learn."

Dakota glances to Finley, making sure she's preoccupied before taking a step towards Ryland and squeezing the girl's hand. "We've got nothing but time."

Seconds later, both girls are flinching, startled by the blaring noise of the car alarm. Finley, wide eyed, turns to look at them.

"Oops."

With the new addition to the driveway, Ryland and Dakota are suddenly transformed into giddy, lovesick teenagers.

"Is it clear?" Dakota slides down the banister, a playful smile on her face.

"She's out like a light," Ryland appears from Red's hallway after making sure she was asleep. "And the upstairs?"

"Both asleep," Dakota nods, hurrying over to Ryland. "You ready?" There's excitement in the air, and Ryland stifles a laugh.

"Shh," Dakota giggles, slowly opening the front door. She pauses, listening for any noise, relieved that Ryland didn't lie about knowing how to dismantle the house alarm. She eventually deems the coast clear and tugs Ryland outside. It takes two tries to get the car started up, but soon Dakota's pulling out of the driveway. Ryland glances over to her, a smile tugging at her lips.

"Where are we even going?" Ryland asks, her eyes trained on Dakota's face. The girl just shrugs.

"Wherever we want," she smirks. "That's the point."

"Take a right," Ryland instructs her. Dakota raises an eyebrow.

"I take it you've got somewhere in mind?"

"Possibly," Ryland shrugs. "Keep going straight."

"Should I be concerned?" Dakota glances over to her, feeling the pavement beneath them slowly fade away, replaced by a narrower, gravel road.

"Park anywhere," Ryland ignores her question. Dakota looks at her questioningly, but obliges. Silence falls over them after she pulls over and takes the keys from the ignition. The engine dies down and she turns to Ryland, but the other girl is already getting out of the car. Dakota's quick to follow.

"I have a recurring fear of being lured out into the wilderness and being murdered by pretty girls, just so you know," Dakota jogs to catch up with Ryland, sticking close to her side.

"Just trust me," Ryland laughs, slowly leading them up a dirt pathway. Wary of her surroundings, Dakota shivers and looks around the dark forest. Something caws in the trees above them, sending her scrambling to grab onto Ryland's arm, latching herself to the girl's side.

"Relax," Ryland grabs the girl's hand, laughing at her sudden outburst. Something inside of her swells with pride at the thought of Dakota looking to her for protection. "Look, we're almost there."

They make their way up the steep hill, with Ryland leaning on Dakota more than she's willing to admit.

"What's that sound?" Dakota furrows her eyebrows.

"You'll see," Ryland smirks.

Once they ascend the steepest part of the hill, Ryland nudges Dakota forward. "Go on," she whispers. "Go look."

"If I die today, tell—," Dakota trails off when she turns, coming face to face with the sight in front of her. "*Woah.*"

Ryland appears by her side moments later. "Told you so."

Dakota inhales deeply, breathing in the cold salty air. They stand high up, on the edge of a cliff that borders a large body of water. The sound Dakota had heard before was the waves crashing against the jagged rock below them.

"Gia dragged me out here once with a bunch of her friends," Ryland explains. "It was pretty hectic then. I like this place better when it's quiet."

"You could totally dive from here if it's deep enough," Dakota notes, taking a step forward.

"Don't even think about it," Ryland grabs her arm, but Dakota just laughs and turns to face her, a playful smirk on her lips.

"What? Don't like heights?"

"I don't like the idea of one of us falling a hundred feet into sharp rocks, no, I don't," Ryland shakes her head.

"You don't have to worry about that," Dakota quirks an eyebrow, taking a step closer and placing her hands on the girl's hips. "I'm already falling for something else."

Ryland rolls her eyes, trying not to focus on the lack of space between them. "That was, by far, the cheesiest thing that's ever left your mouth," she deadpans, a silent challenge.

"It was smooth," Dakota pulls her closer. One hand rests on the small of Ryland's back, the other moves to brush a loose strand of hair from the girl's face.

Ryland struggles to keep her composure, her breath hitching in her throat when Dakota's fingertips ghost across her cheek. "I'm serious," she tries, keeping her voice level. "That was so cheesy I honestly threw up a bit."

Dakota, amused, just meets the girl's eyes and shakes her head. "Shut up and kiss me."

"Where'd you get that line from, Quinn? The—?"

Dakota cuts Ryland off, stealing her words by crashing their lips together. She can't help but giggle into the kiss when Ryland's hands fly to her shoulders to steady herself.

They pull away and Dakota immediately cocks her head to the side. “Still cheesy?”

Breathless, Ryland shakes her head. “Not at all,” she stammers. Her intimidating facade has completely dissolved.

“That’s what I thought,” Dakota grins. Ryland pulls her back, intent on wiping the cocky smirk off her face.

“What are you—?”

Ryland’s cut off when Dakota’s suddenly inches away from her, pushing her against the outside of the car and kissing her for the millionth time that night. They’ve returned back to the house, but Dakota’s in no hurry to go inside.

“Someone’s persistent,” Ryland notes. Breathing heavily, Dakota leans her forehead against Ryland’s, blue eyes searching brown.

“I like kissing you,” Dakota laughs, holding up her hands in surrender. “Sue me.”

Ryland, red-faced, raises an eyebrow. “We really should get back inside.”

“What’s the rush?” Dakota tilts her head to the side. When she moves in for another kiss, however, Ryland grabs her arm, shaking her head.

“My leg,” she mumbles. “It’s starting to…” she trails off and nods downwards. Dakota’s mood quickly flips, and she backs away, but Ryland’s confused when there’s the slightest of smiles on her face.

“What?”

“You told me,” Dakota nods softly, well aware that this was progress. Ryland simply shrugs and looks away shyly, so Dakota grabs her hand and quietly leads her back inside.

"They're gonna start suspecting something soon, you know," Ryland speaks up as she follows Dakota into her bedroom. The younger girl pauses to quirk an eyebrow at her.

"I haven't slept in my own bed in days," Ryland sits down beside Dakota. "Gia's bound to connect the dots. If she hasn't already."

Dakota shrugs. "So let them speculate. Who cares?"

"I do," Ryland nods. "And you should too," she gestures to Dakota, who arches an eyebrow at her. "If Red catches on…"

"We'll get in trouble?"

"Listen, it's happened before between two other girls here," Ryland shakes her head. "Red found out and had to separate them."

"They sent them away?"

"To separate homes, yeah," Ryland nods. "It happens in all places like these, regardless. It's just the way the rules work, I guess."

"What's that mean for us?" Dakota frowns.

"It means we've got to start laying low," Ryland shrugs.

And in all honestly, Dakota doesn't mind. It's quite the opposite, actually. She finds herself excited. She likes the idea of this being their little secret, keeping it hidden may just be part of the fun.

"Can we postpone the laying low until tomorrow?" Dakota rolls to her side of the bed and pats the space beside her hopefully. "I'm sure it can wait a night."

"I suppose so," Ryland laughs quietly, leaning down to steal a quick kiss before moving to undo her brace. Dakota props herself up on her elbow to watch.

"Does it hurt?"

"It always hurts," Ryland shrugs. "Some days more than others."

Dakota frowns, unaccustomed to Ryland talking so openly about her injury. She sighs. "I wish I could fix it."

"M'afraid even I can't do that," Ryland scoots back, laying down next to her. "You help me forget about it, though."

Dakota tilts her head to the side.

"You know," Ryland laughs softly. "You take my mind off it it. Like a pleasant distraction."

"Is that all I am to you?" Dakota teases. "A distraction?"

"No, no, that's not what I—,"

Dakota's created a habit of cutting Ryland off by kissing her. She leans over the girl, finding her lips in the dark and tangling her hands in her hair, rendering her speechless. When the kiss pulls away, too early for Ryland's liking, Dakota smirks. Ryland's stunned.

"I'll be the best damn distraction you've ever seen," Dakota nods, melting into the sheets beside the girl. Struggling to collect her words, Ryland settles for pulling the girl closer into her side.

"I hate to break it to you, tiny, but I have a feeling that this is more than just a distraction," she whispers. Dakota giggles, burying her head in the girl's shoulder.

Chapter 14

WAITING GAME

Laying low is even easier than they thought. And although Ryland always has to slip back into her own bedroom to avoid Gia's suspicions, Dakota's car has begun to make up for that absence. Every chance they get, they embark on adventures, mostly back to the cliffs where they spent their first night. Dakota's nicknamed the spot "Whoops," after accidentally dropping her French Fries over the edge. The name stuck.

With spring break behind them, they're drowning in schoolwork. All girls—with the exception of Finley—graduate in a few months. It's been starting to weigh on Dakota, who has no clue what her future holds.

"Hey Einstein," Dakota flings herself onto the couch beside Ryland, resting her legs over the girl's lap and leaning over to place a notebook between them. She taps her pencil against the page. "Help me out."

"Looks like someone's finally ventured inside," Ryland laughs, reaching out to wipe a smudge of grease from Dakota's forehead using her sleeve. "How's it going out there, Macguyver?"

"It'll be good as new in no time," Dakota nods. She's spent most of her day working on the car, laying flat underneath it with only her feet sticking out. Both Finley and Ryland had wandered out to check on her during the day—Ryland bringing food and stealing kisses, and Finley hanging upside down from the inside of the car to bombard Dakota with car facts.

But now, it's gotten dark, and Dakota's finally returned back inside to get a head start on her homework for the weekend. She nudges her notebook into Ryland's hands and looks to her hopefully.

"Chemistry?" Ryland already knows. Dakota nods. The older girl leans down to study the problem, furrowing her eyebrows. "I showed you how to do this last week."

"It's different," Dakota huffs. "There's more letters."

"They're elements," Ryland shakes her head, tapping the problem with the pencil. "See? *That's* iron, and that's oxygen."

"And *this* is me still being confused"

"Shut up," Ryland laughs, scooting closer. "Watch closely."

Dakota nods, although she struggles to peel her eyes away from Ryland's face. Sometimes she gets a little too entranced.

"The problem's down here, tiny," Ryland smirks, her fingers drumming against the paper. Dakota, flustered, laughs softly and leans against Ryland's shoulder.

"You did it!" Ryland nods quickly. They've been doing Dakota's homework for at least an hour, undisturbed by the other guests.

"I did?" Dakota looks to her in surprise.

"Yes ma'am," Ryland nods. "Now try this one."

Dakota pulls her pencil out from behind her ear, turning her attention to the next problem. She studies it for a few moments before slamming the book shut and shaking her head. "I give up."

Ryland jumps. "But you just—,"

"I know," Dakota cuts her off when she climbs on top of her, shoving her notebook on the floor in the process. "I just wrote random numbers."

Ryland struggles to gather her words with Dakota's face lingering only inches away from her own. "But… you… I…"

Laughing softly, Dakota leans in and kisses her lightly. "I just wanted to kiss you."

"But your homework," Ryland stammers.

Using her foot, Dakota shoves her notebook under the couch, a teasing smile on her face. "What homework?"

Ryland can't help but roll her eyes. "You're going to have to learn eventually."

"But not now," Dakota shakes her head. "I have all weekend. It's Friday night," she leans in closer. "Let's do something."

"Everyone's still awake," Ryland reminds her. "Including Red, so you might wanna…" she rests her hands on the girl's shoulders and guides her off of her lap.

"You're no fun," Dakota pouts, resuming her spot on the couch beside the girl.

"We have to be careful," Ryland reminds her. "We talked about this."

"I know. I just wish we had more alone time."

"Tomorrow's Saturday," Ryland notes, an eyebrow quirked. "I'm sure we can find some time to be alone."

"I'd like that," Dakota nods softly, leaning into Ryland's side and yawning. "We can take the car and drive somewhere."

"Drive where?"

Both girls are startled when Finley appears behind them. Dakota practically leaps to the other side of the couch, distancing herself from Ryland. Finley takes it upon herself to climb over the back of the couch and plop herself down in the spot between the girls. Dakota smiles nervously.

"We were just talking about what we could do tomorrow," Ryland quickly speaks up. "You know, it's Saturday and all."

"Oh," Finley hums. "Where are we going?"

Ryland glances to Dakota, who seems disappointed, but quickly recovers. The dark haired girl just shrugs. "We don't know yet. We're brainstorming."

"How about the aquarium?" Finley tilts her head to the side. "Students get in free on the weekends."

Upon hearing this, Dakota and Ryland glance to one another, both thinking the same thing—the aquarium is a dark labyrinth of hallways, making it easy to "get lost."

"Sounds good to me," Ryland nods. Dakota wiggles her eyebrows when Finley isn't looking.

Somehow Finley convinces Gia to tag along to the aquarium, so the next morning Dakota's woken up by a knock at her door. Ryland peers in with a toothbrush hanging from her mouth.

"Finley just threw our door open to make sure we were getting up," Ryland nods. "Just a warning before she runs in here and gives you a heart attack, too."

"*S'early*," Dakota whines, mumbling into her pillow and tugging the blankets over her head.

"Don't say I didn't warn you," Ryland laughs softly, leaving the door open a crack before she disappears back down the hallway.

And she's right, because an excited Finley shakes Dakota awake only a few minutes later.

However, they never do make it to the aquarium.

It starts out like a normal morning. Red leaves for her weekly meeting with the foster care branch, Finley eats her fruity pebbles three at a time, like usual, and Ryland pulls Dakota into the kitchen to kiss her good morning when no one else is looking. So Dakota figures it's setting up to be a pretty good day. However, she soon learns how things can change in the blink of an eye.

"We should leave soon," Finley speaks up from her spot on the couch. "We don't wanna get stuck in traffic."

"I doubt there will be any traffic at 9am on a Saturday," Gia lights a cigarette, moving over to open a window.

The knock at the door confuses everyone, mostly because they have a doorbell for a reason, but also because the last thing they're expecting at this hour is a visitor. Dakota jogs over as Gia opens the door.

Something shifts in the room as soon as the door is thrown open, as if an integral wire has snapped in Gia. The blonde immediately shoves her cigarette over to Dakota, who scrambles to catch it and then turns to the door in confusion.

"Oh my god, Gia," the man at the door looks as if he's on the verge of tears. He's tall, dressed in fancy clothes, yet his face is weathered. It's off-putting, Dakota thinks.

Gia stiffens the second he moves forward to pull her into a hug. But if he notices her discomfort, he all but acknowledges it. While he's hugging her tightly, Gia is a stone statue, her arms flat at her sides. Finley bolts up from her spot on the couch.

After the hug has gone on for too long for her liking, Gia seems to finally regain enough energy to push him away. And suddenly, Dakota notes, Gia's genuine confidence is gone—replaced by a forced harshness that Dakota's never seen before.

"You're not supposed to be here," Gia's voice is cold. She tilts her chin upwards, trying to match his height.

"I just want to talk," he holds his hands up. Dakota doesn't miss the way Gia tenses. Finley, who's now at Dakota's side, is squeezing her arm so tightly that Dakota's fearful she'll break skin.

"Not interested," Gia deadpans, moving to close the door with both hands. But suddenly, he jams his foot in the door and pushes it back open. Some invisible threshold is broken when he takes a step into their foyer—into their territory.

"*Hey*," Dakota grabs Gia's shoulder, Finley's hands slipping from around her arm. She latches onto Ryland instead.

"What's going on?" Dakota looks to Gia, placing herself between her friend and the visitor.

"I can handle it," Gia's eyes meet Dakota's, almost begging her not to get involved. Uneasy, Dakota takes a step back, but keeps her eyes narrowed at the strange man in the doorway. Ryland fights the urge to reach out and pull her backward.

"How'd you find me?" Gia speaks up again, curling and uncurling her fists.

The man's eyes wander over to the other three girls, focusing on the cigarette in Dakota's hand. Panicking, the girl puts it out on the windowsill. He then steps closer to Gia, as if he's trying to protect her from them. Finley holds her breath.

"I just came here to talk," he puts a hand on her arm but Gia shrugs it off. "This little act has gone on for long enough, Gia, don't you think? Your mother misses you."

Gia's jaw tightens. "I'm sure she does," she mutters. "Your point?"

"I'd appreciate it if you listen to me with an open mind, Gia," he sighs. The way he speaks reminds Dakota all too much of a therapist—concealing their own emotions and forcing themselves to be cordial.

"I'm listening."

"Let's go for a drive," he proposes. "Fifteen minutes, tops."

Gia crosses her arms.

"I brought along some drawings Delia and Jax made for you," he adds, then glances to his watch. "If we leave soon we can probably catch them before school, if you wanted to call them. They always ask about you."

Something changes in Gia when she hears this. After a few seconds of deliberation, she sighs and turns to Finley, tugging her keys from her pocket and handing them to the girl.

"I won't be long," she meets Finley's eyes sternly, unspoken words flying back and forth between them. Finley shivers.

"But—,"

"Finley," Gia's voice is calm, unsettlingly so. "You know."

Biting her lip, the curly haired girl nods quickly, hugging the keys to her chest. "I know."

"*Gia*," Dakota steps forwards, but she's meet with a fake plastered smile.

"I'm fine," the girl laughs and shakes her head. "Don't wait around for me."

As soon as the door slams shut, Finley's turning around and chucking the set of keys across the room in frustration. Dakota flinches.

"What was that?" Ryland speaks up softly. "Should we have let her go?" Finley watches the car back out of the driveway, her hands curling into fists.

"We're not going to the aquarium anymore," she nods in finality. Dakota looks to Ryland, who raises an eyebrow.

"Who was that?"

"Her dad," Finley mumbles, slowly lowering herself down on the couch. Ryland, stunned, moves to sit beside her.

"That's the pastor?"

"He gives me the creeps," Dakota speaks up, pushing the curtains aside and surveying the front yard before locking the door. "We should call Red."

"No!" Finley abruptly jumps to her feet. "We can't do that."

"Why not?"

"Gia said not to."

Ryland raises an eyebrow. "No she didn't."

"You weren't there," Finley mumbles, shaking her head. She retrieves the keys from where she'd thrown them. "Gia can handle it."

"You don't sound so sure," Dakota notes. Finley glances to the door.

"I have to be."

"It's been fifteen minutes," Ryland leans against the windowsill, glancing outside. Finley paces nervously around the foyer, wringing her hands together.

"Finley, come on," Dakota, frustrated, grabs the girl's shoulders. "Why can't we call Red?"

"We can't," Finley shakes her head in a panic. "That's not how it works."

"You know something we don't…" Ryland notes, standing up and approaching the girl. Finley immediately looks away, avoiding their eyes.

"She can't create a scene," Finley sighs. "She says she can't ruin things for Jax and Delia."

"Who?"

"Her brother and sister."

Ryland and Dakota turn to look at her, shocked. Finley peers out the window and taps her foot anxiously.

"So he *does* hit her," Ryland's blunt, crossing her arms and raising an eyebrow at Finley. "That's why she ran away."

Finley swallows nervously, torn between her secrecy to Gia, or Gia's well-being. She keeps her eyes on the driveway, neither confirming nor denying Ryland's suspicions.

"That's it," Dakota shakes her head, trying to be the voice of reason. "I'm calling Red."

"That's not part of the plan!" Finley cries out, flinging her hands down at her sides in frustration, taking both girls by surprise. Dakota freezes.

"What plan?"

"Stay out of trouble until she turns eighteen," Finley mumbles, looking down at the ground. "Stall the court date. Lay low. Keep Jax and Delia safe."

"This is about her siblings?" Ryland speaks up, looking to Finley for answers.

"They don't know," Finley shakes her head. "He doesn't hurt them."

"And?"

"She doesn't want to ruin their lives."

Dakota and Ryland look to one another. "By getting their dad in trouble?" Dakota asks quietly.

"They'd blame her if they something happened to him," Finley nods softly. Suddenly, the situation becomes infinitely more complex. Dakota sighs heavily and leans against the door, now not so sure if calling Red is the best idea.

Ryland speaks up for the both of them, clearing her throat to gain their attention. "Now what?"

"She'll be back," Finley nods softly, her eyes focused on the window. "It's part of the plan."

"I don't know if I trust this plan," Dakota mutters. Simply sitting around and waiting seems like the last thing they should be doing.

But, sitting around and waiting is exactly what they do.

For the next two hours, Finley paces back and forth, dragging her feet against the floor. By now, Ryland and Dakota know better than to disrupt her, although her pacing doesn't exactly help to ease their nerves, either.

When the doorbell finally does ring, Finley's there within seconds. Dakota's close behind, but when they pull the door open, Gia pushes them both out of the way and heads straight into the kitchen. All the girls hurry to follow.

"What happened?" Dakota stands hesitantly in the doorway while Gia digs an ice pack out of the freezer. Her lip is busted, blood running down the corner of her mouth. When she turns and notes Dakota's staring, she rolls her eyes and wipes her mouth with the back of her hand. Slumping down into a stool at the island, she presses the ice pack to her eye, right where it's started to swell. Everyone is quiet—as if a single word could bring forth an explosion.

Sighing heavily, Gia turns to Finley, staring her down from across the counter and speaking her first word since she'd arrived back. "Call 911."

"But your lip—," Finley, distracted, takes a step forward. Gia glares at her.

"*Finley*," her voice is firm. "*Call the police*."

Finley stills, confusion flickering in her eyes. "But you said the plan—,"

"*I know,*" Gia cuts her off. "This is a new plan." She pauses, with Finley staring wide-eyed at her. "You got the license plate number, right?"

Finley nods quickly. "3SV—,"

"*Now,*" Gia's voice is raw. Startled, Finley nods violently and hurries over to the phone. Exhaling slowly, Gia rests her head in her hands.

"Here," Ryland appears by her side, handing the girl a wet cloth. Gia looks to the other two girls, hesitantly takes the cloth, and shakes her head.

"He's hitting Delia," she says, almost casually, not meeting their gaze.

"But Finley said he didn't—,"

"*Before I left,* he didn't," Gia talks as if she's speaking to herself. "I thought if I left it'd all be fine."

"How'd you find out?" Dakota asks carefully. Gia digs something from her pocket—a piece of crumpled paper that she smooths out on the counter. The first thing Dakota notices is the shadow of a footprint across the page, something that propels her to move closer. It's a letter, written in childish handwriting with pink marker. Gia clears her throat and taps the paper.

"Here," she nods, reading aloud. "*We all miss you. But I miss you the most. I fell down the stairs the other day. Please come home.*"

Dakota looks to her, confused.

"That was always *my* excuse," Gia swallows and looks back to the letter. "If they asked about a bruise—I fell down the stairs. But she was smarter than I thought. She must have known."

"And you're sure that's a sign?"

Gia nods. "He basically confirmed it for me," she gestures to herself, bruised and bloody. Dakota bites her lip.

"What about Jax?" Finley appears in the doorway, cautiously taking a few steps forward.

"He'd never lay a hand on him. He's the prized son," Gia shakes her head. "Did you call?"

Finley nods. "But why Delia?"

"She's a girl," Gia mutters. "We need more discipline to keep us in check, remember?" Her voice is bitter. Finley frowns.

"But she's only eight..." Finley sits down, struggling to understand.

"So was I," Gia reminds her, making the curly haired girl clench her jaw. Silence falls over the four of them, causing Ryland and Dakota to exchange concerned glances.

"They said they're on their way," Finley says softly, breaking the tense air between them. Shyly, she pushes the ice pack back into Gia's hands, urging her to keep it on her lip.

"Do you need to go to the hospital?" she adds, noticing the way the girl presses a hand to her ribs and winces. Gia, however, just shakes her head.

"I've had worse," she mutters, making Finley look away.

It's silent until the cops come.

Red arrives home in the midst of the madness, barging her way inside and demanding to know what's going on. She's relieved to find all four girls squished on the couch, and immediately goes to Finley for the full story.

They're questioned for the next few hours, together and separately. And there's a lot of waiting—officers moving to and fro through the front door, making phone calls, pulling Red aside to talk to her. To Dakota, it almost feels like they're the ones in trouble.

When they finally inform Gia that her father's been caught and arrested, all she does is inhale shakily and bring her hands up to her forehead. Finley becomes her voice, speaking on Gia's behalf.

"What about her siblings?" Finley asks tentatively.

"They're conducting an investigation as we speak," Red sits on the coffee table across from them, her hands folded in her lap. "It's all up in the air."

"Can she see them?" Finley continues, tilting her head to the side.

"Not yet," Red shakes her head gently. "They can't run the risk of her coaching them to say anything against him."

"But she wouldn't—,"

"I know, Finley," Red places a hand on the girl's arm. "But *they* don't," she explains, nodding to the police officers in the yard. "The whole process is going to take a little time. We have to be patient."

"She's been patient since she came here!" Finley sits up quickly, the entire couch shifting as she motions to Gia. "She hasn't seen them in a year!"

Slumping back into the couch in frustration, Finley refuses to listen to anyone else's words of comfort. Eventually, Red sends them all upstairs, urging them to take some time to calm down. At the top of the stairs, Ryland, Finley, and Dakota all glance to one another, nodding silently before following Gia into her bedroom.

Ryland and Dakota sit cross legged on Ryland's mattress, and Finley sits on the floor by Gia's bed, where the blonde lays on her back, intently studying the ceiling.

"This is all so stupid," Finley mumbles. "He's so stupid."

"Your mom's no saint either," Gia bites back. Tensing, Finley turns to look at the girl before sighing and and shaking her head. She remains quiet after that.

Red eventually calls them back down for dinner. It's just them once again, and the house suddenly feels too empty. Red tries to create some sort of conversation, but eventually she gives up and the rest of the meal carries on in silence.

That night, Dakota finds it impossible to fall asleep. This happens most nights, but tonight in particular she fights the urge to sneak down the hallway and into Ryland's bed.

It's been a long day. Dakota knows she shouldn't be complaining, considering Gia is the one feeling the brunt of it all, but Dakota knows they're all a bit shaken up following the day's events, Red included. Seeing someone like Gia so beaten and defeated has only served to remind them that they're all not immune.

Maybe that's why Dakota gets a little too excited when her door is nudged open a crack. She sits up slightly. "Ryland?"

"Fraid' not." *Gia.*

"What's going on?" Dakota looks to the girl, cocking her head to the side.

"Get up," Gia nods. "We're going out. You're driving." She tosses the girl her keys. Something in her voice tells Dakota not to question her.

And so, Dakota follows Gia as she sneaks out the back window, climbing down to the ground. Without any words exchanged between them, they pile into Dakota's car, backing out of the driveway in absolute silence.

"Go left," Gia instructs her. At the stop sign, Dakota glances over to the girl, who toys with the radio.

"Are you okay?" Dakota asks hesitantly. Without even looking to her, Gia turns up the radio and leans back in her seat.

"Get on the highway," Gia nods, Dakota's question ignored. "It's a long drive." Dakota doesn't argue. There's an edge to Gia's voice, something that tells her not to test the girl. It's a delicate, fragile silence that falls over them.

The highway is hypnotizing at night. But Dakota's still wide awake an hour later, probably because Gia has the static radio blasting to fill the silence. She's starting to wonder if Gia even has a destination in mind.

"The next exit is ours," Gia speaks up, startling Dakota, who quickly switches lanes.

Gia directs her through a labyrinth of city roads, until the lights slowly start to fade and they venture further into a smaller town, passing vast expanses of land. Eventually, the only thing lighting their way is Dakota's flickering headlights.

"Alright, slow down," Gia warns her, leaning forward to look out the window. They move idly down the narrow road until Gia holds out a hand, a signal to stop.

"Turn off your headlights," she instructs her. "Pull up here."

Dakota begs her car to keep running as they turn onto a dirt road, leading up a steep hill. Gia keeps her eyes peeled. A wooden sign catches Dakota's attention, but it's too dark to read the small lettering.

"Here," Gia calls out abruptly once they reach the top of the hill. "Park here."

As the engine dies down, Dakota studies their surroundings. Things slowly start to piece together when her eyes adjust to the darkness, just enough so she can make out the shape of a small building in the distance. The telltale cross perched atop the roof is enough to let her know exactly where they are.

Meanwhile, Gia leans back to dig in the backseat, retrieving a baseball bat. When Dakota sees this, her eyes shoot wide open.

"Are you crazy?" she hisses, looking to the girl in disbelief. But Gia just smiles, bouncing the end of the bat against the palm of her hand.

"Stay here," she nods, ignoring Dakota's shock. All the girl can do is watch as Gia makes her way over to the small parking lot, dragging the wooden baseball bat behind her. It bounces against the gravel, leaving a trail of dust behind the girl, and Dakota looks around worriedly.

There's only one car in the otherwise vacant lot, and Gia heads straight for it. She can't see much, but Dakota can tell it's a nice car simply by the shape of its silhouette.

Gia circles the car once, twice, like some kind of funeral march. She traces her index finger over the chrome accent that borders the windows, waltzing to a stop directly in front of the car's hood. Almost pensively, she drums her fingers against the metal. And then, taking a step backwards, she grips the bat with both hands. Dakota holds her breath.

The bat comes crashing down into the hood, shaking the whole car and leaving a dent. But that's not enough for Gia. In her collected calm manner, she adjusts her grip on the bat and winds back again, swinging it full speed into the front windshield. She does this three times, until the window finally shatters to pieces. Dakota flinches.

After leaving no window in the car untouched, Gia moves onto the rest, smashing the headlights and kicking in the doors, leaving boot-sized dents on all sides of the car. Dakota finally thinks she's done when the girl drops the bat and takes a step back to admire her work, but instead Gia bends down to pull something out of her boot.

She slashes the tires—flipping open her butterfly knife and yanking it through the thick rubber. The car sinks as she does this, taking its last dying breaths. Once the air is drained, she twirls her knife around her finger and snaps it shut.

Dakota just gapes at the car in utter disbelief as Gia makes her way back over. Her car rocks when Gia slides back in, slamming the door behind her. Taking a deep breath, Dakota pushes back against the steering wheel, replaying what had just happened in her head.

"That make you feel any better?" she asks, for some reason keeping her eyes off of the girl. She hears a heavy sigh from beside her.

"Wish it could," Gia mutters, and when Dakota finally looks to her, she's shocked when she finds the girl's eyes are glassy with tears. Dakota internally panics. Sure, she's seen Finley cry, she's seen Ryland cry, but seeing Gia on the verge of tears makes her short circuit. To be honest, she wasn't even sure if the girl was capable of such emotions.

But luckily Gia breaks the tense silence for her, pulling her hands into her sleeves and wiping her eyes. "We just gonna sit here?" she quips, although Dakota can see right through her act. With a soft nod, she starts the car, and begins the drive back home.

An hour later, when both girls climb back through Dakota's window, a pair of eyes watches them quietly from across the hallway. Gia's the one who notices this, and she raises an eyebrow. The door is pushed open a crack.

"I don't like it when you sneak out," Finley mumbles, poking her head out into the hallway. "I thought you ran away."

"Go to bed," Gia shakes her head, causing the girl to frown.

"I can't."

"Why not?"

"Cause' you might sneak out again."

Sighing heavily, Gia rolls her eyes and crosses the hallway. "If you're so worried about me sneaking out, I'll sleep in here," she kicks the door open, plopping down on the spare bed in Finley's room. "That way you can sound the alarm if I jump out the *fucking* window."

Finley turns to look at Dakota in question, but all she gets is a soft shrug.

As soon as the bedroom door is pulled shut, Dakota's snatching her pillow from her own bed and tiptoeing down the hallway. She nudges Ryland's door open, softly crossing the room and crawling into the space between Ryland and the wall.

"Ryland," she whispers, a smile tugging at her lips. The girl stirs, lifting her head and furrowing her eyebrows.

"What are you… *what*?" she mumbles, still groggy with sleep. Dakota just pulls her closer and finds the girl's hands under the blankets.

"Gia's in Finley's room," she whispers, resting her forehead against Ryland's shoulder. "Go back to sleep."

"Is everything okay?"

Dakota nods softly. "Just wanted to lay with you."

Humming contently, Ryland curls her fingers around Dakota's and tugs her closer. And for a while, Dakota forgets about all that happened earlier. Evil doesn't exist. For a while, it's just her and Ryland and the steady hum of the air conditioning.

(In the morning, when a man in uniform arrives at the door to question Gia about her father's car, Red glares at the girl before turning to tell the officer that it *couldn't possibly have been Gia*, for she was accounted for at all hours of the night. When he leaves, both Finley and Ryland bombard Dakota with questions.)

The days that follow seem to be filled with waiting around. Gia's on edge about the fate of her siblings, and everyone else seems to feed off of her nervous energy.

However, the following Friday, a knock on the door changes everything. Finley, as usual, is the one to answer it, and when she worriedly calls out Gia's name, all three girls come running.

The woman at the door gasps as soon as she sees Gia, brushing past Finley and wrapping the girl in a tight hug. Gia's eyes go wide.

"*Mom*?" she stammers out, noticing the officer on the front porch. The woman grabs her face, looking her daughter up and down. There's still bruises on her skin from her encounter the week before, all dark purple and prominent even when she tries to cover them with makeup.

"Oh, honey," the woman engulfs her in another hug. "I'm so sorry."

Something in Gia snaps in this moment, and she yanks out of her mother's grip. "No you're not," she practically growls. "Where are the twins?"

"Honey—," her mother starts to defend herself, but Gia's already pushing past her and moving out onto the porch. The other three girls watch through the window as moments later, the door of the police car bursts open and a small blur shoots across the yard, jumping into Gia's arms.

"*Delia,*" Finley notes quietly. The girl is practically a carbon copy of her older sister—white blonde hair and all.

"I missed you," the tiny girl wraps her arms around Gia's neck. "They sent daddy away."

Gia kneels down, setting her sister on the soft grass in front of her. "I know," she says quietly, reaching up to comb her fingers through the small girl's hair. "Are you okay? Where's Jax?"

Delia glances toward the car, where her brother sits, arms crossed and eyes staring straight ahead. Gia frowns.

"He doesn't believe me," the small girl says softly. "Daddy told him that I'm a liar. Just like..." she trails off, looking down shyly.

"Just like me?" Gia asks, earning a reluctant nod in response.

"I guess he's lucky," Gia sighs. The smaller girl just wraps her arms around her sister again, holding tightly to her.

"Us girls have to stick together, huh?" A voice appears from behind them.

Gia tenses when she stands up to face her mother. Instinctively, she pulls Delia closer to her side.

"She's my *sister*," Gia says firmly.

"And I'm your mother."

"You can't pick and choose when to be my mother," Gia bites back, lowering her voice. "You already made your choice."

"Honey, I—,"

"No," Gia is firm. "You made your choice when you let me walk out instead of him."

"Gia—,"

"You may have not laid a finger on me, but you are *nowhere* close to innocent," she narrows her eyes. "And then you turned around and let the same thing happen to my *sister*."

This time, her mother doesn't have a response. Gia hugs Delia into her side protectively. There's a tense silence between them.

"We're moving in with Aunt Em for a while," her mother clears her throat, fighting back tears. "It's just temporary. Just until we get back on our feet."

Gia takes a step forward. "If you do *anything* to hurt them..." she lowers her voice. "If you let *anyone* lay a hand on her ever again..."

"I won't," her mother shakes her head, now a crying mess. "I'll make it up to you."

"It's too late for that," Gia deadpans. "Just make sure you won't have anything to make up to them."

Finley, Ryland, and Dakota all watch from inside as Gia's mom pulls her into one last hug, with Gia making a pathetic attempt to peel her away. They watch as Delia bursts into tears and clings to Gia when she realizes her sister isn't going with them. And Gia comforts her, most likely promising to come visit as much as she can.

They watch Gia try to hug her brother, but be rejected when he pulls away, pretending she doesn't even exist. They watch the girl kneel down and shed her sweatshirt, tugging it over her sister's head before hugging her close. And lastly, they watch the officer exchange a few words with Gia before the car pulls out of the driveway.

When Gia storms upstairs, Finley's quick to follow, but she's met with a door slammed in her face. The girls opt for giving her some space for the rest of the night. The house becomes eerily silent.

Chapter 15

COMFORT

Dakota struggles to understand why she's melded with these girls so effortlessly. In the span of weeks, she already feels closer to them than she had ever felt with her old friends. She's discovered that there's an unspoken kinship between them, thanks to their mutual suffering. Even though they originate from different homes and have seen different evils, they find common ground simply because they understand each other in ways that not many other people can.

They come to understand that when Finley starts repeating things—locking doors over and over, flicking the lights on and off, changing channels on the TV—she's having a bad day. And when Finley has a bad day, they know it's best to keep her occupied—which results in them baking lots of desserts and playing hours worth of board games.

They all tread carefully around Ryland on her bad days, which are almost always associated with her leg. On Ryland's bad days, there's a delicate balance between subtly assisting her, but never letting her suspect that she's being coddled. If she notices someone going out of their way to make things easier for her, she'll snap at them. So most of the time Ryland's bad days involve Dakota making her coffee in the morning, Finley scurrying around the house to straighten out the rugs and pick up anything she may trip on, and Gia breaking out her collection of horror movies, dimming the lights, and making a giant bowl of popcorn.

Gia's bad days are few and far between, but when they happen, it's a sudden hurricane. They've come to predict her bad days based on her smoking habits. If she gets up to smoke at the crack of dawn, while everyone else is still in bed, it's a sign of a bad day. And if she starts smoking inside, it's a surefire way to know that hell could break loose at any moment.

On bad days, Gia steals Dakota's keys and disappears for hours at a time. And unlike Ryland or Finley, there's nothing they can do for Gia besides stay out of her way. They've learned the hard way not to try and find out what's wrong. Last time Finley approached her, trying to help, things ended in the slamming of a door, Gia missing dinner, and a very distraught Finley.

But then there's Dakota. She's the newest addition to the group, and usually, based on their history, new residents are the most unstable. Dakota, however, has yet to give them any hint of a breakdown—except for Ryland, who still remembers her sleepwalking incident at the beach. Ryland, in fact, is the only one who has seen any hint of Dakota's true emotions. While all four girls are close, Ryland and Dakota share something different. Something deeper, contained around everyone else, only showing when they're alone. Yet, at times even Ryland struggles to fully understand Dakota.

One thing she knows about Dakota is that touch, to her, is a direct equivalent to comfort. Ryland's yet to understand the extent of this.

It's midnight the following Saturday. Gia and Finley are downstairs, cracking up over some *I Love Lucy* marathon they'd found. Ryland's in her bedroom, immersed in *The Catcher in the*

Rye, she's been reading ahead for English class. Ryland's so absorbed in her book that she doesn't even notice the girl who nudges her door open, gazing into the room tentatively.

Ryland finally looks up when she hears the creak of the floorboards, soft footsteps making their way to her bed. It's clear that something's wrong, evident in the way Dakota averts her eyes and tugs down the sleeves of her sweatshirt.

Ryland's standing up within seconds, placing her hands on Dakota's shoulders and looking her up and down, worried. "What's wrong?"

But Dakota just shakes her head and practically forces Ryland to hug her, hiding her head in her shoulder. Ryland doesn't argue, but she pulls away too quickly for Dakota's liking, concerned.

"Are you hurt?" Ryland asks, confused. But Dakota shakes her head once more and tugs on Ryland's sleeve, nodding gently to the bed, quietly pleading with her.

Ryland obliges, sitting down slowly. And within seconds, Dakota's next to her, leaning against her shoulder and practically melting in her side. Her arms snake around Ryland's. And although Dakota seems content just sitting beside her, Ryland's concern grows.

"Did something happen?" she asks quietly.

Dakota buries her head into Ryland's shoulder, mumbling against her neck. "I don't wanna talk about it."

"But something *did* happen?" Ryland presses.

"*Ryland*," Dakota whines, hugging the girl's arm. "Stop."

"Something's wrong," Ryland shakes her head.

"I don't wanna talk about it," Dakota repeats herself.

"But—,"

"You can't fix it, Ryland," Dakota sighs softly. "I just want you to be here."

"But..." Ryland stops herself, somewhat frustrated.

"We can talk later," Dakota mumbles, shyly nudging Ryland backward, urging her to lay down. "Let's just be quiet for now."

This is where they differ. When Ryland finds a problem, she needs to fix it. And even if she can't technically fix it, she needs to talk about it—to talk it through, give a motivational speech of some sort.

Dakota, on the other hand, is the opposite. Where words fail for her, she's comforted by simply being next to someone. It's innate—starting when she was just a little girl. While Hudson and the other neighborhood kids would run wild in the backyard, Dakota would cling to her mother, climbing into her lap where she was content with just watching.

As she got older, she never talked about her nightmares. She'd just crawl into her mother's bed, comforted by being curled up in her side.

But then she died. And Dakota became even more desperate for comfort. As a tiny seven year old, she'd whine and throw a fit until Hudson would scoot over and make room for her in whatever makeshift bed they had for the night. The Quinn siblings were like that—they never talked anything through. When Dakota was sad, Hudson would let her cry into his shoulder until she fell asleep. And when Hudson would return home, frustrated, Dakota would sit in front of him, curling his hands into fists and pressing on his knuckles, wrapping her smaller hands around them and telling him jokes to try and get his mind off of things.

And while Ryland's aware that Dakota's a touchy person—she's always playing with Ryland's hair, tracing patterns on her arms, pulling her impossibly close and intertwining their fingers at night—Ryland still doesn't get it.

Ryland seeks solution over everything. Unlike Dakota, she didn't have a bed to crawl into when she had nightmares. At all hours of the night, her mother was either throwing a party just a few rooms over, or nowhere to be found, leaving her daughter home alone. At an early age, Ryland developed the habit of rocking herself to sleep. If the house was too loud, or too unbearably quiet, she'd curl up in a ball, knees to her chest, cover her ears with her hands, and slowly rock back and forth, eventually lulling herself to sleep. It's a habit she's yet to fully outgrow—she still finds herself rocking back and forth on her feet when she gets anxious.

So, from the time she would put herself to sleep, Ryland was quick to become self-reliant—a little too much, at times. She tackles things head on, dead set on ridding herself of the problem as quickly as possible.

Plus, it doesn't help that the only touch she's ever known hasn't been comforting. Whether it be her mother's drunken boyfriends, a furious foster parent, or a group of kids throwing rocks—Ryland's always seemed to be at the brunt end of people's frustrations. So at a young age, she shut herself off, building an invisible wall between herself and everyone around her.

So when she first met Dakota, it took some getting used to. While Ryland always had to consciously remind herself to put an arm around the girl, or pull her closer, Dakota's actions were always unconscious—as if she wasn't even aware of what she was doing. Whether it was pulling Ryland's hand into her lap and tracing circles in her palm, or nuzzling her face into her shoulder while they slept, Dakota always seemed to naturally gravitate towards touch.

At first, Ryland didn't know how to handle the girl's incessant closeness. She wasn't used to it. Every time Dakota would randomly run her fingers down her arm, Ryland would practically short circuit, as if her body didn't know how to process it. It didn't exactly make her uncomfortable, per say, because she trusted Dakota, but she'd always tense up and everything else would lose focus. It was just… *different.*

But now, she's used to it—likes it, even. Now, when Dakota randomly leans over the back of the couch to rest her chin on top of Ryland's head and wrap her arms around the girl, Ryland doesn't even flinch. The only difference is that Dakota craves closeness for comfort, and Ryland struggles to understand how simply being held is enough for the girl.

Laying back on the bed, Dakota curls into Ryland's side, head buried in her shoulder and arms hugging her waist. It's quiet except for their breathing. Ryland, fighting the urge to question the girl even more, is frozen for a few minutes. Noticing this, Dakota lifts her head, finds Ryland's hand, and moves it to her head, silently urging the girl to play with her hair. Exhaling slowly, Ryland threads her fingers through Dakota's hair and uses her other hand to retrieve her book from the nightstand.

Sighing contently, Dakota lays her head back down. They exist in comfortable silence for a while, and Ryland can feel Dakota starting to relax. She's slowly starting to realize that sometimes all Dakota needs is to be held. That—for Dakota—it's enough.

"Listen to this," Ryland speaks up softly, a short while later. One hand is around Dakota, the other is holding her book open above them. Dakota lifts her head, resting her chin on Ryland's shoulder and letting her eyes trace the girl's face.

Ryland clears her throat, reading aloud a passage from the book. Dakota studies her, noting how the girl's voice turns thinner when she reads. Ryland pauses, glancing to Dakota for a moment before turning back to the book.

When she looks back to Dakota, the girl just laughs softly and buries her head back in Ryland's shoulder to hide her face. Dog-earing the page, Ryland tosses the book aside.

"You better?" she asks quietly. Dakota glances to her again, nodding softly.

"T'was nothing," she shrugs softly. "Just a bad dream. Felt real."

"Do you want to talk about it?"

"*Ryland*," Dakota giggles. "M'fine. Stop worrying."

"I'm just concerned about you," Ryland mumbles. Endeared, Dakota presses a kiss to the girl's shoulder.

"I know, and I appreciate it," she nods. "But I'm okay now. Promise." She reaches out to trace circles around Ryland's collarbone, an action that causes goosebumps to form on the girl's skin. "I just wanted to lay with you."

"That's all?"

Dakota giggles. "That's all."

"And you'd tell me if something really was wrong?"

"Of course," Dakota pushes herself up with her hands, letting her face linger above Ryland's, her hair cascading down around them like a curtain. She laughs softly, a playful smile on her lips. "I like you."

Gazing up at the girl, Ryland rolls her eyes and plays along. "I like you too."

Laughing, Dakota leans down to kiss her, starting out by just ghosting her lips over the girl's until Ryland's forced to pull her closer, cupping the back of Dakota's neck and making her laugh into the kiss. Things start off slow, but Dakota starts to kiss back harder, spurred by the feeling of Ryland's fingers threaded in her hair at the nape of her neck. Ryland may be practically a stranger to touch, but she's learned a thing or two from Dakota.

When Dakota pulls away abruptly, a teasing smirk on her face, Ryland struggles to catch her breath.

"*Jesus Christ*," is all she can breathe out, amusing Dakota, who tilts her head to the side playfully.

"That bad?" Dakota raises an eyebrow.

"No," Ryland shakes her head, swallowing hard. "Good," she nods, breathless. "Really good."

"You're not so bad yourself," Dakota quips back. She leans down to kiss her again, but Ryland stops her, placing a hand on the girl's shoulder.

"Really?"

Pausing, Dakota studies the girl's face. "Huh?"

"What you said before…"

"About you being a good kisser?"

Ryland nods. "I am?"

"Of course you are," Dakota laughs softly. "I'm surprised no one's ever told you that before."

As soon as the words leave her mouth, Dakota feels Ryland tense up.

"I…" Ryland opens her mouth to speak but changes her mind, clamping her jaw shut. A few seconds pass in tense silence, with Dakota tentatively studying her face, quickly connecting the dots.

"I was your first kiss, wasn't I?" Dakota's eyebrows raise slightly, her mouth agape.

"Technically all those '*firsts*' are just social constructs," Ryland starts to ramble, looking away.

"But I *was* the first person you kissed?" Dakota insists. Ryland refuses to meet her eyes, making the girl laugh softly. "*Ryland*," she whines, giggling and turning the girl's chin to look at her. "Tell me."

"If we're speaking logistically..." Ryland mumbles. "Then you were the first girl I kissed, yes."

"Girl?" Dakota quirks an eyebrow.

"*Person,*" Ryland sighs, correcting herself. "The first *person* I kissed."

Dakota studies her face for a few moments, a small smile creeping onto her own. "You never told me that."

"I didn't see the importance," Ryland tries to look away, embarrassed, but Dakota stops her by cupping her cheek and leaning down to kiss her again. Ryland's breath catches in her throat, caught off guard.

"You're cute," Dakota laughs softly when the kiss breaks, and she plops back down into the space beside Ryland, a smile etched onto her face.

"M'not cute," Ryland mumbles. "I'm tough."

"Shut up," Dakota nudges her shoulder. "You can be both."

"So you've kissed other people?" Ryland blurts out, rolling on her side to face Dakota, who nods softly.

"*Boys,*" Dakota absentmindedly reaches out to run her fingers over Ryland's jawline. "I've kissed boys. Didn't do anything for me. Nothing special," she shrugs. "All those didn't mean anything."

"So you're saying this means something?" Ryland gestures between them, smirking when Dakota's face turns red.

"It's a possibility," Dakota crinkles her nose, a smile creeping across her face. "I'll have to get back to you on that one."

"If it means anything, you're the best person I've ever kissed."

"I'm the *only* person you've ever kissed."

"Exactly."

"Shut up," Dakota nudges her shoulder, rolling her eyes. She turns to lay on her back beside the girl, finding one of Ryland's hands and holding it up, running her index finger across her palm.

"I should probably get going," Dakota half mumbles, hoping Ryland won't even hear her. She glances to the alarm. "Gia will be back soon."

"Don't," Ryland shakes her head. "She hasn't slept in here for the past week because the A/C is too loud." She reaches out, trying to pull Dakota closer. "Stay."

Rolling back over to face her, Dakota raises an eyebrow. "What happened to laying low?"

"It can wait until tomorrow."

"Fine by me," Dakota smiles softly, reaching over to turn out the light. Ryland's hands find hers in the darkness, feeling her chest swell when Dakota melts into her side, sighing contently and pulling Ryland even closer.

"Do you sleep like this with everyone?" Ryland teases, tugging the blankets over them and sinking back into her pillow.

"Nope," Dakota shakes her head. "Just people I really like," she curls and uncurls her fingers against Ryland's stomach, yawning softly. "Just you."

And so, Ryland may not quite understand Dakota's affinity for closeness, but she doesn't mind it, either. In fact, it might be starting to rub off on her, which she realizes when she wakes up in the middle of the night for the sole purpose of pulling Dakota closer.

On Sunday afternoon, Red drives Gia two hours to visit with her siblings. They're gone before anyone else wakes up.

And when Dakota does wake up, she's in Ryland's bed. Ryland is still fast asleep, and Dakota rolls over to face her. However, something else disturbs the peace—the rustling of something in the closet. Dakota lifts her head slowly.

"Oh, good. You're awake," Finley turns around, holding up a blouse and studying herself in the mirror on the back of the door. "Does this look okay?"

Even though Dakota's panicking, Finley doesn't acknowledge the fact that the two girls are in bed together. Cautiously, Dakota sits up.

"What are you doing?"

"Gia said I could borrow something," Finley hums, turning back to the closet and shifting through the hangers. "I need something… professional."

"Why would you need to be professional on a Sunday morning?" Dakota rubs her eyes.

"Job interview," Finley shrugs, pulling out a long skirt, looking at herself in the mirror, and frowning.

"You have a job interview?"

Finley nods. "At noon."

"Where?"

"A country club," Finley says softly. "A friend in my English class told me about it."

"Sounds fancy," Dakota wiggles her eyebrows. Giggling, Finley tugs a white blouse from its hanger and holds it up.

"That one looks professional," Dakota nods. Ryland stirs beside her, mumbling something and rolling over to reach for Dakota. Her eyes flutter open when she feels the girl sitting up. Upon seeing Finley, she freezes, but Dakota just squeezes her shoulder.

Noticing Ryland's awake, Finley holds up the blouse and raises an eyebrow. "Yes or no?"

Ryland, still slightly confused and groggy from sleep, rubs her eyes and looks to Finley. "That's Gia's."

"You should wear that one," Dakota nudges Ryland and sends her a look, but Ryland just groans and shoves her head into her pillow.

A smile graces Finley's face and she looks to her reflection once more. "I think I will," she nods quickly, then slinging the shirt over her arm and disappearing without another word.

They hear the doorknob turn closed 4 times, though, and Ryland lifts her head. "She's nervous," she notes.

"She said she has a job interview," Dakota says softly, running her fingertips up and down Ryland's bare arm. "Sleep well?"

"Mhm," Ryland yawns, rolling onto her back, her eyes scanning Dakota's face. "Are you getting up?"

"Hell no," Dakota shakes her head. "It's Sunday morning, I'm in no rush." Ryland laughs softly, scooting over and patting the space beside her. Soon enough, they're both fast asleep once more, with Dakota's head buried in Ryland's shoulder to block out the sunlight coming in through the windows.

"Little bit of sugar, shit ton of creamer, just the way you like it," Dakota plops down on the couch next to Ryland, passing her a mug of coffee. She can already tell Ryland's leg is bothering her more than usual. Dakota practically had to dive to grab the girl's arm when she lost her footing on the stairs. But she knows better than to bring it up.

"A shit ton of creamer is better than nothing at all," Ryland nods to Dakota's coffee, crinkling her nose. Dakota just shrugs and kicks her feet up on the coffee table.

With Finley going to her interview and Red driving Gia to visit with her siblings, Dakota and Ryland have the house to themselves. When the sky gets dark and the wind starts to pick up,

Dakota digs a pile of blankets and pillows from the hall closet and tosses them onto the couch. She picks an old VHS tape of *America's Funniest Home Videos* reruns and curls up next to Ryland.

As expected, they don't end up watching much television. As the storm rages on outside, Dakota nudges Ryland's chin with her nose and catches the girl's lips as soon as she turns to look at her. Ryland doesn't protest.

They don't hear the doorbell at first.

Dakota's got a case of the giggles, and she's tugged a blanket over her head, pretending to be a ghost. When she ends up bumping their foreheads together, it makes her laugh even harder.

They hear the doorbell the second time, though. And the third. And the fourth. By the time Dakota collects herself and hurries to the door, she's already lost count. Skidding to a stop when she opens the door, Dakota comes face to face with Finley, soaked from head to toe, standing on the front porch looking horribly small and fragile.

Before Dakota can even process this, Finley's ducking under her arm and making a beeline for the couch. She collapses into the corner, burying her face in a pillow hugged to her chest. Dakota turns around slowly, her eyes following the trail of wet, muddy footprints that now litter the foyer. Her eyes meet Ryland's in question, but all she gets is a shrug in return.

"I'm guessing you didn't get the job?" Ryland raises an eyebrow. Dakota glares at her from across the room, but Ryland just holds up her hands in innocence.

"There wasn't even a job to begin with," Finley rubs her eyes furiously, makeup staining her cheeks. "*Not even one to begin with…*" she repeats herself quietly.

"Did you show up late?" Ryland tries a softer approach. Finley shakes her head.

"It was a joke," she mumbles, looking down and sniffing. "It was all just a joke."

Dakota slowly walks over to sit down on the coffee table, pursing her lips and looking to Ryland, unsure of what to say.

"Finley, we have no clue what you're talking about," Ryland sighs, squeezing the girl's shoulder. "Breathe."

"They lied," Finley closes her eyes and shakes her head, prompting Dakota to pass her a handful of tissues. Finley takes them quickly. "There was no job. There wasn't even a country club. I took a two hour bus ride into the middle of nowhere for nothing."

Exchanging confused glances with Ryland, Dakota leans forward. "I thought you said a friend told you about this?"

"I *thought* they were friends," Finley wipes her eyes, wringing out the water from her hair. She pauses for a moment. "They weren't."

"Who?" Dakota frowns. "Who was it?"

"*Don't,*" Ryland shakes her head, placing a hand on Finley's shoulder. "Don't tell her." She knows well enough how Dakota will solve the problem. "We can talk to someone at school tomorrow."

Finley shakes her head violently. "*No,*" she looks to Ryland, her eyes pleading. "That will only make it worse." She tucks her chin to her chest, digging her nails into the pillow.

"We've got to do something," Dakota insists. But Finley simply shakes her head.

"It's not worth it," her voice is weak, defeated. Dakota and Ryland look to one another, unsure of what to do.

"So we just sit back and do nothing?" Dakota tilts her head to the side. Finley nods in return, wringing her hands together nervously.

"That's what I always do," Finley shrugs, having already accepted this. Before the girls can continue to question her, Finley stands up and quietly excuses herself, stealing the box of tissues before slipping upstairs.

Both girls turn to each other at the same time, but all Ryland can offer Dakota is a soft shrug. This isn't the first time they've dealt with this, and at the rate things are going, it's far from the last.

"It's fucked up," Dakota mutters, plopping back down on the couch beside Ryland, who doesn't miss how the girl clenches and unclenches her fists at her sides.

"Punching someone isn't gonna fix it," Ryland raises a knowing eyebrow. Like a child who's been caught, Dakota crosses her arms and sinks further back into the couch.

"It would at least make me feel better."

"Not if you break your hand again."

"It's all healed anyway," Dakota shakes her head. But Ryland knows better. She reaches out, grabs Dakota's hand, and meets her eyes before slowly pressing her thumb down, between her knuckles. Dakota glares at Ryland, bearing the discomfort for as long as she can. But eventually, she hisses in pain and yanks her hand out of Ryland's grip.

Dakota glares at her. "Your point?"

"Your body isn't meant to punch people on a daily basis," Ryland half laughs. However, when she notices Dakota curl and uncurl her fingers, her lip scrunching in distaste, Ryland's smile fades.

"Still that bad?" she raises an eyebrow.

"Don't know why," Dakota lets her hand fall back into her lap. "It should be healed by now."

"I mean, you did hack off your cast like a week after you broke it," Ryland notes. Dakota passes her a half-hearted glare.

"I'm not getting another cast," she mutters.

"You should at least wrap a bandage around it to hold it still."

"I'll look stupid."

Ryland raises an eyebrow. "Who exactly are you trying to look tough for?" All she gets in return is a one-shouldered shrug. Sighing, Ryland gives up on arguing with the girl and leans against her shoulder.

"Today was supposed to be a good day," Dakota grumbles, rolling her eyes. Ryland just nods softly against her shoulder.

The slamming of a car door is just barely audible over the raging storm outside, but it's enough to have Ryland and Dakota scrambling to opposite ends of the couch, pretending as if they've been simply watching television this entire time—very separately, and *very* platonically.

Dakota watches out of the corner of her eye as the door opens slowly. Gia's the first to enter, and Dakota can immediately tell she's the opposite of happy. By the time Red makes it to the doorway, Gia has already stomped up the stairs. Red looks to the two girls on the couch, who both point upward. Just as the woman steps inside, the slamming of a door rocks the entire house.

With a tired sigh, Red just closes the front door quietly. Dakota and Ryland glance to one another when they hear the pitter patter of soft footsteps upstairs. A quiet knock follows.

"Gia?"

"Go away, Finley." Gia's voice is firm, contained.

"But—,"

"I said *go away*, Finley."

Dakota and Ryland hold their breath, well aware that they're one wrong move away from a hurricane.

But luckily, Finley seems to reluctantly take the message. Her footsteps travel back down the hallway, and then follows the faint sound of Finley's door being shut. Ryland rolls her eyes.

"Does anything ever work out for *any* of us?" she mutters, shoving a pillow off of the couch. Dakota watches her, a frown tugging at her lips.

"They may look up for some of us," Red speaks up as she unwraps the large scarf from her neck and holds up an envelope between two fingers. She motions to her. "I need to talk to you, Ryland."

Confused, Dakota looks to Ryland for an explanation, but by the wary look on Ryland's face, she doesn't have one either. Dakota's suddenly aware that she's intruding on a private conversation, and she quietly excuses herself, bringing a game of Scrabble upstairs and gently knocking on Finley's door. From Finley's room, she can just barely hear the hushed voices from downstairs, but she can't make out a single word they're saying.

Sitting across from Ryland at dinner, Dakota raises an eyebrow in silent question. Something's off, she can tell. But all Ryland gives her is a slight shake of the head and a look that reads '*not now*.' The rest of the meal is painfully quiet. Gia doesn't bother to make an appearance, and Finley isn't her usual talkative self. Red blames it on the dark weather, letting them head back upstairs without doing the dishes—she'll take care of it for tonight.

Upstairs, Dakota stands in her doorway and looks to Ryland, hoping she'll say something. But a half smile and a soft shrug is all she gets. Dakota watches Ryland slip into her room down the hallway, disappointed.

Dakota works obsessively on her homework for the remainder of the night. She ends up dozing off midway through a math problem, her pencil rolling from her hand and clattering across the floor.

When she's awoken, it's by Ryland, who's quietly tidying up the books and papers scattered across the bed. Groggily, Dakota lifts her head and glances to the window. It's pitch black and windy—braches whipping to and fro and making patterns in the shadows across her floor.

"What are you…?" Dakota mumbles, her eyes following the girl. Ryland just nudges her shoulder.

"Scoot over."

Dakota obliges, sitting up and rubbing her eyes. Ryland quietly sits down, taking off her brace, well aware that Dakota's watching.

"You alright?" Dakota tilts her head to the side. Ryland nods softly.

"Yeah," she reaches over to turn off the light. "That envelope was a letter from the school. I'm one of the finalists for a scholarship."

Dakota's eyes widen. "Really?"

Ryland shrugs. "Don't get your hopes up," she lays on her back, feeling Dakota hesitantly search for her hand, and squeezing it when she finds it. "Even if I won the money twice over, it still wouldn't be anywhere near what I need."

"That doesn't make sense."

"Welcome to America, kid," Ryland rolls onto her side so she's facing Dakota. "You can't break the cycle you were born into. Once you're down here at the bottom like me, you're a lifer."

"That's comforting," Dakota mumbles, but Ryland just laughs and kisses her forehead.

"You get used to it," the girl yawns. "No big deal."

"You'll figure it out somehow."

Ryland just sighs. "I admire your optimism."

"How was the visit?"

Ryland leans up against the front hood of Dakota's car, next to Dakota. Gia and Finley stand across from them, against a row of bike racks. They've taken up the habit of eating lunch in the parking lot, away from the crowd.

"Alright," Gia shrugs. "Jax still won't acknowledge my existence."

"He'll come around," Finley mumbles.

"Delia's not doing well," Gia admits, shaking her head. "She hates the new house, the new school…" she picks at part of her sandwich and tosses it into the grass. "She broke down when it was time to go. She just… *clung to me*… she kept begging me to take her with me."

Ryland frowns. "I thought that house was a temporary stay?"

"It was supposed to be," Gia rolls her eyes. "But my mom's a wreck. Delia said she sleeps until noon and hasn't made any effort to find a job."

"Stupid," Finley shakes her head.

"S'my fault," Gia mumbles. "I just had to open my big mouth and destroy an entire family."

"He was *hitting your sister,*" Dakota speaks up, reminding her. With a heavy sigh, Gia pinches the bridge of her nose.

"All I did was take her out of one hell and place her in another," she shakes her head. "What good does that do?"

"What if they go to a foster home?" Finley furrows her eyebrows. Gia laughs.

"The system is a whole other level of hell," she rolls her eyes.

"I can attest to that," Ryland speaks up with a nod.

"Everything about this is fucked up," Dakota shakes her head, balling up her trash. Finley frowns, looking back and forth between them.

"If it makes you feel any better, Red says we can order pizza tonight."

That night, Dakota's the only one left downstairs. She's humming to herself, finishing up the last of the dishes from dinner and listening to the radio perched on the edge of the counter. She's in no rush to go upstairs—Ryland's been unusually quiet for the past day or so. Dakota has a feeling it's due to the letter Red had brought home, but she's too afraid to push the subject—she knows how abrasive she can get.

"How was school?"

Flinching, Dakota nearly drops the dish in her hand when Red's voice appears behind her. "I…uh, t'was fine," she nods once, noticing the pensive look on the woman's face.

"Been keeping an eye on Gia?"

Dakota shrugs. "Trying. Not that I'd be able to read her in the first place." Out of all four of them, Gia's the best at putting on a stone cold façade—not allowing anyone to see what she's truly feeling.

"Hm," Red just nods, leaning against the counter. Dakota continues scrubbing the dishes, leaving them in comfortable silence for a while. Eventually, Red wanders over to the refrigerator, plucking a picture from atop it and dusting it off. Pausing, Dakota's eyes follow her as she slowly walks back over to her. She lays the picture down on the counter between them, clearing her throat.

"See that?"

Setting down her dishrag, Dakota leans in closer to get a better look. Her eyes scan the faces, spotting two familiar ones. Ryland, as always, is hiding her face. But Gia's sitting on the front porch steps, unaware that the picture is being taken. Dakota notes her dark black hair.

"This was Gia's first week," Red explains. "Ryland had only been here for a little over a year." She pauses, studying the two other girls in the picture. "The blonde is Tarah," she adds. "She's living with her uncle in New York. He gained full custody of her after her parents gave it up." She taps another face. "That's Jaden. She was one of our first girls."

"Ryland's mentioned her," Dakota nods, hesitating for a moment. "Why?" Putting the picture away, Red glances to her and raises an eyebrow.

"Why'd you do it?" Dakota shakes her head. "I mean, I heard about the things you had to deal with when Finley first got here... and I'm sure Ryland wasn't all that easy to handle," she shrugs. "I could never run a place like this."

Red pauses, appearing to be thinking something over. Then, she sighs and nods for Dakota to follow her. When the girl argues that she has to finish the dishes, Red shakes it off, motioning for her to leave them.

"Ah, there we go," Red mutters under her breath. They stand in her bedroom—which used to be an old office. It's small, with peeling wallpaper and stained ceilings. Dakota watches from the doorway as Red lifts something from a shelf in her closet, exhaling slowly as she lowers a large trunk onto the bed. She dusts it off, coughing and waving the dirt out of her face.

"Well don't just stand there," she looks back to Dakota, slowly sitting down on the bed and patting the space beside her. Shyly—she's never been in Red's room before—Dakota wanders over, sitting on the very edge of the bed and watching curiously as the woman heaves open the top of the trunk.

"Here we are," Red sifts through a pile of old clothes—dresses with lace collars and sheer blouses. The chest even *smells* old. She finally pulls out a small pocketbook—just larger than her hand—and brushes it off. At first it looks like snakeskin leather, but upon getting a closer look, Dakota realizes it's so worn that the material is cracking apart. Red's hands are shaky when she reaches inside, pulling out a small circular object. Dakota thinks it's a coin, but she's quickly proven wrong when Red uses her nails to open it—a locket pendant.

"Take a good look at that," she clears her throat, passing it over to Dakota. Handling it like fine goods, Dakota holds the locket up close, just barely able to make out the picture. It's a baby. She makes the connection quickly, her eyes darting back and forth from Red to the locket.

"That's you?"

Red nods, taking the pendant back from Dakota and tucking it into the pocketbook. "It's the only thing I had on me when my momma left me on the doorstep of the orphanage I grew up in," she holds the pocketbook tight in her lap. "N'fact, it's the only picture taken of me until I was eighteen."

"You're kidding," Dakota's eyes widen. Red just chuckles and buries the pocketbook back beneath the pile of clothes.

"You see, we're not that different—you all and me," Red slowly closes the trunk. "I know all the little tricks y'all try to play. I practically invented them," she laughs and reaches over to squeeze Dakota's shoulder. "Believe it or not, Miss Quinn, I started this place because I was selfish."

"What do you mean?"

"I wanted to be the person I needed when I was as young as you," she explains. "It's a hard job, but someone's gotta do it," she laughs heartily. Dakota slowly tilts her head to the side.

"But isn't it hard when one of us leaves?" the younger girl asks, clasping her hands together in her lap.

"Of course," Red shakes her head. "I cried like a baby after our ol' Jaden left. But *that's* between you and me," she adds with a soft nod.

"Ryland says most kids leave and never come back."

"I can't say I don't blame them," Red sighs, squeezing the girl's shoulder again. "Although, a year or two ago, we had a young girl named Kimberly stay here for a few months. Brightest kid you've ever met—but she was terrified of everyone," she shakes her head at the memory. "But guess where I was just a few weeks before you came in?"

"Where?"

"In New York," Red nods. "Sitting front row for her debut on Broadway." Dakota notices the proud smile curving at her lips.

"Seriously?" Dakota's eyes widen in disbelief. Red just nods and taps her shoulder, drawing her attention to the small framed picture on her bed, amongst others.

"That's her."

Dakota leans in, suddenly realizing that the faces in the collection of frames match the ones Ryland had named off to her weeks ago. She reaches forward, carefully picking up the first image that catches her attention—Ryland. And her face isn't covered, for once. It's more recent, Dakota realizes. She's sitting on the floor across from Finley, her brace out in front of her, leaning over a Monopoly game. Dakota laughs quietly.

"These are all of them? *Us*?"

Red nods. "I like to keep em' here," she admits. "Even the girls that only stay for a few weeks. It's a nice reminder."

Setting the picture down, Dakota slowly sits back on the bed, looking down to her hands and thinking for a moment. "I like it here," she speaks up after a moment of silence, but quickly jumps to correct herself. "I mean, I don't necessarily *want* to be here... But I'd rather be here than the other places Ryland has talked about," she adds, her voice soft.

Red just laughs, standing up and pressing her hand against the trunk, placing her other hand on Dakota's shoulder. "I expect at least one of you four to make it even bigger than Broadway," she teases, before moving to lift the trunk back onto the shelf.

For the rest of the night, Dakota stands in front of the fireplace, looking at the pictures one by one and wondering where each of the girls ended up—where *she'll* end up. It scares her to admit that she's not so sure what her future has in store.

Chapter 16

HIDE AND SEEK

The rest of the week passes by in a blur. Nothing amazing happens, but nothing knocks them off of their feet, either. So, to Dakota, it's been a pretty good week. Not to mention, summer is approaching faster than ever.

Saturday starts off normal, for the most part. Finley makes blueberry waffles for breakfast, and they all sit around the television, humoring Finley by watching Jeopardy reruns.

However, when Ryland is nowhere to be found at lunchtime, Dakota grows confused. Red's out at a meeting, like usual, and both Gia and Finley don't have any answers to offer her. Dakota checks the calendar, suspecting a doctor's appointment, but the entire week is empty.

Gia makes it known that Dakota's worrying for no reason, telling her over and over that Ryland can handle herself. But Dakota can't shake the nervous energy that surrounds her, mostly because Ryland had just disappeared without a word of explanation.

And when Red arrives home, she doesn't even have time to hang up her jacket before Dakota is hurrying to her side, informing her of Ryland's abrupt departure. Red doesn't even bat an eyelash, calmly telling Dakota that it's not against house rules to go out during the day.

So Dakota's the only one driving herself crazy with worry. And it bothers her to no end, mostly because she wants to know where Ryland is, but also because she's never worried this much about someone before.

Ryland's never felt this small.

She thinks it's some kind of joke when they have to pass through a pair of passcode locked gates, past signs sporting "*Smile! You're on camera*!" in bold letters. Ryland scowls. They wind up a hill bordered by perfectly shaped trees and hedges, and Ryland imagines the kind of people that must live here—successful millionaires with government jobs—part of the 'one percent' she always hears politicians talking about. Basically, it's the last place she thought *she* would be headed.

The car slowly rolls to a stop and Red clears her throat, piercing the tense silence and bringing Ryland out of her thoughts. "This is it."

The house itself is bigger than anything she's ever seen. There's tall wrought iron gates that surround the yard, with grass so green that it looks fake. Round, thick columns hold up the second floor balcony. Ryland just finds herself staring in disbelief until Red circles the car.

"I think there's a mistake," Ryland shakes her head, slowly rising to her feet. But Red just laughs and squeezes her shoulder, assuring her they're at the right place.

And so, Red slowly helps her up the steep stone stairs that lead up to the front porch. Ryland doesn't argue when she grabs her arm to keep her steady, but she doesn't acknowledge it either.

Once she stands in front of the door, Ryland just stares at the doorbell, hesitating. But the door winds up swinging open before they even make their presence known.

She's never been in this situation before, and neither has he. So it's awkward for both of them. He moves in for a hug, but Ryland just freezes, so they end up shaking hands. Ryland still hasn't said a word.

Red tries to be the mediator, introducing them both and giving the man a run down of the directions back to the home. But their words all slur together for Ryland, who's craned her neck to see into the house. It looks even bigger on the inside. There's a literal *chandelier* in the foyer. A huge marble staircase winds up onto the second level. She feels dizzy just looking at it all.

"I guess I can take it from here," he laughs nervously. Both pairs of eyes turn to look at Ryland, who quickly forces a painful smile. She's never felt this awkward.

He walks her through the house, talking incessantly about the architecture, the year the house was built, and the name of all the artwork that hangs on the walls. But Ryland's more interested in the little things—the bookcase against the in the living room with volumes of Shakespeare, the world map in the office with clusters of red pins in almost every continent, and especially the wall full of crayon drawings and report cards. It makes her chest tighten.

He notices her staring and joins her, his eyes scanning the wall. "Eliana got that for reading the most books over the summer," he points to a navy-bordered certificate that hangs above his desk. All Ryland can do is nod softly, thinking to her own collection of gold papers and report cards, crumbled and shoved carelessly under her bed.

"Everyone's waiting for us in the dining room," he clears his throat, snapping Ryland out of her thoughts.

"Right," she nods quickly, forcing her eyes away from the wall.

"They're all very excited to meet you," he adds after an awkward pause of silence. "You like spaghetti, right? It's the twins' favorite… we weren't sure what you would—,"

"It's fine," Ryland nods, unable to shake the uncomfortable tension.

The moment she steps down into the dining room, she feels infinitely small, and not from the sheer size of the room. But because now, there's four more pairs of eyes on her, burning into her skin. Ryland shifts uncomfortably. She hates being the center of attention.

"Alright," the man starts out awkwardly. "Everyone, this is Ryland," he motions to her. She wants to disappear.

"Ryland, this is Eliana and Natalia," he gestures to the two youngest girls who sit at the table, dressed in matching dresses and hair bows. One whispers something to the other and they both giggle, their eyes darting back over to Ryland. She shoves her hands in her pockets.

"That's Jonah, our oldest," he nods to the boy across from them, no younger than ten. He seems more reserved compared to his sisters, simply brushing his dark hair out of his face and looking away shyly.

"And *this* is Julienne, my wife," he moves away from Ryland to wrap an arm around the blonde woman's shoulder and kiss her cheek. The woman gives Ryland a soft smile, which Ryland struggles to return.

"I'll go grab the last of the drinks," Julienne speaks up, slipping back into the kitchen. The man then pulls Ryland aside, speaking in hushed tones.

"We haven't told the kids who you are," he explains, glancing over to the table to make sure they're not listening. "Julienne didn't want to confuse them." Ryland suddenly feels even more out of place, but she just nods slowly. She can't blame them. At this point, even she doesn't know who she is.

"Why'd your parents name you Ryland?" one of the twins speaks up from across the table, her head cocked to the side. There's a mischievous look on her face, and Ryland curses herself for feeling so intimidated by an elementary schooler. She just shrugs softly, shaking her food around on her plate.

"My mom thought I was a boy. I was supposed to be Ryan, but..." her voice is weak.

"Coincidentally enough, Ryland was my mother's surname," the man speaks up. "The motto on the coat of arms is '*While I have breath, I hope.*'" Ryland looks to him, suddenly wondering if there's an alternative motive behind her namesake.

"Do you have a sister with a boy's name too?" Both of the twins burst into laughter. Their mother scolds them, but Ryland just shakes her head.

"I'm an only child," she pokes at the food on her plate. It's alright, but she's used to the homemade pasta sauce back at the house, where Dakota doesn't hold back on the garlic. She also doesn't miss the look she receives from the man at the head of the table upon hearing her words, but she refuses to meet his eyes.

The twins occupy most of the conversation, demanding everyone's attention. Ryland's eyes wander, landing on the young boy next to her. Compared to the twins, Jonah favors his father. With dark olive skin and long eyelashes that resemble Ryland's own, he seems to be the black sheep of the family. When Ryland notices the handheld video game he's got hidden in his lap, under the tablecloth, she raises an eyebrow.

"There's a hidden cave with a portal to your left," she whispers, nodding to the game. Startled, he looks to Ryland, back to the game, and then to Ryland again, a shy half-smile forming on his lips. It makes Ryland's blood run cold, though. It's the same one-sided smile that Dakota always affectionately teases *her* about. She looks away quietly.

"So, Ryland," the man directs his attention to her, making her jump. "How do you do in school?"

Ryland shrugs nervously. "I do alright."

"How are your grades?"

"A's."

"All of them?"

Ryland just nods, swallowing nervously when she notes how shocked he is. What had he expected her to be like?

"Bet she didn't get that one from her mother," the woman beside him mumbles. It's an underhanded comment, one that goes right over the heads of the kids, but Ryland hears her loud and clear. And unlike she knows Dakota would, Ryland doesn't say a word.

The man ignores his wife's comment and turns back to Ryland. "What about college?"

"What about it?"

"Any plans?"

"Sure," Ryland shrugs, looking away. "If it was even a viable possibility."

She sees the glance he exchanges with his wife, but just as he opens his mouth to speak, he's interrupted.

"Are you a robot?"

Ryland's attention turns to the opposite side of the table, where the two twins have lifted the dark red tablecloth and are now peeking underneath. Crossing her good leg over her brace,

Ryland looks away at a loss for words. She feels sick to her stomach.

"She's not a robot," the boy next to her speaks up for the first time. "She's a Misty Knight."

"A what?" Both girls look to him in confusion.

"Misty Knight," he nods. "You know? The comic book superhero that hurt her arm so they gave her a bionic one. It's like that."

"Mom says all the comic books you read are gonna melt your brain," the twin on the right scrunches her nose, making her counterpart giggle. But Ryland gives the boy, Jonah, a sad smile.

Ryland's never felt more relieved than she does when the dinner is over and the kids are excused from the table. Now it's just her and the two adults sitting across from her. She can practically *feel* them judging her.

"So, Ryland," the man clasps his hands together. "Do you have any questions for me? For us?"

Ryland just shrugs and looks down.

"Listen, Ryland," he sighs, leaning forward. "I don't blame you if you resent me." Ryland clenches her jaw when she sees his wife squeeze his shoulder to comfort him, as if he's the one who's been suffering all these years.

"But I didn't even know you existed," he shakes his head. "It was only when I heard about your mother's death that I looked into it and discovered she had a daughter."

"She died when I was six," Ryland's voice suddenly runs cold. "You're telling me you didn't think about her at all for *eleven years*?"

"It was a one time thing," he tries to defend himself, although the mood in the room has already shifted. "We only knew each other because we went to high school together."

"*You* were the one who made it a one night thing," Ryland narrows her eyes. "She tried calling you, but *you* refused to talk to her. *You* just pretended she didn't exist. I guess it's pretty easy when you're not the one carrying the child."

He looks shocked. "Who told you that?"

"Who do you think?"

He slams his fist on the table, starling Ryland. "*I* was the one who called her over and over. *I* was the one who showed up at her doorstep. *She* was the one who shut me out. *She* was the one who disappeared."

"And what makes you think I'm going to believe you?" Ryland quips back, her chest tightening.

"What reason do you have to believe her?" He looks to her questioningly.

"She was my *mother*," Ryland speaks through gritted teeth, digging her nails into her jeans under the table.

"And I'm your father."

The words make her blood run cold, but Ryland just keeps her icy gaze on him, shaking her head slowly. "If you were really my '*father*,' you would have been there when I needed one." Her voice is monotone, covering up the fact that her hands are shaking.

She sees his expression falter. The man sits back in his chair, taking a deep breath and clasping his hands together.

"This isn't an ideal situation for any of us," he sighs.

"Well sorry for being a nuisance," Ryland mutters, cutting him off before he can speak again.

"That's not what I meant—,"

"I *know* what you meant," she snaps back, shocking even herself. "I'm sure watching your own mother die, being moved around the system like some circus animal, and crushing all the nerve endings in your leg wasn't the ideal situation for you, either, was it? Life is so hard." She drags out her words, laced with venomous sarcasm.

The room falls silent. Across the table, the woman covers her mouth. Ryland's not sure if it's shock or disgust on her face. Maybe it's both.

"Ryland, I—,"

"*Mom*! Eliana won't let me play with the karaoke machine!" A voice rings out from upstairs, cutting their conversation short. The man sighs.

"I'm supposed to drive you home," he nods softly. All Ryland wants to do is disappear, to shrink down inside of herself and never come back out. Her life feels like it's suddenly been flipped on its head—she's reevaluating everything about her past. The lump in her throat is so big she feels as if she might choke.

Ryland stands awkwardly in the foyer. The man had excused himself to retrieve his keys, but she can hear the hushed arguing coming from the kitchen—making her feel infinitely guilty.

As she's studying the family pictures that line the walls, she becomes aware of the soft footsteps that approach behind her. She's startled when she turns around and comes face to face with Jonah.

"This is Misty Knight," he says softly, rolling out a thin comic book and handing it to her. "You can keep it," he shrugs, looking away shyly. "Mom says I have too many anyway."

Ryland looks down, her eyes scanning the front cover. Jonah gently taps the picture of a character dressed in red.

"That's her," he explains. "Her arm got blown off in an explosion, but now she's got this super cool bionic one that crushes stuff."

“I’ve never heard of her before,” Ryland nods softly, her voice quiet. She traces her fingers over the cover. “You know, I used to collect a bunch of those dollar comics when I was a kid,” she shrugs one shoulder. “I’ve probably still got them in a box somewhere.”

“Really?” his face lights up. “Can you bring them next time?”

Ryland tenses, realizing that a ‘next time’ is expected from her. She opens her mouth to speak but struggles to find the words.

“I-I don’t know,” she looks away. He furrows his eyebrows, studying her for a moment.

“You’re not what I imagined an older sister to be like,” he notes softly. Ryland freezes, looking to him in confusion, but he just laughs.

“I’m not stupid,” he shakes his head. “Dad never has company over. Plus we look exactly the same.” He holds his arm out against Ryland’s, and sure enough, their skin is the same exact color—a golden tan that stays year round, thanks to the Hispanic roots that she now realizes came from her father’s side. Ryland raises an eyebrow.

“Plus I may have overheard them talking about you the other day,” he mumbles. Ryland can’t help but laugh softly, thinking that maybe, just maybe, she’s found an ally.

The drive home is tense.

They exist in silence for a while, with Ryland rolling and unrolling the comic book in her hands nervously.

“I’m sorry about Julienne’s comment.”

The man breaks the silence, but Ryland sits quietly, not even acknowledging his existence. Glancing over to her, he sighs heavily.

"I understand if you're mad at me."

Ryland doesn't say a word.

"Well if you're not going to speak, then I will," he nods, more to himself than anyone. Ryland slumps against the window.

"You don't know how bad I feel about not being there when you were a kid," he shakes his head. "If I'd have known… I would have done *something*."

"And I don't know the extent of what you've been through, but maybe things are looking up now. I hear you won a scholarship," he looks to her for confirmation, but Ryland doesn't move a muscle. He sighs again.

"I shouldn't have expected you to come running to me with open arms, anyway," his voice is quiet. "But I think I can help you, Ryland. I have money. I have friends who are doctors. There's got to be something they can do for your—,"

"I don't *need* your *help*," Ryland snaps back, breaking her silence. "I don't want your pity."

"But—,"

"I've survived for this long on my own, I think I'll do just fine without you trying to buy my love with your money," she clenches her jaw. Her words effectively render him speechless, letting Ryland know that her attitude hadn't come from his side of the family. The rest of the ride is quiet, painfully so, and only when the pull in the driveway of the home does he speak again.

"I'm not asking you to see me as a father," he turns to her. "I'm just—,"

But Ryland's far past the point of defeat. She's already halfway out of the car.

"Thanks for the ride," she mutters, slamming the car door shut and limping up the steps to the front porch. She doesn't go inside until she hears the hum of the engine, waiting for the car to slowly back out of the driveway. Even now, she longs to disappear.

The minute she hears the sound of a key in the doorknob, Dakota's clambering down the stairs.

Everyone else is fast asleep, but Dakota's remained awake, anxiously hoping for Ryland to return. And so, she's standing in front of the door when Ryland nudges it open. As soon as their eyes meet, Dakota's heart drops. Something's wrong.

They just stare at each other for a few moments. Ryland, as if she's been caught, and Dakota, scared that saying something will push the girl away.

But she does. And although she's dying to know where Ryland's been, those aren't the first words that leave her mouth. Instead, she takes a shy step forward.

"What's wrong?" she asks quietly. And for some reason, her voice is just the right mixture of vulnerable and concerned—enough to make Ryland choke back tears, swallowing heavily.

Something instinctual in Dakota makes her hold out her arms slowly. And sure enough, Ryland just crumples, dropping her things to the floor and stumbling the few steps forward into Dakota's arms.

Dakota's stunned, but she's quick to wrap her arms around Ryland, holding her tightly. With her head buried in Dakota's shoulder, Ryland cries for the first time that day. Everything she's kept bottled up comes spilling out, sobs wracking her body. Dakota just keeps her arms wound around the girl, keeping her grounded, as if she'll just float away if she lets go.

What Dakota doesn't see is Red, who peers around the corner to make sure Ryland's home safe. Once she sees Dakota comforting her, though, she quietly leaves her to it.

"Are you hurt?" Dakota asks softly against Ryland's shoulder, relieved when the girl shakes her head. Slowly, Dakota pulls back, cupping Ryland's face with her hands and searching the girl's eyes. Holding her breath to fight back tears, Ryland shrinks under Dakota's concerned gaze.

"Shh," Dakota shakes her head, noting how Ryland's bottom lip trembles. She pulls her closer again, squeezing her tightly. This is the most worked up she's ever seen Ryland, and yet she's doing everything she can to *not* bombard her with questions, even though she's dying to know what's going on. Her first priority is to calm Ryland down.

"Come sit," she says softly, gently ushering the girl into the living room and over to the couch. Once Ryland's sitting, Dakota disappears into the kitchen, emerging a few moments later with a cup of tea and a bag of frozen peas. She hands the mug to Ryland, and then sits on the coffee table directly across from her, placing the makeshift ice pack against the girl's knee. She's not sure if Ryland's leg is even bothering her, but she knows it eases some of the ache regardless.

As they sit there, with Ryland forcing herself to take deep breaths to hold back more tears, Dakota notices how the girl's eyes keep darting to her worriedly.

"I won't ask," Dakota says softly, shaking her head. "I'm here to talk, but you don't have to say a word if you don't want to." Even though everything in her aches to know, Dakota's come to realize that she'll go to any length to see Ryland happy again.

Yet, for some reason, her words seem to have the opposite effect of what she wanted. Setting down the mug, Ryland's head falls into her hands and she chokes back another sob. Within seconds, Dakota's next to her, pulling her into her arms.

"I'm sorry," Ryland finally speaks, her voice rough as sandpaper. Dakota's caught off guard.

"Sorry?" she tenses, looking to the girl, her mind suddenly reeling to find what Ryland could possibly be apologizing for.

"I didn't tell you," Ryland shakes her head, furiously wiping the tears in her eyes with her shirtsleeve. Dakota tilts her head to the side, and Ryland breathes in shakily, pressing her hands to her temples.

"My dad," Ryland whispers, the words hanging heavy between them. "I saw him tonight."

Dakota's eyes widen. "*What*?"

"The letter," Ryland looks away. "He found me. He… he's got a whole family. And a huge house. And an office that's even bigger than my bedroom where they hang their report cards on the wall and—," she cuts her own rambling off, shaking her head and fighting back tears. Dakota reaches up to brush the girl's hair out of her face.

"That bad?" she asks quietly, concealing her own shock.

"H-horrible," Ryland breathes in deeply, holding it in her chest. The waver in her voice compels Dakota to pull her into a hug once again, cupping the back of the girl's neck with her hand.

"I'm so sorry," Dakota whispers, her words quiet against Ryland's shoulder. Even with only the gist of where she's been, Dakota understands how it's managed to shake Ryland to the core. "I'm so sorry," she repeats herself, softer this time. Ryland's arms just wrap tighter around her, clinging to something real. And then, it just slips out.

"I love you."

Dakota's voice is barely a whisper. So quiet, in fact, that Ryland doesn't even hear her over her own shaky sobs. But Dakota hears herself, her own words crashing over her in a wave of realization. It had just spilled out of her without any thought. And suddenly, she's terrified when she realizes how true her words are. Even though the moment is weighed heavy with sadness, her feelings have never been more real. In realizing just how much Ryland's pain spurs her own, Dakota can't deny it any longer. *She loves her.* And even though it terrifies her down to the bone, the only thing she can do is hold Ryland even tighter, praying that maybe, just maybe, she feels the same.

Chapter 17

BROKEN BONES

The next morning, when Finley and Gia wander downstairs, they find Dakota and Ryland on the couch, fast asleep. Dakota's sitting up, her feet resting on the coffee table and her head slumped back against the couch. Ryland's head is in her lap, and she's curled up beside the girl, a pillow hugged to her chest and her braced leg hanging sideways off the couch. Gia and Finley exchange glances, but Finley stops Gia before she can slip an unlit cigarette into Dakota's mouth, which is slightly open.

"Let them sleep," Red's voice rings out from the kitchen, startling the two girls. Red pours herself a cup of coffee and walks over to join them in the doorway. "They've had a long night." Gia looks to her for an explanation, but is only met with a stern gaze.

And so, Gia and Finley quietly gather breakfast and head back upstairs. Gia's confused, but Finley has a content smile on her face—she's known all along.

It's past noon when Ryland finally stirs awake. She groans, blinking her heavy eyelids open and inhaling slowly. She hates crying, simply because she always wakes up feeling like shit the next day. Her surroundings slowly fade into view, and she feels a hand threaded in her hair.

"Morning," Dakota rasps softly, yawning and bringing her free hand up to rub the kink in her neck. Sitting up slowly, Ryland hisses as she moves her leg. Falling asleep in that position hadn't been the best idea.

"Fuck," Ryland mutters under her breath, using her thumb to rub circles in the sensitive skin around her knee. Dakota lifts her head, frowning.

"Hurts?" she asks softly. Ryland nods.

"Hurts."

Scrunching her nose in distaste, Dakota moves to kneel in front of Ryland, her fingers carefully undoing the straps on her brace. Ryland tenses, but Dakota just places a hand on her knee.

"It's fine," she nods softly. "Not like we're going anywhere today, right?" Relaxing softly, Ryland draws her bottom lip between her teeth and watches as Dakota carefully eases the brace from her leg, removing some of the stiff pressure. Ryland slumps back into the couch. Quietly, Dakota crawls back up beside her.

"You're thinking about it," she notes, giving Ryland a knowing look.

"Can you blame me?" Ryland sighs heavily, looking down and picking at her nails. Dakota frowns.

"Do you want to talk about it?"

"I don't even know where I'd start," Ryland mutters. Dakota just reaches over, preventing Ryland from picking at her nails by pulling one of her hands into her lap.

"Start with him," she prompts softly. "What was he like?"

Ryland scrunches her nose. "Alive."

Dakota tilts her head to the side.

"Not dead," Ryland adds. Dakota squeezes her hand, urging her to go on.

"I grew up assuming he was as good as dead," Ryland shakes her head. "He's not."

"He's very much alive," Dakota adds, making Ryland laugh softly. "Was he nice?"

This just earns a half-shrug from Ryland. "He's nothing like I expected."

"What did you expect?"

"Anything but him."

Dakota raises an eyebrow. "That bad?"

"His family is *perfect*," Ryland's voice wavers and she starts to ramble. "He's got this huge map and he's marked all the places they've traveled. Their house is just covered in pictures of them. At the Grand Canyon, swimming with dolphins, hiking up volcanoes..."

"And that's bad?" Dakota furrows her eyebrows.

"That could've been me," Ryland avoids her eyes, her voice shaky and rough in the back of her throat. A wave of realization hits Dakota, her heart dropping. She cups Ryland's hand between her own.

"He only reached out to me to curb his own guilt," Ryland shakes her head, swallowing the lump in her throat. "The minute we were alone he told me he knew doctors that could fix my leg."

Dakota's jaw tightens. "You don't need fixing."

"Tell that to him," Ryland mutters. "I'm just some stain on his bloodline."

Dakota feels the words on the tip of her tongue but she bites them back. Quietly, she pulls her feet up underneath her and curls into Ryland's side.

"I'm too much like my mother," Ryland sighs. "Sometime's it's like I'm doomed to turn out just like her."

"You scare me when you talk like that," Dakota says quietly. Ryland pauses, glancing to her. Their eyes meet and she sighs heavily.

"I can't help it," she draws her bottom lip between her teeth, shivering when Dakota starts tracing patterns into the underside of her forearm. "I can't beat it. No matter what I do I'm always going to be like her."

"No you're not," Dakota shakes her head. "You're nothing like her."

"Well I'm nothing like him, either."

"So?" Dakota lifts her head to look at her. "You don't have to be like any of them. You're you." She gives her a sad smile. "*I'm* nothing like my mom."

Ryland pauses, turning to study the girl. "What about your dad?"

"Dead," Dakota shrugs. "I don't know anything about him. Apparently he was around for a year or so after I was born." She pauses, shaking her head. "I don't remember much of it because he got really sick and moved back home."

Unsure of what to say, Ryland just nods softly, curling and uncurling her fingers around Dakota's.

"You're not where you come from, is all I'm saying," Dakota presses a kiss to her shoulder. "You're not your mom. You're not your dad. You're Ryland," she shrugs. "And if that isn't good enough for him, fuck him. It's good enough for me."

"Thank you," Ryland whispers, squeezing the girl's hand. There's not much else for her to say, so she just sighs softly and rests back against the couch.

"I wish I could make it all perfect for you," Dakota mutters, resting her head on Ryland's shoulder. But Ryland just shakes her head.

"I don't want anything to be perfect," her voice is soft. "How boring would that be?"

This makes Dakota laugh, and she just sinks further into Ryland's side. "Then I'd at least make things easier for you," she sighs.

"You already do," Ryland shrugs. Dakota meets her eyes, a sad smile tugging at her lips. "I can't tell you what I would have done if you hadn't been here last night."

Dakota's close to letting the words slip out. So much so, in fact, that she's scared to say anything. So she just hums softly, pulling Ryland closer and lacing their fingers together.

"So was he like… a douchey rich guy?" Gia leans across the table, dipping a french fry into Dakota's milkshake. "Or a *creepy* rich guy?"

The four girls are squeezed into a booth in the back of Rubio's, a diner that they frequent. They'd gone for a drive, all of them restless and aching to get out of the house. Grainy 80's music plays over the speakers, muffled over the sound of the kitchen.

"I don't know," Ryland shrugs. "He was just…" she shakes her head. "*Weird.*"

In the car ride there, Ryland had reluctantly given the other two girls a brief explanation of where she's been. And now, they've taken to interrogating her.

"Was he really that rich?" Gia continues, stealing one of Finley's potato chips.

"There was practically a chandelier in every room," Ryland nods, raising an eyebrow.

"Hm," Gia hums. "Noted."

"*My dad* is rich," Finley speaks up, picking at her salad. "He worked for the government. They hired him to kill the president and that's why he's in a super secret jail in the middle of the ocean."

Dakota and Ryland exchange glances, but Gia just rolls her eyes.

"We talked about this," she turns to Finley, raising a knowing eyebrow. "That was another one of her lies, remember?"

Finley's face contorts. "What are you talking about?" she looks to Gia in disbelief. "My mom said—,"

"I *know* what she said," Gia cuts her off. "She lied. He's not in jail because he tried to kill the president."

"Then why is he in jail?" Finley cocks her head to the side, a mouth full of food.

"He owed money to a ton of people," Gia shakes her head. "And then tried to run away when he didn't have it."

"So he didn't try to murder the president?"

When Gia shakes her head, Finley mumbles something to herself and rests her chin in her hands. Dakota looks to Gia, confused, but the girl gives her a look that tells her not to say anything.

Stirring her milkshake with her straw, Ryland drums her fingers against the speckled red table. "Summer's almost here," she says softly, trying to create conversation. Dakota perks up.

"What's that mean?" she asks, an eyebrow quirked in curiosity.

"It means endless days of boredom," Ryland rolls her eyes. Finley looks up from her food, pausing her pouting to nod softly

"And broken A/C," Finley deadpans. Despite this, a mischievous smile forms on Gia's face.

"But this summer is different," the blonde notes, nodding to Dakota. "This time around, we've got transportation."

Ryland studies Gia's face, trying to figure out what she's thinking. She steals one of her french fries and points it to her. "I know that look," she nods, taking a bite and raising an eyebrow. "You've got an idea."

"A small one," Gia admits, shrugging. "What would you guys say to a road trip?"

Dakota sits up slightly. "The car still isn't completely fixed."

"Will it be by summer break?"

Catching the hint, Dakota nods once. "If you need it to be."

"Why a road trip?" Ryland inquires, scowling at Dakota when she swipes the cherry from her milkshake. She earns an innocent smile in return.

"Why not?" Gia shrugs. "Take a week and drive up the *golden coast*," she emphasizes her words for dramatic effect. "Stop and do cool shit along the way." She starts to list things off on her fingers. "Go to the beach, go shopping, explore random cities…" Dakota and Ryland exchange glances.

"You think Red would go for it?"

"I think I can print off four summer camp permission slips and get her on board," Gia hums mischievously. Ryland smirks.

"I'm in," Ryland nods, slapping her hand down on the table. She looks to Dakota, who just shrugs and does the same.

"I'm always up for an adventure," Dakota nods. All eyes then turn to Finley, who looks up innocently.

"What?" the curly haired girl furrows her eyebrows.

"You in?" Gia nudges her side. Finley just sighs, setting down her fork and placing her hand in the middle of the table along with the rest of theirs.

"I'm not letting you be idiots on your own," she nods softly. Gia and Ryland celebrate, high-fiving from across the table.

And so, the last few weeks of their senior year drag on.

Gia was right. Red falls for the summer camp excuse, and their plan carries on without a hitch. It's nice to have something to look forward to, Dakota thinks. She's been feeling increasingly restless lately.

Ryland tries not to bring up her dad, knowing it's an awkward topic for everyone involved. No one knows what to say in response. And although Dakota knows it's still on her mind, she's aware that if she pushes the topic, Ryland will only distance herself.

But things are good for the most part, that is, until one Monday afternoon when Dakota doesn't meet them in the parking lot for lunch. Ryland tries calling the house, but there's no answer. Gia shrugs it off, though, convinced that she just went home sick. But that doesn't stop Ryland from worrying. She's reminded of the time when Dakota drove off with Hudson, nearly disappearing without a trace. She'd eventually found her way home, but Ryland's always worried she may not return back one day.

Gia's been serving detention all week after being caught skipping class, leaving Ryland and Finley to walk home on their own. It's a good day for Ryland's leg, and even Finley finds herself struggling to keep up with her.

"What's the rush?" Finley jogs up beside the girl. "It's a beautiful day."

"I'm just walking," Ryland half glares at her, but it's enough to make Finley quickly realize what's going on.

"You're worrying over nothing," she notes, hopping over a crack in the sidewalk. "Gia said she probably just went home sick."

"Gia doesn't know Dakota like I do," Ryland quips back, a bit too fast. She quickly curses herself when she sees the knowing smile form on Finley's face. "Stop it."

"Stop what?" Finley tilts her head, feigning innocence. Ryland just glares at her.

"I haven't said anything, if that's what you're worried about," Finley continues, bending down to pluck a dandelion from someone's yard. "I mean, it's pretty obvious from the way you look at each other," she rambles as if she's talking to herself, twirling the flower between her fingers and then tucking it behind her ear. "You're lucky Gia isn't the best at picking up social cues."

Ryland doesn't respond, mostly because she's afraid to say something that confirms Finley's suspicions. However, her silence speaks for itself, and Finley just hums softly.

When they make it back to the home, Finley steps aside and lets Ryland go first. The girl does her best to ignore the cheeky smile on Finley's face, but she can't hide her urgency as she crosses the yard and quickly digs her keys out of her backpack.

The minute the door opens, Ryland skids to a stop. Finley hurries up to peer over her shoulder. And sure enough, there sits Dakota, slumped over on the couch. Her hair is a mess, half tugged out of the small braids that she'd tied back that morning. Part of her shirt is ripped, stretched and torn around her abdomen. But Ryland focuses on the ice pack she has pressed against her eye, with her head resting in both of her hands and elbows propped on her knees. She doesn't acknowledge the two girls at the door.

Ryland's bag slides to the ground with a thump, and she walks slowly over to the girl. She just stands in front of Dakota for a few moments, waiting for her to say something. But when she doesn't,

Ryland loses her patience, reaches down, grabs the girl's chin, and lifts it upwards to reveal her face.

The first thing she notices is Dakota's lip. It's busted, swollen, blood smeared around the corners of her mouth. And if that wasn't bad enough on its own, Dakota's eye nearly matches. It's already bruised and puffy, a million different shades of purple melted across her face. There's faint traces of blood around her pupil—at least, in the part of her eye that isn't swollen shut. Their gazes meet for a few tense seconds, and Dakota's eyes shy away from her own.

Ryland's hand drops away from her face, and she shakes her head. "*Again*?" she asks, her voice sharp, laced with annoyance. Still looking down, Dakota just shrugs sloppily.

It's then that Ryland notices Dakota's hands, her knuckles cracked and bleeding, already starting to bruise. It's all the confirmation she needs. Frustrated, she just rolls her eyes and storms off into the kitchen. Dakota doesn't make a move to go after her. In fact, she doesn't move at all. Standing awkwardly in the doorway, Finley's eyes dart around the room before she hurries after Ryland.

Finding Ryland in the kitchen, digging aimlessly through the pantry, Finley quietly slips into one of the stools. She watches the girl pensively, knowing Ryland's upset.

"What was that?" Finley finally speaks up, keeping her voice quiet. Ryland whips her head around, startled.

"She's stupid," Ryland mutters, slamming a box of crackers down on the island and leaning against the counter, across from Finley. "She fights everything."

Finley glances back to the doorway, her voice hushed. "She looks hurt."

"No shit," Ryland rolls her eyes. "She brought it upon herself."

Ryland's not sure why she's so bothered. But she hates the sight of Dakota like this, and she hates the fact that fists are the way Dakota solves her problems. Maybe it's because it hurts *her* to see Dakota hurt. Either way, she's outright frustrated with the girl.

They both hear the doorknob at the same time, and they hurry over to peer into the living room. Standing in the front doorway is Red, who crosses her arms and sighs heavily when her eyes land on Dakota. The girl raises her head slowly.

"Get in the car," Red's voice is stern, and she points to Dakota with her keys, flicking them towards the door.

Pressing one hand to her side, Dakota inhales sharply as she rises to her feet. Ryland watches from the kitchen as the girl presses another hand to her pounding forehead, walking stiffly towards the door. Ryland suddenly feels slightly less angry, and a bit more guilty.

When the door slams shut, Ryland lets out a heavy sigh. Finley stands quietly in the doorway, her eyes following Ryland as the girl crosses the room and slams her fist down on the counter, frustrated. Finley raises an eyebrow.

"Looks like Dakota's not the only one who punches things to solve her problems," she notes. Ryland glares at her through hooded eyes.

But before they can say anything else, the front door is thrown wide open and Gia waltzes in, chucking her backpack onto the couch. She pauses, though, when she enters the kitchen to find Ryland and Finley both staring at her.

"Oh, yeah, Dakota got her ass kicked," Gia nods, stealing a cracker. She then pauses, remembering something. Furrowing her eyebrows, she points to Ryland, a mouthful of food. "Something said something about you and she lost it."

Ryland looks at her in disbelief but Finley speaks up first. "How do you know?"

"Kid in detention showed me a video," she shrugs, hopping up to sit on the counter and lighting a cigarette. Ryland's eyes widen.

"Was totally unfair, too," Gia nods to Ryland. "They singled her out in the courtyard and started saying shit to try and piss her off. They had her cornered," she flicks the ash from her cigarette into the trash can. "She lost it when they said something about '*the girl with the leg*.'" The girl pauses in realization. "That's you," she flicks her wrist to Ryland, whose face has fallen expressionless. Finley speaks for her.

"Who was it?"

"A bunch of the stupid football kids," Gia nods. "They wanted her to throw the first punch so they could cry self-defense," she pauses. "Koda got a few good hits in, too. But it was five against one. She didn't stand a chance."

Ryland's blood boils, and her hands curl into fists. "Why the fuck would they do that?"

"Who knows," Gia rolls her eyes. "All I know is things escalated really quickly and they were all surrounding her on the ground when Mr. Ramirez got in the middle to break it up."

"Did they get expelled? Arrested?"

"Suspended," Gia nods. "Dakota, too."

"They suspended *her*?" Ryland's eyes widen in disbelief.

"She threw the first punch," Gia sighs. "They're all out until graduation."

"The entire last week of school?" Finley raises an eyebrow.

"Prom, too," Gia nods. Ryland pinches the bridge of her nose and moves to lean against the counter.

"Not that she would've gone anyway," Ryland mutters, shaking her head. "Now I feel like shit."

"You *were* kinda rough on her," Finley speaks up, earning a glare from the girl.

"Red wouldn't be taking her away, right?" A sudden wave of fear washes over Ryland, and her eyes dart to the front door. "She'd at least give her time to pack her stuff, right?"

Gia shakes her head. "Don't piss yourself. She's just taking her to the hospital."

"Fuck," Ryland mutters. "I hate that fucking school."

"Tell me about it," the two other girls speak in unison, well aware of how she feels. Squeezing her eyes shut, Ryland resists the urge to punch something, knowing the reaction she'll get from Finley.

When Dakota returns home, it's already dark out. The waiting room of the ER was packed, and she had ended up sitting on the floor for 4 hours, waiting to be seen by a doctor. The entire time, Red just looked on disapprovingly. Dakota knows the last thing she needed was a phone call from the school letting her know that one of her girls had been in a fight.

And now, she's home—a new cast on her broken hand, which is even more broken than it was before. Her entire body aches, her head throbs, and the first thing she does when she gets home is pop two of Finley's old sleeping pills. Red doesn't even say anything to her. They're both exhausted, and all Dakota wants to do is crawl under the covers and never come out.

Which is why, at first, she doesn't notice the visitor when she trudges into her bedroom. She doesn't even bother turning on the lights, she just toes off her shoes and tosses her jacket aside.

"Dakota?"

Startled, the girl inhales sharply, stumbling backward. Dakota quickly fumbles for the light switch, groaning and bringing a hand to her head when white light floods her pupils. Her eyes come to focus on Ryland, who sits on the spare bed across the room. She shrinks under Ryland's glare as the girl's eyes scan her up and down.

"You look like shit," Ryland nods once. Dakota just rolls her eyes.

"Yeah, *well*," she mumbles, ignoring the girl and tugging her shirt over her head, digging through her dresser. She slips into an old tank top, wincing when it catches on her cast.

"I heard what happened," Ryland speaks up again. Dakota can't bring herself to look at the girl, so she just shakes her head and slowly pulls down her jeans, her entire body aching when she leans over.

"I got my ass kicked," Dakota mutters, kicking her jeans aside. Now, left in just a tank top and underwear, Ryland can see all the bruises that map across Dakota's torso. Unable to be short with her any longer, Ryland sighs in defeat and stands up, placing a hand on Dakota's shoulder before slipping between her and the dresser. Her eyes scan Dakota's face in concern.

"I'll kill them," she mutters, bringing her hand up to cup the girl's cheek, her thumb ghosting across the swollen skin under her lip. Dakota's eyes shy away from hers, feeling humiliated.

"Sit," Ryland sighs, pushing Dakota back a few steps until the back of her knees touch the bed and she sits down slowly. "Stay here."

Dakota watches as Ryland slips into the hallway, returning from the bathroom with a wet cloth. Carefully, she sits down beside the girl, using a hand to brush the tangled hair out of her face. Slowly, she presses the cloth to the girl's lip, who winces in pain.

"Sorry," Ryland shakes her head, gently dabbing the blood smeared around the girl's mouth. Dakota's eyes radiate sadness and defeat, and Ryland's heart aches. The girl shivers under her touch when Ryland's hand moves up to brush her fingers against the bump on her eyebrow.

"I'm sorry," she repeats herself, subtly noting the glassiness of Dakota's eyes. She's been crying. Swallowing hard, Ryland gently taps Dakota's shoulder and nods, signaling for her to scoot backwards. Dakota does, slowly.

Ryland's hands move up to carefully undo the braids on the side of Dakota's head, already messy and partly undone. Dakota hisses in pain, her scalp still sensitive from the few times hands had managed to grab and yank at her hair. Ryland quickly apologizes, her fingers now moving as gently as possible.

"I'm sorry," Dakota whispers, her voice gravel in the back of her throat. She hangs her head down, feeling Ryland's fingers gently combing through her now-loose hair. The small action brings goosebumps to form on her skin.

Ryland shakes her head. "Don't apologize," she sighs. "I'm not mad. Gia told me what happened." Her fingertips massage the girl's scalp, and Dakota leans her head back slightly. "I'm actually glad you're suspended," she adds. "You shouldn't have to be around them."

"It hurts," Dakota mumbles. Ryland pauses, turning to look at her.

"What does?"

"*Everything*," Dakota shrugs with one shoulder, embarrassed. But Ryland just brushes Dakota's hair out of her face, pressing a soft kiss to her temple. Her lips linger there for a moment and she sighs softly, making Dakota shiver. From behind the girl, she snakes her arms around her waist, clasping her hands together just above her navel. Feeling Ryland's head gently lean against her shoulder, Dakota places her good hand atop Ryland's, squeezing lightly.

"I don't like seeing you like this," Ryland mumbles, her thumb grazing over Dakota's knuckles. But Dakota just sighs, curling her fingers around Ryland's own.

"I don't like *being* like this," she shakes her head, holding up her broken hand and studying the cast in distaste.

"Black?" Ryland notes, raising an eyebrow.

"I got to choose," Dakota nods softly. "I won't take it off this time around." There's a long pause of silence, and Ryland drums her fingers against the cast.

"Dakota?"

The girl lifts her head slightly. "Yeah?"

Ryland hesitates for a moment. "Things are gonna get better, right?"

Dakota pauses. "What do you mean?"

"I just… I feel like I'm always on guard," Ryland breathes in slowly. "It's like… I expect things to go wrong all the time. They always do." Dakota's suddenly aware that Ryland's on the verge of tears, judging by the waver in her voice. "Just… do you…? Do you think one day all this pain will be nothing but a memory?" She pauses. "Things have to look up eventually, right?" There's a pleading tone laced in her words, giving Dakota chills.

"I'd like to hope so," Dakota whispers, feeling Ryland breathe in deeply and rest her head against the back of her shoulder. "If anyone deserves a better future, it's you, Ryland." She feels the girl's breath shake and squeezes her hand.

"Is this about your dad?" Dakota asks carefully, knowing that it's risky. But Ryland just shrugs with one shoulder.

"That too," she says softly, her fingers tracing over Dakota's. "But this isn't any fun, either."

"*This*?"

"You. Being hurt," Ryland whispers, her voice rough. "I don't like it. Don't like thinking about people being mean to you."

"You don't have to think about it," Dakota's quick to shake her head. "I can handle it."

"I can't help it," Ryland mutters, suddenly feeling too vulnerable. She blinks back tears.

"I'm still alive, aren't I?" Dakota looks down to their hands, her bruised knuckles dark and bloody in contrast to Ryland's own. "It's not your battle to fight. It's mine."

"You don't get it, do you?"

Taken off guard by the sudden change in Ryland's voice, Dakota turns around slowly, confusion evident in her features. Their hands detach when she moves to face her, but Dakota quickly finds them again. "What?" she asks quietly, genuine concern in her words. Ryland's breath suddenly catches when she realizes the words on the tip of her tongue. Her jaw shakes and she looks away for a moment, forcing herself to take a deep breath.

"I love you, okay?" her words spill out, half frustration, half desperation. The minute their eyes meet and Ryland realizes what she's said, both girls tense up. Ryland moves to pull her hands away, but Dakota grabs hold of them before she can.

"What?" Dakota's voice is barely a whisper. Ryland's eyes dart away from her own.

"Don't make me say it again," Ryland's voice wavers, suddenly terrified that she's just made a mistake. Dakota pauses, hesitant.

"Ryland..." she shakes her head, giving in and reaching out to cup the girl's cheek, making her face her. "You didn't hear me."

"What?" Ryland shivers, Dakota's thumb ghosting across her skin.

"I told you. The other night," Dakota nods gently. "After your dad's... but you were... you didn't hear..." she shakes her head. "I hadn't even planned on saying it."

Ryland stills, her eyes suddenly searching Dakota's. "Saying what?"

Swallowing her fear, Dakota squeezes Ryland's hand gently. "That I love you," she whispers. "That I love you and... and it really fucking scares me."

Ryland's heart does something weird in her chest and she suddenly feels tears prick at the corners of her eyes. "Scares me too," she nods slowly, blinking back tears. "I've never..." she pauses to take a deep breath. "All my life, love... it just..." she pushes back the sour memories. "It's never been returned."

Dakota's eyebrows furrow together, empathy flickering in her eyes. "It is for me," is all she can whisper before she pulls the girl into a hug, ignoring her soreness as Ryland's arms quickly wrap around her, fingertips clinging to her back as if she's afraid to let go. Dakota just holds her even tighter.

"Please don't be lying to me," Ryland whispers, her voice muffled against the girl's shoulder. Dakota almost immediately shakes her head, feeling tears forming in her own eyes, a rare occurrence.

"Couldn't if I tried," she rests her chin on Ryland's shoulder and rubs circles in her back. "I love you," she repeats herself for good measure, surprised at how simple and effortless the words seem coming out of her mouth. "I do."

Pulling away from the hug, Ryland brings her hands up to Dakota's face, reveling in the intimacy of the moment, in their closeness. "I love you, too," she nods softly, leaning in but hesitating when she remembers the girl's busted lip. Instead, she presses a soft kiss to the corner of the girl's mouth. Dakota's hand cups Ryland's cheek to wipe the few tears that have fallen.

"I'm sorry," Ryland whispers, moving to wipe her own tears. "I'm don't know why I'm so—,"

"It's okay," Dakota shakes her head. "A lot of things are shitty right now. But I can still love you when I'm hurt," she traces her finger across Ryland's jawline, letting her hand drop back down to intertwine their fingers. "That's one thing that doesn't change, yeah?" She gives the girl a sad smile. "And maybe one day I'll love you when we're both happier than we've ever been."

"I like hear you say it," Ryland admits, her voice still shaky. "I was scared you wouldn't…"

"I was scared *you* wouldn't."

Ryland's cheeks flush red and she looks down. "Maybe we need to stop being so scared all the time."

(When they fall asleep that night, Ryland clings to Dakota more than ever before. Everything may be changing around them, and things may be hard, but Dakota's there. And she loves her. And Ryland's found one thing that's constant in the ever changing storm that she calls life. So she holds on, afraid that the wind will carry Dakota far away from her if she doesn't.)

Chapter 18

CABIN FEVER

Within a week's time, Gia, Ryland, and Dakota are all officially high school graduates. They tease Finley about it—knowing she has one more year to go. But however lighthearted they may appear, all three girls are terrified to be thrust into the real world. As much as they may hate high school, it's still a shelter for them. And no matter how unprepared they are, the real world is approaching faster than ever before.

Most of Dakota's time has been spent working on her car, thanks to her suspension. It's a bit difficult with a giant cast on her hand, but she's determined to make their road trip go over without a hitch.

They've split their duties—Gia and Finley planning the route, and Ryland and Dakota in charge of fixing the car and compiling a "*bomb ass summer playlist*"—according to Ryland, who's somehow managed to rig up a speaker system in the car, tapping into the old radio.

Ryland, also, has been avoiding an onslaught of phone calls to the house. But Red had finally forced her to answer, which resulted in an awkward five minute conversation with her father. Long story short, she had no choice but to accept his invitation to attend an awards dinner for his business, along with the rest of his family. She's not looking forward to it, to say the least.

The dinner just so happens to fall on the Friday they're planned on leaving for their road trip. It's also the day of their graduation ceremony, which they're all happy to skip. Good riddance, according to Gia.

Currently, it's Friday afternoon, and Ryland's a bundle of nerves. Gia had helped her get ready for the dinner, pulling her aside, giving her a pep talk, and helping her braid her hair back into a more formal version of her usual ponytail. However, Ryland draws the line when Gia tries to get her in a dress, refusing to wear anything but her jeans. So she settles for a dark purple shirt that the girl lends her.

She finds Dakota outside, her feet sticking out from underneath her car. With a heavy sigh, Ryland sits down in the driver's seat, her the tips of her shoes just barely touching the asphalt. Dakota quickly slides out from underneath.

"Nervous?" she asks, her eyes scanning Ryland as she rises to her feet. "You look good."

Ryland just mutters a "thanks" and shakes her head. Dakota frowns. Compared to Ryland, she's dressed for anything *but* a fancy dinner. She's clad in jean shorts and a white t-shirt, a rag hanging out of her back pocket. Her shirt, hands, and face are covered in smudges of dark grease. Earlier, Finley had teased her for looking like a Dalmatian. Her hair is down, but sections are still wavy from her braids scattered throughout. And of course, there's still a faint purple bruise around her eye.

"When does he get here?" Dakota asks, leaning against the car and studying Ryland's face.

"Any minute now."

"If it makes you feel any better, we leave as soon as you get back," she nods softly. "Oh, and I found an air mattress in the basement. Figured that would help."

"Do we even have any more room in the car?" Ryland raises an eyebrow.

"We'll make it fit," Dakota shrugs, slapping her palm against the roof of the car. "Gia can sit in Finley's lap or something."

"What if I embarrass them?"

Dakota lifts her head, taken aback by Ryland's sudden question. Sighing, she looks around to make sure the coast is clear before leaning down and kissing Ryland's forehead. "Stop worrying. Just talk comics with Jonah." She flashes the girl a hopeful smile.

Ten minutes pass, and Dakota winds up back under the car, tinkering with something and dramatically narrating what she's doing, in hopes it will keep Ryland's mind off of things. When she hears the rumble of tires in the driveway, she moves to scoot out from underneath, but she's stopped by Ryland, who nudges her foot.

"Don't," Ryland's voice is hushed. She stands up. "I'll see you tonight."

However, before Ryland can make her way to the car, the door opens, and the man slides out of the driver's seat. Ryland tenses.

"This yours?" he asks, nodding to the bright red car. Ryland's quick to shake her head.

"It's another one of the girls'," she says softly. He takes a few steps forward.

"Chrysler?"

"Newport." Another voice appears as Dakota slides out from underneath, shooting Ryland a look to silently assure her it's okay. She stands up, tugging the rag out of her back pocket and wiping off her hands. "1967," she nods. "Needs a new paint job, but she runs like a dream."

Ryland watches worriedly as the man studies Dakota, unsure if she should be relieved or terrified when he extends his hand to her. Dakota doesn't flinch, though. She quickly shakes it.

"Lance," he nods, glancing back to Ryland, but making no mention of their relation.

"Dakota," she shoves the rag back in her pocket. To the side, she can see how visibly nervous Ryland is. It's killing her.

"After the place John Lennon was assassinated?"

She shakes her head, taken aback by his random knowledge. "It means friend. It's Native American," she nods slowly. "My mom was a painter and she used to get close the families on the reservation near us when she was working."

"Ah, well, that's a bit more positive" he laughs. Before he can say anything else, the car horn blares from behind them, startling all three. Dakota takes the opportunity to hurry over to Ryland's side, placing a hand on her shoulder.

"We're gonna be late!" the blonde woman in the front seat leans out the window. Impulsively, Dakota pulls Ryland into a "*friendly*" hug.

"Good luck," she whispers as they pull away. All Ryland can offer her is a nervous half smile, and Dakota watches as the car pulls out of the driveway. She's never been religious, but she finds herself whispering a soft prayer under her breath, willing for Ryland's night to go well.

It's dark by the time Ryland returns home. And amidst all the chaos, Dakota's the only one who can tell that something is wrong. Gia and Finley are running around, shoving the last of their things into the back of the car. But Dakota's eyes are on Ryland from the moment she walks in the front door. She starts to move towards her, but stops herself. Ryland's already storming up the stairs.

When Ryland returns downstairs, dressed in something more comfortable, Dakota decides on keeping her distance. She hopes the road trip will be enough to get Ryland's mind off of things.

"And you've got everything you need?" Red watches them lug the last of their things into the trunk. "You've got your medicine, Finley?"

"Mhm," Finley reassures her, holding up her backpack. "Right here."

"And you, Ryland?"

All Red earns in return is a curt nod and a grunt from the girl. But no one pays much attention, except for Dakota, who quietly slips back into the house when Ryland does.

"You excited?" she asks, bending down to help the girl reach her keys that had fallen to the ground. Ryland just meets Dakota's eyes, shrugging softly.

"Talk later?" Dakota asks, looking to her in concern as they head back outside.

"Whatever," Ryland mutters, unable to look at the girl. Dakota's left standing on the front porch, gazing longingly after Ryland. But there's not much time for her to dwell on this, because soon she's in the driver's seat, with Red telling them to have fun at summer camp, and Gia snickering from the back.

Finley's the navigator, seated in the front of the car beside Dakota, a huge map folded out in front of her.

"First stop, Lake Tahoe," she nods, a smile tugging at her lips. Dakota glances in the rearview mirror, frowning when she sees Ryland staring quietly out the window, slumped back in her seat.

Dakota fights the urge to say something, knowing not to bring anything up until they're alone.

Within an hour, everyone's asleep except for Dakota. She's taken a nap during the day, knowing that she would be driving through the night. She steals a glance at Ryland, who's half slumped against the window, fast asleep. She aches to know how the dinner went.

Dakota's driven for about two hours by the time Gia wakes up. Rubbing her eyes, the blonde leans over to study the map in Finley's lap.

"Pull over," she nudges Dakota's shoulder. "My turn."

"But I'm not even—,"

"*I've got it.*"

Although she's confused, Dakota doesn't question the girl. She just pulls over, passing Gia the keys and taking a moment to stretch her legs before she circles the car. As the engine roars to life once more, she slides into the backseat beside Ryland. Noticing the girl's brace is still on, incredibly tight, Dakota sighs and quietly moves to undo it. Pushing it aside, she neglects her seatbelt so she can lay down, curled up with her head resting in Ryland's lap.

She drifts in and out of sleep for a while, the ride rough and bumpy. She's just dozed off for the millionth time when the car rolls to a stop. Confused, she lifts her head.

"Are we already there?" she raises an eyebrow, her voice raspy. But Gia just yanks the keys from the ignition and shakes her head.

"Then why are we stopped?" Dakota rubs her eyes and leans forward to gaze out the window. "Where are we?"

"Stay here," Gia warns her. But just then, Finley's stirred awake by the commotion. She furrows her eyebrows, looking to Gia.

"*Wha…?*" she blinks a few times. "We're here?" However, she answers her own question when she gazes forward, her eyes landing on the dim fluorescent sign of the run-down apartment complex they've parked in front of. She whips her head to look at Gia, wide eyes filled with worry. "*No.*"

Gia glares at her, moving to get out of the car. Within seconds, Finley's scrambling out of her seat and circling the car, grabbing Gia's wrist before she can make it to the door. This stirs Ryland awake, who looks to Dakota in confusion.

"What are you doing?" Finley hisses, her grip on Gia's wrist tightening. "Do you have any idea how much trouble you could get into?"

But Gia just glares at her, her decision already made. She yanks her arm from Finley's grip, storming off around the building. Finley brings a hand to her forehead, exhaling slowly.

"Wild guess, but this wouldn't happen to be where her family is, would it?" Ryland turns to Finley as soon as she plops back into her seat, defeated.

"This can't end well," Finley huffs, leaning to rest her head against the dashboard. "This can't end well at all."

Dakota and Ryland look to one another, unsure of what to say. But all their unspoken questions are answered when Gia reemerges from around the building, holding the hand of a small girl—her sister—clad in a cream colored nightgown and clutching a stuffed rabbit to her chest. Gia hurries over to the car, yanking open Dakota's door.

"Make room," she nods quickly. Dakota scoots over, squished up against Ryland as Gia ushers the smaller girl into the car, tossing a pink backpack onto the floor.

The car tires squeal as Gia speeds out of the parking lot, eyes glued to the road.

Finley glances to the backseat, where the small girl sits, wide eyed and hugging the stuffed bunny to her chest. Glancing to Gia and sighing heavily, Finley turns back to the girl.

"Don't be scared," she says softly, giving Gia's sister a reassuring smile. "It's just a fun little vacation."

Slowly, Delia's eyes scan the car, studying the three other girls. She turns to Dakota. "What's your name?"

"Dakota," the dark haired girl says softly, glancing to Gia, who refuses to look at her.

"*Dakota,*" Delia repeats her, yawning and dragging out her name. And within ten minutes, she's fast asleep, her legs curled up into her chest, tucked into her stretched out nightgown.

When Finley looks back and notices she's asleep, her demeanor finally changes. Her eyes dart to Gia, and she quickly shakes her head. "What were you thinking?"

"*Don't,*" Gia deadpans, her eyes on the road. Dakota leans forward.

"Finley's right," she nods. "You can't just steal a kid."

"She's my *sister,*" Gia mutters. "You don't understand."

"She *does* understand," Ryland speaks up in her defense. "She understands that you're gonna get the cops called on our asses the moment your mom realizes she's gone."

"She won't call the cops," Gia mutters. "I made that clear. I left a note."

"Made what clear?"

"That if she calls the cops, I tell them how much of a shit mother she is," Gia rolls her eyes, curling and uncurling her fingers around the steering wheel. "Now, if you'd calm the fuck down, I'd like to give my sister a little break from the hellhole she's been living in. I'd appreciate it if you didn't make her feel like a fugitive." Her voice is stern, venom laced in her words.

Dakota, Ryland, and Finley all exchange glances, taken aback by Gia's sudden shift in mood. Finley just sighs, slumping back in her seat.

"You better know what you're doing, Gia."

By the time they reach Lake Tahoe, the sun is just starting to rise, peeking over the mountains.

"Koda," Ryland nudges the sleeping girl's shoulder. "Koda, get up, we're here."

Blinking a few times, Dakota lifts her head, taking in her surroundings. She furrows her eyebrows. "Where are we?"

"Gia tried a little off-roading," Ryland laughs, holding out her hand and helping Dakota out of the car. "She claims this is the best campsite this side of the lake," she half smiles. "Come see for yourself."

Dakota lets Ryland lead her past Finley and Gia, setting up tents, and over to the clearing in the trees. Ryland nudges her forward. "See?"

"Woah," Dakota whispers, making Ryland laugh. Her eyes quickly soak in the view of the lake, but then she's turning back to Ryland, her eyes concerned.

"Are you okay?" She asks quietly. "Last night you were… off."

But Ryland's quick to shake her head. "It was fine. I just don't fit in with them."

"You fit in with us," Dakota looks to her hopefully, following her back over to the other girls. Ryland rolls her eyes.

"I fit in with a gang of misfits," Ryland teases, motioning between the both of them with a playful smile. "What an accomplishment."

"Shut up," Dakota laughs, nudging her shoulder. She's instantly relieved to see Ryland in a better mood than yesterday, now able to really enjoy their crazy vacation.

Throughout the course of the day, Dakota finds she's completely forgotten about all of the things that had been weighing heavy on her mind during the past week. The same change is evident in all of the girls, especially Gia, who's at ease now that her sister is safe under her protection.

Gia and Finley swim with Delia for most of the day while Dakota lays on the beach with Ryland, stealing kisses when their backs are turned. Ryland doesn't mind that she isn't able to go in the water, the sun warms her skin and Dakota makes good company.

After they've had dinner, just as the sun starts to set, Dakota gets a fire going, and they all gather around to keep warm. They talk and joke around for a while, but eventually it gets late, and Dakota and Ryland are the only ones left by the fire, a knitted blanket draped around both of their shoulders.

"This is nice," Ryland says softly, snaking an arm around Dakota's waist and pulling her closer now that they're alone. Humming contently, Dakota lets her head rest on Ryland's shoulder.

"I wish we could just stay here forever," Dakota sighs. Her eyes are fixed on the fire, watching tiny embers shoot up and disappear into the night sky. She leans into Ryland's side.

"You and me both, tiny," Ryland laughs softly, kissing the top of the girl's head. "Too bad we just can't run away."

"If only," Dakota nods, pausing for a moment. "Do you want to talk about last night?"

"The dinner?"

Dakota nods. Ryland just sighs and throws a stick into the fire.

"There's not much to talk about," she shrugs. "I found out he owns some super successful computer company."

"Boring," Dakota mumbles, making Ryland laugh.

"He seemed to like you," Ryland adds. Dakota raises her eyebrows.

"What's that mean? That I've got his approval?" she teases.

"We don't need his approval," Ryland shakes her head. "Plus, god knows how he'd react."

"React to what?"

Ryland shrugs. "Us," she motions between them, but Dakota still feigns cluelessness.

"What about us?"

Ryland looks to her. "That we're… you know… together?"

"Like best friends?" Dakota teases, making Ryland roll her eyes when she realizes what the girl is doing.

"Funny," Ryland pushes the girl's shoulder with her own. But Dakota pauses, her eyes scanning Ryland's face.

"Wait, really," she shakes her head. "What are we?"

Taken aback, Ryland turns to look at Dakota, her eyebrows stitching together. "We're just…" she gestures, struggling to find a word. "Together."

"Like boyfriend girlfriend?"

Ryland can't help but laugh. "We're both girls, Koda."

Dakota's face drops for a moment. "*We're both girls*," she repeats Ryland's words, as if she's just now realizing this for the first time. Ryland's eyes quickly scan her face.

"Is that a bad thing?"

Dakota shakes her head quickly. "I just… It just…"

"It scares you?" Ryland asks softly. Dakota nods, swallowing.

"It scares me," she confirms, looking back to Ryland. "Is that bad?"

Ryland shakes her head. "Scares me, too."

"I never really thought about it," Dakota admits. "I don't... when I'm with you, I don't stop to remind myself that you're a girl too."

"Neither do I," Ryland purses her lips. "I don't even know why it scares me. I didn't have a crazy dad like Gia's, I didn't..." she pauses. "I think it's just because it's different from what's '*normal.*'"

"Girls being with girls?"

Ryland nods. "It's still foreign ground. For both of us."

"It's stupid," Dakota mumbles, kicking a pebble towards the fire. "Why does it even matter? I don't love you *because you're a girl.* I love you because you're you. Doesn't matter if you're a girl or a guy."

"So you're bi?"

"No," Dakota shakes her head. "I'm just not stupid enough to let something that small dictate who I should and shouldn't love." She chucks a handful of pine needles into the fire. "Fuck putting people in boxes."

Ryland laughs softly, knowing how much Dakota hates being restrained. She pulls her closer, resting her chin atop her head. "You're cute when you're angry."

"Am I cute because I'm a girl?" Dakota raises an eyebrow.

"You're cute because I love you, idiot."

"Do you *love* me because I'm a girl?"

"I love you because you're you, Dakota."

"There we go," Dakota smiles. "Problem solved. Now we don't have to be scared anymore."

"If only it were that easy," Ryland sighs. Dakota squeezes her hand reassuringly.

"Someday we'll have it all figured out."

Chapter 19

VACANCY

Over the course of the next week, the only worry any of the girls have is whether they'll make it to their next bathroom stop in time. Delia's not much trouble, surprisingly enough. She keeps to herself for the most part, wandering down the beach and collecting seashells, which she makes into necklaces.

One thing Dakota's notices, though, is how quickly the younger Dawson sister will latch onto anyone willing to give her attention. While stopping in Cannery Row, Dakota had bought the girl a snow globe she had her eye on, and for the rest of the day, Delia was glued to her side. Ryland had even pointed it out, wondering aloud if Gia had ever been the same.

They're on the sixth and final day of the trip, driving back down Highway 1, along the coast. Dakota's transfixed by the sight. The sun is just starting to set, casting a golden glow over everything. Ryland, however, is exhausted, and fast asleep against Dakota's shoulder.

They've spent the day in Santa Cruz. Dakota and Gia had attempted surfing while Ryland and Finley opted for a safer approach, taking Delia to the carnival rides at the boardwalk. When they met up later that day, Ryland was limping more than usual, so Dakota had discreetly sent Gia and Finley off to buy dinner while she and Ryland sat with Delia and built sand castles.

With Gia driving, and Finley and Ryland already fast asleep, it's all too easy for Dakota to doze off, pressed between Ryland and the window. However, before she's in a deep sleep, a soft voice lulls her back awake.

"Gia?" Delia sits against the opposite door, playing with a string of beads she's collected. For some reason, when Gia glances back in the rear view mirror, Dakota quickly fakes sleep.

"Yeah?" Gia speaks up softly, her voice losing the usual callousness she uses on everyone else.

Delia pauses, wrapping the strand of beads around her finger. "Do I have to go home now?"

Dakota hears Gia sigh heavily from the front seat. Delia lets the string of beads unravel and fall into her lap.

"I like it better here," Delia adds. "Why can't I just stay with you?"

"I wish I knew," Gia shakes her head.

"Mom's not the same anymore. Not since dad went away."

Gia pauses. "Does she ever hurt you or Jax?"

Delia shakes her head. "Jax is never home. He always goes away to a friend's house." The small girl plays anxiously with her hair. "Mom isn't any fun to be around."

"What about Aunt Em?" Gia glances back to the girl. Delia shrugs.

"Jax says that we're *nuisances*," she nods. "At first Mom said we were gonna move to a perfect cottage in the country, but now she doesn't even look at the house pictures Aunt Em circles for her."

There's a long pauses of silence, and Gia inhales slowly, her grip on the steering wheel tightening. "It's that bad, Dee?"

"Kinda," Delia mumbles. "I liked it a lot better when you lived with us."

"I know you did," Gia sighs. "I'm sorry I left. I shouldn't have tried to run in the first place."

But Delia just shrugs. "I like you here, too," she lifts her head. "You're more fun. Back home you were always too tired to play with us, remember?" Gia just nods softly from the front seat of the car.

"Jax wants to visit dad," Delia blurts out. Through narrowly closed eyes, Dakota sees Gia tense up.

"He does?"

"Mhm," Delia nods. "Aunt Em says she's gonna take him to visit."

"Oh."

"She asked if I wanted to go too. But Jax told me I'm not allowed to."

"Why not?"

"He says I'm a liar."

Gia leans her head back against the seat. "Do you want to go see him?"

"I… I don't know," Delia looks down, still toying with her beads. "Mom says I should forgive him cause' I'm too young to understand. She said that '*now's not the time for overdramatics.*'"

"She doesn't believe you?"

Delia shrugs. "She knows he hurt me. But she says that's just how all dads keep their kids from being bad."

"You know that's not true, right?" Gia's quick to reply. "You know dads aren't supposed to hit their kids like that."

"I dunno," Delia mumbles, her eyes on her lap.

"Hey," Gia's meets Delia's eyes through the rear view mirror. "Listen to me, Dee. I'm gonna figure something out, alright? I'll do whatever I can to get you out of there."

"Mom says you're going to hell."

"Then I'd hate to see where she winds up," Gia mutters, shaking her head. "I'm going to figure something out," she holds back her hand, wiggling her pinky finger. "Promise."

Delia thinks for a few moments before leaning forward and slowly locking their pinkies together. "What about Jax?"

"What about him?"

"Will you help him too?"

"Only if he wants help."

Leaning back in her seat, Delia hugs her arms around her torso. "I just don't get it. Daddy followed all the Ten Commandments." There's a long pause of silence before Gia finally speaks up.

"Sometimes it takes more than a book of rules to determine if someone's a good person."

Dakota eventually falls asleep, only stirred awake when she feels the car slow to a stop.

"My turn?" she asks, rubbing her eyes. But Gia just keeps her hands on the wheel.

"We've got a problem."

"What's going on?" Ryland wakes, the warmth of Dakota's body no longer next to her.

"I don't know what happened," Gia shakes her head. "It said we had half a tank left but then the engine started vibrating. I literally saw the needle drop straight to E," she points to the gas gauge.

"So what's that mean?" Ryland lifts her head.

"That we're out of gas," Dakota nods, earning an eye roll from Ryland.

"I know that, idiot," Ryland nudges her. "I mean, what do we do *now*?"

"We walk," Gia sighs, leaning over to shake Finley awake. "There's got to be a gas station somewhere." Dakota's eyes quickly dart to Ryland, but the girl is already halfway out the car.

"Then let's hurry up," Ryland nods, avoiding Dakota's questioning gaze.

And that's how they end up trekking down the side of a dusty desert highway, with only the last few rays of sun to light the way. Delia skips ahead, excited at the prospect of an adventure. Dakota, however, sticks back with Ryland. It doesn't take an expert to tell that the girl's in pain. But she knows better than to bring it up.

After an hour, Dakota's relieved when they *finally* reach some sort of civilization. There's dim, dusky neon signs in the distance and everyone seems to pick up the pace. Dakota hurries over to Gia, grabbing her arm.

"There's a motel across the street," Dakota keeps her voice hushed. "There's no way I'm letting Ryland walk another hour back to the car tonight."

"Fine with me," Gia nods, not putting up a fight like Dakota had expected. "I'm exhausted, anyway. I'll take Finley with me in the morning and we'll bring the car back here."

When Dakota tells Ryland this, she doesn't miss how relieved she is. And so, they find themselves crossing the street towards a run-down motel. A few of the outdoor rooms sport the blue flickering glow of a television through the windows. Dakota's pleasantly surprised when they end up purchasing two rooms across from one another. It's no question who's rooming with who.

"This place is prehistoric," Ryland notes, coughing and shaking out the curtains in their small room. Dakota just nods in agreement, tinkering with the lock on the door. Ryland sits down on the bed.

"You didn't have to do that, you know."

Dakota lifts her head, raising a questioning eyebrow. "Do what?"

"Make us stay here," Ryland leans down, undoing her brace with skilled hands. She's done this so many times that it's practically muscle memory by now.

"I..." Dakota opens her mouth to argue but struggles to find her words. But Ryland just shrugs.

"Can't say I'm not thankful," she adds with a sigh. Dakota bites her lip, sitting down carefully beside the girl.

"That bad?" Her voice is quiet.

Ryland nods. "More than usual."

"Here," Dakota digs through Ryland's bag and tosses her a change of clothes. "This good?"

"Yeah," Ryland gives her a sad smile. "Thanks."

"I'm gonna take a shower," Dakota gestures to the bathroom. "Yell if you need anything."

However, the peace and quiet is interrupted only minutes later when an ear piercing scream echoes from the bathroom and Dakota comes scrambling out, clutching a t-shirt to her chest and kicking the door shut with her foot. Ryland sits up quickly.

"What's going on?"

Catching her breath, Dakota tugs the t-shirt over her head, leaping from her spot on the floor and onto the bed, which creaks an unhealthy amount. "Either that was a normal sized mouse or an abnormally big spider," she whispers, shaking her head.

Ryland stifles a laugh, raising an eyebrow at the girl. "What happened to the shower?"

"It can wait," Dakota's quick to change her plans. "I'd rather *not* have company."

"Wow," Ryland teases. "I never thought I'd see the day when rough and tumble Dakota Quinn gets taken down by a tiny little spider."

"More like a *dog sized* spider," Dakota shakes her head. "I am not risking my life in there."

"Are you sure this is the same girl who got yelled at for taking her board too far out during the biggest waves of the day?"

"That was worth it," Dakota concludes, falling onto her back and gazing up at the ceiling. "Mouthful of sand and all."

"I don't understand you sometimes," Ryland laughs, scooting back on the bed. Dakota frowns.

"You're gonna sleep in jeans?" she asks carefully. All she gets in return is a one-shouldered shrug.

"You can't get them off, can you?" Dakota looks to her. Ryland shrinks under her gaze. But Dakota's eyes are soft, gentle, and Ryland can't find an ounce of dishonesty in them. She shrugs again.

Sighing, Dakota stands up and extends a hand to Ryland, who just stares at it in confusion.

"Come on," Dakota nods. "I'll help you."

Ryland feels like a helpless little kid, but she knows, deep down, that she won't be able to do it on her own. So hesitantly, she takes Dakota's hand.

It takes a bit of trial and error, but after a few minutes, Ryland's changed into a pair of plaid sleep shorts and is laying on the bed, paging through a book she's brought along.

"What's happening now?" Dakota glances to her through the mirror on the door, where she stands braiding her hair. "Did they kill the bad guy yet?"

"He's not a bad guy," Ryland shakes her head. "His character is a representation of the welfare system in America."

Dakota furrows her eyebrows together. "I don't get it."

Ryland sighs. "No, they haven't killed him yet." She's startled when Dakota flings herself on the bed beside her.

"You almost done that chapter?" Dakota looks to her hopefully, but Ryland doesn't notice, her nose is still buried in the book.

"Three more pages," she nods. Dakota frowns.

"How much longer?"

Ryland finally lifts her head. "What are you—?"

"Shh," Dakota whispers, catching Ryland off guard when she pushes the book down, out of Ryland's gaze, and leans in to catch the girl's lips with her own. Ryland's breath hitches in her throat and she scrambles to mark her page, tossing the book aside as Dakota climbs on top of her.

"This okay?" Dakota asks, catching her breath. With wide eyes, Ryland looks up to her, nodding softly.

Dakota laughs breathily, her eyes skittering down to meet Ryland's once more. This time, Ryland's prepared when she kisses her again, and her arms wrap around Dakota's shoulders, fingers coming up to play with the baby hairs at the back of the girl's neck. Ryland giggles into the kiss when she feels Dakota shiver.

"Rude," Dakota teases when the kiss breaks, playfully dodging Ryland's advances when she tries to kiss her again. Ryland whines, letting her head fall back against the pillow.

"Need something?" Dakota smirks, her face impossibly close to Ryland's. The girl underneath her manages to keep a straight face, until Dakota starts trailing her lips up her jawline, which is when Ryland loses the battle of wills and balls her hand in Dakota's shirt, tugging her into a kiss, to which Dakota doesn't argue.

"I love you," Dakota mumbles against her lips. She tilts her head, their noses brushing together, before her kisses begin to slow down. Her fingers ghost across Ryland's sides, which Ryland doesn't think much of, until she feels those same fingers begin to toy with the hem of her shirt. Something instinctual takes over in that moment, and Dakota nearly gets the wind knocked of her when both of Ryland's hands fly up to her chest to separate them.

All Ryland can do is shake her head, and Dakota immediately pulls her hands away from the girl, sitting up on her knees. Her light eyes search Ryland's questioningly.

"*No*," Ryland breathes out. Dakota's confusion is replaced with fear, and there's a look of hurt that flashes across her face, but she's quickly moving from atop Ryland, creating a safe amount of space between them. Catching her breath, Dakota's wide eyes look to Ryland for answers.

"That's what you're supposed to say, right?" Ryland's voice shakes, her pupils huge. "Right?"

"I-I don't know what you're—,"

"You're supposed to say no," Ryland shakes her head, a far-away look in her eyes. "If you don't want it, you say no, right? So then when you're in the courtroom they won't think you're just overreacting and then—,"

"*Ryland*," Dakota cuts off Ryland's nervous rambling, her voice grounding the girl. Ryland's mouth hangs open for a few seconds before she clamps it shut. It takes all of Dakota's restraint to keep her from moving towards the girl. But she keeps her distance, knowing they've both entered foreign territory. Part of Dakota understands, though, and she sits down slowly.

"Ryland… I would never—,"

"I'm sorry," Ryland sits up quickly, shaking her head as if she's just awoken from some sort of trance. "It's not you, I just… I just—,"

"Hey," Dakota shakes her head. "Breathe."

Inhaling slowly, Ryland hesitates to meet Dakota's eyes. There's a long pause of silence before she speaks again.

"I can't," Ryland swallows hard. "I'm sorry, I just… I'm not… It's too…"

"Ryland," Dakota starts to move forward but freezes. Her eyes dart to Ryland, a silent question, and when she's met with no resistance she quickly finds the girl's hand and cups it between her own. "Don't apologize."

"But you—,"

"I shouldn't have," Dakota shakes her head. "I wasn't thinking."

"I'm sorry."

Dakota holds up her hands as if she's surrendering. "I'm not mad."

"I'm just not used to…"

"I know," Dakota whispers gently, moving to lay down beside the girl. "Then now isn't the right time," she shrugs. "No big deal."

"You're not mad?"

"Of course not," Dakota looks to her in disbelief. "I would never even think about… *you know*."

"I don't deserve you," Ryland mumbles, shaking her head. Within seconds, Dakota is sitting up, confused.

"Are you kidding me?" Her eyes search Ryland's. "Ryland... I'm not a luxury item," she shakes her head, squeezing the girl's hand. "I'm just a decent human being," she laughs softly. "You deserve all that and more. You deserve the world."

Ryland thinks about her words for a few moment before shaking her head. "I don't want the world," she whispers. "I'm fine here with just you and me in this shitty hotel room." She gives the girl a soft smile, tugging on Dakota's hand. Dakota immediately pulls her closer, resting her head on her shoulder.

"Just you, me, and the giant spider rat," Dakota mumbles, making Ryland laugh. Dakota lifts her head, studying the girl's face for a few moments. "I'm serious though, Ryland. I'm not as great as you think I am."

"Eh, you know, maybe you're right," Ryland teases. "You kinda suck."

Dakota knows Ryland's changing the subject, well aware that she can only handle so much seriousness for one day. So she just mumbles a "*very funny*" and curls up against Ryland's side, absentmindedly playing with the girl's fingers.

"Dakota?"

"Hm?"

"You don't give yourself enough credit."

When Dakota's awoken, she assumes it's time to get back on the road. But, confusion washes over her when she realizes the room is still pitch black, and the digital clock beside the bed blinks 2:42.

"You awake?" Ryland's voice is quiet, her hand on the girl's shoulder. Dakota rolls over to face her.

"I am now."

Ryland hesitates. "I need to tell you something."

"Right now?"

'I-I…"

Dakota sits up, suddenly concerned. "What's going on?"

"Don't freak out," Ryland grabs Dakota's arm, knowing that if Dakota makes a big deal out of it, she won't be able to avoid it either. "It's about the dinner."

"With your dad?"

Ryland nods.

"I *knew* something happened," Dakota clenches her jaw. Ryland tenses, hesitating for a few moments. The words are on the tip of her tongue. She takes a deep breath.

"My dad…" she nods slowly. "He wants to pay for my college."

Dakota's eyes widen almost immediately. "Really?"

"Really. He talked to me about it before—,"

She's cut off when Dakota wraps her in a tight hug, catching her off guard. "That's amazing, Ryland," the girl smiles widely. "That's like… your dream."

But Ryland's quick to pull away from the hug, shaking her head. "You don't get it, Dakota," she places both hands on the girl's shoulders. "Going to school is my dream. Taking someone else's pity money isn't."

Confused, Dakota cocks her head to the side, eyebrows stitching together. She gives herself a moment to think. "So it's a pride thing."

"What?"

"You won't accept his help because you're too scared to admit you need it," Dakota says carefully.

"I…" Ryland hesitates. "I can't do it. I can't owe him anything."

"But it's your dream…" Dakota's eyes search hers.

"I *know*," Ryland's voice turns sharp. "I know it is. But… I just…"

"You're scared," Dakota notes. Ryland sighs in defeat.

"I'm scared," she admits, feeling Dakota's hand find hers under the blankets. "Why would he want to do that in the first place? What does he want from me?"

Dakota shrugs softly. "Maybe he's doing it out of the kindness of his heart, maybe he's doing it to try and ease his guilt." She squeezes Ryland's hand. "Either way, Ryland, this is a huge opportunity. And from what you've told me, I don't think this will make a significant dent in his bank account." Dakota pauses, noticing the conflicted look on Ryland's face. Her voice turns to a soft whisper. "Maybe it's time for you to be selfish for once."

"But what if…"

"Don't start imagining what could go wrong, Ryland," Dakota shakes her head. "If he ever starts to use it against you, you stop taking his money and figure another way around it. You always do."

With a deep breath, Ryland runs her thumb over the back of Dakota's hand, a silent reassurance. "I'll think about it," she nods once.

"That's all I ask," Dakota whispers, relaxing back down into the bed beside Ryland. "I know how much it means to you."

Ryland just nods softly, her thoughts racing. "I don't want to go back home," she admits. "I don't want reality anymore."

"This week *was* nice, wasn't it?" Dakota hums softly. "Let's just stay here forever."

Ryland can't help but laugh quietly, a sound Dakota never grows tired of. She pulls Dakota closer, letting the girl settle into her side.

"You turn eighteen soon," Dakota whispers hesitantly. It's something they're both been trying to avoid, pushing it to the back of their minds, in hopes that it won't happen at all. But they both know well enough that Ryland's birthday is approaching faster than ever. It bothers Dakota more than she's letting on.

"Are you counting down the days?" Ryland teases, but her expression softens when Dakota just shrugs.

"What happens then?" Dakota looks to her anxiously. "Where will you go?"

"Not far," Ryland shakes her head. "Me and Gia have been looking at places right outside the city. So you and Finley can come visit whenever you like."

"But Gia isn't eighteen yet."

"She will be," Ryland nods. "Her birthday's a little over a month after mine."

"So you'll be by yourself in an apartment for that long."

Ryland raises an eyebrow. "Are you worried about me?"

All she gets in return is a soft shrug from Dakota. "That's a big change."

"I've handled my share of big changes," Ryland reassures her, humming softly. "At least I have control over this one."

"But you're not scared?" Dakota looks up to her.

"Terrified," Ryland laughs. "But excited, too."

"But what about me and Finley? You're leaving us behind," Dakota pouts, teasingly.

"I'm sure Red will bring in new people," Ryland nods. "But you'll be eighteen soon, too. And then you can hightail it out of the system."

"And then what?"

"That's up to you, tiny."

"I'll be able to see my brother again," Dakota notes. Ryland quirks an eyebrow.

"You don't sound too excited."

"I am," Dakota shakes her head. "I'm just... scared. I don't want him thinking we can just run off and relocate again."

"He would do that?"

Dakota gives her a soft nod. "But I like it here. I like California."

"I like you here, too," Ryland half smiles. "Now quit worrying. We've got time."

"Not much," Dakota mumbles. But Ryland just shakes her head.

"We've got tonight," she squeezes Dakota's hand. "One step at a time."

Early the next morning, even before the sun's fully risen, the girls pile back into the car, making the final stretch home. Dakota's driving, making Ryland pass her up apple slices as she does so.

It's a teary goodbye for Delia, who refuses to let go of Gia until their mother appears to pull her away. A heated conversation ensues between Gia and her mother, but she refuses to talk about it once she storms back over to the car, simply ordering Dakota to "get us home."

And by the time they get home, they've agreed on a story of how their week at "summer camp" went—giving Red no reason to suspect that they were anywhere else.

That night, when Dakota tiptoes into Ryland's room and crawls into bed beside her, she assumes the girl is already asleep.

Which is why she's startled when—as she's slipping under the blankets—Ryland's voice appears.

"I think I'm gonna do it."

Dakota jumps, lifting her head. "Huh?"

"I just called my dad," Ryland whispers. "I think I'm gonna do it."

"College?"

Ryland nods. "On a few conditions," she adds. "He lets me pay as much as I can, and he promises to never use it against me."

"Fair enough," Dakota nods, smiling softly. "Are you excited?"

Judging by the smile that Ryland fails to fight back, she's more than excited. Dakota just leans down to kiss her, whispering her own excitement against the girl's lips.

Chapter 20

MANY LONG GOODBYES

Summer seems to be flying by. Ryland and Gia have been wrapped up in apartment hunting. Dakota has become Ryland's personal chauffeur, taking her to college visits multiple times a week. She doesn't mind, though. It's worth being able to see the light in Ryland's eyes when she rambles on about her own excitement.

Dakota even tags along on a few, feeling wide eyed and out of place in the expansive lecture halls, surrounded by kids her age who know exactly what they want to do with their lives. It's a bit unsettling. While she sits next to Ryland, who goes on and on about all the majors that interest her, Dakota can't help but think of herself. What will she do? Even if she had all the money in the world, she's not sure if college is for her. It comes easy to Ryland—she's smart. But Dakota doesn't thrive in a classroom. While Ryland reads books, Dakota hangs upside down and carves vines into the bed posts. While Ryland watches long documentaries that Finley fishes out of thrift store boxes, Dakota's outside, trying to replace the headlights on her car with blue light bulbs. And while Ryland lights up at the idea of going to school, Dakota shrinks at the mere mention of a classroom.

Ryland tries to talk to her about it, even offering to help her find scholarships, going as far as to leave brochures on Dakota's nightstand. But every time, Dakota changes the subject. That's how she deals with things—she avoids them at all costs. She winds up snapping at Ryland, saying how she doesn't have someone to pay the bills for her. Ryland doesn't take it personally, but after that incident she does her best to avoid the topic.

All the pent up worry and frustration about her own future is what eventually pushes Dakota to agree to accompany Finley for three weeks, working as a camp counselor in Nevada. The pay is fine, and she figures three weeks will be enough time to clear her head and keep herself busy. Ryland's surprised when Dakota presents her with the news, but Dakota exaggerates and says Finley had begged her to go because Red wouldn't allow her to travel alone.

But there's a catch—the camp starts the day after Ryland's birthday, meaning the latest Dakota and Finley can leave is 3am the morning after. Ryland's not too excited at the prospect of them being separated for three weeks, but Dakota promises to write as often as possible. But for the time being, they try not to focus on it.

So, in the long weeks of summer leading up to their departure, Finley and Dakota team up. While Ryland and Gia begin the final stretch in hunting for apartments, Finley and Dakota huddle together in Finley's room, planning Ryland's 18th birthday. The girl may have let it slip at dinner that she'd never had a real birthday party, and Finley and Dakota had immediately exchanged knowing looks from across the table.

(Later that night, when Dakota had brought it up, Ryland admitted to never even knowing when her real birthday was until she was fourteen. Dakota burns July 2nd into her brain, promising to never forget it.)

So now, with only a week left until Ryland turns eighteen, things start to pick up. Ryland and Gia finally decide on an apartment, a small two bedroom space just outside the city. All four girls drive out to see it, with Dakota and Gia lugging two sets of thrift store furniture up the stairwell. They all order pizza that night, sitting on the floor and planning the perfect future before they head back to the home.

Around that same time, Ryland's invited over to her father's once more. He wants to throw her an early birthday party. She's hesitant at first, not one to enjoy large gatherings focused on her, but when he proposes a smaller dinner at his house—just the family—she accepts. She's surprised when he goes out of his way to ask her for her favorite meal, and whether she prefers chocolate or vanilla cake. She opts for red velvet, feeling uneasy when he chuckles and reveals that it's his favorite, too.

Dakota offers to drive her there, to Ryland's relief. She'd much rather avoid the awkward car conversations with her father. When they pull into the driveway, Dakota makes sure they're not being watched before tucking Ryland's hair behind her ear and kissing her for good luck.

When Ryland steps into a house, lugging a heavy box in her arms, the twins are the first to run up to her.

"Is that for us?" Eliana asks, trying to reach for the box. Ryland, still struggling to tell the two sisters apart, moves it away from their reach.

"It's for Jonah," she explains, resulting in pouts from both of the girls. However, when Jonah comes forward and Ryland sets the box down, revealing her old comic book collection, they quickly lose interest. Jonah, on the other hand, sits on the floor with Ryland and digs through the box curiously.

"You know," he looks up once it's just them in the foyer, waiting to be called in for dinner. "I read once about a lady with a knee brace who got stranded in the wilderness and survived."

Ryland raises an eyebrow. "Yeah?"

"Yeah," Jonah nods, pulling out another comic book and paging through it. "So, you've got an even better chance of surviving on a deserted island." He leans forward to study her brace, and Ryland tenses, but he just nods in approval. "You could totally sharpen that into a weapon."

And to her own surprise, she laughs. Jonah talks of her injury so nonchalantly, making Ryland feel more at ease.

Eventually, they're called into the dining room for dinner—pizza, upon Ryland's request. She'd figured it was something everyone would eat. Table conversation actually isn't as awkward as last time, she realizes, mostly because Jonah talks animately about the comic books she's brought.

Her father inquires about her college search, but his stern glare tells her that his involvement is a secret. So Ryland answers vaguely, relieved when one of the twins starts babbling on about what she wants for her birthday.

When the cake is brought out—red velvet with white icing—Ryland sinks down into her seat. They sing her happy birthday, which is the most embarrassing thirty seconds of her night. Not to mention, she doesn't miss the bitter looks Julienne sends her way.

Ryland's relieved when the night comes to a close. It could've gone worse, she figures. As she sits on the porch waiting for Dakota to show up, she hears the creak of the door. She looks up just as the man sits down beside her.

"I know you requested no presents, but this is an exception," he clears his throat. With a raised eyebrow, Ryland watches as he holds up his hand, uncurling his fingers and letting a necklace dangle down.

"It was your mother's," he explains, his words compelling Ryland forward to take it into her own hands. She runs her fingers over the chain, studying the ruby red ring fashioned around it.

"I found it in my jacket pocket a few weeks after we… you know," he clears his throat awkwardly. "I tried to return it but she refused to see me. I guess I held onto it because it seemed important. There's initials on the inside."

Picking up the ring, Ryland studies the intricate carving. *RJM*. Blurry memories of gray hair, herb gardens, and the smell of homemade bread flash through her mind. She shivers.

"Ramona Jane," she says softly. "My mother's mother." Ryland pauses, remembering things she'd thought she'd forgotten. "I lived at her house one summer when I was really little and my mom couldn't take care of me."

She surprises even herself with the information she's disclosing. Her eyes remain on the necklace, her fingers curling around the ring—the only remaining link she has left of those who came before her. A lump forms in her throat.

Unsure of how to handle her quietness, her father changes the subject. He clears his throat and rubs his hands together. "Do you remember that intern I introduced you to at the awards dinner? Malcom?"

Ryland shrugs. "I think so."

"He mentioned you the other day," her father continues. "He's a really nice kid. Got into college on an academic scholarship and everything."

Ryland suddenly realizes the direction this conversation is going, and she slips the necklace into her pocket. "I'm sure he's great," she says softly.

"He comes by the house every Monday as part of his training," he notes, his voice suggestive. "I could invite him to stay for dinner one night."

But Ryland just shakes her head. "I appreciate the offer, but I'm not… looking for anyone." She can't help but mumble a quiet "*I'm taken*" under her breath, which he hears.

"Oh," he's quick to apologize. "I didn't realize there was already someone." There's a long pause of silence. "What's his name?"

"I…" Ryland struggles to form a coherent sentence. She's cut off, however, by the slamming of a car door followed by rushed footsteps.

"Are you okay?" Dakota skids to a stop in front of them, her eyes searching Ryland's in concern. "I just—I saw you sitting down and thought…" she motions with her hand. "Your leg?"

Ryland's quick to shake her head. "S'fine." She doesn't miss the look on her father's face when Dakota holds out her hand, offering to help Ryland to her feet with a shy smile. Ryland doesn't look to him, but she places her hand in Dakota's and allows the girl to pull her up.

"Good timing," Ryland whispers under her breath as her father stands to his feet. Dakota looks to her questioningly, but Ryland gives her a slight shake of the head.

"Thanks for the dinner," Ryland paints on a forced smile, exchanging rushed goodbyes before tugging a confused Dakota back to the car.

"What was that?" Dakota asks as she slides into the driver's seat. But Ryland doesn't answer, her eyes are fixed on the house. A few tense seconds pass between them, but as soon as the front door closes and the porch light flickers off, Ryland practically deflates like a balloon. Exhaling heavily, she fishes something out of her pocket.

"He gave me this," he voice is shaky, barely a whisper. Dakota slowly holds out her hand, palm turned upward, allowing Ryland to press the cold metal into her fist. Hesitantly, Dakota holds up the necklace to study it.

"It was my mom's," Ryland swallows the lump in her throat. "That was her mother's ring."

Dakota doesn't say anything, she just nods softly, knowing well enough the meaning of the things left behind by those who are no longer there. She twirls it around, the ruby sparkling a brilliant red in the dim light.

Then, without any words, she leans over, her fingers gently brushing Ryland's hair to one side. She can feel the girl hold her breath as she carefully clasps the necklace around her neck, the ring cold against her bare skin. Once she's finished, she presses a kiss to Ryland's temple and starts the car. As she reaches over to lace their fingers together, she feels Ryland squeeze her hand, understanding how sometimes pure silence can be the best company.

(The only words uttered on the drive home is a quiet "I love you," whispered by Dakota when she glances over to find Ryland watching her, tears glimmering in her eyes.)

That night, when Dakota rolls over to face Ryland, she finds the girl already asleep, one hand around her waist, and the other clutching the ring on her necklace, holding it tightly in her fist. A soft smile spreads across Dakota's face, and she can't resist leaning in to kiss the girl's forehead before wiggling out of her grip and tiptoeing down the hallway.

"Look at this," Finley holds up the laptop as soon as Dakota appears downstairs. The girl hops over the back of the couch, landing next to Finley and studying the recipe she's found.

"That makes enough for 24 people, it says," Dakota taps the screen. "There's only four of us. Plus Red."

Frowning, Finley continues scrolling. Dakota leans over her shoulder, occasionally telling her to bookmark a certain page.

"What about presents?" Finley speaks up, raising an eyebrow. Dakota's quick to shake her head.

"She's already gonna kill us for throwing a party," Dakota explains, glancing to the stairs. "We'll be dead twice over if we get her presents," she laughs under her breath.

"Then the food better be extra good," Finley nods.

"Gia's making her homemade guacamole," Dakota reminds her. "And I was thinking we could convince Red to make that legendary strawberry shortcake you guys always rave about."

Finley's eyes widen and she nods in excitement. "Yes, good idea," she grins, leaning forward to jot something down on her notepad. "The last time Red made that was when—," she cuts herself off, shaking her head and turning her attention back to her laptop.

Dakota raises an eyebrow. "When what?"

Finley looks away. "When Ryland… she…"

Now concerned, Dakota nudges Finley's shoulder. "What?"

"Red made it when she came home from the hospital."

Dakota's heart does something unexplainable in her chest and she sits up quickly. "What are you talking about?"

Confused, Finley tilts her head to the side. "She didn't tell you?"

Dakota shakes her head.

"Then I don't know if I should—,"

"*Finley.*"

"It was just this weird… leg thing. Some infection," Finley shakes her head, intimidated by the tone in Dakota's voice. "Red sat us all in a circle one day and told us she might not make it."

Dakota frowns. "What…?"

"They wanted to take off her leg," Finley adds. "They thought it would help. But Ryland wouldn't let any doctors near her. Then she slept for 3 days—that's when Red talked to us."

"That bad?"

Finley nods slowly. "She had all these tubes in her," she holds up both arms, pointing to her own veins. "But then she woke up cause' the medicine started working and she got to come home a week later. And Red made the cake to celebrate."

Dakota just stays quiet, taking it all in. She breathes out slowly.

"It was actually kinda funny," Finley adds. "Red says when a pastor came into the hospital room, she threw a spoon at him and threatened to send him to heaven early," she giggles softly.

But Dakota doesn't laugh, she just wrings out her hands nervously. Then, she quickly finds an excuse to disappear upstairs, leaving a confused Finley in her wake.

She climbs into Ryland's bed, squeezing into the space between the girl and the wall. Unable to help herself, she pulls the girl closer, holding onto her and pressing her forehead against her back. She doesn't mean to wake her, but when Ryland stirs, Dakota just holds tighter to the girl.

"Koda?" Ryland's voice is groggy, confused.

"You're too stubborn," Dakota mumbles against her back. It takes Ryland a few long moments to process this. When she realizes, she sighs.

"Finley told you, didn't she?" Ryland asks, knowing it was only just a matter of time. Finley can't get enough of the spoon story.

"You could've died," Dakota whispers, indirectly answering her question. Sighing heavily, Ryland rolls to her side so she's facing the girl, who looks at her with concern flickering in her eyes.

"But I didn't," Ryland shakes her head. "I'm right here."

One of Dakota's hands moves up to cup Ryland's cheek, as if she needs confirmation of her words. The girl squeezes her eyes shut. "You could've died," she repeats herself.

"Dakota…" Ryland's suddenly hit with a wave of guilt. "It's really not that big of a deal."

"It could've been," Dakota mutters. "You could've died just because you're so damn stubborn."

Ryland sighs. "The only thing that mattered to me at the time was keeping my leg," she admits. "I didn't care if I died, but I sure as hell wasn't going to let them take my leg."

"*So fucking stubborn*," Dakota mumbles under her breath. "I don't care if they cut off both your legs. I just want you alive."

"Then I'd be useless."

"Shut the fuck up," Dakota lifts her head, startling Ryland. "You? Useless? Never."

"Funny."

"I'm serious," Dakota glares at her. "Everything you need is up here," she taps the side of Ryland's head. "You're anything but useless."

"I admire your optimism," Ryland sighs, resulting in a frown from Dakota, who notices the way Ryland toys nervously with the ring on her necklace, dragging it back and forth across the chain.

"You're thinking about something else," Dakota notes. Ryland simply shrugs.

"More like thinking about *everything* at once."

Furrowing her eyebrows together, Dakota pushes Ryland's hair out of her face. "Talk?"

Ryland half shrugs. "It's late."

"Sleep?"

Yawning, Ryland nods softly. "Just lay with me."

"Will do," Dakota offers her a soft smile, settling back down in the space beside Ryland. "Love you."

"Love you too," Ryland whispers, the words falling from her lips so effortlessly. And although things may not be perfect, she feels a hell of a lot safer with Dakota next to her, her arms holding to her tightly.

"Sepsis," Finley clears her throat, cracking open an encyclopedia at breakfast the next morning. Dakota's homemade waffles had somehow managed to rouse Gia from bed before noon, a near impossible feat. All four girls sit at the kitchen table.

"Can we please not do this?" Ryland mutters, hanging her head down. But Finley's already tapping her finger against a large paragraph.

"*Sepsis is an extreme immune system response to an infection that has spread throughout the blood and tissues. Severe causes of sepsis often cause extremely low blood pressure, which limits blood flow to the body and can result in organ failure or death,*" Finley reads aloud, nodding once when she's done.

"Yep, that's it," Gia swallows her food, pointing to Finley with her fork. "That's the one."

Dakota, still confused, looks back and forth between the girls. Her eyes settle on Ryland, though, who avoids her gaze.

"I don't even remember much of it," Ryland mumbles, shrugging as she skates her food around on her plate.

"I do," Gia nods, oblivious to the glare that Ryland sends her way. "They had her doped up on all sorts of drugs. Finley was afraid of her," she shakes her head before turning to Dakota. "She's downplaying it. It was scary as fuck."

Finley nudges Gia's arm with her elbow. "Tell her what Jaden did."

Laughing, Gia nods. "One of the old girls that used to live here wrote threats on Ryland's leg with a sharpie so they wouldn't cut it off."

"*Don't even think about it*," Finley recites. "It made the doctor laugh so hard that he had to go out in the hallway."

"Can we change the subject?" Ryland's fork clatters against her plate and she glares across the table. Finley sinks down in her seat.

"We can talk about tomorrow," Dakota speaks up, cutting the tense silence and turning to Ryland. "You're finally gonna be eighteen."

"And?"

Dakota just shrugs, casting a knowing glance in Finley's direction. "Just figured you'd be more excited."

"*I'm* excited," Gia speaks up. "With Ryland gone, and you two at camp, I get the whole house to myself."

"Don't get too ahead of yourself," Red appears in the doorway, a towel wrapped around her head. "We're moving you into Finley's room and most likely getting a new resident within a few weeks."

"That soon?" Ryland raises an eyebrow.

Red nods. "Summer always brings in more kids."

"So when me and Dakota come back the house is going to be full of strangers?" Finley frowns.

"That's how this place works, Finley," Red nods. "You were all strangers at one point, too." Dakota and Ryland glance to one another.

The next morning—Ryland's birthday—starts out with Red sending Gia and Ryland out to run errands. Errands, coincidentally, that will take much longer than originally intended. Thanks to Gia, who when they're already halfway home, realizes that she'd "*forgot*" to stop at the dry cleaners—derailing them for at least another two hours.

By the time they finally arrive back at the house, Ryland is annoyed and hungry. As they make their way inside, she trails behind Gia, lugging an armful of groceries. Almost immediately, she notes something is up. It's too quiet.

She stops just short of the kitchen, a knowing look on her face. 'I'm not in the mood, Finley," she deadpans, well aware of Finley's affinity for hiding behind corners and jumping out to scare people.

There's a long pause of silence and Ryland rolls her eyes. "Very funny," she mutters, giving in and making her way into the kitchen. "But don't get mad at me when I punch—,"

"SURPRISE!"

Ryland stumbles backward, a loaf of bread falling out of her arms. Finley tugs a string on a small plastic bottle, causing confetti to burst out and rain down on them.

Recovering, still slightly startled, Ryland's eyes scan the kitchen—the colorful streamers, the cake in the middle of the island, and the cut out letters hanging above the table. She cracks a smile. “Impressive.”

Dakota takes the groceries from her arms, pushing them aside atop the counter. “You like it?” she asks, tossing Gia a bag of chips. “I was afraid you'd kill us all.”

“I'll save that for later,” Ryland teases. She's honestly still a bit shocked, considering she'd nearly forgotten her own birthday, but she plays it off the best she can. “Where's Red?”

“Visiting family,” Gia nods. “You're a legal adult now. You can be our babysitter.”

“We've got until 3am to do absolutely nothing,” Dakota adds, leaning against the counter. “We got takeout, too. Plus an extra thing of that spicy sauce you like.”

“Not too bad, tiny,” Ryland laughs, nudging Dakota's shoulder.

(For Dakota, the look of surprise on Ryland's face is more than enough.)

“This is the last time it's just gonna be the four of us,” Finley speaks up, stealing a piece of chicken from Gia's plate with her chopsticks. They've all congregated in the living room, eating Chinese food and waiting for their usual Friday movie marathon to start.

“Don't remind me,” Gia rolls her eyes. “I'm not in the mood to deal with a bunch of new kids.”

“At least you'll be out in a month,” Dakota reminds her. “Me and Finley are stick here.”

“At least you guys get free food,” Ryland adds, laughing softly. Dakota scoots closer to her, pretending she needed to reach something on the table. Ryland teasingly ruffles her hair.

"It's starting," Finley hisses at them to be quiet. She hops up to turn off the lights, bouncing back onto the beanbag. Ryland grabs the blanket hanging over the back of the couch, slinging it around Dakota's shoulders and pulling her closer.

Dakota's not sure when she falls asleep, all she knows is that when she wakes up, it's to Ryland nudging her shoulder gently.

"Koda," she whispers. "It's almost time."

That's how Dakota ends up following Ryland upstairs, reality hitting her when her eyes land on Ryland's half of the room, barren except for a suitcase and a few boxes stacked on the bed. Soon, she's helping the girl lug the last of her belongings down to the trunk of her car—she'd agreed to drop Ryland off at the apartment when she and Finley departed for Nevada.

"That's the last of it," Dakota closes the trunk, brushing her hands off on her jeans. Her eyes finally meet Ryland's, and she can sense the girl's nervousness for the first time that night. She takes a step forward.

"I'm on my own now," Ryland half-whispers, giving Dakota a sad smile. "I thought it would feel more liberating."

"Feels scary?" Dakota asks softly, earning a soft nod from the girl. Dakota pulls her into a hug, breathing her in and holding her tightly. "It's not just you," she whispers, her words muffled against Ryland's shoulder. "You can't get rid of me that easily."

Laughing softly, Ryland pulls away, brushing Dakota's hair back and taking a moment just to study her face. "Everything's gonna start changing," she says, almost as if she's warning the girl, giving her a chance to back out early. But Dakota doesn't even flinch.

"Bring it on," she nods in finality, placing a hand on Ryland's shoulder and leaning up to kiss her. For Ryland, her words provide relief, confirmation that Dakota's willing to stay through whatever's thrown their way.

The car ride is quiet. Gia's agreed to spend the night at Ryland's apartment for her first night. Meanwhile, Dakota and Finley have a grueling four-hour drive ahead of them. Everyone's mind is racing.

When they finally pull into the parking lot of the apartment building, Ryland doesn't make a move to get out. Sighing, Dakota circles the car, opening Ryland's door and quietly helping her to her feet.

"This is it?" Ryland asks softly, even though she already knows the answer. She's doing her best to stall Dakota's departure for as long as possible.

"It's just three weeks," Dakota reminds her. "You have the mailing address, right?"

Ryland nods.

"Oh, and..." Dakota pauses, holding up a finger to signal for Ryland to wait as she retrieves something from her jacket pocket. "Happy Birthday," she whispers, pressing something into Ryland's palm, curling her fingers around it. With furrowed eyebrows, Ryland holds up the small bronze key.

"You'll see," Dakota nods. Ryland gives her a questioning look, but Dakota just laughs and shakes her head. "You'll like it. I promise."

"You leaving or what?" Gia appears from the back of the car, carrying a box on her hip. Finley peers out the window.

Dakota just nods quickly and turns back to Ryland, throwing her arms around the girl and hugging her tightly. She hears Ryland whisper a soft "I love you," against her shoulder, and she does the same.

"Three weeks," Ryland nods when they pull away. Dakota just smiles softly.

"Three weeks."

As the car drives away with Finley and Dakota in tow, Ryland stands beside Gia, fingers curling and uncurling around the key in her hand.

"C'mon, Romeo," Gia shakes her head, tossing a duffel back to the girl. Snapping out of her trance, Ryland hurries to follow her. Once they're in the elevator, she raises an eyebrow at the girl.

"Romeo?" Ryland questions. "Are you implying I'll die in four days?"

Gia just smirks and shakes her head, unlocking the apartment and nudging the door open. Ryland's about to question her once more, but she's distracted as soon as they venture into the apartment.

"*I wonder who that could be from,*" Gia deadpans knowingly. Against the wall in the small living room space is a tall bookshelf. Ryland looks to Gia, but she just motions for the girl to continue before disappearing into the kitchen.

Ryland, still confused, slowly makes her way across the room. She can smell wood stain, immediately letting her know that this must be one of the projects Dakota had locked herself away in the garage to work on. What catches her attention, though, is the bottom portion of the piece of furniture. Instead of shelves, there's two doors, a small brass lock between them. Looking down to the key, she raises an eyebrow.

Carefully, Ryland lowers herself to one knee. It takes a bit of effort to turn the key in the lock, but once she does, the doors slowly swing open.

Sitting inside the small outcove are three things. First is a record player. It's an older antique, Ryland can tell by the weathered brass embellishments. Her eyes travel over to the small stack of records beside it. And last but not least, there's a small note, folded up and taped to the inside of the door. Ryland smiles as soon as she recognizes the cream colored paper from Dakota's journal. She carefully unfolds it.

Ryland,

I wasn't sure what to get you, because one—you hate presents, and two—you don't suit normal presents. The only jewelry you wear is your mom's necklace. Plus I suck at picking out jewelry. (That much money for a rock? Really?) But then when I went with you to help carry stuff into the apartment, I noticed something. You only brought the things you needed. A bed, a dresser, a desk—all the bare necessities. And then I realized that applies to everything you do. You only take what you need, and sometimes not even that. But I figured it was about time someone gave you a little bit more. Maybe that's why I'm here.

I wish I had all the money in the world so I could give you absolutely everything. But for now, I found this bookshelf on one of me and Finley's thrift store adventures and fixed it up a bit. I figured you could put your books on here instead of shoving them in the back of your closet. The record player is in case you get lonely. Music always helps. And you can lock it all away when you're done, because I know your obsession with things that lock—that belong to only you. Here's to being eighteen and free from this shitty ass system.

I love you,

Dakota

Ryland reads the letter once, then twice, and then folds it up into a small square and tucks it into her back pocket. After she closes and locks the small cabinet, she stands up. Carefully, she undoes the clasp of her mother's necklace and strings it through the small bronze key, letting it fall into place right beside her grandmother's ring. Taking a deep breath, she curls her fingers around the key before turning her attention to the boxes by the door.

Gia emerges from the kitchen to find Ryland carefully placing her books into the new shelf. Keeping quiet, she leans against the doorframe and watches as Ryland takes a few steps backward to study her work before shaking her head and moving forward to switch two books. Gia snorts.

"You've got it bad, Moreno," Gia shakes her head, tossing a chip into her mouth. Startled, Ryland whips her head around and looks to the sudden intruder with wide eyes. It takes her a few moments to process the girl's words.

"I don't know what you're talking about," she quickly shakes her head, turning away from Gia's knowing gaze. Her hand comes up to toy with her necklace.

"Oh come on," Gia rolls her eyes, amused at how Ryland's still trying to keep it hidden. "You're eighteen now, dumbass. Doesn't matter what you do anymore." She raises a teasing eyebrow. "Doesn't matter who you hug… who you kiss… who you f—,"

"*Alright*," Ryland cuts her off, glaring at the girl. "Alright, Gia, I get it."

"What?" Gia feigns innocence, not missing how red Ryland's face has turned. "I was gonna say fancy."

"Doesn't matter who I *fancy*?" Ryland raises an eyebrow. Gia just laughs.

"Seriously though, kid. I'm happy for you," Gia walks over and slaps a hand on Ryland's shoulder. She pauses for a moment. "Just don't do it on my bed," she adds before disappearing down the hallway.

"There it is!" Ryland calls after her, trying to compose herself. "I knew you couldn't be sincere!"

"Yeah, yeah," Gia pauses by her bedroom door. "You love me."

Ryland rolls her eyes half-heartedly. "Fuck you."

"You know, I'd say it back, but I'll leave that job to Dakota," Gia smirks, watching Ryland's eyes widen just as she closes her bedroom door behind her.

Chapter 21

LETTERS

Dear Dakota

This may be too early to send you a letter, but it's the first night in my apartment alone and I can't sleep because there's noises coming from the room below mine. Loud music or something. Gia left around lunchtime. She's got another job interview.

I got your note and stuff last night. Thank you. I have The Mama's and Papa's record on right now. It's nice. It makes the space feel less empty.

I thought a lot about what you said in the note—about me being obsessed with things that lock. I think that's what you get for being a product of the system. Nothing's ever really yours, so you hold onto anything you can—and you lock it away so it only belongs to you. I used to have this metal change box that I stole from a Girl Scout's table when I was younger. It had a key and everything. I kept all my treasures in there. Which wasn't much, considering I was just a little kid—a deck of cards, a bouncy ball, a pair of mittens my old teacher had given me from the lost and found… but then when they picked me up at school to relocate me after the foster mother said she couldn't deal with me, they never bothered to pack the lockbox. Probably because I kept it shoved in the back of a dresser drawer to keep it hidden.

It's funny now, because my apartment is essentially a lockbox of its own. It's pretty empty right now, though. Maybe I should try decorating a bit.

I hope you're having fun. I was looking over the camp brochure that Finley brought home and it looks like everything you could ever dream of. Just be careful on the zip-lines, daredevil.

Come back soon. It's boring without you. There's a little cafe across the street that I think you would like. Maybe we can go there when you get back.

Love you,

Ryland

Ry,

Are you sad? You sound sad in your letter. I wish I could be there but maybe you should call Gia and ask her to keep you company. I bet Red wouldn't mind if you paid her a visit, either.

Camp is really nice, but it's hot as hell. To be honest, I didn't even read the brochure before I got here. But yes, I did go zip-lining. And yes, it was fucking awesome. I even convinced Finley to try it.

They have me working in a girl's dorm with 4th and 5th graders. They're insane. I wouldn't be able to handle it on my own. There's another counselor here. Her name is Laura and she's engaged to some guy she met online. But the kids like me more. I can tell.

You should see Finley, Ry. She's like a whole different person. She spends all her time in the Arts and Crafts cabin with the group of special ed kids. What happened to the girl who failed art, right? I have no clue. But she works so well with the kids. I stopped in one day to see what she was doing but I could only sit still for so long. It was like magic, man. Those kids love her. They just get each other.

I'm sending you a picture that Finley took. It's kinda dark, but that's me in the tree with a few of the kids from my cabin. That night we were watching fireworks from across the lake. They went crazy on the 4th of July, you should have seen them. Finley's hair almost caught on fire. Remind me to tell you that story when I get home.

I feel bad that I'm all the way over here, getting to zip-line and go swimming, while you're back there all alone. Did you listen to the Elvis record? The gold one? That's one of my favorites. Finley picked out the Bon Iver one, but maybe you shouldn't listen to that one yet, cause' it's kinda sad. But I think you'll like some of the others.

And don't worry, once I get back we can get into all sorts of trouble together. I'll climb up onto your balcony and sweep you off your feet like some Romeo and Juliet shit. Or was that Rapunzel? Either way. It'll be the best summer ever, Ry. Promise. (And yes, I'd love to go to the cafe with you.)

Are you keeping in touch with your dad? And have you heard from any colleges? I'll write again as soon as I can.

Love you (more),

Koda

Koda,

I'm not really sad. Just kinda… stuck. I'm thinking of getting summer job with Gia, but she's got an interview at Sonic and I don't think my leg would take kindly to standing all day. So when I say I'm stuck, I guess that just means I'm bored. And kinda lonely.

It sounds like both you and Finley really like it there. I'd rather die than be left in charge of a group of 5th grade girls, to be honest.

I don't know how you do it. The picture was cute, though. You look tan as hell. Do I have competition?

And yes, I did listen to the Elvis record. I figured it'd be your favorite, just cause' all the songs are loud and fast. Do you ever listen to slow music? Oh, and also, both Rapunzel and Romeo and Juliet involve climbing up balconies. But I don't think my hair is long or healthy enough for you to climb up it. So you're on your own on that one, kid.

My dad actually called this morning. He wants me to come camping with their whole family this weekend. I didn't really give him an answer. Sleeping on the ground would kill my leg. I don't know, Koda. No matter how much time I spend with them, they don't feel like a family to me. He doesn't feel like a father. At this point I'm not sure if he ever will. (Or, if I even want him to.)

It's funny, because this is the kind of thing I would have dreamed of as a kid. I mean, how much better could it get? Finding out you have a rich father and an entire family. But honestly, it just makes me feel more isolated. Is that weird? These are the people I'm supposed to fit in with, but I don't. It just makes me think, you know? Will I ever find a place where I fit in?

Damn, Ryland, way to kill the mood. But hey, I'm happy you're having so much fun. Send more pictures. Oh, and Gia says hi.

Love you (even more),

Ryland

Ryland,

What's worse? Feeling sad or feeling stuck?

Tell Gia I say hi back. Has she been hanging out at the apartment a lot? Oh, and Finley says hi, too. I'm writing this while

I'm sitting next to her in the arts and crafts cabin. They're making some sort of poster with pressed flowers.

We spent all day on the water. One of the leaders rented a boat and tied this inflatable tube to the back of it. You should've seen how much air we got. It was insane. Finley tried to take pictures but they all came out blurry.

Just because your dad is filthy rich doesn't mean he's perfect, Ry. His money doesn't entitle you to feel anything for him. You may be family, but he knows close to nothing about you. He wasn't there for eighteen years. Hell, Red knows you better than he does. I don't believe that whole "blood is thicker than water" bullshit. Sure, family matters, but it's not the world. Loyalty trumps blood, any day. And people can become a part of your family without sharing the same blood as you. I mean, look at our friendship with Gia and Finley. They're like my sisters.

And hey, if it counts for anything, you fit in with me. I'm not perfect, but it's better than nothing, right? Gia and Finley too. We're a shitty little family of our own. And me and you… well, I think no matter what happens between now and the future, you'll always be important to me. I couldn't forget you if I tried.

(I can't help falling in love with you—Elvis said it himself.)

Dakota

Koda,

Neither is worse, just different.

Gia's spent the last two nights here because we've been painting all the rooms. She's doing hers dark red. Mine is gonna be blue. Robin's egg blue, to be exact. I'm feeling a bit better. It's just taking some time to adjust to being on my own. Sometimes I lose track of time and forget that no one's gonna call me downstairs for dinner. Oh, and you're gonna be back in a week. That's a plus.

I got all the pictures you sent. It's gorgeous out there. I appreciate your love for taking pictures of weird ass trees. And sunsets. Send some more of you guys.

I went to dinner with my dad the other night. It was just the two of us this time and it was super awkward. He kept trying to bring up my mom. I feel like he has no right to talk about her. It was uncomfortable. Like talking to a stranger. Maybe even worse.

You'll always be important to me, too. You came around right when things were really shitty and made them… a lot less shitty. Just having you there is enough to make things easier.

You help me to be strong, Koda. I love you.

Ryland

Ry,

This may not get to you before I get home, but it's worth a try.

I miss you too. I stole one of your hoodies when I was packing. Have you noticed? The maroon one? Yeah. I wear it every night. I even wear it at our bonfires, even though it's anything but cold. Good luck getting it back.

There's not much else to say because I'll be home soon, but I think it's good you're still making an effort with your dad. It's good for you. He's your dad, after all. If anything, you can learn a little more about yourself. And at least he's making an effort, right? He seems to want to make up for lost time.

See you soon. I love you.

Dakota

Chapter 22

HOMECOMING

If there's one thing Ryland likes about living on her own, it's the privacy. It's nine o'clock at night and she's eating a bowl of cereal on the couch, in nothing but her underwear. She's watching some documentary about astrophysics, nearly falling asleep, when a knock at the door startles her back awake.

Deep down, she knows who it is, which is why she doesn't bother looking through the peephole. But she's still confused, because Dakota wasn't supposed to be home until tomorrow afternoon. She makes her way over to the door, unsure if she's hearing things.

However, it all hits her when she opens the door and there stands Dakota, a soft smile on her face. She's tan, considerably more than before, and the sun has brought out faint freckles, scattering them across the bridge of her nose and under her eyes. Her hair is thrown up into some half up, half down style that she hasn't given much regard to. Ryland's eyes scan her up and down—flip flops, white shorts, and a mustard yellow camp t-shirt, covered in sharpie signatures and crudely drawn smiley faces. There's a beach ball tucked under her arm, and the faded colors of a temporary tattoo on her cheek.

"Hey, stranger," Dakota speaks up when Ryland doesn't say anything. She balances her duffel bag on her hip, a smile tugging at her lips. "You gonna let me in or are you just gonna keep staring?"

Snapping out of her daze, Ryland quickly steps aside and holds open the door. "I thought you were…" she stumbles over her words, gesturing vaguely to fill in the gaps. "Tomorrow?"

"Drove through the night," Dakota shrugs, standing in the middle of the living room and taking it all in. The apartment looks completely different than it had when she left. For starters, the living room walls are now a muted green, no longer plain white. There's a few new pieces of furniture, two small lamps and a beanbag chair tossed in front of the television—Gia's doing. A smile tugs at Dakota's lips when she notices a few of the pictures she'd send from camp, now taped in a row on the bookshelf.

"I wasn't expecting you," Ryland shakes her head, flustered. She grabs two dirty glasses from the table beside the couch and hurries to put them away. But Dakota stops her, suddenly at her side and placing a hand on her arm.

"Hey, it's been three weeks," the girl quirks an eyebrow. "Don't I at least get a hello?" There's a smile on her face, but she grows uneasy at Ryland's odd behavior.

"You do… it's just," Ryland shakes her head. "I'm…" she motions vaguely. Dakota's eyes scan her up and down.

"In your underwear?" Dakota furrows her eyebrows together, but she just shrugs. "Nothing I haven't seen before."

"That's not it," Ryland shakes her head, swallowing hard. "All those times were in the dark."

"Yeah, so?" Dakota looks to her in utter confusion.

"My leg."

"What about it?"

"It's... *it.*"

"And?"

"It's... scarred."

Dakota tilts her head to the side.

"Like, really fucking ugly."

"No it's not," Dakota quips back, but Ryland's too flustered to think rationally. She starts to move back toward the kitchen but Dakota snatches the glasses from her hands before she can even take a step, setting them back down on the table. Her eyes never leave Ryland's.

"You're complicating this more than you need to," Dakota steps in front of her, blocking the pathway to the kitchen. "You really think I care what your leg looks like?"

Ryland shrinks back. Truth is, even *she* gets dressed in the dark to avoid looking at her reflection in the mirror. She's a mangled version of herself, a shell of the body she used to be. After the accident, not only was she left with raised white scars from stitches and a surgery that tried (but failed) to save the nerves in her leg, but she was also left with a series of bruises that just... never went away—dark purple watercolor patches, prominent on her skin as a result of muscle damage. When Ryland sees this, she sees weakness, failure—a reminder that she'll never truly recover.

But to Dakota, who can't help but glance downward for a split second, all she sees are battle scars. Unlike Ryland, disgust doesn't bubble in her stomach at the sight. She doesn't feel compelled to avert her eyes. It's not as bad as Ryland's making it out to be, she thinks. For Dakota, it's simple. It's just Ryland. Nothing more, nothing less.

"Ryland..." Dakota sighs when the girl in front of her just shakes her head and lets her hair fall in front of her face, shielding herself. "C'mon, Ry, it's just me," she takes a step forward, her fingers brushing the inside of Ryland's wrist. "We haven't seen each other in three weeks and that's the first thing you think? That I'm going to be… I don't know… *disgusted* at the sight of you?"

Ryland's eyes finally lifts to meet hers, passing a silent question between them.

"I'm serious," Dakota keeps unwavering eye contact. "I don't care," she nods once. "And you shouldn't either."

"Koda…" Ryland starts, but trails off. Dakota makes it sound so simple that even *she's* starting to believe the girl's words. Ryland's come to know when Dakota's lying, and this isn't one of those times.

Ryland opens her mouth to speak again, but closes it slowly when Dakota's eyes flicker down to her necklace. Her breath catches in her throat when, stepping forward, Dakota's fingers find the key around her neck. The girl's lips curve into a smile, and suddenly, with Dakota so close to her, Ryland's stomach does something unexplainable.

"S'cute," Dakota nods softly, twirling the key around her finger. Just as Dakota's eyes flutter back up to Ryland's, Ryland is hit with a wave of newfound confidence, and Dakota has to grab her shoulders for support when Ryland's lips crash against hers, taking her by surprise and nearly making her lose her balance.

"*Woah,*" Dakota breathes out, pulling away from the kiss. Blinking rapidly, she looks to Ryland, her eyes searching the girl's. "Wh-why?" she struggles to compose herself. Her heart has suddenly kicked into overdrive.

"Three weeks," Ryland shakes her head. "S'been three weeks."

With a soft nod, Dakota allows the girl to pull her closer, arms looped around her waist, resting at the small of her back. Within seconds, the roles are reversed—Dakota's the one at a lost for words, Ryland's fingers tracing spirals over the fabric of her shirt, just beneath her shoulder blades.

"Dakota," Ryland whispers, just for the sake of saying her name. Her words ghost across the girl's lips. It's a declaration that she's there, finally, standing in front of her. Dakota just nods, some sort of confirmation. Her wide eyes bore into Ryland's, waiting for the girl's next move. She's already putty in her hands.

However, they're interrupted by a crash of thunder that practically shakes the walls. Dakota jumps, grabbing Ryland's arms and looking to the window. Lighting flickers in her eyes, flashing across the room.

"Are you staying the night?" Ryland rasps, gaining Dakota's attention once more.

"I mean, I-I figured..." Dakota stammers. There's a change in the air, and she's pretty sure she can already guess what's just moments ahead of them, but she struggles to think straight with Ryland this close to her. It's intoxicating.

"Good," Ryland just nods once, tugging Dakota's wrist and nodding back towards her bedroom. Like a lost puppy, Dakota follows closely behind her.

"Blue," Dakota whispers once she's standing in Ryland's doorway, letting her eyes scan the bedroom. Her duffel bag slides off of her shoulder, landing on the ground with a thud. She makes a mental note to do something about the lack of pictures of Ryland's walls. "I like it."

"Reminds me of your eyes," Ryland nods. She throws Dakota for a loop when, sitting down on the end of the bed, she motions for the girl to come closer. Dakota doesn't argue. Her heart starts to race as she quickly toes off her shoes and takes the few steps forward to close the gap between her and Ryland.

"Cheesy," she mumbles, gaining a bit of her confidence back. But, before she can say anything else, Ryland tugs her forward by her shirt and kisses her hungrily. Dakota nearly falls on top of her. When they pull away, she struggles to catch her breath. There's a silent question passed between them,

"Are you sure?" Dakota whispers, her face lingering dangerously close to Ryland's. Ryland's eyes never leave hers, though. She just laughs softly.

"It's been *three weeks*," she stresses her words, a smile tugging at her lips. "I'm sure."

But Dakota doesn't move. Her eyes are still on Ryland's, questioning her. She hesitates to take this any further, knowing exactly what had happened the last time things got heated between them. Her head falls to the side slightly, an eyebrow arched in silent question. Ryland raises one back.

"Are *you* sure?" Ryland asks, studying Dakota's face. The girl nods without hesitation.

"I'm... *yeah*," Dakota breathes out. "I just want to make sure that you're... you know."

Lightning flickers through the room, but this time neither of the girls even notice it. Ryland, fed up with talking, just balls her hands in the collar of Dakota's shirt and kisses her again. This time, Dakota's quick to respond. As their lips battle for dominance, Dakota's fingers trail up Ryland's back, gently tugging the girl's hair out of its ponytail. The kiss breaks, giving Ryland just enough time to shake out her damp hair before Dakota's nudging her shoulder, urging the girl to scoot back on the bed.

Pulling herself back with her hands, Ryland tenses when she feels her brace catch on the sheets. Panic flickers in her eyes, but Dakota can read her like a book. Within seconds, Dakota's hands deftly move to undo the brace. Even she's become more skilled at this, and the brace fumbles to the floor in no time at all.

"Not so bad," Ryland laughs, although she's still slightly embarrassed. But Dakota makes her forget all about it, demanding her full attention when she crawls up the bed beside her. Ryland follows her lead, slowly resting back against the mattress as Dakota climbs atop her, one knee resting on each side of her waist. Straddling Ryland, she falls forward, catching herself with her hands pressed into the mattress, her face dangling just inches above Ryland's.

"Three weeks, huh?" she cocks her head to the side, a teasing smile on her face. Her hair slips down from behind her shoulders, framing her face and creating a curtain around them. But Ryland somehow manages to keep her cool, even throwing a playful smirk back in Dakota's direction.

"I missed you, too," Dakota murmurs in passing, finding Ryland's lips only moments later.

And then it happens. And Ryland isn't scared anymore. Because for the first time in a long time, she has someone she trusts. Dakota's yet to let her down.

It's nothing like she expected it to be, either—and not in a bad way. Dakota is still Dakota, giggling and cracking jokes. And Ryland finds herself thinking how stupid it is that she's supposed to have "lost" something tonight. Truth is, she doesn't feel empty… or much different at all. She hasn't lost anything, Ryland decides. It fact, it might just be the opposite.

Dakota doesn't even remember falling asleep, all she knows is that one minute she was peppering sloppy kisses down Ryland's jawline, and then she wasn't. When she wakes up, she's half on

Ryland, her hair splayed across the girl's bare chest. It takes her a moment to remember the previous night's events, and when she does, she's blinking rapidly and letting her eyes rake over the girl's sleeping figure.

Entranced, and still filled with disbelief that last night actually happened, Dakota props herself up on one elbow. She ghosts her fingertips up Ryland's abdomen, leaving goosebumps in her wake.

Dakota doesn't think this could be any more perfect. It's peaceful, quiet except for their soft breathing. Complete silence is a rarity for Dakota, but now it's just them, white sheets tangled around their legs, the sun leaking in through the windows and casting a soft pale glow across the bed. There's no worry of interruption or missed appointments. It's just an impenetrable now, and Dakota thinks she could lay like this forever. She could drown in it.

"Take a picture. It lasts longer."

Ryland's words startle Dakota, snapping her out of her daze. Her eyes flutter down to meet Ryland's, who's looking at with the faintest of smiles on her face. Dakota's expression softens.

"Did I wake you?" Dakota's voice is raspy from sleep. Her fingers curl and uncurl absentmindedly, her hand resting on Ryland's hip.

"I don't mind," Ryland half shrugs, rolling onto her side and mimicking Dakota by propping herself up with one elbow, now facing the girl. Reaching out, Ryland combs Dakota's hair out of her face, brushing it past her shoulder. She mumbles a "*that's better*," not missing the flush in Dakota's cheeks that follows.

"You got freckles," Ryland notes, her voice gentle. Dakota just nods softly.

"From the sun," Dakota mumbles, her gaze following Ryland when she traces a thumb over the soft skin under her eyes. "Got it from my mom."

"S'cute," Ryland whispers, wetting her lips. Her eyes flicker down to Dakota's own, leaning in just seconds later. Dakota's hands find her way up the curve of Ryland's shoulders, her fingers threading themselves into the hair at the nape of her neck. Kissing her back softly, Dakota submits rather easily, letting Ryland take the lead.

When the kiss breaks, Dakota looks wide eyed up at the girl, who remains lingering inches above her face. Something flashes in Ryland's eyes, something that causes her to fail at fighting back a smile.

"I have something to show you," Ryland nods, pushing off the bed and rolling over so she's within reach of the nightstand. Dakota watches curiously as Ryland digs something out of her drawer. When she turns back over, she slaps and envelope onto Dakota's chest.

"Read it," Ryland urges her when Dakota raises an eyebrow in question. She drums her fingers against the envelope, giving her a slight nod of the head. "Go on."

Now intrigued, Dakota sits up, tugging the sheet around her shoulders. Ryland's eyes follow Dakota's hands as she slips the letter from the envelope and unfolds it, leaning in closer and squinting to read the small print.

Dakota half-mumbles the words as her eyes scan the letter. It takes her a few beats to realize what she's reading, but when she does, she scrambles to grab the envelope again, eyes skating across the return address. The letter falls from her hands.

"Stanford?" She whips her head to look at Ryland, her mouth agape. "You got into *Stanford*?"

Ryland, failing to hide her own excitement, just nods softly. Dakota can only stare at her in disbelief for a few seconds before looking at the letter again, reading it twice over.

"It was my reach school," Ryland adds softly. "I honestly wasn't even gonna send in my application, but..."

"But you did," Dakota smiles and holds up the letter. "You got in."

Ryland just shrugs, flustered. But Dakota can tell she's excited, it's practically radiating off of the girl. This is the first time she's even seen Ryland act even vaguely proud of her own accomplishments. It rubs off on Dakota.

"This is huge," Dakota glances at her, unable to wipe the smile from her face. She slips the letter back into the envelope. "Wait until Red finds out."

Ryland smiles at the thought. "I just got the letter last night. I was gonna tell you earlier but then... you know," she laughs softly. "I'm majoring in psychology."

"Psychology?" Dakota tilts her head to the side. "What happened to astronaut outer space shit?"

"That stuff's just for fun," Ryland shrugs. Dakota furrows her eyebrows.

"You study that stuff *for fun*?"

"That's not the point," Ryland laughs, nudging the girl's arm. "I talked to my dad about it... and he said he'd help me get into law school after I get my Bachelor's. If I want."

"Law school?" Dakota's eyes scan Ryland's face.

"Yeah," Ryland nods. "Sounds cheesy, I know. But I wanna be a child advocate. For kids like us," she shrugs softly. "I figure the only person who can help those kids is someone who's survived it all and knows exactly how they feel; you know?"

"Even if the system is fucked, they still need someone to fight for them," Ryland adds with a soft shrug. "I never had that."

"I'll fight for you," Dakota tilts her chin upwards defensively. Ryland can't help but laugh, and she places a hand on Dakota's knee.

"I know you will, tiny," she rolls her eyes playfully. "I meant when I was younger. One of my social workers didn't even know my name. She called me Riley for over a year. I had all these people making life-changing decisions for me when they'd never even met me before."

"Like separating me from my brother."

"Exactly," Ryland squeezes the girl's knee. "I know I can't fix the entire system, but I guess I'm just hoping I'll be able to keep one kid out of a shitty situation. That's a start, right?"

"So you're still going to be working in the system you hate?" Dakota raises an eyebrow, somewhat confused.

"I'll be working *against* the part of the system that dehumanizes people," Ryland explains. "Protecting the kids from it."

"So that's why you said child *advocate*," Dakota realizes aloud. Her lips curve into a smile. "It fits you," she says softly. "Who better to help them than you?"

Ryland just shrugs, surprised at at how much Dakota's approval means to her. She sits up so she's leaning against the girl's shoulder.

"You know, they have scholarships for foster kids," Ryland speaks up tentatively, studying Dakota's face. She knows it's a sensitive topic. "I bet if you send in a few essays you'd get the money, easy."

Dakota's quiet for a few moments before she glances to Ryland. "I don't know," she admits. "The idea of going to school again is kinda terrifying. And not the healthy kind."

Pursing her lips in thought, Ryland absentmindedly trails her fingers up and down Dakota's arm. "But then what are you going to do?"

There's a long pause of silence followed by a sigh from Dakota. "M'not sure," she confesses. "I don't see myself doing the same thing for the rest of my life. I can't stand the routine. I just… I want to do everything and nothing all at once."

"What happens when you turn eighteen?"

"Whatever comes along," Dakota shrugs. "Maybe me and Finley will do the same thing you are Gia are doing," she motions around the apartment. "I really don't know."

"Well, whatever you wind up doing, you'll kick ass at it," Ryland nudges her shoulder, smiling softly.

"Alright, Miss Stanford," Dakota teases. She rests her chin on top of Ryland's head, running her fingers through the girl's hair. "M'proud of you," she hums, allowing Ryland to pull her down with her so they're laying on their backs. With her arms wrapped around Dakota, Ryland skates the tips of her fingers up and down her stomach, giggling when Dakota shivers.

"What's on the agenda for today?" Dakota asks, turning and nuzzling her head into the crook of Ryland's neck.

"I've got nothing planned," Ryland hums, feeling Dakota relax into her side. The girl giggles, allowing herself to be pulled closer.

"Works for me,"

They do absolutely nothing all day. And it's wonderful. They end up on the couch, watching old movies and sharing a bowl of popcorn. They don't have to worry about being interrupted, and Dakota hadn't realized how much of a luxury that could be.

Eventually, though, Dakota convinces Ryland to come back with her to Red's for dinner. When they pile into Dakota's car, Ryland realizes just how much she'd missed it—holes in the floor and all.

Going back to Red's for the first time since she left feels a bit odd to Ryland. But she knows she's not intruding, Red's made it more than clear that all of her girls are welcome back whenever they please. But Ryland would never take advantage of that.

As soon as they walk back into the house, Ryland's tackled into a hug by Finley. Dakota has to grab her arm to keep her from falling backwards.

"You're crushing me," Ryland laughs, peeling Finley off of her. "But I appreciate the enthusiasm."

Even Red pulls her into a hug. Ryland's become a daughter figure to her, having lived in the house the longest. She remembers when Ryland had first showed up, newly fifteen, with only a checkered pillow and a drawstring bag of clothes to her name. But now, she's blossomed into a young adult, graduating at the top of her class and onto bigger things.

Which is why, when Dakota snatches the letter from Ryland's pocket and waves it in front of Red, the older woman struggles to fight back tears. She pulls Ryland into another hug, squeezing her tight and letting her know how proud she is.

"Who would've thought," Red places both of her hands on Ryland's shoulders and looking her straight in the eyes. "The same little girl who refused to leave her bedroom for weeks when she first got here is the same one who's going to Stanford." She hugs her again. "I knew you'd prove them wrong."

"Thank you," Ryland whispers, reveling in the fact that she's made Red proud. "I don't think Stanford would have even been an option if you hadn't put up with all my bullshit."

"You would've done it with or without me," Red shakes her head. "I just gave you a place to stay."

Eventually, after they're through with the sappy conversation, they all sit down for dinner. Turkey burgers—Finley's specialty. Conversation immediately turns to Finley and Dakota, who babble incessantly about camp. Gia steals food from Ryland's plate when she's distracted, and to Ryland, it's as if she never left.

"Acrobatics."

"We did that one already."

"Fine. Aerodynamics."

"Good one," Finley nods from her spot on the beanbag, flipping through the thick encyclopedia on her lap. Dakota's just gotten back from dropping Ryland off at her apartment, something that turned out to be surprisingly difficult. Leaving Ryland by herself in an empty apartment is something she knows she'll grow to hate. But she also knows it won't be long before they see each other again.

"So how was it?"

Dakota jumps when Gia plops down on the couch beside her. She just looks to the girl in confusion. Meanwhile, Finley's reading aloud a lengthy paragraph about aerodynamics, unaware that no one is listening.

"You totally did it," Gia shakes her head in disbelief. "I knew it."

Dakota glances to Finley, who's preoccupied, and then back to Gia. "What are you talking about?"

"You know," Gia raises an eyebrow at her. "You and Ryland…"

"What did we do?" Dakota's still oblivious.

"*It*."

"Oh."

The word just slips out of Dakota's mouth upon realizing what Gia is hinting at. Within seconds, her face is bright red. Panicking, all she can do is look away from Gia's knowing gaze.

"Y'all couldn't even wait one day," Gia shakes her head. Dakota, embarrassed, throws a pillow at her and covers her face.

Gia's teasing may seem lighthearted, but when they disperse upstairs that night, she lingers in Dakota's doorway.

"Hurt her and I hurt you," Gia nods once, rapping her knuckles against the wall before pushing off the doorframe and disappearing into her own room, leaving a startled Dakota in her wake.

(That night, Dakota gets in trouble because she stretches the phone cord down the hallway and into her bedroom, which Gia trips over in the middle of the night. But Dakota just moves to call Ryland on the downstairs phone, eventually falling asleep on the couch.)

Chapter 23

TIPPING POINT

Within just a week's time, Gia's packed up and moved out of the house. She takes Delia out with her for her 18th birthday—stealing Dakota's car for the night. And while Dakota's relieved that Ryland isn't living on her own anymore, she's also a little disappointed that it isn't her who gets to move in with the girl.

To make things even worse, there's two new girls in the house. Step sisters. Blair and Zoe. They don't seem to mind that their parents fell victim to a tragic boating accident, either. Their only concern is what's going to happen to their father's money, and how many calories that meals at dinner are. Even Finley, who's usually nothing but welcoming, starts to subtly avoid them. So within the course of a day, the entire dynamic in the house has changed.

One night, after Finley's nearly brought to tears when the two girls criticize her cooking, Dakota helps her gather up her things and move them across the hallway. She's not sure why they start sharing a bedroom—but she knows there's strength in numbers.

Dakota gets a job across the street from Ryland's apartment, waiting tables in a sports bar. And even though she's not supposed to, she somehow manages to lie about her age and get shifts working behind the bar—the tips are better, and god knows she needs the extra money. But, this means she's working an unhealthy amount of hours, exhausted by the time her shift ends. And since Ryland's apartment is just across the street, she finds herself spending more nights there than she does at Red's—sneaking up the fire escape and crawling in through the bedroom window.

"You look exhausted," Ryland notes on night when Dakota heaves open the window a bit later than usual. The lights are still on, and Ryland sits on the edge of the bed, watching as Dakota throws one of her legs over the windowsill and rolls inside.

"Long night," Dakota mumbles, moving to stand in front of the mirror. Her lips curl in disgust when she sees her reflection.

"You stink," Ryland stands up, crinkling her nose.

"Yeah, well, that's what happens when you get an entire tray of drinks spilled on you," Dakota sniffs. Ryland suddenly notes how flustered the girl is. Before she can say something, though, Dakota shakes her head.

"I need to shower," Dakota mutters, yanking off her shoes and disappearing into the hallway. All Ryland can do is watch in confusion.

When Dakota finally emerges from the bathroom fifteen minutes later, she reenters Ryland's room and steals a change of clothes. Ryland raises a questioning eyebrow at her.

"You good?"

Rolling her eyes, Dakota leans against the edge of the bed and combs her fingers through her damp hair. "I don't know," she confesses, balling her hands into fists. Even though her broken hand is fully healed, her knuckles pop every time she clenches her fists hard enough, a surefire sign of her frustration.

"Long night?" Ryland scoots closer and tilts her head to the side. Dakota just shrugs.

"I don't know," she repeats herself. "I can't do this shit for the rest of my life," she squeezes her eyes shut, forcing herself to take a deep breath. "I can't."

"Do what, Koda?"

"Waiting tables," Dakota mumbles. Ryland grows confused.

"Who told you that you have to wait tables for the rest of your life?"

"Well what else am I gonna do?!" Dakota snaps, whipping her head around to look at Ryland, who's startled by her sudden outburst.

"What do you mean?" Ryland furrows her eyebrows together. "If it's that bad, why don't you just quit and find another job?"

"You don't get it," Dakota sighs, her voice harsh. She shakes her head and looks away. "You just don't."

"Then *talk to me*, Dakota."

"I'm gonna be stuck in this phase for the rest of my life, *Ryland*," Dakota presses two fingers to her temples. "I don't get to go to *Stanford*. I'm not smart enough," she mutters. "But I'm also not braindead enough to deal with drunk assholes all night and then fucking pretend I don't hear the shit they say when they think I'm not listening."

"But apparently that's all I'm good for," Dakota mumbles, holding a deep breath in her chest. She kicks at the carpet. "Just a stupid kid with dead parents and no talent whatsoever."

"You have talent," Ryland shakes her head. She opens her mouth to say more, but Dakota beats her to it.

"Yeah, I'm sure Stanford would *kill* to have me."

"Dakota..."

"Don't '*Dakota*' me!" The girl snaps, jumping to her feet. "You're a fucking genius, Finley's practically got a photographic memory, and Gia doesn't even care!" She flings her arm to the side. "Hell, even the two new assholes at Red's have more money in their bank accounts than I'll ever make in my life! How is that fair, huh? Tell me."

Ryland just stares at her, at a loss for words. Dakota hands curl and uncurl into fists as she paces over to the window.

"But I'm just fucking average," she mutters. "Just like every fucking report card I've ever gotten. Just *average*." Ryland watches as the girl gazes out the window.

"Koda..." Ryland bites her lip, hesitant. "Can you not...?"

"I'm not gonna fucking *jump*, Ryland," Dakota snaps at the girl, glaring at her from across the room. Ryland sinks back into herself, remaining silent.

When Dakota looks back over, her expression falters as she realizes what she's said. She opens her mouth to say something but hesitates, just long enough for Ryland to shake her head, turn away, and flick off the bedside lamp before Dakota has a chance to argue.

As the room becomes engulfed in pitch blackness, Ryland can hear Dakota linger for a moment or two. But then, the only thing she hears is the creak of the window being shoved back open and the pang of footsteps as they disappear down the fire escape. She takes a deep breath.

Ryland's worried about Dakota, even more so after she'd snapped at her. And maybe Ryland should understand, because Dakota's been working non-stop for the past three weeks—waking up in the earliest hours of the morning just so she can sneak back into Red's and pretend she wasn't out late. And she does understand, a little.

But she's also hurt. And she's not sure why. Either way, it's what makes her hesitant to call Dakota the next morning after she wakes up to an empty bed. Part of her had held onto the belief that Dakota would find her way back to her side, the entire night forgotten. But she hadn't.

She spends the whole day planning some sort of apology speech for when Dakota clambers back up her fire escape that night, but she doesn't show. Ryland hates to admit that she lays awake all night, waiting for the sound of the window cracking open. She even leaves her light on, just in case the girl does decide to return.

Ryland thinks maybe she should call Dakota, but she has no clue what she'd say. Or how she'd expect Dakota to answer. And even though it wasn't exactly a fight between them, there's still a tiny ounce of stubbornness in her. Insecurity, even. Telling her—*if she loves you so much, she'll call you first*. So Ryland waits.

Maybe she's overreacting a bit. Maybe Dakota could care less. But also, Ryland thinks, maybe Dakota never wants to see her again. Maybe they're broken up. Were they ever really together? Ryland gives herself a headache just thinking about it.

Little does she know, just across town, Dakota's been doing the exact same thing. For some reason, being the one to break the silence between them would mean showing weakness. At least—that's the worry that keeps Dakota from picking up the phone. Hell, she works across the street from Ryland's apartment. On the second night of silence between them, she'd made it halfway up the fire escape before she panicked, psyching herself out and scrambling back down to her car.

And although she took her anger out on Ryland, she's more mad at herself. Dakota's ashamed to face Ryland again under the pretense of what she'd said. Because it still bothers her. And although the delivery was a bit rough around the edges, all the fears she had voiced still ring true. Ryland got into Stanford.

Stanford. Of course Dakota's proud—she's the one who hung the letter up on the fridge and spelled out "GENUIS" in alphabet magnets—but she can't help but size herself up next to Ryland.

Ryland's smart. She can turn anything into a mathematical formula and do long division in her head. She can read a novel a day and write a five page essay in less than an hour. She reads books on astrophysics *for fun*. Next to Ryland, Dakota feels like a dollar store knockoff of a person. And as much as she tells herself she's being stupid and selfish, she just can't help but feel insecure.

Dakota can't do long division in her head. Hell, she probably doesn't even remember how to do it on paper. Whenever Ryland's watching space documentaries, Dakota's the one who steals the remote and changes the channel to *American Ninja Warrior*. She failed English twice because no matter how hard she tried, she couldn't get past the first chapter of a Charles Dickens novel. She'd only passed the third time because Ryland had written her final essay for her. And even then, Ryland and Finley had scoured over the paper, dumbing down some of Ryland's fancy language so the teacher wouldn't suspect Dakota of cheating.

She'd taken the job at the bar to try and earn money for when she moved out. But as the long hours started to add up, piling shift after shift on top of one another, Dakota's slowly become struck by the fear that *this is it*—this is what she'll be doing for the rest of her life. Ryland will go to law school and change lives. Finley will win a Nobel prize. Hell, even Gia will probably discover the cure to cancer on accident while trying a new recipe. But where does that leave Dakota? She's just another kid with dead parents feeling a little too sorry for herself.

All of the restless nights and breaks at work had piled up into a ball of red hot rage inside her chest, probably to cover up her own crippling anxiety. And on that particular night, when she realized she'd gotten double the usual amount of tips just because she'd been wearing a low-cut shirt, she had spent the entire walk back to Ryland's house in boiling anger. She would've snapped at anyone, but Ryland just happened to be there. And god, she just *had* to allude to her mom. Right away, she'd known she hit a nerve. She wants to take it back—she really does. But she's hesitant to face Ryland.

Their combined stubbornness and insecurity doesn't help, either, because they're both hesitant to be the one who picks up the phone. So the silence drags on between them, palpable and suffocating.

What finally brings them together, though, isn't by choice.

It all starts with a knock on the door. Not at the normal time of day, either. It's nearly 3am when Ryland's roused from her sleep. At first, she thinks she's hallucinating. But, the incessant knocking appears again, more rushed, and when she doesn't hear Gia stir in the room beside hers, she groans and fumbles for her brace in the darkness.

She's not sure who she's expecting at this time of night, but it certainly isn't Finley, who has a wide smile on her face when Ryland cracks the door open to peer out.

"Finley?" Ryland's hit with a wave of confusion. "What are you…? How did you…?"

"Do you have Fruity Pebbles?" The girl tilts her head to the side.

"I think there's some in—," Ryland starts, but by then Finley's already halfway across the room. The first thing Ryland notices is that Finley's soaking wet. Granted, it's been raining all night, but…

"Did you *walk* here?" Ryland connects the dots, eyes widening. She hurries to follow Finley into the kitchen. But if Finley hears her question, she ignores it—she just searches through the cabinets until she finds a bowl. Well, actually, the first thing she finds is a plastic container they use for leftovers, and all Ryland can do is watch in confusion as Finley pours milk into it. Tucking the box of cereal under her arm, Finley brushes past Ryland and heads into the living room as if Ryland's not even there.

Ryland's snapped out of her trance when she hears the television click on in the other room, gradually growing louder. By the time Ryland scrambles in to snatch the remote from Finley's hands, the sound is blaring so loud that it's painful.

"What are you doing?" Ryland hisses, frantically turning down the volume on the remote. "It's the middle of the night, Gia's asleep!"

"Not anymore."

Gia's voice startles Ryland, and Finley takes the chance to slip the remote from her hands. Gia, still groggy from sleep, raises an eyebrow at the dripping wet girl on their couch. She turns to Ryland, expecting an explanation.

"Don't look at me," Ryland holds her hands up as if she's surrendering. Finley doesn't seem to be paying them any attention. She just surfs through the channels and counts out three red flakes, dropping them into the container of milk.

"I think she walked here," Ryland adds. Gia circles around the couch, standing in front of the television and studying Finley, who just cranes her head to the side to see past her.

"That's way too far," Gia furrows her eyebrows together in thought. "But how else…?" She trails off, thoroughly confused.

"Quiet," Finley mumbles, holding up a hand to silence the girls. Gia and Ryland exchange concerned glances, but Finley continues watching some black and white movie and shoveling cereal into her mouth, as if it's a completely normal thing to do at 3am.

"Scoot," Gia sighs, nudging Finley's shoulder and plopping down on the couch beside her. Finley moves over, but doesn't peel her eyes from the television. Ryland raises an eyebrow at her, but Gia just shrugs. At this point, she's never quite sure what to expect from Finley.

What they don't expect, though, is a phone call an hour later. Ryland's dozing off on the couch beside Finley, but she's quickly snapped out of her slumber by the shrill ringing of the phone. She hurries to answer it.

"Hello?"

"Ryland? Ryland—it's Red."

"What's going on?" Ryland can instantly tell something is wrong.

"It's Finley. She's gone. She—,"

"She's here," Ryland jumps to interrupt her, keeping her voice down and glancing to the girl on their couch. "She's at our apartment."

"Oh thank god," Red sounds relieved. Ryland can hear muffled speaking in the background. "I'm on my way over right now. Ryland, listen to me, whatever you do, do not let her leave."

"What are you—?"

"Am I clear?"

"Y-yeah," Ryland shakes her head, overwhelmed. "What's going on?" she asks, but by then, the line's already gone dead.

Slowly, running over Red's words in her mind, Ryland hangs up the phone. Gia looks to her—a silent question—but Ryland just shakes her head. Something tells her letting Finley know that Red's on her way isn't the best idea. So, taking a deep breath, she slowly sits back down.

"Who was that?" Gia asks. Finley seems completely oblivious. She just drops three more green flakes into her milk, her eyes trained on the television.

Ryland meets Gia's eyes and shakes her head, giving the slightest of nods in Finley's direction. She's confused, but Gia senses her seriousness and doesn't question her further.

They sit there for a while longer, and suddenly Finley abandons her cereal and hops to her feet, announcing she has to go to the bathroom. As soon as they hear the door at the end of the hallway close, Gia and Ryland huddle closer. Ryland does her best to summarize the phone call.

"She sounded panicked," Ryland nods quickly, glancing back down the hallway. "Like... *really* panicked."

"I mean, anyone would panic when someone goes missing, right?" Gia tenses, suddenly nervous. "She's Finley, for god sakes. They probably just ran out of Fruity Pebbles at the house and so she thought it was perfectly normal to come here... Right?" She talks as if she's trying to convince herself.

"But Red—," Ryland starts, but clamps her mouth shut when they hear the bathroom door close. Finley appears at the end of the hallway moments later.

"Thanks for the cereal," she smiles widely. Ryland notes how it almost looks fake. And then, the girl heads towards the door. Ryland's eyes widen.

"Don't let her go," she hisses to Gia, who looks as confused as ever, but doesn't argue. Both girls jump to their feet and Gia's the first to get to Finley, sliding in between her and the door just as she reaches for the doorknob. Ryland can see Finley's entire body tense.

"Where are you going?" Gia asks, glancing to Ryland over Finley's shoulder. They're both a bit lost on how to handle this.

"Out," Finley nods quickly. But something's off. Gia scoots to the side to block her when she reaches for the doorknob again.

"Out where?"

"Gia..." Finley shakes her head.

"*Finley.*"

"Why are you being like this?" Finley tilts her head to the side. But there's an air of falseness to her actions. It's off putting. Gia takes a step forward, holding her hands up in innocence, an attempt to calm Finley down.

"Finley, I—"

But she's cut off. As soon as the doorknob is free, Finley bolts for it. Gia immediately whirls around and tries to grab for her, but her hands slip out of her grip on Finley's shirt.

Luckily, Finley doesn't make it two steps down the hallway before she's slamming into Red, nearly knocking the woman over. She even tries to dodge around her, but Red reacts fast, grabbing Finley's arm before she can run.

Stunned, Gia and Ryland look to one another with wide eyes. And while Red starts studying Finley, leaning in close and narrowing her eyes, someone else bursts into the apartment. *Dakota.*

She doesn't say anything, she just hurries across the room. Something's horribly wrong, Ryland realizes.

"*Hey,*" Ryland speaks up as Dakota brushes past her, as if she doesn't even exist. She grabs the girl's arm and looks at her questioningly, but Dakota just yanks out of her grip, her dark hair whipping behind her.

Ryland's hurt, but only for a second. Because Dakota's disappearing down the hallway, and her attention is drawn back over to the front door, where Red's grip on Finley's arms has tightened as the girl tries to twist her hands out of her hold.

"*Red*," Dakota reappears, only speaking a single word. Her voice is loud, panicked yet cold as stone. She stands at the end of the hallway, an unreadable expression on her face as she holds up an empty bottle. Ryland's painkillers.

Everything escalates. Gia immediately catches on, and before Ryland can even process what's happening, Red and Gia are wrestling a panicked Finley into the bathroom. Gia doesn't hesitate to practically shove her fingers down Finley's throat, an iron grip on the girl as she forces her to vomit up whatever she's swallowed. Finley's screaming as if she's under attack, trying to fight her way out of their grip as she coughs and sputters and struggles to breathe through her own tears. Dakota stands in the doorway of the bathroom, unsure of what to do, and Ryland lingers at the front of the hallway, a few uneasy steps behind her.

Ryland practically has to slam herself backward against the wall when Red pulls a struggling Finley back to her feet and half drags, half carries her down the hallway. Gia rushes after them, followed by Dakota, but Ryland stands frozen.

"Go start the car," Red looks to Gia, her voice laced with panic. "Now." And for once, Gia doesn't argue. In fact, she practically sprints for the door.

"Let's go," Red nods towards the door, her grip on Finley unwavering. But Dakota hesitates, glancing over to Ryland for the first time that night. Her decision is made as soon as she sees the look on Ryland's face.

"You go," she shakes her head. "We'll stay here. We shouldn't overwhelm her."

Ryland opens her mouth to protest against Dakota making decisions for the both of them, but Red's too focused on Finley to pay much attention. By then, she's already leading the girl down the hallway.

Finley's cries of protest slowly die out, and eventually, after standing frozen in silence for a good amount of time, Dakota slowly moves to close the door. Only when the door slams shut, and it's just them, does a wave of realization hit Ryland. She balls her hands into fists to stop them from shaking. The past three days are instantly forgotten as Dakota rushes over to her side.

"Don't panic," Dakota breathes out, grabbing Ryland's shoulders and looking her straight in the eyes. "Don't panic."

Ryland's breathing fast. "What… what was…?" she stumbles over her words, sloppily motioning to the door.

"Ry…" Dakota glances around the room before urging Ryland to sit down on the couch. And she does, but her eyes fall down to her lap and she digs her nails into her thighs, doing whatever she can to stop her hands from shaking. Dakota's immediately beside her.

"Don't panic," Dakota repeats herself, placing her hand on top of Ryland's own. A rush of guilt runs through her when she feels just how badly the girl is shaking. "Stop thinking about it. Stop."

"What happened?" Ryland lifts her head to look at Dakota, her eyes pleading. Dakota hesitates for a moment but eventually gives in.

"Her mom…" Dakota swallows hard. "They found her… she…" she shakes her head. "She tied her bedsheets together and hung them up and… you know…"

"She's dead?" Ryland's eyes widen. Dakota holds her hand tighter between her own, pulling it into her lap. All she can offer is a slow nod.

"Finley was the one who answered the phone," she explains, pausing to take a deep breath. "They're supposed to relay any information to Red first but… they didn't. And then I woke up to go to the bathroom and Finley was gone. She wasn't in her bed or downstairs… so I woke up Red."

"This isn't the first time she's ran off, so I guess Red's first instinct was to call the hospital where her mom is at… cause she's tried to run away to her mom before," Dakota nods slowly. "That's when Red found out what had happened."

"That she's dead?"

"Don't hyperfocus," Dakota warns her, knowing how Ryland's mind can be her own downfall. "But that's when we realized it was serious."

"That's when Red called here," Ryland notes. Dakota nods.

"And then…" she motions around the room, taking a deep breath and hoping Ryland can fill in the gaps. "Yeah."

"They were mine," Ryland whispers after a few seconds of silence. Dakota shakes her head almost instantly.

"Finley would've found a way no matter whose pills they were," Dakota's quick to respond. "Doesn't matter—,"

"No," Ryland cuts her off, even though her voice is soft. "Not Finley."

Confused, Dakota tilts her head to the side, scooting even closer to the girl. "Your mom?" she asks carefully, knowing she's treading fragile ground.

"They were mine," Ryland closes her eyes. "Her autopsy… my ADHD pills… really strong ones… they're what killed her. She took them and… she…"

"Ryland..."

"She could have lived!" Ryland snaps, slamming her hands down onto the couch. "I... I..." she stammers, unable to choke out any words. It's then that Dakota just pulls the girl closer, wrapping her arms around her and holding to her tightly. Surprisingly, Ryland doesn't argue. In fact, her arms come up to cling onto Dakota just as willingly.

And she cries. She sobs for the first time in ages, her head buried into Dakota's shoulder. The girl just holds her closer, now crying too. Dakota's crying because she hates seeing Ryland like this, but she's also terrified for Finley, shaken by everything that's happened in the past hour. And any quarreling between them is forgotten, because they're both thinking about if it had been the other who had taken the pills. The thought of losing one another is terrifying. Enough that neither Dakota nor Ryland has any intention of letting go.

"It's not your fault," Dakota whispers over and over, her own words muffled in Ryland's shoulder. "Ryland. Please don't. Don't think about it. It's not. Finley's gonna live because *you were here.* Please don't blame yourself."

All Ryland can do is nod against Dakota's shoulder, feeling the girl curl up on the couch, her feet tucked underneath her.

"We should stay awake..." Ryland holds her breath to keep back tears. "By the phone... they could call."

And even though Dakota nods in agreement, sleep beckons to them almost immediately. They don't put up a fight. They can't. They're too drained. Ryland's the first to fall asleep, and Dakota thinks it's better to let her rest, mostly because it's a relief she's not shaking anymore.

Dakota tries to stay awake, she really does. But somehow she ends up with her head drooped down against Ryland's shoulder, her eyelids shut tightly and her hand still holding the girl's own.

Chapter 24

PLAYING GOD

Dakota hates the smell of hospitals. It's too clean. Not human, either. A feeling of dread washes over her. Usually she avoids these places at all costs, but this time it's a bit different. This time, it's Finley. And this time, Ryland's with her, following her down the hallway with a stack of books tucked under her arm.

They both stop in front of the door, and Dakota double checks the room number she's scrawled on her hand in blue ink. She then glances to Ryland, who looks even more nervous than her. It takes her a moment to realize that Ryland's track record with hospitals has been anything but normal. So, taking a deep breath, Dakota knocks on the door and waits a second before poking her head into the room.

"It's us," she says softly, finding Red sitting in a plastic chair beside the bed. After Red nods for them to come in, Dakota nudges the door open and pauses to scan the room.

Finley and Gia sit cross legged at opposite ends of the bed, facing each other over some sort of card game spread out between them. Gia glances up when they enter the room, but Finley doesn't even acknowledge them. She has her head hung low, her ruffled hair keeping her face hidden. All she does is slap another card onto the bed in front of Gia.

Finley's wearing a blue hospital gown that's slightly too big for her, hanging off of one shoulder. Dakota's eyes trace the collection of wires stuck to her back, keeping track of her vitals. Ryland nudges the stack of books into Dakota arms and moves closer to the monitor hung on the wall.

"S'low," she says softly, pointing to one of the numbers and looking to Red.

"It's rising," Red nods. "They pumped her stomach last night. She's still recovering."

With furrowed eyebrows, Ryland slinks back over to Dakota's side. Well aware that Ryland's uncomfortable, Dakota takes the lead, walking forward and plopping the stack of books onto the bed.

"We brought these," Dakota nods, drumming her fingers on top of Finley's encyclopedias. "Figured you might want them."

"She won't talk to you," Gia speaks up. Finley doesn't move. "She won't talk to any of us."

"Give her time," Red sighs. "It's been a long night."

"Tell me about it," Gia huffs, tossing her deck of cards onto the middle of the bed. Finley tenses, but doesn't look up.

"Gia—,"

"I need a smoke," Gia announces, snatching her bag from the chair and trudging out of the room. Dakota hops to her feet, but hesitantly glances to Ryland. As soon as she receives a nod from the girl, she's hurrying off after Gia.

After hovering by the door for a few moments, Ryland quietly moves to sit down at the edge of the bed. She picks up the deck of cards Gia had abandoned and shuffles through them.

"Go fish?" she asks softly, but Finley doesn't respond.

"Crazy eights," Red speaks for her, offering her a comforting smile. She stands up and squeezes Ryland's shoulder. "I'm gonna go see if I can talk to a doctor. You'll be alright?"

Ryland nods hesitantly, her eyes following Red until she disappears from the room, leaving her alone with Finley. Ryland just sits there, unsure of what to do next. She's startled when Finley slaps a card down on the bed between them.

Raising an eyebrow, Ryland looks to Finley for an explanation, but the girl still doesn't lift her head. Slowly, Ryland studies her own deck, plucking a card from her hand and pressing it atop Finley's, tapping it gently.

They carry on like this for a bit, playing cards in dead silence. Meanwhile, outside the expansive hospital building, Dakota finally catches up with Gia, spotting a blonde head of hair sitting on the curb. Carefully, Dakota approaches the girl, who blows a cloud of smoke into the air.

"Bum me one?" Dakota sits down beside the girl, holding up two fingers and tapping them together. Gia raises an eyebrow.

"You smoke?"

"Not regularly, but…" Dakota shrugs. Gia just shakes her head and shoves her pack of cigarettes back into her bag.

"Then I'm doing you a favor," she nods curtly, pushing Dakota's hand away. "Saving you from lung cancer or some shit."

Dakota studies the girl for a moment, slowly drawing her hand back into her lap. She's quiet for a beat, digging at a fray in her jeans and making the rip even bigger. "If you know it's bad for you, then why do you do it?"

"We all do stupid things," Gia flicks the end of her cigarette, raining ash down onto the asphalt between them, which Dakota stomps out with the tip of her shoe. "Smoke cigarettes, down a bottle of pills…" Gia motions with her hand. "Some more than others."

When Gia puts out her cigarette and immediately reaches for another, Dakota's quick to snatch the lighter from her hands. Gia glares at her, but Dakota just shoves the lighter into her pocket.

"Doing you a favor," Dakota nods, ignoring when Gia rolls her eyes. She digs her heel into the old cigarette, crushing the ash into the pavement.

"You know about her mom?" Dakota asks carefully. Gia snorts.

"Yeah, the bitch finally up and offed herself," her voice is bitter. "T'was only a matter of time."

Dakota furrows her eyebrows together, surprised at just how angry Gia sounds. She trains her eyes on the pavement. "You're upset?"

"Who wouldn't be?" Gia looks to her in disbelief. "She can't just do that to Finley. That's her *daughter*." She scoffs. "What a fucking coward."

"You're not supposed to say that," Dakota says quietly, wary of making Gia angry.

"Says who?"

Dakota shrugs. "Everyone. You're supposed to think they're brave for holding on that long."

"Bullshit," Gia scoffs. "That's just what they say to do damage control."

"So Finley's a coward for trying?"

Gia hesitates, looking away and sighing heavily. "The way I see it…" she speaks up after a long pause of silence, gaining Dakota's attention. "You don't kill yourself because you want to die. It's human nature to avoid death," she looks down at her hands, picking at her nails until she nearly draws blood. "That's why it's impossible to drown yourself. You can only hold your head underwater for so long."

"So what are you saying?" Dakota pauses to look over at the girl.

"You kill yourself because you want an escape," Gia turns the unlit cigarette around in her hands, almost pensively. "You think Finley would've washed down a handful of those pills if she had someone next to her offering her a chance to start over with the perfect life?" She pauses. "It's an escape. That's all it is. We're all killing ourselves in different ways," she holds up the unlit cigarette and traces a circle in the air. "Some just go about it faster than others."

Dakota takes a few moments to process Gia's words, realizing the girl next to her has likely spent countless hours thinking this over. She takes the cigarette from Gia and turns it around in her hands, studying it. "So you're saying it's cowardly to want to escape?"

"If it is, then we're all fucking cowards," Gia shakes her head. "I'm saying it's stupid to kill yourself with no regard to the damage you leave behind."

"Damage?"

"For god sakes, Dakota! Look at Ryland!" Gia flings her arm back towards the hospital building, making Dakota flinch. "Look how fucked her life is all because *mommy dearest* decided to mix herself up a pill cocktail," she sighs heavily, letting her hand drop back into her lap and pinching the bridge of her nose. She takes a moment to calm herself down.

"It's a fucked up chain of destruction," Gia mutters, shaking her head. "When you kill yourself, you leave a void where your body used to be, and everyone else around you gets sucked into it. Like a black hole."

"So that's why Finley...?" Dakota motions vaguely.

"Her mom killed herself in the same hospital they're gonna ship Finley off to," Gia shakes her head. "Like mother, like daughter." She finally throws the cigarette down and stomps on it. "Only difference is that Finley gets to live to see all the destruction she could have caused."

Dakota watches Gia dig the heel of her shoe into the asphalt, swallowing roughly. "But you can't just be... mad at her..."

"I'm not mad," Gia quips back. "I'm a lot of other things. Not mad."

"Like what?"

"Frustrated, Scared, Worried," Gia counts them off on her fingers. "Disappointed," she pauses. "Disappointed that she didn't care enough to think of how we'd feel."

"I'm sure she thought about it..."

"Yeah, well it sure didn't stop her, did it?" Gia rolls her eyes and pushes herself up to her feet. "Give me your keys."

Dakota's taken aback, looking up at the girl who holds out her hand. "What are you doing?"

"Going home," Gia wiggles her fingers. "Come on."

Hesitantly, Dakota stands up and fishes the keys from her pocket. She looks back and forth from them to Gia, unsure if she should hand them over.

"For god sakes, Koda," Gia huffs. "I just want to take a nap."

Dakota raises an eyebrow.

"Don't worry, I'm not gonna off myself," Gia rolls her eyes sarcastically. "We can only handle so much in one day."

With that, Gia snatches the keys from Dakota's hand and storms off. But Dakota makes no move to stop her. She just stands frozen on the sidewalk, running over the girl's words in her head.

As she watches Gia walk away, she feels for the lighter in the pocket. For some reason, she's relieved that it's still there.

"They wouldn't have killed you, you know."

Ryland still sits with Finley in the hospital room, and Finley's silently crushing her at a game of cards. When Ryland speaks up for the first time in a while, Finley tenses and doesn't put down her next card. Instead, to Ryland's surprise, she finally lifts her head, quietly looking up at her.

Ryland holds her breath. Finley looks horrible. There's no sugarcoating it. Ryland realizes there's nothing beautiful about this type of suffering. For starters, her eyes are dark and bloodshot. They're not Finley's eyes, Ryland thinks. Her face is red and blotchy from crying, puffy around her eyes—which are still glassy, as if tears could spill over at any moment. They bore into Ryland's questioningly.

"The pills," Ryland nods once. "They wouldn't have killed you."

Finley gently sets down a card, and her head slowly tilts to the side, prompting Ryland to go on.

"You'd need a lot more of those painkillers to actually stop your heart," Ryland slaps down another card. "With the amount you took, you'd either wind up in a coma or spend the rest of your life hooked up to a machine without any muscle function." She pauses. "Oh, and you'd probably go blind. Fun, right?"

She sees Finley shudder. The girl quickly scrambles to put down another card, averting her eyes from Ryland's. But if Ryland notices, it doesn't stop her from talking.

"If you really wanted to kill yourself, you would've taken more than one type of pill. Target as many different organs as possible," Ryland slaps down another card, startling Finley.

"And if you really wanted to go out with a bang, you would've downed it all with a bottle of vodka and slit your wrists for good measure," she nods once. "Vertical," she adds, her voice cold. "Everyone knows they can't stitch that up."

Shakily, Finley sets down another card, quickly drawing her hand back into her lap.

"You should really do your research next time," Ryland mutters, tossing her card down. It slides across the bed and Finley has to grab it before it falls to the floor. "Killing yourself isn't as simple as it seems."

"And how would you know?" Finley's voice is barely audible. Shaky, but accusatory. Even though they're the first words she's spoken since they've been there, Ryland doesn't even act surprised. She just laughs bitterly.

"You think I haven't thought about it?" Ryland tilts her head to the side, feigning a chilling type of innocence. "You think seeing my mom all cold and dead and motionless didn't plant a little seed of wondering in my head?"

Finley looks away, but Ryland just keeps talking.

"Who would have found you, Finley?" Ryland tilts her head to the side. "Would it have been Red…? Dakota…? *Me*? Would you have been the second person I found dead thanks to a bottle of pills?" She pauses, letting her words sink in. "Or would it have been Gia? You already know how she blames herself for everything. I'm sure your death would just be another checkmark on her list." Finley shivers.

"You don't get to die, Finley. And neither do I," Ryland shakes her head. "It's not that easy. That's not our choice to make."

"But my mom…" Finley's voice wavers. Ryland almost doesn't hear her.

"And look where she ended up!" Ryland slams her hand of cards down. "*Dead*. My mom? Dead too. You don't think they had even a *moment* of regret? That, maybe, just maybe, they changed their minds when it was too late?"

"I…"

"Jesus Christ, Finley! You can't even decide where to stick a fucking sticker because it's too permanent of a decision!" Ryland shakes her head in frustration. "And yet you try to kill yourself? Does that make sense to you?"

Ryland looks to Finley for an answer, tilting her head to the side, but Finley just shies backwards and shakes her head. "Ryland…"

"You don't get to play God, Finley. No one does. You don't get to—,"

"You're scaring me!" Finley finally snaps, her voice hoarse.

"Good!" Ryland throws her hands down to her sides. "That's the point! It's supposed to scare you, Finley! This is terrifying!"

At this point, Finley's crying, and Ryland's on the verge of tears. Shaking her head and taking a deep breath. Ryland leans back on her hands.

"Listen, Fin…"

"*Finley*."

"*Finley*, sorry," Ryland quickly corrects herself. She sighs. "Listen, I know how it feels. You know I do. Out of everyone, I know. And it fucking sucks."

Finley just nods softly, slowly beginning to rearrange the cards that Ryland had thrown across the bed. "It does," she whispers, her voice barely audible.

"But you can't… you can't just follow them down," Ryland swallows. Her bitterness is gone, replaced with an overwhelming amount of empathy. "And I'm sorry, I am. I'm sorry your mom turned into a ticking time bomb. But that's not you, Finley. I know it isn't." She pauses. "You know that, right?"

All she gets in return is a half hearted shrug as Finley makes a feeble attempt to wipe the tears from her eyes with the back of her hand. With a sigh, Ryland decides she's had enough lecturing for the day, and simply stands up to pull the girl into a hug.

"It's gonna be okay," Ryland nods softly. Finley doesn't return the hug—she's still withdrawn, but it doesn't turn Ryland away. She knows Finley needs it, whether she says so or not.

Later that night, Red drops Ryland and Dakota off back at the apartment, silently giving Dakota permission to spend the night. It's been a long day for all of them, especially after they'd watched Finley hesitantly climb into the ambulance that would transfer her to the psychiatric hospital she'll be staying at temporarily.

Dakota's relieved to find Gia fast asleep on the couch when she follows Ryland into the apartment. Snoring, nonetheless.

Even though Dakota's shaken up, it's obvious to her that Gia and Ryland have taken this the hardest. Ryland, because painful memories are resurfacing. And Gia, well, Dakota's not so sure. Either way, she quickly falls into some sort of leadership position, making Ryland sit down and relax while she rushes into the kitchen to find something for dinner.

She winds up making pancakes, mainly because she knows they're one of Ryland's comfort foods. Gia wakes up and they force her to eat something. An odd silence falls over them and Dakota feels like a bomb could drop at any second.

But it doesn't. It's so painfully quiet that Dakota honestly wishes someone would snap. But Gia's dead silent, zombie-like, and Ryland just bounces her leg nervously.

Eventually, Dakota dismisses herself to Ryland's bedroom. And that's where Ryland finds her later that night, curled up against the headboard with a book in her hands. Lingering in the doorway, Ryland traces the girl's figure with her eyes. She looks incredibly small in comparison to the big bed.

"Reading?" Ryland eventually speaks up, raising an eyebrow. Startled, Dakota's head jerks up.

"Trying to," she shrugs and shakes her head. "I've been reading this same paragraph over and over but I just can't focus." Setting the book aside, she looks Ryland up and down. "You good?"

"Long day," Ryland wanders over to her dresser, but something else catches her eye. She holds up the jacket thrown over the back of her chair. "This yours?"

Once Dakota nods, Ryland's shedding her t-shirt and tugging on Dakota's hoodie. She wanders over to the bed, sitting down on the very end and fumbling with her brace. Dakota crawls over to sit next to her.

"She'll be okay," Dakota tries to reassure her, resting her chin on Ryland's shoulder. "She'll get better."

Her resolve crumbling, Ryland's shoulders slump and she shoves her brace aside. "Will she?" Ryland's hands fall limply in her lap. "*Will we*?"

"We?"

"All of us," Ryland motions around the room. "With everything we've been through, will we ever fully recover?"

Dakota shivers at the thought, also reminded of Gia's words from earlier that day. She doesn't like the hopelessness that's been draped over them. But then again, what words of encouragement can she offer that Ryland hasn't heard a million times before? What string of speech could possibly make up for everything?

She opens her mouth to speak but all that comes out is a strangled "*I'm sorry.*" Ryland just sighs, her shoulders losing their stiffness. Dakota's about as lost as she is, she realizes. They're both figuring this out together.

"No one's fault," Ryland says softly. Dakota's hands reach up to pull Ryland's hair out of her ponytail, running her fingers through it. She sighs and presses her forehead against her shoulder.

"We'll get through it," Dakota whispers, talking more to herself than anyone. "We have to."

Up until now, Dakota's never realized how much of a kinship she's formed with the girls. Losing Finley would be like losing a part of them. It's become the four of them against the world, a shelter that Dakota realizes she relies on more than she thought.

"You okay?" Ryland turns to face the girl. "You've been quiet all day."

With a soft shrug, Dakota leans forward and gently massages the area around Ryland's knee, a habit she's picked up after watching Ryland do it for so long. "Last night was… a lot," she admits, looking up to Ryland. "Never dealt with something like that before."

"You seemed pretty level headed all day," Ryland notes. Dakota shrugs again.

"I had to be," Dakota nods. "You and Gia seemed… *off.*"

"Yeah…" Ryland whispers, embarrassed. "It's a lot."

"Your mom?" Dakota asks knowingly, earning a hesitant nod in return.

"Thought so," Dakota whispers. Ryland doesn't say anything, just looks down softly. Scooting closer to her, Dakota brushes her hair of her face.

"There's someplace better," she says quietly. "There has to be."

"You think so?" Ryland lifts her head. The pleading look in her eyes is unsettling.

"It's what I tell myself," Dakota nods. "All of this…" she motions around the room. "It all means too much to just… disappear."

"I try not to think about it," Ryland admits. "When I was little, I used to tie letters to balloons and send them up to heaven.

Dakota can't help but laugh softly. "That's logical," she scoots back on the bed, propping a collection of pillows up against the headboard. "I used to start my journal entries as a letter to my mom instead of saying 'Dear Diary.'"

Ryland gives her a sad smile, moving over to lay beside the girl. "It scares me that Finley's going to have to go through all that."

"Me too," Dakota whispers, looking down at her hands. "I guess we've just gotta be there for her. That's about all we have to offer."

Ryland needs her pills.

She's been taking them almost every night when she wakes up to a painful numbness in her leg, similar to the 'pins and needles' sensation after her foot falls asleep. But this is worse. Way worse. Her veins *burn*.

She's gotten used to it, though. Mostly because she's been able to fumble her way across the hallway and into the bathroom to retrieve her painkillers. This time, however, it takes a bit of searching through the medicine cabinet until the realization hits her. And when it does, she's slamming both of her fists against the counter and groaning in frustration.

It's no surprise that, moments later, a very sleeping and very confused Dakota is scrambling across the hallway. She's still a bit on edge after Finley's incident. Wide eyed, she looks to Ryland. "What's going on?"

"The last of my pills," Ryland mutters, too tired to try and hide her pain. "There's none left." She throws the empty bottle down and leans on the counter to keep herself standing.

"Bad?" Dakota whispers, a look of concern washing over her face.

All it takes is a nod from Ryland, and Dakota's launching herself into battle mode. Ignoring the girl's protests, Dakota ducks under Ryland's shoulder and helps lead her back into the living room, where she props her leg up with pillows and presses the TV remote into her hands.

"I'll be back," she promises, pressing a rushed kiss to Ryland's forehead and disappearing out the front door. Ryland doesn't even have time to argue, and when she tries to get up and go after her, the pain that shoots through her leg is enough to make her fall back onto the couch and cry out in pain.

Dakota may hate her job, but right now she's pretty goddamn thankful for the connections it has given her. She doesn't even bother taking her car, she just tugs on her jacket and hurries across the street.

The bar is still open, and she hurries inside, keeping her head down until she arrives at the corner booth in the very back of the restaurant. Imitating what she'd seen many do before, she slams both hands down on the table. Sure enough, the man slumped against the booth stirs, cracking a smile when he looks up to find Dakota staring him down.

"Haven't seen you here before," he comments, looking her up and down. "What is it you need?"

"Pills," she nods, glancing around and pulling a twenty dollar bill from her pocket. "Painkillers. Strong ones."

He just laughs. "I'm afraid pills aren't my turf, little lady. But I do have—," he reaches to pull something from the inside of his jacket, but Dakota cuts him off by slamming her hands down again, an urgent look in her eyes.

"Do you know where I can get some?" she keeps her voice firm. "Painkillers. Prescription kind. M'not interested in any recreational shit."

The man raises an eyebrow, but slips the twenty from her grip and studies it, snapping the bill a few times between his fingers. "I might have something that could help you."

And that's how Dakota ends up breaking into a pharmacy. Well, is it considered breaking in if she has a magnet strong enough to wipe the entire security system? Either way, she pries her way inside through the back door and quickly deactivates the alarm.

She's thought her days of breaking and entering were long behind her, confined to the countless times she and Hudson had shoved things under their clothes in gas stations or picked the locks on the back of vending machines, stuffing their pockets with change and their backpacks with candy. Sure, it made her feel guilty, but it was what they had to do to survive. She figures this time, it's the same thing.

She knows Ryland will freak if she finds out what she's doing, but she's willing to risk that if it means easing just a fraction of the girl's pain. She finds Ryland's pills right away, having memorized the long scientific name on the bottle. They're locked away, but there's a ring of keys hanging on the wall, making it all too easy for her to shove a handful into her jacket pocket. To ease her own conscience, she slips a twenty into the cash register before disappearing out the back door.

It would be an understatement to say that Ryland's relieved when she hears the familiar sound of Dakota climbing back up the fire escape. She sits up as soon as Dakota hurries into the room, shoving a water bottle into her hands and digging the pills from her pocket. She's been gone a considerable amount of time, and in that time, it's only gotten worse. The searing pain has moved up to her thigh, and by the time Dakota hands her two pills, she doesn't even question where they came from.

For the rest of the night, as the medicine takes its time to kick in, Dakota holds Ryland and rocks her back and forth through the pain, quietly telling her stories from her childhood to try and keep her mind off of things. And that's how Gia finds them the next morning, fast asleep in each other's arms.

With Finley in the hospital, there's a few small changes.

First and foremost, every night at 6 o'clock sharp, without fail, Gia is on the phone. She's practically memorized the number of the hospital, and she's figured out when to call at just the right time, so she catches the nurse that gives Finley fifteen minutes to talk, instead of ten. Ryland and Dakota try and linger around the living room, catching bits and pieces of their conversation. Most of it is Gia nagging at her, making sure she's eating enough, and keeping track of the changes they've made to her medicine on a little notepad she keeps by the couch.

But some days are worse than others, and those are the nights Gia hangs up the phone and yanks the cord from the wall. Those are the nights she rants on and on about how Finley sounds like a robot, and how the last thing she needs it to be "*locked up in a fucking prison for weeks.*"

It goes unspoken that things haven't been going very well lately. Which is why Dakota's wary when Ryland calls her at Red's and asks her to come over. It worries her even more because Ryland wouldn't tell her what it was about. So, waiting until Red's asleep, Dakota sneaks out her window and takes the familiar route to Ryland's apartment.

Ryland's practically waiting at the door when she gets there, and she quickly lets Dakota in.

"I did something," Ryland breathes out right away, clasping her hands together. Her nervousness makes Dakota feel uneasy. "I did something and you might not like it. But I had to."

"What are you talking about?" Dakota tilts her head to the side. Ryland just shakes her head and hands Dakota an envelope. It's already been opened, so Dakota just eyes Ryland suspiciously and slips the letter from within.

It's addressed to her, and as soon as she reads the first few sentences, she's looking to Ryland in utter confusion. "What the fuck?"

Ryland's quick to try and defend herself, shaking her head and moving forwards. "Don't be mad," she pleads. "Just hear me out."

"Ryland—,"

"It's just a small state college," Ryland desperately tries to plead her case. "I didn't want you to just… *not try*. There's a ton of majors. Hell, you could just take general studies classes. And I can help you. Plus, it's cheap, but it's rated really good and—,"

"You sent in an application for me?" Dakota raises an eyebrow. Ryland struggles to decipher how she's feeling, which worries her even more.

"I… I just thought you'd want to have options," Ryland says softly. "You didn't read the rest but they're, uh…" she averts her eyes. "They're offering you a scholarship based on your essay."

"My essay?"

"Yeah," Ryland clears her throat awkwardly. "I sent in one of your journal entries. Revised, of course, but…" she bites her lip.

"You did *what*?" Dakota narrows her eyes.

"Please don't be mad," Ryland takes a step forward and reaches for her, but Dakota moves away. She just shakes her head.

"I don't—," she cuts herself off, handing the letter back to Ryland. "I can't. I… I've got to go."

"Dakota…" Ryland makes a feeble attempt to convince her, but Dakota's already made up her mind. Breathing in deeply, Ryland looks down at the letter in her hands. But even once the door closes behind Dakota, something in Ryland makes her save the letter, slipping the envelope between a stack of books on her desk.

Chapter 25

HEALING

It takes Dakota exactly three days to reach her breaking point.

It's not that she's avoiding Ryland, because she isn't. It's just that work has been practically consuming her life. It also doesn't help that she's on the verge of punching Blair or Zoe in the face. Even though they've lost their parents, they don't seem to care. They act as if they haven't suffered a day in their lives, treating Dakota like some poor little misfit toy with broken circuitry. Granted, maybe Dakota's internalizing it too much, but she doesn't miss the glares they throw her way, judging her every move.

It all happens on a Wednesday. For starters, she's working from 5:00 to 2:00 without any breaks, which probably isn't legal, but she can't argue, she needs the money. Things just don't go the way they should that afternoon. She spills the ramen she was rushing to eat all over her good shirt, and she practically has to tug on another blouse as she's hurrying out the door. When she gets in the car, her eyes narrow. In an attempt to extend an olive branch, she'd let the devil sisters borrow her car that morning. But now it stinks like smoke, something even Gia wouldn't do. She spends the entire ride with the windows down and prays the smell doesn't stick to her clothes.

To make matters worse, she gets to work a few minutes late and receives an earful from her boss. Then, one of her coworkers doesn't show up, and she has to scramble to work the bar all by herself. Dakota manages to stay on top of things for a while, but as the night carries on, more regulars make their way inside and they all seem to want to stay and chat. She tries her best to listen to a guy describing his ex while she simultaneously makes a drink for another customer, all the while taking an order from halfway across the bar.

But of course, something snaps, and somewhere amidst the whirlwind she ends up dropping an entire bottle of vodka to the floor. The expensive kind, too. It shatters to pieces, drawing the attention of everyone in the bar. She just stands there for a moment, staring down at her feet and swallowing hard. Fuck.

"Really, Quinn?"

Her boss's voice echoes across the entire room, and she usually doesn't pay his comments much mind, but now he's storming over to her in front of *everyone*, and suddenly she's reminded that she's only seventeen years old. This is too much. She braces herself.

"Get the man his drink and then clean this mess up," he glares at her, speaking through gritted teeth. Dakota turns, intent on following his instructions, but moments later she skids to a stop. Someone's clapping. One of the guys across the bar whistles his approval to the boss, as if he's "put her in her place," and for some reason, Dakota's hands curl into fists. Slowly, with shaky fingers, she unties the apron from her waist and turns back around.

"I quit."

"What was that?" he chuckles, looking down at her.

"I *quit*," Dakota raises her voice, tilting her chin upwards and taking a step forward. She's terrified, but it doesn't show through her hardened exterior. Her eyes lock with his, daring him to challenge her.

"You can't just quit," he laughs, rolling his eyes. All of his employees have threatened to quit at one point or another. But Dakota doesn't waver. She takes a step closer, glass crunching under her shoes.

"Watch me," she looks him dead in the eyes, holding up her apron and letting it drop to the ground. She storms past him, not looking back as the door swings shut behind her.

She doesn't stop walking. In fact, she tugs her hair up into a ponytail and picks up the pace into a light jog. And then, she's running.

She used to do this back when she lived with Hudson. Whenever she was mad or angry, she'd run, bursting out the back door and sprinting until her lungs ached, until she couldn't even remember what she'd been mad about in the first place.

And that's what she does tonight. Even though it's pitch black, she runs. Her feet pound against the pavement, buildings passing by in blurs. Which is how, sometime later that night, she finds herself outside Ryland's apartment, staring up at the old metal fire escape.

At first Ryland thinks Dakota's dying when she climbs in through the window, breathing heavily. Ryland's already taken her brace off and is in bed, but she still scrambles to sit up and turn on the light. As soon as she sees Dakota, red faced and bent over to catch her breath, she moves to stand up.

"Don't," Dakota holds out a hand to stop her. So Ryland hesitates, feet hanging off the bed. Her eyes meet Dakota's questioningly.

"I need to shower," Dakota clears her throat, grabbing a towel thrown over Ryland's desk chair. "Will you be up in like... fifteen?" she asks shyly, her eyes fluttering down to the ground.

"If you need me to be," Ryland whispers, her voice weathered from sleep. Dakota just nods, clutching the towel to her chest and disappearing into the hallway without another word.

When Dakota returns, she's dressed in one of Ryland's burgundy hoodies and a pair of striped socks she always steals from Gia, which purposely don't match. Even though it's the middle of a California summer, the apartment always seems to be freezing. (Not that Dakota minds. She likes wearing Ryland's sweaters.) She's lazily brushed through her hair, leaving it damp and hanging down her shoulders. Ryland raises an eyebrow when she wanders in the room, looking hopelessly lost.

"You gonna tell me what happened?" Ryland asks, struggling to keep her voice soft. She sits up, forgetting the book she had been reading and taking a moment to study the girl, who hesitates in the doorway. Ryland pats the space beside her, to which Dakota is thankful for.

Crawling onto the bed and sitting cross legged, Dakota takes a moment to compose her words. She's never been one to admit that she's wrong, or even close to it. It's probably a fear of showing weakness, she thinks. Her entire life has conditioned her to constantly be in survival mode—where there's no room for vulnerability. Being able to feel those emotions is something she's still getting used to.

"I was thinking," Dakota speaks up quietly, her eyes looking anywhere but Ryland's, as if the moment their gazes meet, Ryland would be able to see right through her. "The college," she swallows nervously. "They wouldn't happen to have a degree in fire science, would they?"

Ryland raises an eyebrow at her, but quietly retrieves her laptop from her nightstand and surfs through it for a moment. Clearing her throat, she drums her fingers against the space bar and quietly passes it over to Dakota. She doesn't say anything, in fear of ruining whatever fragile progress they've made. Dakota's eyes scan the screen, leaning in slowly as she reads.

"So… with this," Dakota taps the screen, glancing to Ryland quickly. "Someone could go into firefighting or some shit, right?"

"If they had the proper training, yeah," Ryland nods slowly. Dakota doesn't notice the eyebrow she raises in question.

"Training?" the girl tilts her head to the side. "What do you mean?"

"Do you want me to find out?" Ryland eyes the girl. Dakota shrinks under her knowing gaze, but nods slowly and passes the laptop back over to her. Ryland notices how she subtly moves to lean over her shoulder as she google searches the requirements, fighting back a smile when Dakota's practically hovering overtop of her.

"Here," Ryland taps her nails against the screen and glances up at Dakota. "You've gotta get volunteer hours and shit, and CPR training, but that's about it."

"So if someone went to college for fire science, and got all the training they needed, they'd be able to be a firefighter?"

"Pretty much," Ryland nods softly, studying Dakota, who fights to avoid her gaze. "Does this *someone* happen to be sitting next to me?"

Crossing her legs underneath her, Dakota shrugs one shoulder. "Just thinking, that's all."

"Is this wishful thinking? Or serious thinking?"

"It's '*I quit my job and I have no other options*' thinking," Dakota mutters, still reading an article on the laptop.

"You quit your job?"

"T'was bound to happen eventually."

Almost intuitively, Ryland grabs Dakota's hand, turning it over and running her thumb over the girl's knuckles. Dakota can't help but laugh.

"I didn't punch anyone," she reassures the girl, shaking her head. "Almost did. But didn't."

"But you quit."

"That I did."

"Why?"

Sighing heavily, Dakota glances to the window from which she came. "Just got to be too much," she cracks her knuckles. "Boss yelled at me and I guess that was about it."

"You okay?" Ryland scoots closer, biting her lip. Dakota leans into her side, but shakes her head.

"Just glad it's over," she admits. "But lost on what to do next."

"Then talk to me," Ryland squeezes her shoulder. "Why a firefighter?"

Dakota thinks for a moment, rubbing the material of Ryland's hoodie between her thumb and forefinger. "I thought about what you said. About wanting to be a child advocate because of your past. And I got to thinking about my own past…"

"And the fire," Ryland notes softly, Dakota nods.

"Yeah," Dakota whispers. "I mean, I figured I'm enough of an adrenaline junkie to handle it."

"You've thought about this a lot?" Ryland asks, tilting her head to the side just slightly. Dakota closes the laptop and nods.

"I have," she breathes out. "I think I'm gonna do it."

"Elements of American Literature, page 371," Ryland nudges her forwards, pointing to the stack of books on the desk. Dakota looks to her questioningly, but slowly rises to her feet and pries the heavy textbook from the bottom of the pile. She flips through it, quickly finding the object in question—the same envelope she'd shoved into Ryland's hands just a few days ago. With her back turn to the girl, she reads over it again. Then, with a deep breath, she turns back around and holds it up.

"What's the next step?"

Ryland can't fight back her smile, and she motions for Dakota to come closer. When she does, Ryland tugs on her hand so she'll sit back down.

"We'll figure it out together," she says softly, kissing the girl's forehead. "I'm proud of you."

"M'proud of you, too," Dakota mumbles, a playful smile tugging at her lips. She nudges Ryland's chin with her hand, finding the girl's lips and kissing her as she lowers her back down onto the bed. Ryland immediately knows where this is going. Not that she minds, though. In fact, given the opportunity, she pushes Dakota's knee with her own and flips them over so she's on top. Dakota's back hits the bed, her hair sprawled out around her, and she looks up to Ryland with wide eyes.

"Hi," she breathes out, making Ryland laugh and roll her eyes. And when Ryland leans down to kiss her again, everything else is forgotten. Ryland's her spark, her aphrodisiac, and Dakota thinks she'll never grow tired of being close to her.

Dakota could possibly be the world's deepest sleeper.

The knocking on the apartment door doesn't stir the girl, but it does manage to pull Ryland from her sleep. She glances over to

Dakota beside her, pulling the sheets over her before sitting up and retrieving her brace from the floor.

Her father is the last person she expects to see when she peers through the peephole. But he's there, and Ryland immediately notices the wrapped box in his hands as she opens the door. She rubs her eyes and looks to him in confusion.

"I'm sorry it's early," he apologizes, glancing back into her apartment. "I wanted to bring you something on the way to work," he adds. Ryland can tell he's nervous, and it starts to rub off on her. "I heard about Stanford." There's a smile on his face, and Ryland purses her lips. Is he proud? She slowly steps aside, nudging the door further open.

"You can come in," she says softly, her eyes nervously scanning her own apartment. "Sorry it's messy."

He shrugs it off, stepping past her and taking in the small room. Ryland watches him, curious. Nodding, he turns to her and hands her the box in his hands.

"Noticed you needed one of these," he explains. Ryland raises a questioning eyebrow, but quietly moves over to the kitchen table and sets it down. It's quiet, awkwardly so, but she proceeds to carefully unwrap the present.

"Holy shit," her eyes widen, but she quickly catches herself and apologizes for her language. He just laughs and nods for her to look at it.

"Figured every Stanford student could use one," he chuckles, cupping the back of his neck. "That's a big deal, you know."

Ryland swallows. "I know," she nods softly, studying the brand new laptop he's gotten her. And she knows he can't buy her friendship with his money—of course—but she realizes he'd gone out of his way to notice her old, junky laptop note that she was well due for a replacement. His effort means more to her than whatever monetary amount he spent.

"Are you excited?" he asks, watching her. Ryland nods.

"It's intimidating," she admits, drumming her fingers against the table.

"It should be," he shrugs. "A little bit of fear is a good thing."

"More like a *lot* of fear," Ryland corrects him, surprised when he chuckles.

"Even better," he nods once.

"I'm gonna go… put this away," she speaks up, still feeling a bit uneasy around him. She curses herself as she moves toward her bedroom. Their relationship has definitely improved, but god, she still has so many walls up. She's consciously aware of it, and yet she struggles to move past it.

She slips into her bedroom, quickly setting down the box on her desk. However, her mind is so scattered that when she exits her bedroom, she doesn't understand why he's looking at her with an unreadable expression. She tilts her head to the side in utter confusion.

"Is this the same one?"

Now even more confused, Ryland furrows her eyebrows. However, when she realizes his gaze has moved behind her, she quickly turns around. That's when it hits her—her eyes widen as soon as she sees the tangle of dark hair poking out of her sheets. Panicking, she quickly moves to shut her door. Her face is bright red.

"I-I…" she swallows roughly, feeling infinitely embarrassed when she meets his gaze again. He, however, doesn't seem fazed.

"She's the same one? Dakota?" he asks again. Ryland leans against the door. All she can over him is a slow nod, hesitant to see his reaction.

"Hm," he nods. Is it approval? Ryland bites her lip. "Well, at least you're not like your mother."

As soon as the words leave his mouth, Ryland tenses, and he immediately regrets what he's said. "I didn't mean it that way," he quickly apologizes. "I didn't—,"

"I get it," Ryland interrupts him, holding up her hands to show she's not mad. "I get it," she repeats herself. "I really need to stop idolizing her," she admits, looking away nervously.

It's awkward, and Ryland silently pleads for Dakota to stay asleep. Luckily, he just nods, and an empty silence falls over them. God, Ryland wishes she was better at conversation.

"Hey," he speaks up, walking over to the coffee table and picking up the book she'd been reading. "Dialogues of Plato?"

Ryland nods quietly.

"God, that's some dense stuff," he laughs, flipping through the pages. "Interesting though."

"I have to reread a lot," Ryland admits, moving away from the door and over to the couch. "We do this thing where we go to thrift stores and randomly pick out books to read."

"We?"

"Me and Dakota," she says softly, concealing her own nervousness.

"So… you two…" he glances back to the door and then motions to Ryland. "You two really are…?"

"*Together*, yeah," Ryland nods once. "For a while now."

"You seem scared."

Ryland shrugs, feeling as if she's shrinking under his gaze. But god, why does she care what he thinks? When did she start caring? "It's weird."

"What's the big deal?" he looks to her in confusion. Ryland pauses. She doesn't know.

She doesn't know. It just now hits her that she's eighteen, in control of her own life, and able to make her own decisions. So, really, what is the big deal?

"Nothing," Ryland shakes her head. "Thank you for the laptop, by the way. God knows I needed it."

He laughs, remembering the bulky computer she'd been lugging around with her before. "No problem," he clears his throat. "Oh, and Jonah wanted me to give you this," he adds, remembering the paper in his pocket. "It's an invitation to his 5th grade graduation. Big deal," he chuckles. "You don't have to go if you feel—,"

"I'll go," Ryland nods, not even looking at the invitation. She surprises even herself by saying this. "It's this Saturday?"

"We're all going out to dinner afterwards," he confirms. "I was… well, me and Julienne talked it over, and I mean, it looks like you're alright with being a part of our lives now. We thought it was fit to tell the kids… *who you are.* I wanted to ask you first, though."

"Jonah knows," Ryland says the only thing that comes to mind. "He already knows."

Her father just laughs and rolls his eyes. "Of course he does. I should've known."

"But the twins?"

"Clueless," he shakes his head. "Julienne's hesitant to tell them, but I think it's only fair. That is, if you plan to stick around."

"I, uh…" Ryland hesitates. "Whatever you think is best."

"Then we'll see how things go," he nods and gives her a soft smile. "I'd stick around for a bit, but I've got to head to work."

Ryland nods softly, and he turns for the door, but at the last minute something pushes her forward. "Wait," she speaks up, surprising herself. He pauses.

And then she hugs him for the first time. It just feels like the right timing. He might not feel like her dad—she's not sure if she ever will—but he's starting to feel like a friend. And a bit like family. And even though she's still hesitant around him, there's something comforting about having him in her life. He's started to prove himself to her, just by staying there. Not many people have, she realizes.

"Thank you," she says softly. She notes the surprised expression on his face and falters for a moment. But he just smiles and squeezes her shoulder.

"I'll see you Saturday," he nods. Ryland takes a deep breath.

And, ironically, as soon as she closes the door behind him, she turns around to find a very sleepy Dakota padding out of her bedroom. She's clad in only her underwear, hugging a blanket around her torso. Yawning, she rubs her eyes and finds Ryland across the room. She tilts her head to the side. "Mornin'?"

"Good timing," Ryland laughs, glancing back to the door before walking over to her. Dakota's eyebrows furrow together. She looks adorably exhausted with her hair tousled all over the place.

"Hm?" Dakota walks towards her, leaning her head against Ryland's shoulder when the girl wraps her arms around her.

"My dad just stopped by," she admits. Dakota looks up at her, concerned.

"Nothing bad," Ryland's quick to shake her head. "He brought me a laptop for school. Oh, and he saw you."

"Huh?" Dakota raises her eyebrows.

"I told him about us," Ryland nods. Dakota tilts her head to the side.

"Did you now?" she smirks, earning a playful nudge from Ryland.

"Go put on a fucking shirt before Gia wakes up," she urges her back to the bedroom. Dakota pouts, but agrees, stopping to send a cheeky smile in Ryland's direction.

As Dakota gets dressed, Ryland wanders over to the window, leaning with her hands on the windowsill and watching the sun as it starts to peek over the buildings around them. Things are looking up, she thinks. And a few minutes later, the pair of arms that wrap around her waist and the airy giggle that follows only serve to remind her of one of the reasons why.

In the upcoming weeks, Dakota thanks god for Ryland. If it wasn't for her, she wouldn't have a clue how to navigate starting school once again. But with Ryland, it's surprisingly easy.

However, there's one more order of business they have to attend to before it's smooth sailing. And that's Finley. Who today, for the first time, they finally get to see. She's going on her fourth week in the hospital, which means she's now allowed to have visitors who aren't immediate family. Red had seen her the week before, which is when Gia stole Dakota's car and drove over to hear every single detail from Red.

But now, Ryland, Gia, and Dakota are all seated in a freezing cold waiting room, nervous yet eager to finally see Finley. Four weeks feels like an eternity, especially to Dakota, who's now outnumbered at the home. Thankfully, Red doesn't seem to mind all the time she spends at Ryland and Gia's apartment. Dakota's pretty sure Red can't stand Blair and Zoe either, though she'd never say it aloud.

"How long do you think they're gonna keep her here?" Dakota asks, looking to Gia, who's aimlessly picking at a loose string on her jeans. The blonde shrugs.

"Red said the average visit is five weeks," she nods. "So hopefully soon."

"Do you know how she's doing?"

"Red said she seems better," Gia finally looks up, although Dakota can tell she's worried. "But there's really no telling what's going on inside her head."

"But—,"

Dakota's interrupted by two beeps and the sound of two metal doors sliding open. Everyone in the room looks up hopefully, but the nurse who enters scans the chairs before pointing to the three girls and motioning for them to follow her. They all practically leap to her feet.

"Don't act like it's a big deal," Gia hangs back, trying to coach Dakota and Ryland. "Don't freak her out."

However, the moment the nurse steps aside, holding the door open to a small bedroom, it's Finley who jumps to her feet and throws her arms around Gia. Gia tenses in shock, but she quickly hugs her back, forgetting just how small the girl is. The nurse tells them they have a little less than an hour, leaving the four girls in the tiny room.

Dakota looks around. There really isn't much to see, Finley doesn't seem to have made any effort to make herself at home. Dakota notes that it's probably a good thing.

"Did you cut your hair?" Finley notices, tilting her head to the side and twirling a strand of Dakota's hair around her finger.

"Just a few inches," Dakota nods. "Ryland did it."

"Oh," Finley sits down on the end of her bed. "What else is different?"

"Not much," Gia answers. The three girls all look to one another before shrugging and sitting down against the wall, across from Finley. It feels more like an interrogation, though, so Gia hops up to her feet to sit on the bed beside her.

"Has Red said anything… about me?" Finley asks hesitantly, pulling her hands into her lap. "About school?"

Dakota thinks for a moment. "Your first priority is getting better," she glances to Gia, who nods.

"But I can go back to school?"

"You want to?"

Finley nods quickly. "I want to go to college."

"Well, good," Dakota smiles softly. "There's an open apartment a few doors down from Ryland's, I'm still in if you are."

"You still want to…?" Finley tilts her head to the side, shocked. And now, everyone else is confused.

"That was the plan, right?" Dakota asks, but all she earns is a shrug from Finley.

"I didn't know you wanted to… after I…" Finley motions with her hand, her eyes skittering down to her lap. "I thought you'd be mad at me."

"You thought we'd be mad?"

Finley nods slowly.

"Well that's stupid," Dakota laughs. She earns glares from Gia and Ryland, but she ignores them. "Why would we be mad?"

"Because I…"

"We're not mad," Dakota quickly shakes her head. "We just… we just don't want you to do it again."

"I won't," Finley looks up, conviction in her voice. "I won't."

"Then prove it," Gia adds, nudging her shoulder. "You scared the hell out of me."

Finley laughs, but she's still nervous. She feels embarrassed. She hadn't intended for them to see everything that happened. But they did—and now she feels painstakingly exposed. They witnessed a side of her that even she didn't know existed.

"Come on, kid," Ryland stands up, plopping down on the bed beside her and squeezing her shoulder. "You think we're perfect? We're all a little rough around the edges," she shrugs, glancing over to Dakota. "Doesn't matter if you're dealing with shit. Whatever you need to do, we'll make it work."

"We always do," Dakota nods, standing up and squeezing onto the bed beside Ryland.

Slowly, Finley glances to all three of them. And then, she's blurting out the first thing that comes to her mind. "My mom died."

Dakota and Ryland panic and look to one another, but Gia doesn't even flinch. She seems rehearsed. "She did," is all she says, nodding softly.

"I… I'm sad about it," Finley admits, her eyes trained on her hands. "But… I'm also… not sad…."

"Relieved?" Ryland asks, raising an eyebrow. Finley nods hesitantly.

"That's not bad," Ryland shakes her head, speaking from experience. "It was the same way for me. I mean, I was six years old and practically taking care of my own mother whenever she would come home drunk. When she died… I mean…" she pauses, glancing to Dakota, who grabs her hand and squeezes it. "It was horrible to lose her, obviously, but… it took a weight off my shoulders."

"It's not that I'm *happy* she's dead," Finley shakes her head, her own words making her tense. "But I think… I think I knew it was coming… for a while now."

"She used to have good days, she really did," Finley adds, nodding quickly to prove her point. "But then she started to have bad days. And I started to count them," she traces tally marks in the air with her finger. "But I lost count after a while," she adds, quieter. "She was gone before she was *gone*, you know?"

"I think that's the smartest thing you've ever said," Gia offers her a sad smile. Finley just shrugs and looks down, but her cheeks turn bright red.

"We've all lost people," Dakota speaks up. "Whether it be physically or emotionally," she glances to Gia, who shrugs softly. "All of us know how it is. Take it from me, Finley, the worst part is over."

Finley smiles sadly, nodding her head. Luckily, their optimism is rubbing off on her. She thinks for a moment before her eyes widen. "Do you think Red will make strawberry shortcake when I come home?"

For some reason, Dakota can't help but burst into laughter, and it's not soon before the other three girls follow. They're laughing for a lot of reasons—sadness, happiness, and everything in between. But it's the four of them against the world, and she can't help but feel like things will turn out just fine.

Chapter 26

THE EPILOGUE WE DESERVE

"You're late."

Dakota jumps when she walks into her apartment to find Ryland sitting on her couch, her feet propped up on the coffee table. There's a book in her lap and an Amy Winehouse record playing in the background.

"I had to clean out an engine. Lost track of time," Dakota nods, letting the duffel bag over her shoulder slide to the ground beside the door. She tosses her backpack next to it, stretching out her shoulders. Ryland marks the page in her book and raises an eyebrow at her.

"C'mere, greaseball," she teases, patting the space beside her. Dakota doesn't argue, falling back onto the couch and yawning. "When're they actually gonna let you fight fires?"

"When they think I'm ready," Dakota shrugs. Ryland wipes at a smudge on her face with her sleeve before leaning against the girl's shoulder. "How was school?"

"Intense," Ryland laughs, motioning to the stack of books on the table across from them. "You know anything about Quantum Physics?"

Rolling her eyes, Dakota scoffs and leans her head on Ryland's shoulder. "Do I look like I know anything about Quantum Physics?" She nudges Ryland's arm, making the girl laugh. "May I ask why you're doing homework in my apartment instead of at your desk?"

"Gia and Finley kicked me out," Ryland rolls her eyes half-heartedly. "They're having a movie night with Delia."

"Another no show?"

"What do you think?"

Dakota sighs and leans back on the couch, curling up against Ryland's side. They exist in comfortable silence for a while, Dakota resting for the first time that day, and Ryland mumbling softly to herself, flipping through a textbook and scrawling things down on a sheet of graph paper.

Dakota's eyes scan the room slowly, amused at the collection of random pictures and drawings that line the walls. Compared to Gia and Ryland's apartment, the apartment she and Finley now share is a bit more... eccentric. And although they've yet to move in officially, they've still managed to make it their home. Finley's already set up a fish tank in the living room, tacked pictures and magazine clippings all over the walls, and has laid piles of blankets in almost every room.

A lot has changed in the past few months, Dakota realizes. Finley was discharged from the hospital, on a trial run with new medication that's surprisingly making a difference. They've all started school—Ryland at Stanford, Dakota at a smaller college, Finley at the same high school, and Gia's begun an internship with Red, tagging along to meetings and spending more time at the group home.

Since she's started school, Dakota's days have grown longer. She's shaken awake at the crack of dawn by Ryland, who's always the first one up. After she drops Ryland off at 8am, Dakota drives back across town to her first class. (Ryland's offered to take the bus, but Dakota doesn't mind the extra fifteen minutes it takes her to drop Ryland off.) Dakota surprisingly doesn't hate school, either. Probably because she spends mornings at the college, and the rest of the day as a volunteer firefighter at the station down the street. And although she's yet to *actually* fight fires, she's content with knowing it will happen eventually.

According to Ryland, Stanford is "*kicking her ass, but in a good way.*" She's challenged, sure. And sometimes it's a bit overwhelming, but her teachers have seen her potential and gone out of their way to help her. That's something she's never had before. She's always seemed to slip through the cracks. Dakota has noticed just how much that extra effort means to Ryland.

As for her father, things still aren't perfect. But, just a few weeks ago, he finally told the kids about their half sister. And surprisingly enough, the twins didn't freak out. Sure, it's an odd concept to them, but Ryland actually thinks it's made them more accepting of her. She still receives death glares from Julienne, his wife, but it doesn't bother her as much as it used to. Ryland's decided that she'll just have to deal with it.

Red's become more and more lenient about the time Dakota and Finley spend at the apartments. They're almost out of the system, anyway. And Dakota knows she trusts them the most out of all the girls in the house. At first, Dakota had been disappointed that the house didn't feel the same when Ryland and Gia left. But now, that same feeling of protection is always around when she's with all four of the girls. It wasn't the home that made her feel safe, she realizes. It was the people. She likes to think they'll remain friends for a long, long time.

But, there's also a new addition to their group. Gia's late nights and random disappearances were all for a reason—one that she announced to them not long ago. With help from Red and a lawyer, she's gained partial custody of her sister. So, now that she's eighteen, Gia is Deila's legal guardian. Delia stays at the apartment on the weekdays, and goes home with her mother on the weekends. Gia's still fighting for full custody, but she practically has it already. More often than not, Delia's mother doesn't show up to pick her up on the weekends. Not that Delia minds, though. She's quite fond of Gia's company, and her three surrogate sisters.

As for Jax, Gia's not so sure. She's reluctant to think he'll ever come around. While she and her sister witnessed a darker side of their father, Jax was never subjected to it. So, unfortunately, Gia understands why he resents them. She's made it clear to him countless times, though, that she will always be there if he needs her. She's extended the olive branch, and that's about as much as she can do.

Finley, the youngest of the four, has been plagued with school and doctor's appointments. However, a week or so after her mother's funeral, she was contacted by a lawyer. Thanks to insurance and a bank account her mom had set up when she was an infant, she has a good sum of money waiting for her when she turns eighteen. Enough, in fact, to help her get into college. She'd shown up at Ryland's apartment when she found out, sobbing. At first, they thought something was wrong, but Finley just kept mumbling on and on about how *relieved* she was. So now, combined with her inheritance, a new therapist, and a job at the local daycare, she's ready to tackle college head on. And although things are yet to be perfect, she's formed a unique bond with Ryland—who empathizes with her due to their similar experiences. And now, for the first time in a long time, Finley's able to open up.

To say the least, things have started to look up now that they've begun taking control of their own lives. With the reins handed over to them, it's taken a while for all four girls to realize just how much they can overcome.

Dakota eventually winds up asleep, curled up against Ryland, still in her work uniform—a black tank top and khakis. Ryland doesn't mind, she just wraps an arm around the girl and spreads the textbook across both of their laps so she can read.

She's still reading when Dakota wakes up once again. Except this time, they're both startled by a knock at the door. Dakota looks to Ryland, confused, but Ryland just shrugs and moves to get up.

"I've got it," Dakota stops her, hopping to her feet before Ryland can. She runs a hand through her messy hair and jogs over to the door. Ryland makes a mental note to start making Dakota use the peephole, because she's a bit uneasy when Dakota just throws the door wide open.

Dakota had all intentions of giving the unwanted visitor an earful. It is the middle of the night, *some people* are sleeping. She's jutted out her hip and crossed her arms, but the moment she recognizes the face in the hallway, her act vanishes.

"*Hudson*?" she breathes out, rubbing her eyes as if it's some sort of dream. She blinks rapidly, looking back to him again. Her brother just chuckles and holds up the heavy duffel bag he's carrying with him.

"Happy Birthday," he studies his younger sister, only slightly taller than she had been when they last met.

Dakota, still recovering from her sleep, looks to him in confusion. "It's not even...?"

"It's 12:05 on October 4th," he grins. "You're eighteen."

Realization setting in, Dakota glances to Ryland and then back to her brother in the doorway. Before Hudson can even ask about the girl sitting on the couch, Dakota's launching forwards and tackling him in a hug. To be honest, she hadn't realized how much she missed him until just now.

"I'm going to college," she pulls away, grabbing his shoulders and rushing to fill him in on everything that's happened since he's been gone. "And I'm working as a volunteer firefighter and soon I'll be able to go on drills with them, see?" She turns around, retrieving a certificate from the fridge to show him. Ryland watches, amused at just how badly Dakota needs to impress her older brother.

"And look, Hudson," she tugs on his arm, leading him inside. "This is my apartment."

His eyes scan the room, until they land on the girl on the couch. He motions to her. "This your roommate?"

"Nope," Dakota shakes her head. "That's Ryland."

Hudson looks to his sister for an explanation. Pausing, Dakota glances back to Ryland, raising an eyebrow. But Ryland just shrugs at her, giving her a soft nod of the head.

"She's my girlfriend," Dakota turns back to Hudson, grabbing his arm again. "C'mon, you've gotta see the—,"

"Girlfriend?" Hudson doesn't budge. Letting go of him, Dakota's eyes grow wide with worry and she looks to her brother carefully.

"Yeah," she says softly, suddenly concerned that she's walking on eggshells. "She's my... we're both... yeah." She holds her breath.

"Well," Hudson pauses, glancing between the two of them. "This is new."

"She goes to Stanford," Dakota blurts out, as if she has to plea Ryland's case. "She's smart as hell, Hudson," she rambles, eyes darting around the room until they land on the bookshelf, and she hurries over to pluck a book from it. "She even reads Socrates, see? And Plato!"

"Hudson," her brother rolls his eyes at his younger sister and extends a hand to Ryland. Dakota's still going on about Ryland's accomplishments, while meanwhile, Ryland stands up and shakes Hudson's hand.

"Ryland," she nods once, glancing over her shoulder to Dakota. "Don't listen to her. She's—,"

"I know how she is," he laughs, cupping the back of his neck and shaking his head half-heartedly. When Dakota realizes they're talking over her, she quickly hurries to stand in front of Ryland, something protective igniting within her. Even *she's* not sure why she's suddenly this worried about what her brother will think of them.

"Don't be mad," she blurts out. Hudson and Ryland look to one another in confusion.

"Why would I be mad?" her brother notes how she's wedged her way in-between them. Ryland places a hand on Dakota's shoulder to try and calm her down.

"Cause' before—,"

"Because I've been a dick to all the old guys you used to bring around?"

Dakota shrugs. "That too."

"I don't care that you're both… you know," Hudson gestures to the both of them. "I mean, I wasn't expecting it, but… it doesn't *matter*. Are you happy?"

Dakota pauses, glancing to Ryland and then nodding softly. "It's different... with her." She feels Ryland squeeze her shoulder, a silent acknowledgement.

"Well, then," Hudson shrugs. "Isn't that all that matters?"

(When Dakota pulls her brother into another hug, relieved, Ryland flashes him a shy thumbs up from behind her back.)

"I want a milkshake and fries."

"You can't get a milkshake for dinner."

"Why not?"

"Cause—,"

"It's my birthday, and I say she can get a milkshake," Dakota speaks up from her seat at the table—squeezed between Ryland and her brother. Gia and Finley sit across from them, and Delia's off at the front of the restaurant, spending a handful of quarters on arcade games.

Dakota had requested things be simple for her birthday, which is why she's perfectly content with spending it crammed into a booth at their favorite diner. In fact, if she could have anything, she'd probably still choose this.

"I'm getting the biggest strawberry milkshake they've got," Finley nods in finality, sticking her tongue out at Gia, who rolls her eyes half-heartedly. Ryland nudges Dakota's foot with her own, and just smiles when the girl looks over at her.

"You come here a lot?" Hudson asks, drawing Dakota's attention.

"Every Friday," she nods, finding herself proud of their tradition. "They practically know us by name."

Stirring his drink with his straw, Hudson pauses for a moment. "So you've really made your home here, huh?"

Dakota doesn't miss how he looks to Ryland as he says this, who's absentmindedly drumming her fingers against the table. All Dakota can do is nod softly.

"I'm tired of running," she admits, keeping her voice down as conversation around the table beings to pick up. "I feel like I'm finally building something here, Hudson. I'm not on edge anymore."

"So this is it."

"What do you mean?" Dakota grows concerned.

"No more running," Hudson nods once. "You're staying here."

"I mean—," she hesitates, glancing back to Ryland. "Yeah," she bites her lip. "But you..."

"California's a big state," Hudson shrugs. "I'll find work somewhere.

Dakota's eyes widen. "Really?"

"You're not the only one tired of running, kid," he chuckles, ruffling her hair like he used to do when they were kids. Dakota just glares at him playfully, though she can't deny how relieved she feels. Everything's starting to come together.

(And for once, she's not plagued with the fear that it will all fall apart.)

With a soft smile on her face, Dakota leans over to whisper something in Ryland's ear. As soon as she does, Ryland's entire demeanor shifts.

"Really?" the girl perks up. She couldn't help feeling a bit uneasy when Hudson had showed up, knowing that the last time he'd seen Dakota, she'd almost lost her. So with Hudson's unexpected arrival, she's been concerned that he's still planning a grand escape.

But four words whispered by Dakota—"*I'm not going anywhere,*"—have managed to crush all of Ryland's worries. Nothing her shock, Dakota just nods, giggles, and leans into her side to steal a sip of her drink. She feels at home. *This* feels like home.

Dakota can't help but feel like this is both an ending and a beginning, arriving hand in hand. There's a weight that's no longer on her shoulders—she's eighteen, she's in charge now. She never imagined that it would feel this liberating. But it does. For once, she's looking forward to the future, to the unknown—when before, she used to cower in fear.

They arrive back at the apartment, and all four girls pile onto Ryland and Gia's couch to watch a movie. Delia disappears into one of the bedrooms with a pile of Ryland's books, something she's made a habit of doing. As the movie plays, Dakota wanders over to check on Hudson periodically, who's in the kitchen using Ryland's laptop to look for work.

"Do I look like her?"

Hudson is startled when Dakota randomly breaks the silence. She's been sitting next to him at the kitchen counter, watching quietly. But the thought had entered her mind and she didn't have time to think before blurting it out.

"What?" Hudson looks to his younger sister in confusion. She freezes, as if she's just now realizing what she's said.

"Mom," Dakota swallows. "Do I look like her?"

Hudson's taken aback by her question. These are the kind of things the Quinn siblings don't usually talk about.

"I'm serious, Hudson," she shakes her head. "I... I'm afraid I'm going to forget her. Or that I already have and I don't even realize it."

Hudson studies her, running over her words in his head before sighing and turning his attention away from the laptop. "Sometimes I think you look *too* much like her," he admits. "Even she used to say that the only thing you got from your father was your hot-headedness."

"Really?" Dakota tilts her head to the side and leans forward, even more interested. "What else do you remember?"

Sometimes she thinks it's unfair that Hudson got to spend more time with their mother. Dakota would give almost anything to be able to see her one last time. She seems to have an endless list of questions without answers.

"I don't know, Koda," he shakes his head. "I know she loved us both an awful lot."

"Keep talking," Dakota mumbles, urging him to go on. She rests her elbows on the table.

"Why does it matter all of a sudden?"

"It's always mattered," she nudges his shoulder. "Come on, you remember more than I do. I just want to know about her."

He pauses, thinking for a moment before shrugging. "She almost got in a fight with our neighbor because he made you cry when he told you not to pick the flowers in his garden," he laughs and rolls his eyes. "She would have let you get away with anything."

"Was she as happy as I remember her?"

"Around us," Hudson pauses. "She was always worried about money, though. That's why our phone and cable were never on. She only cried when she thought we weren't around."

Frowning, Dakota rests her chin in her hands, revisiting old memories she thought she'd forgotten. The image of her mother is only a ghost to her, blurry around the edges and skipping like a broken record. But she can still remember the sound of her voice, soft and comforting, etched into the deepest parts of her conscience.

"Would she be proud of me?" The words slip out of her mouth without abandon. Her eyes find Hudson's, almost pleadingly.

"She always was," Hudson pauses to look at her, stitching his eyebrows together. "Why would you even ask that?"

"I..." Dakota hesitates. "I just... think about it a lot. I know it sounds cheesy, but... I'm just... I'm scared she wouldn't like how I turned out."

"Why wouldn't she?" Hudson looks to his younger sister, not understanding why she's suddenly so fixated on this idea. But when she looks away nervously, it's almost as if he can read her mind. "This is about Ryland, isn't it?"

The way Dakota freezes gives him enough of an answer.

"C'mon, kid, she wouldn't care," Hudson chuckles, squeezing her shoulder. "She wasn't like that," he shakes his head. "I remember one time another mother in the neighborhood told her how the boys would be *all over you* when you were older, but mom told her that it wasn't how she wanted to measure your worth," he pauses to think. "And another time, when you were disappointed that you couldn't be Batman because you weren't a boy, she gave you a long speech about how you could be "*the best damn batman this town has ever seen*" and then made you a mask and a cape with our old curtains and hot glue. You didn't take those things off for weeks, not even when you went to bed." He laughs at the memory, but Dakota just frowns.

"What's that got to do with it?"

"It's got everything to do with it, Koda," Hudson shakes his head. "She loved you because you're *you.* And if this is who you are, then I guarantee you she'd love that part of you, too."

"I never planned on this," Dakota says softly, after a long pause of silence. Hudson looks to her in confusion.

"Planned on what?"

"Ryland," she whispers, too shy to make eye contact. "With her, it all just... *happened.* I didn't even have to try."

Hudson raises an eyebrow. "It's that serious? You really do like her?"

"I love her, Hudson," Dakota shakes her head, her voice soft. Hudson's shocked by her words—normally used to his younger sister's hard exterior, the side of her that runs at any sign of emotion. But now, there's a different air around her. It's honest. Admitting love, to Dakota, still feels a bit like admitting vulnerability.

"Oh, woah," Hudson looks to Dakota, realizing just how serious she's being. "It's like... that?"

Dakota finally lifts her head, nodding carefully.

"Then why're you acting so scared?" he furrows his eyebrows. "Is something wrong, Koda?"

"I was scared you'd be..." she hesitates, the words heavy in the back of her throat.

"C'mon, Koda, how many times do I have to tell you that it doesn't matter?" He shakes his head before throwing an arm around Dakota's shoulders and ruffling her hair. "And if I had gotten mad at you for that, I hope you would have punched me in the face and kept on doing whatever makes you happy, regardless of what anyone says," he laughs. You're my sister, you idiot. I love you no matter what."

Dakota finally cracks a smile and Hudson pulls her into a hug, kissing the top of her head and squeezing her tight. "I missed you," he admits. Dakota just laughs and punches his shoulder.

"Missed you too, idiot," she hums, hopping to her feet. "Now get back to work."

Just as quickly as she'd let her walls down, she's built them back up again. However, Hudson's thankful for the moment of vulnerability he'd gotten a glimpse of. There's something different about Dakota, he realizes. Something new, youthful, as if an internal flame has been reignited. It's a breath of fresh air to see his sister free of the worries that used to plague her. He has a feeling the brown eyed girl in the other room has something to do with it.

Hudson watches as Dakota scampers back into the living room and hops over the back of the couch, plopping down into place beside Ryland. He sees the way Ryland's arm absentmindedly wraps around the girl, and how Dakota curls up against her side, fitting snugly like a missing puzzle piece. When Dakota glances back over her shoulder at him, and he sees the genuine smile tugging at her lips, he has to admit—he has a good feeling about this one.

"This movie's boring," Ryland whispers, nudging Dakota's shoulder with her own. Yawning, Dakota looks over to her and raises an eyebrow.

"Wanna call it a night?" Ryland urges. Dakota knows something's up, but she just nods softly, figuring Ryland's leg is bothering her. And she *is* tired, after all.

Clearing her throat, Ryland hands the remote off to Finley and slowly stands up. "I'm gonna walk Dakota back to her apartment."

"It's literally right across the hallw—," Gia starts, but is cut off by Finley, who elbows her in the side. Gia glares at her, but Finley glares right back, motioning for her to be quiet.

Dakota doesn't have time to question the suspicious behavior, because Ryland is practically pulling her to her feet and dragging her out into the hallway. As soon as they're alone, Dakota raises a questioning eyebrow at the girl.

"I've gotta give you your present," Ryland smiles knowingly. Dakota narrows her eyes.

"I thought we agreed on no presents?"

"More like you said no presents, and I kept my fingers crossed behind my back when I nodded," Ryland deadpans, tugging on Dakota's arm. "Come on, Koda, you'll like it. Promise."

Giving in, Dakota sighs and hands over the key to the apartment. Ryland shoots her an excited smile, letting herself in and motioning for Dakota to follow her.

"So," Ryland starts, clearing her throat when they stop in front of Dakota's soon-to-be bedroom. She's yet to live in it. In fact, it's empty except for a new mattress on the floor, unused. "You go first."

Raising her eyebrows, Dakota places a hand on the doorknob, but pauses to look back at Ryland. "Should I be scared?" she teases. But Ryland, impatient, nudges her forwards.

"Alright, alright, I'll go," Dakota holds her hands up in surrender, rolling her eyes playfully. She opens her mouth to speak again, but it clamps shut the moment she steps into the room. "Holy shit."

"Like it?" Ryland smirks, following Dakota's gaze up to the ceiling. There, scattered across the space above them, is a detailed painting of the entire solar system. Dakota's eyes scan over the expanse of it, covering the entire ceiling. She just stares straight upwards for a few moments before her gaze shifts back to Ryland.

"You did this?" she asks in disbelief. A smile tugs at Ryland's lips and she nods softly.

"Finley helped, too," Ryland explains. "For the girl who failed high school art, she's pretty talented."

"You got up on a ladder to do this?" Dakota grows concerned. But Ryland just laughs and shrugs her shoulders.

"I survived, didn't I?" she smiles softly. "Although, painting like that really kills your neck."

Scooting closer to her, Dakota leans against Ryland's back and rests her chin on the girl's shoulder. "I love it," she whispers. "But isn't the landlord gonna kill us?"

"Oh come on," Ryland laughs. "This place is barely up to code, it's not wonder you got it for so cheap. He should be thanking me for an excuse to redo this place."

"Sneaky," Dakota giggles against her shoulder. She starts to wrap her hands around the girl's waist, but Ryland stops her, pulling away and holding up a finger to make her wait.

"That's not all," Ryland shakes her head. Dakota sends her a death glare, but Ryland just smiles and motions for her to stay put before slipping out of the room.

She returns a minute later, carrying a wooden box and dragging a long cord behind her. Dakota's eyes follow Ryland as she sets it down in the middle of the room, placing her hands on her hips and thinking for a moment.

"Kill the lights," she nods to Dakota, who raises a confused eyebrow but decides against arguing. Once the room is pitch black, she hears Ryland fumbling with something near the wall. There's a flash of light that makes her jump, but soon her eyes are darting around the room in amazement.

"Woah," Dakota breathes out. Somehow, the box is projecting hundreds of tiny stars all over the room, casting a gentle blue glow over the both of them. Ryland smirks.

"Cool, huh?" She wanders over to Dakota and nudges her shoulder. "Made it myself."

Dakota's eyes widen. "How?"

"Light bulbs… and a box with some holes it it," Ryland laughs softly, absentmindedly reaching up to brush Dakota's hair away from her face. "Like it?"

"I'm never turning it off," Dakota fails to fight back a smile. She pulls Ryland closer to her, her lips suddenly lingering inches away from the girl's own.

"You may want to… be careful… it could o-overheat," Ryland stammers, losing her composure due to their sudden closeness. She can see the smirk playing on Dakota's lips, and can feel her entire face turning bright red. Noticing this, Dakota giggles and places one of her hands right underneath Ryland's collarbone, flat against her chest.

"Your heart's racing," she says softly, meeting Ryland's eyes once more. And god, Ryland hates how the way Dakota shyly bites her lip makes her pulse skyrocket even more.

Dakota giggles when Ryland looks away in embarrassment, and she quickly takes one of Ryland's hands, pressing it against her own heart. "It's not just you," she whispers, managing to make Ryland crack a smile. Dakota's yet to fully understand why Ryland's the one who can make her feel this way. She's not sure if she wants to. She likes the mystery.

Without saying anything else, Dakota takes a step closer, closing the gap between them and finally finding Ryland's lips with her own. Ryland catches on instantly, resting her arms around the girl's neck and kissing her back, as if it's second nature. For Ryland, Dakota's become almost an extension of herself, a best friend, a girlfriend, a partner in crime. Hell, Ryland doesn't believe in soulmates or star-crossed lovers, but kissing Dakota feels like magic in it's purest form, and Ryland likes to think that something caused them to cross paths just when they needed each other. That alone is enough to make her believe in miracles again.

"One more thing," Ryland breathes out when the kiss separates. Dakota's eyes follow hers, wide and curious as she digs something out of her pocket. An object pressed into her palm, and Dakota slowly holds it up. A cord necklace dangles down between them. Strung onto it is a small key.

"For my apartment," Ryland explains, her voice raspy and still winded from merely kissing the girl. "Figured you'd need a copy, now that you live across the hallway and all."

Dakota swings the necklace around one finger, catching the key with her other hand and holding it up to study it. "This is big for you, isn't it?" She asks gently. Ryland just shrugs when Dakota looks up at her.

"You always keep things locked away to protect yourself, you told me that," Dakota nods to herself. "Yet you've just given me a key."

"I handed you the key a long time ago," Ryland admits, knowing Dakota will understand what she means. "Never thought it'd be you who I let in… but I'm glad it was."

"I love you," Dakota breathes out. The key rests cold against her chest as Ryland gently pulls the necklace over her head, and she clutches it in her fist. Dakota takes a moment to take it all in—

the room, the stars on the walls, the girl in front of her—who's looking back at her as if she's the entire universe. In that moment, Dakota *feels* it—it goes without saying—Ryland loves her. And by the look on Ryland's face, she can feel it too.

(Though she'll never grow tired of saying it.)

"Goddamn it, Dakota Quinn, I'm in love with you," Ryland shakes her head in disbelief, making Dakota laugh and pull her even closer. And when Ryland kisses her again, Dakota's eyes fall shut and she breathes it all in. She's spent so much of her life looking for a home, but she's realized she'd been searching in all the wrong places; until the day it stood right in front of her, hidden behind a pair of dark brown eyes.

She can't help but look at the two of them and feel victorious, as if they've both won a battle that was waged against them. And sure, there's a whole future of uncertainty ahead, but Dakota decides they've become warriors. From the ashes of the fire meant to destroy them, Dakota's certain that they will rise hand in hand.

AFTERWORD

Why did I write this book?

I had a moment—just after I had finished writing the first draft—when I sat back and asked myself where this story had come from. When you write, sometimes it just spills out of you without abandon, and that's how this story and these characters had come to be. But parts of yourself always seem to leak through—whether it be a thought, an idea, a catch phrase—you are always leaving parts of yourself behind in your writing. I learn more about myself by proofreading my own works than I ever thought I would.

I write because I am a control freak. I write because I'm unable to trust someone else to tell the story that I want to be told. I write because I'm too shy to speak the words that I eventually put to paper. So if everything I write is so integral to my own being, how did this story come to be?

At first glance, this book is a cheesy love story. And alright, alright—it is. Obviously it's not your typical Disney romance, but a main part of the story is about Dakota and Ryland. And... oh yeah, they're girls.

People are gay—let's just get that out there. There are girls who love girls, boys who love boys, and every possible combination in between. I assume if you've read this book, you understand that. And this day in age, it seems that a large majority of people "accept" us into their society. My problem is, whether it be acceptance or tolerance, are we really included?

There are stories to be told. If you look at mainstream media—*the perfect example of diversity, right?*—you'll see all sorts of people getting their stories told. Boy meets girl, girl meets boy, they fall in love, blah blah blah... We know. We've seen it a million times before.

Now, of course, portrayal of LGBT+ persons in the media *has* improved. Show runners just love to throw in a token gay character to drive someone else's plot forward. And hey, maybe you get a good love story every now and then. However, in the name of being "realistic," so many of these stories seem to end in tragedy. Don't believe me? I'll try to keep it simple.

- *1976, Executive Suite, Julie — When her lover attempted suicide after realizing her sexuality, Julie died while trying to save her.*
- *1992, Northern Exposure, Cicely — Took a bullet intended for her girlfriend, shot by someone who didn't approve of homosexuality.*
- *2002, Buffy the Vampire Slayer — Stray bullet to the head. (Sense a recurring theme?)*
- *2002, Family Affairs, Kelly Hurst — Pushed down stairs by her lover's husband.*
- *2006, Battlestar Galactica, Helena Cain — Shot to death by her former lover.*
- *2010, Sons of Anarchy, Amy Tyler — Girlfriend wanted to frame her for murder, shot her in the neck.*
- *2011, All My Children, Marissa Tasker — Shot to death by her ex-husband.*

- *2012, Pretty Little Liars, Maya St. Germain — Killed by her ex-boyfriend.*
- *2014, Defiance, Kenya Rosewater — Poisoned by her lover.*
- *2015, House of Cards, Rachel Posner — Hit with a car by a man who had an obsessive crush on her.*
- *2015, Murdoch Mysteries, Lillian Moss — Killed by the husband of her ex-lover.*
- *2016, The 100, Lexa — Killed by a stray bullet.*

I could go on, but I like to think you get the point by now. I listed these particular deaths for a reason—the stereotypes they emulate.

1. If you're gay, you probably want to invest in a bulletproof vest. Otherwise, you'll either take a bullet for your partner, or a stray one will find its way to you.
2. If you so much as *think* you're gay, you probably should never experiment with a guy. He'll lose his shit if he sees you with a girl. So make sure to lock your doors, check your drinks, yadda yadda...
3. If you're gay, you're either involved with a married woman, or *you're* the married women cheating on your husband. (If you haven't gotten the bulletproof vest yet, you definitely need it now.)
4. Oh, yeah, and if you're gay, don't even talk to men. At all. They'll probably fall madly in love with you, stalk you, and then murder you when the feelings aren't returned.

THESE ARE UNHEALTHY STEREOTYPES.

Listen, I know many of these probably weren't intentional. But, intentional or not, the unconscious biases we get from the media about LGBT+ characters and their community can be extremely harmful.

Having a character with whom you can identify is something we may talk for granted. When I was little, I was *in love* with Kim Possible. I wanted to be just as cool as she was. In my pre-teen years, I wanted to be like Alex from Wizards of Waverly Place, with her "take no shit" attitude. And now, my favorite character on TV currently is Octavia Blake from The 100—a kickass female with a warrior's heart.

You can piece apart these characters and see yourself in them. But if you get older, like me, and struggle with the idea of sexuality, wouldn't it be nice to see someone else going through the same thing? And in a realistic way? The stories being told about LGBT people in the media today are scary. *We don't want to imagine ourselves in their shoes.* And even lazily written LGBT characters are few and far between—thrown into a show to bait a certain audience. They don't get diverse storylines. They're not main characters. They're sidekicks, pushed to the background.

It's time that we became main characters. It's time that we write our own stories, drive our own plots forward, make our voices heard. **Representation is important.** Whether you like it or not, mass media influences our society.

And so, maybe I wrote this book, created these characters, and told this story because *I'm tired*. I'm tired of someone else trying to tell my story for me. I'm tired of a community so large being silenced—because silence can be just as oppressive. I'm not a background character, and I never will be.

And so, this story was made to perpetuate a different set of stereotypes—the right ones.

1. Gay people exist as complex, diverse, wonderful human beings, independent of their sexuality! *What a radical concept.*

2. Nothing physical is "gay." No item of clothing, no dialect, nothing. You can be gay and paint your nails a different color every day. You can be gay and shave your head. If you say you're gay, guess what? You are.

3. And if you don't want to say you're gay—that's fine too. Labels are socially constructed because some people find comfort in falling under that umbrella. But some of us don't. It doesn't have to be complicated. You love who you love. (Like Dakota says, she doesn't love Ryland *because she's a girl.* She loves her because she's, well, Ryland.)

4. People are tolerant. I'm sure there's a few outliers, but most people *won't* murder you if you tell them you're gay. Shocker, right? Sure, it may take some getting used to for them. They're new to this, too. But the true friends, the true family… they love you because you're *you*. Sometimes they need time. And sometimes it can be relieving when you find out that they've suspected it all along. And if there's people out there who don't agree with who you are, consider yourself lucky. You've just filtered another toxic person out of your headspace. They've done you a favor. (As my friend says "Take out the trash.")

And lastly, my main reason for writing this story was for normalization. Hand in hand with correct representation, these two concepts are the best ways to combat negative stereotypes.

In this book—in their world—the topic of sexuality isn't talked about much. Not because it's frowned upon, but just because these girls don't really mind. Dakota and Ryland have only one scene where they explicitly talk about their sexuality, and that's it. I'm not against stories that put focus on their characters figuring out their sexuality, but that's also not all that defines them. Both Dakota and Ryland have storylines and backstories that are *completely* separate from their romantic preference.

(Revisiting positive stereotype #1 - Gay people exist as complex, diverse, wonderful human beings, independent of their sexuality.)

And so, in the story, they take their relationship for what it is. They don't complicate it. The people around them don't scrutinize them for it. Hell, Finley had an inkling all along and didn't even bat an eyelash. And I know, I know, this isn't the case for everyone. *But god, isn't it nice to read a story where they get a happy ending for once*? Don't we deserve a few of those?

Not every story is happy. But not every story ends in tragedy, either. Sometimes it's a happy middle. (Sometimes, your bulletproof vest ends up saving your life.) You think Stanford is going to be a breeze for Ryland? Probably not. You think Dakota's not going to have to worry about money to pay for school ever again? Nope. Their struggles with still go on, but they've surrounded themselves with people who support them. Gia, Finley, Red, Hudson… And god, they're in a *way* better place than they were at the start. That's the kind of hope and persistence I want to be taken away from this story.

The title "From the Ashes" was based on the mythological story of the Phoenix—a great, powerful, beautiful bird that appears as a symbol in ancient literature from all over the world. The

Phoenix is used to represent renewal and resurrection, by literally *rising from the ashes*. It lives countless lifetimes, being consumed by fire only to rise again. That's why I chose this title. Because god, who wouldn't aspire to be that powerful? There's beauty in healing. There's beauty in admitting weakness and being able to emerge from it.

And finally, thank you for reading. For those of you who have been with me the beginning, thanks for sticking around. Here's to taking charge of our own stories.

— Lena

Keep Up with The Author

Twitter: @lenajfc

Tumblr: txrches.tumblr.com

Email: txrches@gmail.com

Printed in Great Britain
by Amazon

65150835R00260